Judgment Call

ALSO BY J. A. JANCE

Joanna Brady Mysteries

Desert Heat
Tombstone Courage
Shoot/Don't Shoot
Dead to Rights
Skeleton Canyon
Rattlesnake Crossing
Outlaw Mountain
Devil's Claw
Paradise Lost
Partner in Crime
Exit Wounds
Dead Wrong
Damage Control
Fire and Ice

J. P. Beaumont Mysteries

Until Proven Guilty
Injustice for All
Trial by Fury
Taking the Fifth
Improbable Cause
A More Perfect Union
Dismissed with Prejudice
Minor in Possession
Payment in Kind
Without Due Process

Failure to Appear
Lying in Wait
Name Withheld
Breach of Duty
Birds of Prey
Partner in Crime
Long Time Gone
Justice Denied
Fire and Ice
Betrayal of Trust

and

Hour of the Hunter
Kiss of the Bees
Day of the Dead
Queen of the Night
Edge of Evil
Web of Evil

Hand of Evil
Cruel Intent
Trial by Fire
Fatal Error
Left for Dead

JUDGMENT CALL

J. A. JANCE

HARPER LUXE

An Imprint of HarperCollins*Publishers*

JUDGMENT CALL. Copyright © 2012 by J. A. Jance. All rights reserved. Printed in the United States of America. No part of this book may be used or reproduced in any manner whatsoever without written permission except in the case of brief quotations embodied in critical articles and reviews. For information address HarperCollins Publishers, 10 East 53rd Street, New York, NY 10022.

HarperCollins books may be purchased for educational, business, or sales promotional use. For information please write: Special Markets Department, HarperCollins Publishers, 10 East 53rd Street, New York, NY 10022.

FIRST HARPERLUXE EDITION

HarperLuxe™ is a trademark of HarperCollins Publishers

Library of Congress Cataloging-in-Publication Data is available upon request.

ISBN: 978-0-06-212838-6

12 13 14 ID/RRD 10 9 8 7 6 5 4 3 2 1

To Loretta, in memory of Randy. Semper Fi.

Judgment Call

Chapter 1

Late on a Thursday afternoon, Sheriff Joanna Brady sat at her desk in the Cochise County Justice Center outside Bisbee, Arizona, and studied the duty roster her chief deputy, Tom Hadlock, had dropped off an hour earlier.

Her former chief deputy, Frank Montoya, had been lured away from her department with the offer of a new job—chief of police in nearby Sierra Vista. Looking for a replacement, Joanna had tapped her jail commander to step into the job. Tom was well qualified on paper, but he had found Frank's tenure as chief deputy to be a tough act to follow.

When Frank had been Joanna's second in command, he had handily juggled several sets of seemingly unrelated responsibilities—media relations, routine

whole point. Otherwise, it would be a lot like being struck by lightning. God reached out and got you and you had no idea what was coming. That wasn't what this trip was about; wasn't what he was about. For him this was far more personal.

He pressed the button on the key fob, opened the back hatch, and removed the blanket he had used to cover her. As soon as the blanket came off, she began to struggle. That was all right. They were far enough away from civilization that no matter what she did, it wouldn't matter. No one would hear her. Out here in the cold night air of the Arizona desert, the two of them were entirely alone except for the occasional mournful cry of a coyote.

"Up and at 'em, sunshine," he said. "You ready for a game of hide-and-seek?"

She shook her head desperately back and forth and made a whimpering noise that was probably some form of the word "please." Through the duct tape, that was difficult to tell. Grabbing her by the underarms, he hauled her up and out of the vehicle and stood her upright, barefoot and swaying unsteadily, on the rough surface of the dirt road. She looked up at him. He could see the terror in her wide-eyed stare. He liked that. He had spent years anticipating this moment, and he didn't want to rush it.

"I'm going to take off the gag," he said. "You can scream your head off if you want. No one will hear you."

He had watched enough forensic TV to know that the cops loved looking for DNA on pieces of duct tape, so he had no intention of leaving any of that behind. Ditto for the nylon tie straps he had used to secure her hands and feet. Those had ID numbers that could be traced back to certain retailers. He would take those with him as well. Ditto his brass.

When he peeled off the duct tape, she surprised him. She didn't scream. "You don't need to do this," she said. "Please let me go. Please."

"No," he said. "That's not how this is going to work. I'm going to let you loose now and give you a running start. Who knows? You may be able to run faster than I can shoot. Or maybe I'll miss."

"I can't run," she said. "I'm barefoot."

"That's your problem. If you want to live, you'll run."

When he pulled the box knife out of his pocket, she cringed away from him. That was fine. He liked the idea that she was afraid of being cut, but cutting wasn't what he had in mind. Instead, he used the knife to slice through her restraints and then stuffed them in his pockets along with the duct tape.

"There you go," he said. "I'll give you to the count of ten. You run. I shoot. If I miss, you win. If I don't

miss?" He shrugged. "Well, I guess that's the end of the story."

"Please," she begged again. "Please."

She didn't need to say any more than that. He knew what she wanted, and he had no intention of giving it to her.

"You'd better get started, because as of now, I'm counting. One!"

She hesitated for only a moment, then she wheeled and started off into the desert, back the way they had come. That surprised him. He had expected her to cross the wash and then stick to the road. That would have given him a clear shot. If she managed to duck into a nearby thicket of mesquite trees, he'd have to go trailing after her.

So he didn't bother waiting until the count of ten. He got as far as four and then pulled the trigger. The first shot caught her in the leg. Stumbling forward, she fell to the ground as the second shot went over her head. She was still trying to get away, scrabbling forward on the rocky ground, dragging her crippled leg, when he came up behind her. He shot her three more times after that. The shots were meant more to maim than to kill. He had wanted her to suffer. If she died instantly, she missed the point. This was punishment, payback.

While she lay moaning on the ground, he went looking for his brass. He had shot her with a .38. He found all five casings and pocketed them as well.

Immediately after the first gunshot, a stark silence had fallen over the desert. Gradually, though, the night sounds returned. A nearby coyote howled, and another one off in the distance yipped a response. Far away he heard what sounded like a dog barking, but the barking stayed where it was without coming any closer. The shooter wasn't especially worried about anyone hearing the gunfire. After all, it was three o'clock in the morning, and the killing ground was suitably remote.

He didn't bother moving the body. For one thing, he didn't want to bring any blood evidence back into the car with him. Besides, with the coyotes out and about, he was sure they would deal with the body in their own time-honored fashion.

She was still alive and breathing shallowly as he turned to walk away. "Ashes to ashes, and dust to dust," he said. "And it serves you right."

Prologue

The car stopped in the middle of a stretch of rough dirt road. In the silvery moonlight, the road was a light-colored ribbon cutting straight north through a forest of newly leafed mesquite trees. He had hoped to drive much farther before he stopped the car, but his study of Google Maps had let him down. This was a far more primitive road than he had been led to believe it would be. He had managed to pick his way around the boulder-littered crossings at the first two washes, but this one was impossible. The unfamiliar low-slung Passat wasn't going to make it.

There was a noisy thumping from inside the trunk. That meant she was awake, and that was fine with him. He wanted her to be awake and aware. He wanted her to know what was happening and why. That was the administrative chores, and information technology issues—with unflappable ease. Now, after more than a year in the position, Tom was finally growing into the job and had a far better handle on what needed to be done than he'd had in the beginning. Unfortunately, he still wasn't quite up to Frank Montoya standards.

After months of struggle, Tom had finally tamed the duty roster monster, handing Joanna a flawlessly executed copy of the upcoming month's schedule two days before she absolutely had to have it in hand. At this point, he was hard at work preparing a first go-down of the next year's budget. Joanna knew that he had placed several calls to Frank asking for pointers on both the budget and IT concerns, and she was grateful Frank had been willing to help.

The one place where Tom was still sadly lacking was in media relations. Faced with a camera or a reporter, the former jail commander morphed from your basic macho tough guy into a spluttering, tongue-tied neophyte. Six months of participation in a Toastmasters group in Sierra Vista had helped some, but it would take lots more time and effort before Tom Hadlock would be fully at ease in front of a bank of microphones and cameras.

When the phone on Joanna's desk rang, she glanced at her watch to check the time before picking it up. At home her husband, Butch Dixon, was battling a tough deadline for reviewing the copyedited manuscript of his latest crime novel. As a consequence, Joanna was on tap to pick up the kids. Her nearly sixteen-year-old daughter, Jenny, worked two hours a day after school as an aide in a local veterinarian's office. With equal parts anticipation and dread, Joanna was looking forward to the day, coming all too soon, when Jenny would have a driver's license of her own. Once that happened, driving her back and forth to work and school activities would no longer be a necessity.

Joanna and Butch's two-year-old, Dennis, spent five hours each afternoon at a preschool that operated in conjunction with their church in Old Bisbee. Dennis was a gregarious kid. When the older members of what Joanna termed the "gang of four"—Jenny and the housekeeper's two grandsons—had gone off to school in the fall, Dennis had been lost on his own. When a spot had opened up in the preschool program at Tombstone Canyon United Methodist, they had signed him up for a half day four days a week.

Joanna's first thought was that the phone call would involve some hitch in picking up the kids. Or maybe Butch needed her to stop by the store to grab some last-minute item for dinner before she went home to High Lonesome Ranch. When she answered, however, it turned out that the call had nothing to do with the home front and everything to do with work.

"Jury's back," Kristin Gregovich said.

Kristin was Joanna's secretary, and the returning jury in question was only a few steps away from Joanna's office at the Cochise County Justice Center, a joint facility that housed not only the sheriff's department and the jail, but also the Cochise County Superior Court offices and courtrooms. The case currently being tried there was one in which Joanna Brady had played a pivotal role.

More than a year earlier, an elderly woman named Philippa Brinson had gone AWOL from what was supposedly a state-of-the-art Alzheimer's group home near the Cochise County town of Palominas. Sheriff Brady had been one of several officers who had responded to the original missing persons call on Ms. Brinson.

But Caring Friends had turned out to be a far worse can of worms than anyone expected. For one thing, arriving officers had been dumbfounded by the appallingly unsanitary conditions in what was supposed to be a healthcare facility. The kitchen had been a food handler's nightmare, and they had found evidence that helpless residents had been routinely strapped to beds and chairs and left, trapped in their own bodily filth, for hours on end. A subsequent investigation had brought evidence to light that several Caring Friends patients had died as a result of serious infections that started out as bedsores.

It was while Joanna and her deputies were at the crime scene that they had been confronted by Alma DeLong, the owner of Caring Friends as well as several other Alzheimer's treatment facilities. Outraged to find police officers on the premises, she had launched a physical attack against them and had been hauled off to jail in a Cochise County patrol car.

Hours later, Philippa Brinson had been found safe. Confined to a chair in her room, she had managed to use nail clippers to cut away her restraints. Out on the highway, she had hitched a ride into Bisbee and had made her way to the old high school building. To her way of thinking, she had been on her way to work in her old office, a place from which she had retired some thirty-five years earlier. After that misadventure, she was placed in the care of a niece and had gone off to a different facility—hopefully a better one—in Phoenix, while Joanna's department had been left to clean up the mess revealed by Philippa's brief disappearance.

Alma DeLong, arrogant and utterly unrepentant, had brought in high-powered attorneys to fight all the charges lodged against her. For years, Joanna had held a fairly low opinion of Arlee Jones, the local "good old boy" county attorney, and that antipathy went both ways. The county attorney didn't approve of Joanna any more than she approved of him. Arlee was a political animal—well connected, smart, and lazy. Everyone knew that whenever possible, he preferred plea bargains to the work of actually going to trial.

When Arlee had offered Alma a plea bargain on a single count of negligent homicide that would have resulted in less than four years of jail time, Joanna hadn't been happy, but Alma had turned that option down cold, choosing instead to take her chances with a judge and jury. Annoyed and galvanized, Arlee Jones had gone after Alma DeLong with a vengeance, charging the woman with three counts of second-degree homicide, which in terms of seriousness was two whole steps up the felony ladder from negligent homicide. DeLong was also charged with assaulting a police officer and resisting arrest.

After more than a year of legal maneuvering and stalling on the defense's part, the case had finally come to trial. Because Joanna had been a part of that initial investigation, she had been called to testify. She had spent a day and a half on the stand being grilled first by Arlee and later by Alma's defense attorney. Now, a full day after beginning their deliberations, the jury was finally back.

Because Alma was a well-known Tucson-area businesswoman, the trial had attracted a good deal of media attention. Rather than throw Tom Hadlock up against what was likely to be a mob of reporters, Joanna ducked into the restroom long enough to check her hair and lipstick before leaving the office and walking across the breezeway to Judge Cameron Moore's courtroom.

Once inside, Joanna slipped into an empty seat next to Bobby Fletcher. His mother, Inez, was one of the Caring Friends patients who had died. Bobby's sister, Candace, had been more interested in winning a financial settlement than anything else. She had been notably absent throughout the criminal trial. Bobby, on the other hand, had been in the courtroom every single day, observing the testimony with avid interest. Bobby was a man with plenty of deficits in terms of social skills and education, and some criminal convictions of his own. When he had finally straightened up, Inez had taken him in and been his unwavering refuge. A guilty verdict wouldn't bring his mother back from the grave, but it would go a long way toward giving her grieving son a measure of justice.

As the jury filed into the courtroom, Bobby said nothing. Looking for reassurance, he reached out and took Joanna's hand.

"Madam Forewoman," Judge Moore intoned. "Have you reached a verdict?"

"We have, Your Honor."

The piece of paper was passed to the judge. While the judge perused it, the defendant, flanked by her attorneys, rose to her feet.

"How do you find?"

"On the first count of homicide in the second degree, we find the defendant guilty."

Bobby Fletcher shuddered and covered his face with his hands, sobbing silently as the jury forewoman continued: "On the second count of homicide in the second degree, we find the defendant guilty. On the third count of homicide in the second degree, we find the defendant guilty. On the charge of assaulting an officer of the law, we find the defendant innocent. On the charge of resisting arrest, we find the defendant guilty."

The last two struck Joanna as incomprehensible hairsplitting. How could someone be innocent of physically assaulting an officer—something Joanna had witnessed with her own eyes—and at the same time be guilty of resisting arrest? But Bobby Fletcher had heard the single word he needed to hear. Alma DeLong was guilty of killing his mother. She had been free on bail. Now, once the judge granted the prosecutor's request to rescind her bail, a deputy stepped forward to lead her across the parking lot to the county jail, where she would be held while awaiting sentencing.

Walking side by side, Joanna and Bobby Fletcher moved to the courtroom door, where Bobby came to a sudden stop. "I want to wait here and talk to Mr. Jones," Bobby said. "I want to thank him."

Not eager to face the media throng that was no doubt assembled outside, Joanna waited, too, but she was also amazed. Bobby had spent huge chunks of his adult life as a prison inmate. The idea of his having a cordial conversation with any prosecutor on the planet was pretty much unthinkable. But then, to Joanna's astonishment, when Arlee Jones appeared, she found herself in for an even bigger shock. The county attorney approached Bobby Fletcher with his hand outstretched and a broad smile on his face.

"We got her," the county attorney gloated, pumping Bobby's hand with congratulatory enthusiasm. "We still have the sentencing process to get through, but one way or another, Alma DeLong is going to jail, starting today. Her bail may yet be reinstated, pending an appeal, but for now she's a guest in your establishment, Sheriff Brady. Unfortunately, the accommodations there will be somewhat better than what her victims experienced at Caring Friends."

"Thank you, sir," Bobby Fletcher said.

"You're welcome, Mr. Fletcher," Arlee replied. "I'm not sure I ever mentioned this, but back when I was a kid, I used to deliver newspapers to your folks' place over on Black Knob. Even when times were tough, your mom always made sure I got a tip when I came around collecting. Depending on whether it was winter or summer, she also offered me either hot chocolate or iced tea. Inez Fletcher was a good woman. Sending her killer to jail is the least I can do."

The unguarded sincerity in that statement caused Arlee Jones to move up several notches in Joanna's estimation. She usually dismissed Jones as being a pompous ass in a mostly empty suit. Now she momentarily reconsidered that opinion. And that was the thing that Alma DeLong hadn't realized, either. Bisbee was a small town. The invisible spiderweb of connections running from one person and one family to the next was another reason Arlee Jones had tackled this case with unaccustomed zeal.

"So are you ready to talk to some reporters?" Jones asked.

"Who, me?" Bobby asked. A look of dismay spread across his face. "Are you kidding?"

"Yes, you," Arlee said, placing a guiding hand on Bobby's shoulder. "And I'm not kidding. As far as the people following this trial are concerned, you're the living face of the victims. You're the stand-in for every family that ever made the mistake of placing a loved one in a Caring Friends facility. You and the other families did so expecting that their father or mother or grandmother would be well cared for, even though we know now that that wasn't the case.

"Having you speak to reporters tonight serves two purposes. It shows families that they can't just drop their loved ones off at one of these places and then not monitor what goes on once the doors slam shut. They have to be vigilant. And it also serves to show people like Alma DeLong that if they deliver inadequate care, there will be consequences. Can you do that?"

"All right," Bobby said uncertainly. "I guess."

Witnessing this, Joanna felt her approval needle on Arlee Jones dip back down a bit. No doubt the man would make plenty of political hay from this incident. Having Bobby standing beside him during the press conference would provide a compelling segment on the evening news, and it would probably allow him to bank any number of sound bites that would work well the next time Arlee had to stand for election.

Joanna followed the two men out onto the covered outdoor breezeway. Content to be on the sidelines for a change, she stood next to Arlee Jones and listened in while a number of reporters piled on with a bombardment of questions. To Joanna's surprise, Bobby Fletcher answered all of them in the unassuming but straightforward manner that had made him an effective prosecution witness during the trial. He hadn't just dropped his mother off at the facility. He had seen the quality of care going down the tubes, and his attempts to rectify the situation had come to nothing.

All Joanna had to do was listen and smile and nod. The press conference ended without her having been asked a single question. That was exactly how she liked it, and her makeup had been on straight and her hair had been combed properly. Things didn't get any better than that.

Once the press conference was over, however, a glance at her watch told Joanna she was running late. The day-care facility closed at six, and she had exactly five minutes of grace time to pick up Dennis. After that, she would begin accumulating late fines to the tune of twenty-six dollars for every additional five-minute period. Being late was not an option.

Joanna raced out through the back door of her office, jumped into her Yukon, and headed for Dr. Millicent Ross's veterinary office in Bisbee's Saginaw neighborhood, calling Jenny's cell phone as she went.

"I'm on my way," she told her daughter. "Meet me outside. Then I'll drop you off at the church so you can go in and sign Dennis out. If I have to mess around with finding a parking place there, we're not going to make it on time."

As directed, Jenny stood by the entrance to the clinic's driveway, leaning against a gatepost with one strap of her backpack flung over her shoulder. A stiff breeze blew in out of the north, and Jenny's long ponytail fluttered like a blond flag in the turbulent air. Back in high school, Joanna had been a tiny redhead who had often been referred to as "cute." Jenny, on the other hand, was beautiful in a tall, slender, blue-eyed way that would never be considered cute.

It came as no surprise to Joanna that Jenny, an accomplished horsewoman, would be a natural choice for the title of Bisbee High School's rodeo queen at some point in the course of her four years of high school. The surprise had been in the timing. Joanna had expected it to happen later on. Being rodeo queen as a senior would have been just about right, but Jenny had won the crown as a mere junior, leaving Joanna as the mother of a rodeo queen somewhat earlier than she'd thought possible.

Once she had made the mistake of mentioning all of that to her own mother. Eleanor Lathrop Winfield had responded with a singular lack of sympathy.

"It's one of those surprises that comes with being a parent, and you don't even have time enough to dodge out of the way," Eleanor had told her. "Besides, you're better off as the youngish mother of a rodeo queen than being an underage grandmother."

The implications in her mother's statement were quite clear, as in, your daughter's a fifteen-year-old rodeo queen. Mine was an unmarried, pregnant seventeen-year-old. Which do you prefer?

Guilty as charged, and that was pretty much the end of Joanna's taking issue with the rodeo queen situation.

"Hey," Joanna said as Jenny dropped her backpack on the floorboard, scrambled into the passenger seat, and fastened her seat belt. "How are things?"

"Good," Jenny said.

"And work?"

"Okay."

The older Jenny got the harder it became to get her to reply to any given question with something other than a single word.

"School?" Joanna ventured.

"School was weird."

That was more than a one-word answer. It was long on worrisome implications but short on meaning. "What do you mean, weird?"

"When the buses were leaving this afternoon, the parking lot was full of cops."

"Really?" Joanna asked. "How come? Did something happen? Was the school on lockdown?"

And if it was, she asked herself, *why didn't I know about it?*

"Ms. Highsmith is missing or something."

Debra Highsmith, the high school principal, was someone with whom Joanna had crossed swords several times, most notably when Joanna had been invited to speak at career day and was notified that, due to the school's strict "zero tolerance of weapons" policy, she would need to leave both her Glock and her Taser at home. Joanna had gone to the school board and had succeeded in obtaining a waiver of that policy for trained police officers.

"Ms. Highsmith is missing?" Joanna asked.

Jenny shrugged and nodded. "She wasn't at school this morning. When I took the homeroom attendance sheets down to the office, I heard Mrs. Holder talking to Mr. Howard about it—that Ms. Highsmith hadn't come in and that it was odd that she hadn't called to let anyone know. After that, I didn't hear anything else until we were going out to the buses. That's when all the cop cars showed up."

Wondering what had happened but not wanting to grill her daughter, Joanna changed the subject. "How was driver's ed?"

"Mr. Forte is having a hard time finding a stick-shift vehicle for me to practice on."

Jenny had won her local rodeo crown, but there were other titles to conquer. If she intended to run for or win any of those, both Jenny and her horse, Kiddo, needed to attend the far-flung competitions, a reality which had underscored the fact that they needed suitable horse-hauling transportation.

With that in mind, Butch had gone on Craigslist and found a bargain-basement used dual-cab Toyota Tundra pickup complete with a heavy-duty towing package. It was a good enough deal that he had snapped it up on the spot. The only sticking point had to do with the fact that the Tundra came with a manual transmission, and all the vehicles used for Bisbee High School's driver's ed classes were automatics.

"If Butch finishes going over his copyediting, maybe he can take you out for a spin tomorrow since you don't have school."

"I'm working tomorrow," Jenny said. "We're planning to do the driving thing on Saturday."

Faced with severe budget shortfalls, the school district had switched to four-day weeks, leaving the schools shuttered on Fridays and weekends. It cut down on utilities and transportation costs, but it left working parents scrambling for something to do with their kids each Friday when school was out and the parents still had to work. Joanna was fortunate. On those days when extra kids had to be accommodated at the church-run preschool and day care, Dennis was usually able to be at home with Butch. When Butch wasn't available, they could call on Carol Sunderson, their part-time house-keeper, and her two grandsons.

Joanna pulled over to the curb, and Jenny dashed inside to get her brother. While she was gone, Joanna called Alvin Bernard, Bisbee's chief of police. She was still on hold when Jenny came out with Dennis in tow. As Jenny strapped her little brother into the car seat that was a permanent fixture in Joanna's patrol car, Alvin finally came on the line.

"Sorry to make you wait so long," Alvin said. "I'm busier than a one-legged man at a butt-kicking contest."

Like Arlee Jones, Alvin Bernard was a good old boy of a certain vintage. When Joanna was first elected sher-iff, Alvin hadn't exactly welcomed her to the local law enforcement community with open arms. Over time, however, they had buried the hatchet and learned to work together.

"What's the deal with Debra Highsmith?" Joanna asked.

"Sorry, I suppose I should have given you a call about this," Alvin said, "but it's been crazy. When she didn't show up at school this morning and didn't call in, we sent out officers to do a welfare check. They found nothing—zip. Her purse and cell phone were there, but her car keys and car are missing. And there's a pair of shoes on the floor beside the door, as though she kicked them off as soon as she came inside. There was no sign of forced entry. No sign of a struggle. It's as though she went home after school yesterday afternoon and then both she and her vehicle simply vanished into thin air. We've checked with all the neighbors. No one admits to having seen or heard anything out of the ordinary with her or with her dog."

"She's got a dog?" Joanna asked.

"A big Doberman," Alvin replied. "The neighbors tell us she's only had him a couple of weeks, but he's gone, too. Dog dishes and doggy doo-doo are everywhere. No dog, but with the car and keys gone, it's unlikely that the woman's on foot, and chances are the dog is with her. All the same, we're searching the neighborhood in case she went out for a walk with the dog. It could be she suffered some kind of medical emergency and ended up in a ditch where no one can see her. Or else she's in a hospital. I've got someone calling hospitals in the area just in case."

"Where does she live?"

"Out in San Jose Estates, so there's some distance between the houses. I've had uniforms out canvassing up and down the street. No one remembers seeing her out and about on foot or otherwise. However, we did find something pretty interesting."

By then Joanna had put the Yukon in gear and was driving down Tombstone Canyon with Dennis jabbering happily in the backseat. His brand of nonstop talk was pretty much lost on everyone but his sister, who seemed to understand his every word. Neither of them appeared to be paying the slightest attention to Joanna's side of the conversation.

"What's that?"

"Remember when she gave you all that crap over her zero tolerance of weapons at school?"

"Yes," Joanna said. "I remember it well. Why?"

"I knew she had applied for and received a concealed-weapons permit. After her giving you so much grief about bringing a weapon to school, I guess I never thought she'd go the distance, but she did. Guess what we found in her purse? One of those two-inch Judge Public Defenders loaded with five four-ten shotgun shells."

A Public Defender loaded with shotgun shells certainly wouldn't have been Joanna's first choice of weapon. It was designed to do serious damage, and it wasn't something that lent itself to harmless practice shooting on a firing range.

"You've got to be kidding. She had one of those in her purse?"

"Yes, ma'am," Alvin said. "Big as life. Considering her very public attitude toward firearms, I thought you'd get a kick out of that."

As far as Joanna was concerned, "kick" wasn't exactly the word that came to mind.

"Sounds like she was worried about something," Joanna said. "You don't go around with a handgun in your purse, especially one loaded with shotgun shells, if you haven't a care in the world."

"Who has a gun in her purse?" Jenny asked.

If Jenny was tuning in, that meant that Joanna's part of the conversation was over. "Keep me posted if you learn anything more," she said. "I need to get my kids home to dinner."

Alvin took the hint. "Okay," he said. "Talk to you later."

"You still didn't say whose gun," Jenny objected.

"Police business," Joanna said.

In her family those two words carried a lot of weight, just as they had years earlier when her father had used them with Joanna. It was a conversational Do Not Cross line that was every bit as effective as a strip of yellow crime scene tape. It meant the subject was off-limits and any further discussion forbidden.

"I'm not a baby, you know," Jenny complained.

"No, you're not," Joanna agreed. "Which means that you understand I'm not allowed to discuss an ongoing investigation with anyone."

"I'll bet you'll discuss it with Dad," Jenny said.

Joanna's heart did a tiny flip. She and Butch Dixon had been married for years, but this was the first time she ever remembered hearing Jenny refer to him as "Dad" rather than "Butch." Although the whole idea gladdened her heart, she didn't want to screw it up by overreacting. Besides, there was always a chance that, in this case, Jenny was deliberately zinging her mother.

"What do you want to bet?" Joanna asked.

"Never mind," Jenny said. "I didn't want to know anyway."

With that Jenny lapsed into a brooding silence that lasted the rest of the way home. Joanna tried not to take any of it too seriously. When it came to parenting teenagers, bouts of surly silence were par for the course. When they got to the house, Jenny grabbed her backpack, darted out of the car, and slammed her way into her bedroom before Joanna managed to drag Dennis and all his toddler gear into the house.

"What's up with Jenny?" Butch asked.

From the complex aroma in the kitchen, Joanna could tell that dinner was all but cooked. Butch was busy setting the table.

"Nothing five years won't fix," Joanna said with a laugh.

"Oh, that," Butch said, giving first her and then Dennis quick pecks on the cheek as they walked by. "Wash your hands, little man," Butch added to Dennis. "Dinner's almost ready."

Chapter 2

When Joanna Brady was first elected sheriff, she had dutifully followed in the footsteps of her father, who had once held the same position. Her own election had come about in the aftermath of the shooting death of her first husband, Andrew Roy Brady, who had been running for the office of sheriff when he was killed by a drug kingpin's hit man. Friends of Andy's had prevailed on Joanna to run in his stead. When she was elected, everyone had more or less written her off as a figurehead, sheriff in name only, but she had rejected those assumptions, making the effort to learn the job by sending herself off to the police academy.

In the process Joanna had surprised both her supporters and her critics; she had also surprised herself. She soon discovered that law enforcement fever ran in her veins. Being sheriff wasn't just a job, it was her passion. Like her father, D. H. Lathrop, before her, she lived and breathed the job, working too many hours and bringing home mountains of paperwork to do in the evening at the dining room table. Before long she was living to work instead of working to live. Big difference.

She hadn't anticipated falling in love again, and the idea of having another baby had never crossed her mind. Both of those had come as complete surprises. When first Butch Dixon and later Dennis came into her life, those two additions had caused a sudden reordering of Joanna's priorities. Yes, her job was still important to her; yes, she still loved it; but now she made a conscious effort every day to maintain a balance between home and work.

A big part of achieving that balance had to do with the fact that, in their two-career family, Butch and Joanna were beyond lucky in having good help. A year or so earlier, Carol Sunderson and the two grandsons she was raising had been left homeless when an electrical fire had swept through their mobile home, taking the life of her invalid husband. At the time, Joanna's old house on High Lonesome Ranch had been rented out and was left in terrible shape by departing tenants who had torn the place apart before they skipped town without paying the rent. In a stroke of enlightened self-interest, after fixing it up Joanna and Butch had offered the house to Carol at a reasonable rent while at the same time hiring her as part-time household help.

It had turned out to be a match made in heaven. Having Carol to backstop Butch with cooking, housework, and child care gave him more time to devote to his writing. Now that his third crime novel was due to be published in several months' time, Carol's capable presence made it feasible for him to go on a book tour—which his publisher definitely wanted him to do.

When dinner was over and the dishes done, Butch retreated to the office to finish reviewing his copyediting and Jenny shut herself up in her room to do homework, leaving Joanna to spend some one-on-one time with Dennis. They went out into the yard and turned on the yard light. Long after sunset, she and Dennis continued playing a rousing game of fetch with their two remaining dogs—Lucky, a deaf black Lab, and Lady, the shy Australian shepherd. The dogs didn't tire of fetching and Dennis didn't tire of throwing.

Jenny had taught Lucky to respond to sign language, and he was more her dog than he was anyone else's. When they had first rescued Lady, Joanna was the only member of the family the dog would tolerate. Now, to everyone's surprise, she had switched loyalties by taking

Dennis under her wing as though he was her special charge. When Dennis was home, inside or outside, Lady literally dogged his heels wherever he went. She had even abandoned her special spot on Joanna's side of the bed, choosing instead to sleep on the rug next to the trundle bed in Dennis's room.

It was fully dark before they finally went inside. Once Dennis was bathed and in bed, Joanna settled down with a book in the family room where the model trains on Butch's train track were, for once, mercifully still. She was reading quietly when, well after nine, Butch finally emerged from his office.

"Done?" she inquired.

Nodding, he picked up the remote control and switched on the TV. "Mind if I turn on the news?"

"Help yourself."

"Thanks for chasing after Denny tonight," he said. "The manuscript needs to go out by FedEx tomorrow so it can be in New York on Monday. I needed to finish it tonight, especially since both kids will be home from school tomorrow. When they're here, it's almost impossible to work. Besides, Jenny and I have to schedule some stick-shift driving lessons over the weekend."

"You're fearless," Joanna said. "By the way, Jenny gave you a promotion this afternoon. She actually called you Dad."

"That is a promotion," Butch agreed, "but why was she so grumpy at dinner? She barely said a word and seemed really out of sorts."

"We had a disagreement coming home in the car," Joanna said. "She overheard part of a conversation about a current investigation, and she was put out that I wouldn't spill the beans about what was going on."

"What investigation?" Butch asked.

The ten o'clock news was just coming on with a teaser about a missing high school principal. "If you watch the news," Joanna said, "you'll know exactly which investigation. You'll also understand why I couldn't discuss it with her."

As expected, the story about the missing school principal was right there at the top of the news broadcast.

"Tonight, authorities in Bisbee are searching for Bisbee High School's principal, Debra Highsmith, who went missing sometime last night," the news anchor said. "When Ms. Highsmith failed to show up at work today, police officers were dispatched to her home to do a welfare check, but failed to find her. Our reporter Toni Avila is on the scene. What can you tell us, Toni?"

"According to a spokesman for the Bisbee Police Department, when officers were dispatched to Ms. Highsmith's residence in Bisbee's San Jose neighborhood, they found no evidence of a struggle or of foul play. Her vehicle, a white 2006 VW Passat with Arizona plate number AZU-657, is also missing. At this point, officers assisted by K-9 teams are doing a thorough search of the nearby area. They're also checking with area hospitals to see if Ms. Highsmith may have suffered some kind of medical emergency. Anyone with knowledge of her whereabouts is urged to contact the Bisbee Police Department."

"Let's hope they're able to find her," the anchor said, "but it turns out Ms. Highsmith's disappearance isn't the only news from Bisbee today. What else is going on?"

"As many of our viewers realize, we've been doing daily coverage of the trial of Alma DeLong, a Tucson-area businesswoman who owned Caring Friends, a now-defunct organization that operated inpatient care for Alzheimer's patients all over southern Arizona. Second-degree homicide charges were lodged against Ms. DeLong in the deaths of three people who died while being housed at the Caring Friends Palominas facility. After a weeklong trial in Cochise County Superior Court and after almost two days of deliberation, the jury returned their verdict late this afternoon. Ms. DeLong was found guilty on all three homicide charges and on the charge of resisting arrest. She was found innocent on a related charge of assaulting a police officer.

"Here's what the son of one of the victims had to say after the verdict was rendered."

The screen switched over to a view of Bobby Fletcher standing outside the courtroom door, flanked on one side by Arlee Jones and on the other by Joanna.

"Hey, why didn't you tell us you were going to be on TV tonight?" Butch wanted to know.

"Because I didn't know for sure that I was. Besides, it was a walk-on appearance only. No spoken lines."

"And the case Jenny's annoyed about is the one involving the missing principal?"

Joanna nodded. "That would be it, since Debra Highsmith happens to be Jenny's principal."

"Was that a live feed just now?" Butch asked.

"I think so. Why?"

"That means they still haven't found her."

"Evidently."

"If it's not your case, what's the problem with talking to Jenny about it?"

"What if she ended up carrying tales to school about it? That could cause trouble down the road, especially if what happened to Debra Highsmith turns out to be something more serious than her just going out for a solitary evening drive."

"The reporter made it sound like she might have landed in a hospital somewhere."

"Let's hope that's all it is," Joanna said. "Debra Highsmith has never been one of my favorite people, but I'd hate to see something bad happen to her."

A few minutes later, when the weather came on, Butch switched off the television set. "This is Arizona. The weather tomorrow is going to be just like the weather today. What say we go to bed?"

They did. Their bedroom door had a lock on it, and they made good use of same. Afterward, Joanna slept like a baby. When the rooster-crowing ring of her cell phone jarred her awake the next morning, it was full daylight and the clock on the nightstand said 6:47. When she saw Jenny's number on the caller ID readout, Joanna assumed Butch had forgotten to unlock the bedroom door before they went to sleep.

"Mom, Mom," Jenny sobbed into the phone. "You have to come quick. I just found Ms. Highsmith."

Joanna sat up in bed, trying to get her head around what was going on. "You found her here?" she demanded. "At the house?"

"I'm not at the house!" Jenny replied indignantly. "I woke up early and decided to take Kiddo out for a ride before breakfast. I found Ms. Highsmith here, beside the road."

"That's a relief," Joanna said. "Is she all right?"

"She's not all right!" Jenny declared. "She's dead. I think someone shot her."

By the time Jenny finished that last sentence, Joanna was out of bed and scrambling into her clothes.

"You're sure it's her?" Joanna demanded.

"She's still wearing her name badge. I can read, you know."

"Where are you?" Joanna asked urgently, switching her phone to speaker. "Tell me exactly."

"When Kiddo and I go out for an early-morning gallop, we always head up High Lonesome. We're just this side of the third wash north of our house."

High Lonesome Road runs north and south along the base of the Mule Mountains. On those rare occasions when it rains, rushing water comes flooding down out of the mountains to drain into the Sulphur Springs Valley. Wash beds that are only a few feet apart up on the mountainsides spread out like the spokes of a wheel at lower elevations. During those periodic deluges the gullies run wall to wall with roiling water, sometimes ten to fifteen feet deep. Once the floods are over and the water drains away, the sandy beds are often left littered with man-size boulders.

Faced with budget cuts, the county had finally quit blading the rocks out of the way, which left High

Lonesome Road north of the High Lonesome Ranch impassable for through traffic. The washouts may have been hazardous to most vehicular traffic, but Joanna realized they presented no barrier for someone traveling on a speeding quarter horse.

"I'm getting dressed," Joanna said. "I'll be there as soon as I can. You're sure she's dead?"

"Yes, Mom," Jenny said. "I'm sure."

"Don't touch anything," Joanna cautioned. "Especially don't touch the body."

Jenny's earlier panic morphed into indignation. "Mom," she said, "do you think I'm stupid or something? Besides, why would I touch it? It's gross. There are flies and bugs. It smells awful."

"All right," Joanna said. "How's the road?"

"Pretty bad. Her car is stuck in the first wash. At least I'm pretty sure it's Ms. Highsmith's car, and it's blocking the road."

"Don't worry," Joanna said. "I have four-wheel drive. That shouldn't be a problem, but if it is and I can't make it to where you are in the Yukon, I may have to walk. That could take a while."

By then Joanna was on her way through the kitchen where Butch was overseeing Dennis's breakfast.

"What's up?" Butch asked as Joanna hurried past him.

"Jenny and Kiddo went out for a ride and found a body," Joanna said. "I've got to go."

"A body? Whose? Where?"

"She says it looks like Debra Highsmith. They're up the road," Joanna said. "Up High Lonesome."

"Do you want me to come with you?"

"No," Joanna said. "You stay with Dennis. I'll get some deputies out here. We'll be fine."

In the garage, Joanna put the Yukon in gear, backed out, and sped away up the driveway. At first she intended to get on the radio and call out the troops. Ultimately she changed her mind. She wanted to be on the scene in person and see the lay of the land before she ran up the flag for help. With Jenny involved, she wanted to have a clear idea of the challenges her people and the medical examiner's crew would encounter in trying to reach the body.

As she approached the first wash, the road narrowed from two lanes to one. As she crested the hill, the Passat was completely hidden from view until she started down into the dip. The moment she saw the stranded vehicle, Joanna understood that Jenny was right. The vehicle had plowed into the sand and then had turned sideways where it had high-centered on an invisible boulder hidden under a thin layer of sand. The driver's fruitless attempt to free it had torn up the surrounding sand, making a bad situation worse. Stopping short of the wash, Joanna climbed out of her SUV to survey the scene. She realized that if she attempted to drive around the Passat at low speed, even with four-wheel drive, there was a good chance the Yukon would end up stuck as well.

"I told you," Jenny said.

Joanna looked up in time to see Jenny pull Kiddo out of a trot on the far side of the wash. "Come on," she said. "We can ride double. It'll be faster than walking."

Avoiding the churned-up sand, Joanna crossed the wash. With Jenny's help, Joanna managed to get a foot in the stirrup and clamber up onto Kiddo's back, where she clung to Jenny's waist. As soon as Joanna was onboard, Jenny urged Kiddo into a fast canter. Jenny was a capable rider; Joanna was not. As Kiddo raced along in the rocky roadway, Joanna clung to her daughter for dear life.

Joanna estimated that they covered the better part of a mile between the first wash and the next. After that, when the road became even rougher, Jenny slowed Kiddo to a walk. A mile later, Jenny pulled Kiddo to a halt and nodded toward something beside the road. It resembled a fully clothed rag doll lying in an awkward heap. Only on closer inspection did the heap resolve itself into a woman's body.

Joanna slid off the horse. While Jenny remained on a restive Kiddo, Joanna moved toward the body. She stopped short several feet away and stood still, giving herself a chance to examine both the victim and the nearby surroundings.

The body of a woman, with her head twisted to one side, lay prone in a flat expanse of rocky dirt. The victim had been there long enough for carrion eaters to have made inroads on her facial features, leaving her unrecognizable. She was dressed in the kind of clothing someone might have worn to work—a dirt- and blood-stained white blouse and tailored navy blue jacket and skirt. A name badge, still pinned to the lapel of her jacket, identified her as DEBRA HIGHSMITH. Her bare feet showed the laddered remnants of a pair of panty hose. It looked as though she had been shot in the back. Joanna counted four different entrance wounds, one in her right leg and the others in her torso. She hadn't died instantly, but Joanna knew she couldn't have survived for long because there wasn't much blood. What there was had turned brown in the sun.

After ascertaining there were no visible footprints that would be disturbed by her presence, Joanna stepped closer. That sudden movement sent a black cloud of flies milling skyward. The distinctive stench of decomposition was thick in the air. Fighting down her gag reflex, Joanna didn't need a medical examiner to tell her Debra Highsmith had been dead for some time, probably more than a day.

"There's not a lot of blood," Jenny observed from the sidelines. "She must have died right away."

Joanna gave her fifteen-year-old daughter an appraising look. Joanna had tried her best to protect Jenny from some of the grim realities of growing up in a law enforcement family, but clearly she'd been paying attention. Her astute observation warranted an acknowledgment.

"You're right," Joanna said. "Let's hope she didn't suffer too much."

"Maybe not after she got shot," Jenny said, "but what about before?"

That one rocked Joanna, too, because once again Jenny's conclusion was on the money. There was enough visible bruising around the victim's wrists and ankles to show that she had been restrained for some period of time before being shot. Given that, there was no way to tell what kind of damage might have been inflicted prior to shooting.

"Yes," Joanna agreed. "After."

She plucked her phone out of the pocket of her uniform and punched the speed-dial combination that would take her to Dispatch. Larry Kendrick, her lead dispatcher, took the call.

"Good morning, Sheriff Brady," he said, greeting her by name before she said a word. In the world of nearly universal caller ID that was hardly surprising. "What's up?"

"I believe Jenny and I have found the body of that missing high school principal. I'll need a full-court homicide call-out ASAP."

Joanna's homicide unit consisted of three detectives—Ernie Carpenter, Jaime Carbajal, and Deb Howell—as well as her two-person CSI unit, which included Casey Ledford, a fingerprint tech, and Dave Hollicker, her crime scene investigator. Ernie, the senior detective, was off on vacation, taking a Rhine River cruise with his wife, Rose. That left detectives Jaime Carbajal and Deb Howell to pick up the slack.

"Dave Hollicker and Jaime are already here at the department," Larry said. "I'll send them right out. As for Howell and Ledford? It's Friday. You know what that means."

Joanna did know what that meant. Both Deb Howell and Casey Ledford were single mothers of school-age children whose work lives were impacted by the school system's four-day week. The two women were generally not scheduled to work on Fridays, and they wouldn't be able to show up unless and until they were able to arrange for child care.

"Tell them to come as soon as they can," Joanna said. "We're about three miles north of my place on High Lonesome Road. The road's a mess. Most of the way the road is wide enough for two cars, but it narrows down to one lane in the dips. Ms. Highsmith's Passat is blocking the road at the first wash. We'll need a tow truck to get it out of there. Pass the word that everyone will need four-wheel drive to get here." Joanna paused and then added, "Oh, and I'll want the K-9 unit, too."

"You got it," Larry said. "What about the M.E.? Are you going to call him or am I?"

In the old days, when Dr. George Winfield had been the Cochise County Medical Examiner, the call-out could have come from any number of people inside Joanna's department. Unfortunately, George had fallen in love with Joanna's mother, Eleanor, and she had packed him off into a retirement that now included an annual snow-bird migration back and forth between Arizona and Minnesota.

Both in public and in private, Joanna's relationship with George Winfield had been businesslike and virtually trouble free even after he'd married Eleanor Lathrop. As sheriff and M.E., they had continued to work together with little difficulty. So it had come as something of a shock to Joanna and to other members of her department to discover that Doc Winfield's replacement, Dr. Guy Machett, was anything but trouble free.

For one thing, Dr. Machett—never Doc Machett—insisted that everyone follow a strict chain-of-command hierarchy. If his services were required, he expected the call to come from Joanna herself and not from someone who reported to her.

"That's my next call," Joanna said.

"Good," Larry said.

The relief in his voice spoke volumes. Larry had endured more than his share of Guy Machett temper tantrums. He didn't need another one.

The clock in Joanna's cell phone said 8:01 AM as she scrolled through her contact list to find Guy Machett's number. He was nothing if not punctual, so she dialed his office number.

"Medical examiner's office," Madge Livingston drawled.

Forty years of smoking unfiltered Camels had left Madge with a throaty voice that might have been sexy if it hadn't been punctuated by periodic fits of coughing. A sixty-something peroxide blonde, Madge had worked for county government all her adult life, moving from one department to another because no one had balls enough to put her out to pasture. Madge's last remotion, one that had moved her out of the county office complex, had landed her in the M.E.'s office. Like Joanna, Madge had gotten along just fine with Doc Winfield. Her relationship with Dr. Machett was something less than smooth sailing.

Dr. Machett was a man with a very high opinion of himself, someone who felt he was doing the world a favor by sharing his vast knowledge and abilities with the lowly folks in Cochise County. Unfortunately, there weren't many other people who agreed with that assessment.

"Sheriff Brady," Joanna said. "Is he in?"

"I believe he's on the other line," Madge said. "Can you hold?"

In the old days, Joanna would have passed the information along to Madge with no further muss or fuss because Madge would have informed George of the situation. These days it didn't work that way, and both Joanna and Madge knew it.

"Sure," Joanna said. "I'll hold."

While she waited, Joanna tried to imagine what had been going on when Debra Highsmith was gunned down. There was no way to tell where the victim had been standing in relation to her killer. As far as addresses were concerned, High Lonesome Road was a fine place to live—Joanna had lived there with Andy and she lived there now with Butch—but it struck Joanna as a hard place to die. It had been true for Andrew Roy Brady and it was equally true for Debra Highsmith.

"Who's calling?" Guy Machett asked when he came on the line.

Madge Livingston knew very well who was on the phone. Not telling her boss who was calling was his secretary's way of getting a little of her own back.

"Sheriff Brady," Joanna said. "We've located a body on High Lonesome Road."

"Where the hell is High Lonesome Road?" he demanded. "Sounds like it's out in the sticks somewhere."

"It is. It's just down the road from where I live," Joanna told him, "also on High Lonesome Road. Take Highway 80 east from Bisbee and take the turnoff to Elfrida. Turn left almost immediately. That's High Lonesome Road. Come north three miles. You'll probably need four-wheel drive to get here."

"Is that how you got there?" Machett asked.

"No," Joanna said quite truthfully while at the same time trying not to betray the grin that had suddenly tweaked her face. "I came on horseback."

Chapter 3

Joanna's next call was to Bisbee's chief of police. "We found Debra Highsmith's body," she said without preamble.

"You're sure it's her?" Alvin Bernard asked.

Joanna sighed. "Yes, I am."

"Where?" Chief Bernard wanted to know. "When?"

"My daughter went out for an early-morning ride and found the body on High Lonesome Road, about three miles north of our place. I'm no medical examiner, but I'd say she's been dead for more than a day."

"How?" Alvin asked.

He seemed to be stuck in the world of one-word questions.

"I counted at least three gunshot entrance wounds in her back and one in her leg. I'd say he used the leg shot to bring her down and then finished her off execution style."

"Ugly," Alvin said.

"Yes," Joanna agreed. "Very, but since this looks like a joint case, I'm calling to see if you want to send out a detective."

"Due to budget cuts, I've got only one investigator to my name, Matt Keller. He does the whole nine yards—property, homicide, whatever. I'll be glad to send him along."

"Does he have a four-wheel-drive vehicle?"

"Are you kidding? This is Bisbee," Chief Bernard said. "We don't have four-wheel-drive anything."

"The road out here is rough. You might want to send Keller down to the Justice Center so he can hitch a ride out to the crime scene with Jaime Carbajal. I'll tell him to wait until Matt shows up."

"I'll get right on it," Bernard said. "Thanks for letting me know."

After calling Larry Kendrick back with a request that Jaime wait for Detective Keller, Joanna turned to her daughter. Jenny and Kiddo were standing on the far side of the wash, where Kiddo was contentedly munching on several carrots Jenny had brought along in her pocket.

"Are you okay?" Joanna asked.

"I'm fine, Mom," Jenny said. "I mean, I've seen something dead before."

"Someone," Joanna corrected, "and so have I. But to see someone shot like this? It's still upsetting."

"Even for you?"

"Even for me."

Jenny took a bite out of a carrot and passed the remainder to Kiddo. Joanna managed to keep from asking if Jenny had washed the carrots before sticking them in her pocket.

"How did the bad guy leave?" Jenny asked. "If his getaway car was stuck in the wash, where did he go?"

"He must have left on foot," Joanna said.

That made it possible that the killer had walked right past High Lonesome Ranch. Not a comforting thought, but Joanna needed to know for sure.

"That's why I called for the K-9 unit," Joanna continued. "Terry and Spike might be able to pick up his trail and at least give us an idea of which direction he went."

"What if he walked by our house?"

Not for the first time, Joanna was forced to consider the mysterious workings of DNA. Jenny seemed to have a mental GPS that was following her mother's every thought, spoken or unspoken.

"If he had come anywhere near the house, I'm sure Lady would have raised a fuss, and just because Lucky happens to be deaf doesn't mean he isn't up to the job. If someone posed a threat to you or anyone else in the family, I have a feeling that big black lug of yours would tear the bad guy limb from limb."

Jenny nodded. "Probably," she said.

"Speaking of dogs," Joanna said. "Did you see any dog prints around here?"

Jenny shook her head. "Why?"

"I understand Ms. Highsmith had a dog."

"Giles," Jenny said. "That's the name of her dog."

"You knew Ms. Highsmith's dog?"

"I only saw him one time. His first owner, a guy out at Fort Huachuca, was being deployed and had to get rid of him—free to a good home. Ms. Highsmith brought him to the clinic for a checkup, to update his shots, and to have him chipped. He's a Doberman. He looks fierce, but he's a good dog."

Joanna spent a few minutes looking but could find no visible dog prints. She had the sick feeling that if Debra Highsmith was dead, so was her dog.

Finally, Joanna turned back to Jenny. "You and Kiddo should probably head home," Joanna said. "The crime scene team will be here soon."

"Won't somebody need to interview me?" Jenny asked. "I mean, on TV the cops always interview the person who finds the body. The person calling it in usually turns out to be some kind of suspect or some-thing."

"The person who finds the body usually isn't my daughter," Joanna responded. "If anyone besides me needs to interview you, I'll send them by the house."

"Okay," Jenny said, but she clearly wasn't happy about it. She turned away from Joanna, put a foot in the stirrup, and then vaulted easily up into the saddle. She was doing exactly what Joanna had asked her to do, yet somehow it felt like a rebuke.

"I'm your mother," Joanna said. "I'm only trying to protect you."

"I'm almost grown up," Jenny said, with a defiant toss of her blond hair. "You can't always protect me, you know."

With that, she touched her heels to Kiddo's flanks, and they raced off down the road, leaving Joanna stand-ing in the cloud of dust kicked up by the departing horse's galloping hooves. With a sigh, Joanna pulled out her cell phone and called home.

"Incoming," she said, when Butch answered. "Jenny's on her way home and she's bent out of shape again. She thinks I'm being unreasonable for sending her home instead of having her hang around here to be interviewed by one of my detectives."

"Doesn't sound unreasonable to me," Butch said.

"Maybe you can convince her of that. In the meantime, I'm waiting for my crime scene team to show up. Debra Highsmith's vehicle is stuck in the first wash and blocking the road. It'll have to be towed out of the way before anyone else can get here. I'm not sure how long that's going to take."

"I guess I should have packed you a lunch."

"Too late for that," Joanna said. "I'll stop off and grab something on my way to the office. In the meantime, rather than inadvertently messing up some evidence, I'm walking back to the first wash. Since no one can get in or out for the time being except on foot, I'm deeming the crime scene secure."

"You're walking?" Butch asked.

"Yes, the Yukon is on the far side of the first wash."

"How did you get from there to the body?"

"Jenny gave me a ride on Kiddo. The fact that she didn't offer me a ride back gives you some idea of how mad she is."

"Sometimes parenthood sucks," Butch said, "but since she bestowed the honorary title of dad on me yesterday, I guess I'd better see what I can do to calm the troubled waters once she gets home."

"Thanks, Butch," Joanna said, and she meant it.

Call waiting buzzed. "Phone call," she said. She clicked over to find Deb Howell on the line.

"I'm stuck on the far side of the first wash," Deb said. "No sign of the tow truck so far."

"I'm coming that way on foot," Joanna said. "I'll be there when I can, but how did you make it there so fast? I thought you'd be the last to arrive."

"If I'd had to track down a babysitter, I probably would have been, but Maury's here today and tomorrow. Ben and I were supposed to go ATVing with him today. Now Maury and Ben are going without me."

A year earlier Maury Robbins, a 911 operator in Tucson, had called in a homicide that had occurred at Action Trail Adventures, a combination RV/all-terrain vehicle park north of Bowie in the far-northeast corner of Cochise County. During that investigation, Maury had exhibited more than a passing interest in Deb Howell, one of the detectives on the case. When Ernie Carpenter had mentioned as much, Deb had replied with an immediate denial, insisting that it was all about work. In the months since, however, Ernie's assessment had been proved correct. Deb Howell and Maury Robbins were now a romantic item. Although he still lived in Tucson, he spent many of his days off in Bisbee, parking his Jayco pop-up camper at the RV park in Old Bisbee, a few blocks from the home on Brewery Gulch that Deb shared with her son.

The news that Deb trusted the man enough to let
Ben go ATVing with him alone struck Joanna as significant, but she didn't make any comment to that effect.

"What's going on?" Deb asked. "Larry said something about your finding a body."

"I didn't find it; Jenny did," Joanna replied, "and
it's not just any body. It's Debra Highsmith, the missing high school principal. Jenny found her near the
third wash, which is about two miles north of your
current location."

"The high school principal?" Deb asked.

"That's the one. So this will be a joint investigation,"
Joanna explained. "Chief of Police Bernard is sending
Matt Keller, his only detective. Due to budget cuts, the
city had to lay off all their forensics folks. Fortunately,
we've still got ours. So we'll be handling all the crime
scene and forensic lines of inquiry. And since you're
the first to arrive, you'll be lead investigator."

Deb was the greenest of Joanna's three detectives.
With a high-profile school principal involved, Debra
Highsmith's murder was bound to garner plenty of
publicity. Someone else might have opted for a more
senior investigator, but Joanna thought that leading the
charge on this one might help give Deb some much-
needed street cred. In order for Detective Howell to
carry her weight inside the department, people on the

outside needed to know that she was capable of doing the job. This case was her chance to prove it.

"The tow truck's here," Deb reported.

"Crap," Joanna said. "I was hoping Casey Ledford would show up first. Ask the driver to hold off until Casey has a chance to dust the doors and door handles as well as the steering wheel, gearshift, and emergency-brake handle for prints."

Deb was off the line for a moment. In the background Joanna could hear her negotiating with the tow truck driver. Eventually she came back on the phone.

"He's not happy about it, but I told him this is a homicide investigation. He'll wait. I didn't exactly give him a choice."

"Good," Joanna said. As far as Sheriff Brady was concerned, in dealing with the tow truck driver, Detective Howell had just passed her first test in being lead investigator.

"While you're waiting, you might have a look around the general area," Joanna said.

"Isn't this still a long way from the actual crime scene?"

"Yes, but it looked to me like whoever was driving the Passat spent some time and effort trying to get it out of the sand. While he was concentrating on that, he might have inadvertently dropped something that would help us identify him."

"You believe the killer was leaving the scene when the car got hung up?"

"Yes," Joanna replied.

"Where'd he go from here and how did he do it—on foot?"

Joanna didn't bother pointing out Deb's sexist assumption that the killer was male, because she shared the same opinion.

"Terry Gregovich and Spike are on their way," Joanna said. "If he did walk away, I'm hoping Spike and Terry will be able to pick up the scent."

"Your place is the closest one to where the car is," Deb said. "Do you think he might have gone there?"

"I doubt it. At least I hope not," Joanna said. "Still, you might have a uniformed deputy stop by Carol Sunderson's place and ours and take a look around the outbuildings just in case he did head there and hunker down for the night." The idea that an unsuspecting Jenny could have walked into the tack room that morning and come face-to-face with a killer was chilling.

"I'll get right on it," Deb said. "Casey just showed up. And the M.E. I need to go."

"I'm almost there," Joanna said. "I can see the tow truck."

By the time she finished that last sentence, Detective Howell was long gone. Joanna trudged on. It was only a little past eight, but she felt as if she'd been up for hours. This was April, and the Arizona sun was giving a clear warning that summer was coming. She was hot, dusty, sweaty, and thirsty. She had a bottle of water in the back of her Yukon. Right at that moment, Joanna needed the water bottle in her hand, not in her vehicle.

She crossed the wash in time to hear Guy Machett berating Deb Howell.

"How long is this going to take? You mean we can't even get near the body until she finishes taking fingerprints?"

"The body is a good two miles from here," Deb responded. "If you want to walk that far, fine. Otherwise we'll have to wait until Casey finishes lifting whatever prints she can find."

"This is ridiculous," Machett replied. "You can't expect me to stand around here twiddling my thumbs and doing nothing for who knows how long. Where's Sheriff Brady?"

"I'm right here, Dr. Machett," Joanna said, slipping through the knot of investigators. "And Detective Howell is simply following my orders. We believe this vehicle was driven by the killer, and we need to make every effort to gather any available information before the vehicle is moved."

"That could take hours."

"No," Joanna said. "Ms. Ledford won't be dusting the entire vehicle. She'll work on the parts that might be disturbed by the process of getting the Passat pulled out of the sand and loaded onto the tow truck. The remaining investigation will be conducted in the garage at the county's impound facility."

"It's still damned inconvenient to expect me to show up and wait."

Joanna felt like saying that he was getting paid for waiting, but she didn't. There were too many people around. She didn't want to provoke a firefight that might become fodder for public consumption. A year earlier, Joanna's rivalry with the head of the county health department had made a splash in the local media. She didn't need a similar situation between her department and the M.E.'s office showing up on the evening news.

"As Detective Howell told you, the body's about two miles north of here," she said. "I just walked it. If you want to go on ahead and start the process, we can bring your vehicle and equipment along once the road is clear."

Given a choice between walking or waiting, Guy Machett didn't take long to make up his mind. "I'll wait," he said. "Who is this person again?"

"I believe her name is Debra Highsmith. She's the principal at the high school. The high school secretary reported her missing yesterday morning."

"Married?"

"Not that I know of," Joanna answered.

"I suppose I should call the school district office and try to get a handle on next of kin."

Joanna was pretty sure Deb Howell had already made a call like that, but she let the M.E. make his own. Guy Machett was touchy enough under the best of circumstances. He would no doubt go ballistic if he thought someone was making investigative inroads inside the boundaries of what he considered his bureaucratic territory.

By the time the remaining members of Joanna's team were assembled, Casey Ledford had finished lifting the prints that were in danger of being disturbed by the towing process. At the tow truck driver's request, she shifted the Passat into neutral. There was no need to release the emergency brake. It hadn't been set. Then they all stood and watched as the Passat was winched out of the wash and loaded onto a flatbed truck.

Once the roadway was cleared, however, the wash still wasn't passable. Not wanting to risk having another vehicle stuck in the torn-up sand, Joanna had Dave Hollicker lay down two tracks of interlocking plastic pavers that created a solid enough surface across the churned sand that even the M.E.'s front-wheel-drive minivan could cross the wash with no difficulty. In the meantime, Terry Gregovich and his German shepherd, Spike, had been searching the surrounding area in ever-widening circles.

"Hey, boss," Terry called. "Come look. I think we found something. I've got a set of footprints heading that way."

Unfortunately, the direction in which he was pointing was also the same direction they had all come from—down High Lonesome Road and directly past the ranch.

Clearly reading the concerned expression on Joanna's face, Deb offered welcome reassurance. "I've already got uniformed deputies on their way to check out all the outbuildings at your place and at Carol Sunderson's."

"Thank you."

Joanna stared down at the faint remains of a shoe print left in a patch of dust along the shoulder of the road. "Good spotting," she told Terry. "When Dave is done with the pavers, I'll have him come check it out. This one doesn't look well-enough defined for a plaster cast to work, but he can at least take some measurements."

"You want us to try following the trail?" Terry asked.

"Please," Joanna said. "If you come across any better prints, let Dave know so he can try to get plaster casts."

As Joanna turned back north toward the wash and the collection of vehicles, she spotted a vulture drifting in ever narrowing circles on the air currents far above them. There was little question about the carrion eater's target.

"We'd better get a move on," she said. "Otherwise the buzzards will be back there before we are."

"Dr. Machett would not be pleased," Deb said.

"No," Joanna agreed. "It would give him one more thing to complain about."

And blame on me. She thought that last sentence, but she didn't say it aloud.

Detective Jaime Carbajal arrived on the scene. He drove up to the vehicles collected at the wash, then pulled a U-turn and came back.

"Dave has the pavers in place," he said. "Time to head out."

The second wash, with a bed of mostly undisturbed sand, was far easier to cross than the one that had been blocked by the stalled car and torn up by the towing process. Minutes after crossing the first one the caravan of official vehicles, led by Dave Hollicker's aging Tahoe and with Dr. Machett's far newer minivan second in line, arrived at the actual crime scene. Everyone else waited while Dave and the still-disgruntled M.E. walked toward the body. Joanna might have followed them, but her phone rang just then.

"Two of your deputies just gave our place a clean bill of health," Butch said. "They're headed for Carol's place next. You're not overreacting, are you? Do you really think a guy who had killed someone would be dumb enough to stop off at the sheriff's place on his way out of Dodge?"

"Nobody ever said crooks are smart," Joanna said. "The K-9 unit is trying to follow the trail. It seems to lead straight south on High Lonesome."

"Okay, then," Butch replied. "I'll tell Jenny that the next time she decides to go out for an early-morning ride, she needs to wake me so I can walk down to the barn with her."

The idea that their kids might need that kind of protection in order to be safe in their own backyard was beyond disturbing.

"Sad but true," Joanna agreed. "I need to go. I'll stop back by the house when we finish up here."

Joanna and her people stayed out of the way while Dr. Machett completed his preliminary examination of the body and while the M.E. and his recently hired assistant loaded the bagged remains. As Dr. Machett's minivan drove off in a cloud of dust,

Joanna caught sight of an arriving vehicle, which pulled aside to let them pass. Due to the remote location of the crime scene, Joanna hadn't posted a deputy to secure it. When the white RAV4 stopped beside her, Joanna realized that had been a serious oversight on her part.

The new arrival turned out to be one of Sheriff Brady's least favorite people, none other than Marliss Shackleford. A woman of indeterminate years, Marliss was a longtime employee of the local paper, the *Bisbee Bee*. Her signature column, "Bisbee Buzzings," was more of a gossip column than anything else, one that served up the paper's bread and butter, a plethora of local names. In recent years, however, the economic reality of running a small paper had caught up with the *Bee*. Marliss still wrote her column, but she was also the paper's sole reporter, covering everything but sports, which were handled on a part-time basis by a retired BHS football coach.

Joanna was not happy about any reporters showing up at a still-active crime scene. That went double for Marliss, who maintained a close personal friendship with Joanna's mother and who was married to Richard Voland, a local private eye who had once been Joanna's chief deputy. Neither of those relationships did a thing to endear Marliss to Joanna.

As the reporter's vehicle slowed, Joanna stepped forward to cut her off, motioning for her to roll down the window.

"This is a crime scene," she said brusquely. "You need to move along."

Instead, the reporter shifted her Toyota into park, switched off the ignition, and stepped out of the car with her iPad in hand. Marliss was dressed in a brightly chartreuse pantsuit. Her brassy mane of recently frosted curls glowed in the sunlight. The combination of the green pantsuit and the aggressively blond hair put Joanna in mind of an ear of corn. She allowed herself a mental smile but didn't indulge in a physical one.

"Is it true you've found Debra Highsmith's body?" Marliss demanded.

What Joanna needed right then was to have her chief deputy on hand to run media relations interference. Unfortunately it was after nine on a Friday. That meant Tom Hadlock was already on his way to monitor that week's regular meeting of the county board of supervisors.

Marliss's arrival at the crime scene and her premature knowledge of the victim's name meant that she had somehow obtained access to unauthorized information about both the crime scene and the victim's identity.

That left Joanna to draw the disconcerting conclusion that either she had a leak inside her own department or Guy Machett had one in his. While hoping for the latter, Joanna made an effort to maintain her game face.

"Come on, Marliss," she said. "You know the drill. No comment at this time. We don't release any information about the victim until we've made a positive ID and until we've notified the next of kin. Once we do that, we'll be sure to let you know."

Marliss wasn't dissuaded.

"Right," she muttered. "Along with everyone else. This is a big story, Joanna." In a piece of gamesmanship of her own, the reporter deliberately avoided the use of Joanna's official title. "A big local story. You can't expect me to sit on a scoop like this indefinitely."

Marliss had been divorced for a long time when she scored big by marrying a man a decade and a half younger than she was. Since then she had invested in any number of "image-enhancing" procedures. In the harsh sunlight, when her lips shifted into a pout, glimpses of her history of cosmetic changes showed through her carefully applied makeup, making it clear that she was far older than a first impression might have indicated.

"It's exactly what I expect," Joanna replied firmly. "We'll have a press briefing maybe later on today. In the meantime, I'd like to know where you're getting your information."

"Have you ever heard of freedom of the press?" Marliss shot back. "I'm a reporter, and I'm under no obligation to reveal my confidential sources."

"True," Joanna said, "but you also don't get preferential treatment."

"I don't have to not publish something I know just on your say-so."

"What you think you know," Joanna corrected. "And you're right. You're welcome to publish whatever you want. Putting something about a victim in your paper prior to our notifying the family would be reprehensible, but it wouldn't be against the law. You should leave now."

Marliss's cheeks glowed with fury and her Botoxed lips pulled into a sneer, but she kept her tone civil. "Very well," she said. "I'm leaving." She reached out to open the door on the RAV4. Then she stopped and turned back to Joanna. "By the way," she said, "how's Jenny doing these days?"

It was an out-of-the-blue question. As far as Joanna knew, Jenny's only meetings with Marliss had occurred mostly during coffee hours after Sunday services at Tombstone Canyon United Methodist Church, although she supposed Jenny could have encountered Marliss when she was out with Joanna's mother.

"Jenny's fine," Joanna answered.

"Good," Marliss replied with a smile that was as unsettling as it was insincere. "Glad to hear it."

Once in the SUV, she slammed it into gear, made a quick U-turn, and then took off, leaving Joanna standing there in a cloud of gravel and dust. She looked down at the grimy uniform she had put on clean only a couple of hours earlier. She'd have to shower and change before she showed up at the office.

Chapter 4

Joanna sent Deb Howell off to start tracking down the victim's next of kin while Jaime, Dave, and several uniformed officers stayed at the crime scene conducting a systematic search of the area. Unfortunately, they came up empty-handed. The killer had evidently picked up all his brass. In spots where there might have been footprints, there was evidence that the ground had been swept clean. Dave was able to make casts of one set of tire tracks, but it seemed likely that they would match the tires on Debra Highsmith's vehicle, which had now been hauled off to the department's impound lot.

The only conclusion to be drawn from this was that the perpetrator was someone who was careful enough to cover his tracks—literally.

By the time Joanna finally got back home to High Lonesome Ranch to shower and change, she was famished and hoping for breakfast, but Butch had Dennis in his car seat, and the two of them were just pulling out of the garage.

"I'm on my way to FedEx first," Butch said. "You probably don't remember, but it's Friday, when kids get all-they-can-eat tacos for three bucks at Daisy's. Jeff and his kids and Dennis and I are meeting there for lunch, then we're going to the park. Care to join us? I already know the park excursion is out, but you still need to eat."

Jeff was Jeff Daniels, the stay-at-home husband of Marianne Maculyea, the pastor of their church. Marianne and Joanna were lifelong friends. Now their husbands and kids were friends as well. Jeff and Marianne's daughter, Ruth, now nine, was an adoptee from China. Their biological son, Jeffy, had arrived as something of a surprise some time after they had adopted Ruth. Because of the long friendship between Joanna and Marianne, Jeffy's full name was Jeffrey Andrew in honor of Joanna's first husband, Andrew Roy Brady. Jeffy was more than a year older than Dennis. Despite the age difference, they were great pals.

"You're sure I won't be horning in on your guy time?" Joanna asked.

"Hardly," Butch said with a laugh.

"All right, then," Joanna said. "Order a machaca chimichanga for me, and I'll be there once I get cleaned up."

Twenty minutes later, showered, newly made up, and dressed in a fresh uniform, Joanna arrived at the restaurant, where she was astonished to see her former mother-in-law, Eva Lou Brady, stationed at the hostess stand and handing out menus.

"What are you doing here?" Joanna wanted to know.

"Jim Bob and I came in for an early lunch," Eva Lou explained. "Junior was here when we got here, but there was some kind of problem. He got upset about something—really agitated. Daisy had to call Moe to come take him home. This is the week that Daisy's is serving lunch to that whole out-of-town Plein Air painting group in the back room every day. With Junior off the floor, I could see they were really under the gun, so I offered to fill in. I told Daisy that if Junior can figure out how to make change, hand out menus, and bus tables, so can I."

Years earlier, Junior Dowdle, a developmentally disabled man in his midforties, had been abandoned by his caregivers at an arts festival in Saint David. Realizing the man was incapable of caring for himself, Joanna had brought him back to Bisbee with her. Eventually the owners of Daisy's Café, Moe and Daisy Maxwell, had taken him in. Later, they had gone to court to become Junior's official guardians. In the years since, Junior had become a fixture at the restaurant and in the community, greeting people with his constant smile and perpetually cheerful attitude, conducting customers to tables, and then handing out menus.

As for Plein Air? Once Bisbee stopped being a copper-mining town, it had morphed into an arts community and tourist attraction. Three years earlier, Maggie Oliphant, a relatively new arrival in town, had decided it was time to make a difference. The well-to-do widow of a retired army officer, she had spent years living on post at Fort Huachuca. After her husband's death, she had returned to southeastern Arizona, but she had decided against living in Sierra Vista. She had wanted a new life that was different from her old one. She had settled in Bisbee, and seeing a need, she had decided to fill it.

Living the vagabond life first as an army brat and later as an army spouse, Maggie had found art to be her salvation. It had done the same for her two daughters. When she returned to Bisbee, she found that things had changed from the time when her girls were attending school. When loss of revenue caused the school board to make budget cuts, art was an easy target. So not only was art out of the curriculum, Bisbee's school-age kids were also at loose ends on those school-free Fridays.

Maggie Oliphant's favorite credo was "If it is to be, it is up to me," and she lived by those words. She had established the Bisbee Art League and had raised enough money to rent a suite of rooms in the once abandoned and now repurposed Horace Mann School, where, on Fridays, qualified art teachers taught pottery making and charcoal drawing along with pastels and oil painting. When Maggie needed money to pay the rent or pay the teachers, she found it by writing grants or raised it by holding fund-raisers.

One of her fund-raising ideas consisted of bringing people to town to participate in weeklong hands-on workshops or, as Butch Dixon liked to call them, writers' conferences with no writing. She managed to cajole name-brand painters, potters, and sculptors into teaching what she termed "master classes." On the Saturday night of each weeklong workshop there was a celebratory dinner and one-man show for the workshop's lead artist. On the Sunday afternoon at the end of each conference week, there was an end-of-conference reception where guests were encouraged to purchase work done by the various participants during the week, with the art league receiving a commission from every sale.

Of all the workshops offered, the Plein Air master classes held in April of each year were by far the most popular. This year's Plein Air session was being led by M. L. Coleman, a well-respected Sedona landscape artist with an international following. Maggie considered Michael Coleman a big enough catch that she had gone to the trouble of creating a Saturday-night gala in his honor. The event, including both a one-man show and an auction, was booked for the clubhouse of Rob Roy Links, in Palominas, with art collectors from all over Arizona expected to attend.

During the conferences, workshop participants stayed at local lodging establishments that, depending on their financial situation, ranged from economical rooms in private homes to upscale B and Bs. When the light was right—in the early mornings and late afternoons—attendees spread out around town to do their individual painting wherever they chose. During the middle of the day, they gathered in one of the foundation's repurposed junior high school classrooms where the session's moderator conducted workshop-style classes. At lunchtime, the fifteen Plein Air painters as well as their spouses and significant others gathered at Daisy's to eat and chat. The back room at Daisy's was the only place in town large enough to accommodate a group of thirty on a daily basis.

Having Junior blow a gasket in the midst of Plein Air week had obviously created a problem.

"I hope whatever's going on with Junior isn't serious," Joanna said.

"That's what I hope, too," Eva Lou agreed, "but Moe and Daisy were both clearly upset."

"It's good of you to help out," Joanna said, giving Eva Lou a quick hug on her way past.

The fact that Eva Lou had taken it upon herself to step in and help out was typical. Jim Bob and Eva Lou Brady were good people who, in the aftermath of their son's death, had continued to treat Joanna more like a daughter than a daughter-in-law. When their son's widow had married again, they had welcomed Butch Dixon into their lives, and they were as much Dennis's grandparents as were Joanna's mother, Eleanor, and her husband, George Winfield.

"It's a shame about that poor Ms. Highsmith," Eva Lou said as she escorted Joanna toward the corner booth.

Joanna stopped in midstride. "What about her?" she asked.

Eva Lou seemed flustered. "Well, she's dead, isn't she?"

"Who told you that?" Joanna wanted to know.

She and Alvin Bernard had agreed that her department would be handling all media relations dealing with the Highsmith homicide. At this point, no official information about the homicide victim's identity had been released, at least not as far as Joanna knew.

"Those kids over there," Eva Lou said, nodding toward a booth where four high-school-age kids were huddled together, their attention focused on a cell phone that they were passing around.

"You're sure they mentioned Ms. Highsmith by name?" Joanna asked.

"Absolutely. When I came up to the table, they were all staring at one of those little cell phone things, talking and laughing and pointing at a picture. At first I couldn't make out what was on the screen, but finally I did. It looked like one of those crime scene stories on TV.

"About that time, one of them—the tall, lanky, string-bean guy in the corner next to the wall—was downright gleeful," Eva Lou replied. "I heard him say something like, 'Way to go, Ms. Highsmith! The wicked witch is dead!' Considering the woman was their principal, I thought that was in very bad taste. One of the two girls—the one with the long, dark hair—was saying that maybe the school board would end up having to cancel school for the rest of the year."

Eva Lou had been leading Joanna on a trajectory that would have taken her directly to the corner booth where Jeff Daniels, Butch, and the three kids, now joined by

Joanna's former father-in-law, Jim Bob Brady, had all settled in for lunch. Instead, Joanna again stopped short.

"They were looking at a picture?" she asked.

Eva Lou nodded. "On one of those little iPhone kind of things. When I walked up to the table the tall kid again—the one in the corner—tried to cover the screen, but it didn't work. Ever since my cataract surgery, my distance vision is perfect."

"Maybe I should go ask them about it," Joanna suggested.

"Maybe so," Eva Lou agreed.

Veering off in another direction, Joanna dodged away before Dennis saw her coming. She hurried toward the booth where the group of teenagers seemed to be preparing to leave. Joanna stopped in front of their booth and then pulled over an extra chair from a nearby table, effectively blocking their exit.

"I'm Sheriff Brady," she said. "Good morning, or is it afternoon already? Mind if I join you?"

She recognized at least three of the kids. Two of them—Tiffany Brazile and Dena Carothers—were on the cheerleading squad. Billy Stout was a big man on campus, a key player in every sport. The other boy, tall and skinny, was someone Joanna didn't know. Faced with her uniformed presence, the four teenagers exchanged guilty glances. The expressions on their faces said they did mind having Joanna join them, but none of them had nerve enough to say so. Without waiting for an invitation Joanna sat down.

"I understand that a little while ago, you were overheard discussing one of our ongoing investigations—the disappearance of Ms. Debra Highsmith. Do you mind sharing whatever information you might have?"

"We don't really know anything," Tiffany said too quickly. "We were just looking at a picture on Facebook. It's no big deal."

"Excuse me, but it is a big deal," Joanna corrected. "You seem to be in possession of details concerning the investigation that have not yet been released to the public. I need to know exactly what you know about my case and how you came to have that information."

"What if we don't want to tell you?" The speaker was the boy in the corner.

"This is a homicide investigation," Joanna said flatly. "So far this is simply an informal conversation. If you would prefer something more official, I could always throw all of you in the back of a couple of patrol cars and take you on a field trip out to the Justice Center. In that case, we'd be having this discussion in one or two of my department's interview rooms. Your call."

"If I ended up in jail, my parents would kill me!" Tiffany exclaimed. "Go ahead, Marty. Show her the picture."

"My parents would do the same thing," Dena said. "Show it to her."

Shaking his head, the boy named Marty pulled an iPhone out of his shirt pocket. After scrolling through several pages, he handed the device over to Joanna. She recognized both the scene and the subject—Debra Highsmith, lying dead, struck down by a hail of gunfire on the rock-strewn shoulder of High Lonesome Road.

Sheriff Brady prided herself on her ability to maintain a poker face, but it took a superhuman effort for her to keep her facial features utterly neutral in the face of that damning photo. She knew that photo could have come from only one source—her daughter, Jenny.

"You believe this to be . . . ?" Joanna prompted.

"That's Ms. Highsmith, our principal," Dena said quickly. "That's her hair, and she's wearing her favorite suit. She wore it to school every week."

Joanna turned her unblinking gaze on the owner of the iPhone. "What's your name?" she asked. "I don't believe I've seen you before."

"Marty. Martin Pembroke. My dad's the new doctor at the hospital."

"I'm glad to meet you, Marty," Joanna said without offering her hand. "My source tells me you weren't exactly overwhelmed with grief when you learned Ms. Highsmith might be dead. My source says that you seemed downright gleeful and said something to the effect that the wicked witch is dead."

"She was a witch," Marty said.

"I'm assuming that means she wasn't one of your faves," Joanna said.

These kids already knew Debra Highsmith was dead. There was no point in Joanna's trying to maintain otherwise, so she didn't bother.

"Earlier this year she suspended me for ten days for no reason," Marty Pembroke grumbled. "If my father hadn't appealed to the school board, I wouldn't have been able to make up the work and might not have been able to graduate with my class."

"Well, boo-hoo-hoo," Joanna said, making zero effort to tone down the sarcasm. "You claim she suspended you for no reason? Really?"

"It was all because some jerk put a can of beer in my locker. The beer wasn't even mine. It was one of my friends' idea of a joke. She blew it all out of proportion."

"Excuse me," Joanna pointed out, "but being a minor in possession of alcohol is against the law." She passed the phone back to him. "Saying you were suspended for no reason isn't exactly being fair to Ms. Highsmith. It turns out there was a reason for your suspension—and a valid one at that. As for having a beer at school? That certainly compounds an already difficult issue. Did you mention to Ms. Highsmith that you thought someone else had put it there?"

"No," Marty said. "What do you think I am, some kind of snitch?"

"There you are," Joanna said agreeably. "You didn't rat out your pals, and you're the one who got suspended. Fair enough. You pays your money and you takes your choice. Still, does a ten-day suspension warrant being glad someone is dead?"

"All we were doing here was talking, and just because I said it doesn't mean I meant it," Marty muttered. "Besides, all any of us know about what happened is what we saw in the picture—just her body lying there."

The intervening conversation had given Joanna a chance to get a grip on herself. It didn't matter whose Facebook site had the photo on it; Joanna knew the origin of the original. It had to have come from either the killer or Jenny. Unfortunately, between those two options, Jennifer Ann Brady as the source of the photo seemed the more likely, although Joanna wasn't aware that her daughter even had a Facebook page.

"Tell me about Facebook," she said. "Where is that photo posted? Whose account?"

"We don't have to tell you that," Marty Pembroke replied. "Isn't that like freedom of speech or something?"

"If you won't tell her, I will," Dena said. Obviously Marty's reluctance to be a snitch didn't extend to Dena. "It's Anne Marie Mayfield's page. She's the one who posted it. She didn't like Ms. Highsmith, either. Neither did I."

"What was your beef with her?" Joanna asked.

"She sent us both home to change clothes," Dena replied. "She said Anne Marie's skirt was too short, and my neckline was too low. It's like she turned into the fashion police or something. She probably would have been happier if we'd all had to wear uniforms to school."

"Sounds to me like she was doing her job," Joanna said.

The four kids in the booth, exchanging a set of disparaging looks, remained duly unimpressed.

With the conversation seemingly at an end, Joanna pulled out a pen and a notebook that she opened to a fresh page. "I'll need your names and phone numbers," she said.

Dena had struck Joanna as being the weakest link, so she handed the writing equipment to her. Without a word, she wrote down the required information and passed it along. Since Dena had complied without objection, so did everyone else.

When they finished and handed the pen and notebook back, Joanna stood up and returned her chair to the other table. Then she reached into her pocket and pulled out a packet of business cards.

"You're all welcome to go now," she said, passing one card to each of the young people in the booth. "You should expect to hear from one of my investigators sometime in the very near future, and if you happen to stumble across any information that might be helpful, please feel free to call."

As Joanna turned away from the booth, the idea that any of them would call her for any reason at all seemed more than unlikely.

Again she headed for the corner booth. From the sloppy debris field littering the table, Joanna gathered that lunch was mostly over. As she walked up, Butch looked at her and grinned.

"Without that layer of red dust, you clean up very well," he told her, "but is something wrong? You look upset."

"Yes, something's wrong," Joanna answered stiffly. "I am upset, and I'm here to tell you, Jennifer Ann Brady is in deep caca!"

"What's caca?" Dennis asked, smiling up at his mother over a last fistful of taco.

"Mommy will tell you later," Butch assured their son.

Joanna knew she'd just been thrown under the bus. Since she was the one who had used the term, that was only fair.

"What did Jenny do?" Butch asked.

Joanna shook her head. "I'd better not talk about it right now. Obviously, little pitchers have big ears. Am I too late for lunch?"

Butch moved over far enough so Joanna could sit down next to him. He passed her a glass of iced tea. "This is yours," he said. "Your chimichanga is ready, but I told Daisy to keep it under the salamander until you got here. She'll bring it out in a minute."

"After we have our ice cream, we're going to the park," Jeff said. "Can you come, too?"

"No," Joanna told him. "I have to go to work."

Daisy Maxwell arrived at the table, personally delivering a platter with Joanna's steaming chimichanga on it. Daisy set the plate down in front of Joanna and then started away from the table without saying a word. Her customary smile was missing in action. Seams of worry lined her face.

"I'm sorry to hear Junior is under the weather," Joanna said. "Let him know we're sending him get-well wishes."

Daisy paused long enough to nod her thanks. "I'll tell him," she said, but clearly Joanna's words had done little to lighten the woman's burden of worry as she marched back to the kitchen.

Joanna pushed a fork into the chimichanga's crusty tortilla shell, letting some of the steam leak out into the air. She wished she could let some of the steam out of her head at the same time.

"You heard about Junior, then?" Butch asked.

Joanna was grateful he had changed the subject. "Just what Eva Lou said."

"I've been noticing it for the last few weeks," Jim Bob told them. "It used to be whenever Eva Lou and I came in, he greeted us by name. Now he acts as though he's never seen us before. This morning, the people next to us asked him for water. He said he'd bring it. When the guy reminded him—and that's all he did and not even in a mean way—Junior went ballistic. It was out of character and completely over the top. Daisy had to come out of the kitchen and talk him down. He was so upset that she had to take him back to the kitchen with her. When the next set of customers came in, Eva Lou decided it was time to help out."

"She's doing a fine job of it, too," Jeff Daniels added.

Their waitress came by, checking to see if any additional tacos were needed. Fortunately all three of the kids had reached their taco limit. By the time they were done with their single servings of ice cream, Joanna had gobbled down half of her chimichanga and had the rest of it boxed up to take back to the office.

"In other words," Butch said, when she stood up to leave, doggie bag in hand, "we shouldn't be surprised if you're late for dinner."

On a day that had started out with a homicide investigation, that was a good guess. Joanna was grateful that he didn't say anything more than that, something that might have turned their private discussion into fodder for the local gossip mills, which were already operating at full capacity.

She leaned down and gave him a kiss, picking up the collection of checks on the table as she did so and making the move before either Jeff Daniels or Jim Bob could object.

"See you when you get home," Butch said. "Are you going to stop by the clinic to see Jenny?"

Joanna nodded.

"Don't be too hard on her," Butch said. "Whatever it is, she probably didn't do it on purpose."

Chapter 5

I took a while to exit the restaurant. Joanna was leaving at the same time the thirty diners from the back room were paying for their lunches, separate checks all around. A man in his sixties, dressed in a red flannel shirt topped by a brown vest, seemed to be in charge. He hustled around trying to hurry the process.

Eva Lou was a willing worker, but that kind of crush was more than she could handle. Eventually Daisy herself had to emerge from the kitchen and take charge of the cash register.

Most of the participants seemed to be much the same age as their leader, fifties to sixties or even older. They were all chatting away, discussing their plans for the afternoon and evening. One of them who seemed to be several decades younger than his fellows gave Joanna a sidelong look through a pair of fashionable wire-framed glasses.

She had been on the receiving end of looks like that numerous times. Usually the look was followed by a rude comment that had something to do with the unlikelihood of women being qualified to serve as sheriffs. She often responded to those folks with a flip comment about getting her badge out of a Cracker Jack box and her uniform from a costume shop. This time, before she had a chance to say a word, he nodded at her and smiled.

"Nice hair," he said. The man was the last customer in the Plein Air line. He had short reddish hair and a matching well-trimmed beard. His unexpected compliment took Joanna by surprise, and she found herself blushing.

"Thanks," she said. "Yours isn't bad, either."

"Yes," he agreed with a grin. "Redheads rule."

He left then, allowing Joanna to step forward with her several checks in hand.

"How was your lunch?" Daisy asked.

"Better than the rest of my morning," Joanna said. "It sounds like yours wasn't all smooth sailing, either."

"I've been happy to have the extra business this week," Daisy said, "but I think that's what pushed Junior over the edge. He's used to all the regulars, but couldn't handle so many strangers."

"He's going to be all right, isn't he?" Joanna asked.

Daisy shook her head. "No," she said. "I don't think so. His doctor says he believes it's early-onset Alzheimer's. It's not that unusual in cases like Junior's."

Daisy's eyes filled with sudden tears as she punched the numbers into the register. Joanna wanted to offer some kind of comfort, but as two additional customers stepped into line behind her, she kept quiet rather than risk upsetting Daisy even more.

Back in her dust-covered Yukon, Joanna put the vehicle in gear, backed out of the parking lot, and headed for Dr. Millicent Ross's veterinary clinic in Bisbee's Saginaw neighborhood.

In the early fifties, before the opening of Lavender Pit, clusters of frame houses that had dotted the hillsides and canyons of Upper Lowell, Lower Bisbee, and Jiggerville had stood in the way. One at a time, the houses were pried off their foundations, loaded onto axles, and then trucked through town, where they were attached to new foundations that had been dug on lots that had formerly been company-owned land in neighborhoods that would ultimately come to be known as Bakerville and Saginaw.

As far as Joanna was concerned, this was all ancient history—almost as lost on her as the fact that townspeople in Bisbee had once sheltered in mines when Apaches had threatened to ride through town causing trouble. Joanna remembered seeing photos of the houses being moved, but that was all. By now, those houses had been in place on their "new" lots long enough that mature trees and bushes had grown up around them.

On arriving in town Dr. Millicent Ross had bought two adjoining houses in a part of Saginaw that fronted on the highway. She lived in one with her partner, Jeannine Philips, who was head of Joanna's Animal Control unit. The other housed Millicent's veterinary clinic as well as a pet boarding and day-care facility. Jenny worked at the boarding area—feeding and walking animals who were either recuperating from procedures or being boarded. Her shifts ran for two hours a day after school, for several hours on Fridays, and sometimes on weekends as well, if working didn't conflict with a scheduled rodeo. Jenny's work for the clinic was ostensibly done on a volunteer basis, but Dr. Ross had assured her that once Jenny was ready to go off to college and vet school, there would be a college fund awaiting her in exchange for her hours of work.

Joanna and Butch had regarded this unorthodox arrangement as a win-win situation all the way around. Through her own efforts, Jenny was making a very real down payment on her college education, and she was far too busy with work and school to get into any trouble. Up to now, that is.

Joanna pulled into the small parking lot in front of the clinic. A chain-link fence surrounded a yard between the clinic and Dr. Ross's home. Through the chain-link mesh, Joanna could see Jenny walking a placid pit bull who seemed totally unconcerned about the plastic surgical cone fastened around his broad neck. Joanna used a self-locking gate to let herself into the tree-shaded yard. Only up close did she see the straight line of stitches going down the dog's right rear leg.

"Hi, Mom," Jenny said. "This is Prince. He got out of his yard and got hit by a car. Dr. Ross had to install rods and pins in his leg to put it back together. He's really doing good."

"He's doing well." Joanna corrected her daughter's grammar automatically. "I'm glad to hear that, but it's not why I'm here. You're in trouble, young lady."

Jenny frowned. "I am?"

"Yes, you certainly are."

"How come?"

"Because you took an unauthorized photo of Ms. Highsmith this morning before I got to the crime scene. What did you use, your cell phone?"

Jenny nodded, her blue eyes wide. "I did," she replied, "but I only sent it to Cassie."

Cassie Parks, Jenny's best friend, lived in a decommissioned KOA campground near Double Adobe that her parents had turned into a mobile-home park.

"She may be the only person you sent it to, but Cassie must have passed it along to someone else. Now it's all over the Internet. Someone, one of the students from the high school, has even posted it on her Facebook page. I saw that one with my own eyes. Because of the photo Marliss Shackleford is threatening to write an article identifying the homicide victim without bothering to wait for a next-of-kin notification, something my detectives have not yet been able to accomplish."

Jenny's bright blue eyes widened even more. A flush of embarrassment flamed the skin of her cheeks and neck.

"I'm sorry," she said. "I never meant for that to happen."

"I can understand that this isn't at all what you intended," Joanna conceded, "but it's what has happened, and it's serious, Jenny—terribly serious. What if this is how Ms. Highsmith's family members find out about her death—because some uncaring idiot posted a gory picture of her body on the Internet?"

To Joanna's astonishment, Jenny sank to the ground. She sat there with her knees pulled up to her chest, sobbing inconsolably. With a grateful sigh, Prince, the wide-load butterball pit bull, sank down beside her. Resting his muzzle on his front paws, he closed his eyes contentedly.

"I just wanted to get her back," Jenny said. "That's all."

"Get who back?" Joanna asked. "What are we talking about?"

"Cassie. It's like we're not even friends anymore," Jenny hiccuped through her tears. "She's going to be a cheerleader next year, and she thinks that makes her a really big deal. She has all kinds of new friends. The only time I even get to see her is in class or on the bus on our way to school. I thought if I sent her that picture, she'd feel like I was giving her some special inside information and that we'd be friends again. Instead, she did this. How could she?"

Crouching next to her devastated daughter, Joanna came face-to-face with her own culpability, served up with a huge helping of motherly guilt. How long had Jenny and Cassie been on the outs? As Jenny's mother, how had Joanna not known about this crisis that was tearing away at her daughter's well-being? How could she have left Jenny to make her way through such a painful loss on her own?

With all that in mind, the idea of Jenny's taking and sending the photo was still wrong, but it was certainly more understandable.

Quieter now but still sniffling, Jenny mumbled, "Am I grounded then? Are you going to take my cell phone away?"

Joanna and Jenny's birth father, Andy, had never been on quite the same page when it came to disciplining Jenny. With Butch, Joanna had found a partner who was a master at presenting a united front.

"We'll need to talk it over with Dad," Joanna said.

The day before, Jenny was the one who had first used the term "Dad" to refer to Butch. This was the first time Joanna tried it. To her surprise Jenny voiced no objection.

"Okay," she said, drying her eyes with her sleeve. "I'm really sorry, Mom. Honest."

Joanna patted her daughter's shoulder. "I know," she said consolingly. "Sometimes that's the only way to get smarter—to learn from our mistakes. We're a law enforcement family, Jenny. That makes us different. That's why I didn't discuss the Highsmith situation with you yesterday. I didn't want you to mention the case to friends and classmates. Some of the things that are discussed around our dinner table are things you shouldn't talk about with anyone outside our immediate family."

"You mean like it's privileged information or something?" Jenny asked. "Like what clients tell their lawyers?"

"Not exactly like that," Joanna said. "There isn't a legal requirement that I not tell you about Ms. Highsmith. It's more a matter of discretion."

"You mean like using common sense."

"Yes," Joanna replied.

Jenny stood up and dusted off her jeans.

"I'm sorry about you and Cassie," Joanna said. "I wish you had told me."

Jenny bit her lip. "It started last fall, after she made the JV cheerleading squad. I kept thinking it would get better. It's like she's fine when we're on the bus going to school, but once we get there, she acts like I'm invisible. It hurts my feelings, Mom. I can't help it."

Joanna remembered all too well her own struggles in high school. First it had been because the kids were wary of being friends with the sheriff's daughter. Then, after her father was killed by a drunk driver, Joanna had been considered the odd kid out because her father was dead. It was like people thought being without a father was somehow contagious. Her social situation in high school was one of the things that had made an "older man," Andy, so attractive to her. Through it all, even in the face of a hurried "have-to" wedding, Marianne Maculyea had been Joanna's true-blue loyal friend. Was then; still was. Unfortunately, Jenny's friend Cassie wasn't made of the same stuff.

"Of course it hurts your feelings," Joanna agreed. "Have you talked about it with Butch?" She couldn't quite justify playing the "Dad" card twice in the same conversation.

Jenny shrugged. "I guess I thought you'd notice."

Joanna smiled at her daughter. "We didn't," she said. "You're probably giving us way too much credit. We'll talk about it tonight. All of us together."

"Except Dennis."

"Yes," Joanna agreed. "Except Dennis."

Bored with what must have seemed like endless prattle, Prince continued to sleep, snoring soundly. Pit bulls may have had a reputation for being scary and fierce; Prince was anything but.

"You'd better get that big guy up and back inside," Joanna added, nodding toward the snoozing dog. "Dr. Ross is going to be wondering what became of you."

As Jenny and Prince meandered back inside, Joanna returned to the Yukon. She had handled the Jenny situation to the best of her ability, but there were still outstanding issues on that score, not the least of which was making sure Debra Highsmith's family was notified in a timely fashion. That included getting the jump on whatever story Marliss Shackleford was getting ready to publish.

Joanna was in the Yukon and had already turned the key in the ignition when she remembered Marliss's unusual question about Jenny that morning while Joanna had still been at the crime scene. Even that early on, the reporter must have had a good idea that Jenny was the source of the photo. So where was she getting her information?

Removing the key and picking up the doggie bag from Daisy's, Joanna hurried back into the yard just as Jenny came outside again. This time she had a miniature long-haired dachshund on a leash. Prince had outweighed this tiny thing ten times over, but this dog was clearly ten times the trouble. She went into a paroxysm of barking, each bark lifting her stiff little legs off the ground.

"Quiet, Heidi," Jenny ordered, jerking on the leash.

Heidi paid no attention. Jenny looked uncomfortable, as though she was afraid Joanna was going to give her more grief. Instead, Joanna handed her daughter the doggie bag.

"I only ate half my chimichanga at lunch," she said. "I brought you the rest."

Jenny's face brightened. Bean and cheese chimichangas were her second-favorite food, right after pepperoni pizza. "Thanks," she said. "I didn't have time to pack a lunch."

"Wouldn't want you to starve," Joanna told her with a smile, "but I have one other question. What time did you send the photo to Cassie?"

Jenny shook her head. "I'm not sure. It was while Kiddo and I were waiting for you. Why?"

"I was just wondering. Can you check your call history?"

With Heidi still barking her head off, Jenny put down the bag, just out of the dog's reach, and pulled her cell phone out of her pocket. With a one-handed dexterity that amazed her mother, she scrolled through her calls. "Seven sixteen," she said at last. "That's when I sent it."

"Okay," Joanna said. "Thanks."

Walking back to the Yukon a second time, Joanna pulled out the notebook and located the page where the four kids from Daisy's had listed their names and phone numbers. She found Dena's name as well as her numbers. Dena had listed both her home phone number and her cell. Joanna called the latter.

"It's Sheriff Brady," she announced when Dena answered. "I'm wondering if you could do me a favor. You're one of Anne Marie Mayfield's Facebook friends, right?"

"Right."

"Could you please access her Facebook page and see if you can tell me what time the photo was posted?"

As a law enforcement officer, Joanna was painfully aware of the problems with cyberpredators stalking the Internet to find likely victims. She and Butch had installed the latest and greatest parental controls on their home computer system for just that reason. The situation with Jenny and the crime scene photo taught her that there was as much of a problem with information going out as there was with bad guys trying to get in. Besides, by using her cell phone to take and send the picture, Jenny had cleverly outmaneuvered them. The parental controls were on her computer, not her phone. That would have to change.

It took the better part of a minute, but finally Dena came back on the line. "Eight ten," she said. "That's what it says."

In other words, Joanna thought, it took a little less than an hour to get from Jenny to Cassie and from Cassie to the whole school!

"You're not going to be calling my parents, are you?" Dena asked. "They'll be really upset if I get called in to talk to a detective."

"Don't worry," Joanna said reassuringly. "Before this is over, we'll probably be talking to everyone at the school."

That was a little white lie. Joanna didn't have the man- or womanpower to interview everyone at Bisbee

High School, but knowing how the school social networking system worked, she had effectively put everyone on notice that she intended to do so. With any kind of luck, that little bit of intimidation would be enough to smoke out some useful information.

This time, when she started the car, she drove away from Dr. Ross's clinic and headed for the Justice Center, dialing Deb Howell's number as she went.

"Detective Howell here."

"Any luck with the next-of-kin situation?"

"Sorry, boss," Deb said. "I've run into a brick wall. As far as I can tell, Deb Highsmith doesn't have any next of kin. The contact listed with the Department of Licensing is Abby Holder."

"Mrs. Holder?" Joanna repeated. "That old battle-ax who's the secretary at the high school?"

"One and the same," Deb replied. "I'm on my way to see her now. I have to say, that woman absolutely terrified me when I was going to school. I never saw her in any color but black."

"She had the same effect on me," Joanna said, stifling a chuckle when she remembered how the kids at Daisy's had expressed similar kinds of fear about Debra Highsmith. "Isn't that the way it's supposed to be when you're in high school?" she asked. "If the kids aren't scared to death of the principal and the people in the principal's office, something's wrong. It's a control issue. It's been that way forever. Is Abby Holder at school today?"

"I already checked," Deb said. "The kids are out of school for the weekend and so are the staff members. I'm headed to her house."

Joanna had a choice. If she went to the office where she could tackle the day's paperwork, she would also be a sitting duck for anyone Marliss Shackleford happened to send her way. If Joanna was out on an interview with Deb Howell, she would be a moving target rather than a stationary one.

"Mind if I tag along?"

"I'd love to have you come along," Deb said. "She lives at 2828 Hazzard."

"All right," Joanna said. "I'll meet you there in a few minutes."

Chapter 6

Abigail Holder was a few years younger than Joanna's mother. It was mostly through Eleanor Lathrop Winfield that Joanna knew some of Abby's history. She had grown up on the Vista, an upscale neighborhood in Bisbee's Warren neighborhood, one that had long been home to the town's white-collar elite—the mine supervisors along with a selection of judges, doctors, and lawyers.

Growing up and walking to school from her parents' far-lower-class home on Campbell, Joanna had been jealous of the people who lived on the Vista. The large, mostly brick houses with shady front porches and yards usually required the regular attention of a gardener. The houses on East Vista and West Vista faced each other across a block-wide, five-block-long expanse of park that had once been the neighborhood's center-piece. Joanna had heard that the park had once been a grassy oasis, complete with a bandstand and huge trees. The bandstand and trees were both gone now, and the lush grass had been allowed to go to weedy ruin due to the prohibitive costs of watering and mowing it.

Hazzard was the last street in Bisbee's Warren neighborhood, a final outpost of civilization before town gave way to desert. When Joanna pulled up in front of Abby Holder's small frame house on Hazzard, it was clear that this one was very different from the brick-clad mansion where she had grown up. The ramshackle wooden structure was built on a terrace, several steep steps above street level. A concrete wheelchair ramp zigzagged across the small front yard up to the terrace, and then again up onto a tiny front porch. In the early afternoon, the porch still offered some shade, but as the sun went down in the west, Joanna knew the shade would disappear. In the summer, the setting sun would turn the front room of the house into a virtual oven.

Joanna parked out front, just behind Detective Howell's Tahoe. Together the two of them walked up the wheelchair ramp. When they reached the front door, Deb, ID in hand, stepped up to the door and rang the old-fashioned doorbell. From somewhere deep inside the house a tuneless jangle announced their presence.

Moments later the door cracked open and Abby Holder peered outside at them. "Yes," she said. "What do you want?"

"I'm Detective Howell with the Cochise County Sheriff's Department," Deb explained, "and this is Sheriff Brady."

In response, Abby opened the door wider. For the first time ever, she wasn't wearing all black. She was dressed in a faded red-and-gray Bisbee High School tracksuit, complete with the school's familiar Puma logo. Drab gray hair was pulled back in a tight French twist. She wore no makeup, however, and the grim expression that had petrified generations of schoolchildren was firmly in place.

The formal introductions were interrupted by an aggrieved voice, calling from somewhere inside the house, "What's going on? Are we having company? Why didn't you tell me?"

Abby turned away from the door. "It's about school, Mother," she said. "I'll take care of it."

Pulling the inside door shut behind her, Abby Holder stepped out through the screen door and onto the porch. "This is about Ms. Highsmith, right?" Abby asked as she studied Detective Howell's ID. "I already heard you found her body. One of the teachers called me."

"Yes, and that's why we're here," Deb continued. "At the Department of Licensing, you're listed as her next of kin. You're not related, are you?"

"No, not at all," Abby replied.

"Close friends, then?" Deb asked.

Abby shook her head. "Not really, although we worked together every day for several years. When she told me she was going to put me down as her emergency contact, I was a little taken aback—uncomfortable, really—but she said there was no one else."

"No relatives of any kind?" Joanna asked.

"None that I know of. That's what she told me, anyway. That she was an only child, that her parents died in a car accident years ago, and that she wasn't close to any of her cousins. I wondered about it at the time, if maybe she was in the witness protection program or something. I didn't ask her that, of course. I just wondered about it."

"When did she list you as her emergency contact?" Deb asked. "Was this a recent development?"

"Oh, no," Abby answered. "It happened when she first got here and was filling out all her paperwork."

"Did she ever mention where she was from?"

"Back east somewhere," Abby replied. "From one of those tiny states—Vermont or New Hampshire or Connecticut. I can never keep those straight in my head."

"I believe there's a life insurance rider on your group insurance policy," Joanna said.

That was a lie. Joanna didn't believe it was true; she knew it was true. For years before she ran for and was elected to the office of sheriff, Joanna had worked for the Davis Insurance Agency. She had handled the paperwork on the transaction when her boss, Milo Davis, had won the bid to handle the school's group insurance program.

"Yes," Abby agreed. "There are some differences in coverage for certified as opposed to noncertified personnel, but we all have a life insurance benefit."

"Do you have any idea who she might have named as the beneficiary on that?"

"No idea whatsoever," Abby answered. "You'd have to check with the school district office for that information, or there might be something about that in her files at school."

"What about a cell phone?" Deb asked.

Joanna knew that no cell phone had been found at the crime scene or at the victim's home. She also knew that cell phone records might lead them to people who were part of Debra Highsmith's social circle but weren't necessarily known to the people with whom she worked.

"Oh, yes."

"Do you happen to know the number?"

Abby reeled it off from memory. Deb punched the number into her cell phone and tried dialing it. Unsurprisingly, it went straight to voice mail.

Just then there were several sharp raps on the closed door behind Abby. The blows were hard enough that the three stair-step windowpanes jiggled in their mahogany frames, threatening to come loose.

"I know you're still out there, Abigail," her mother said imperiously. "It's very low class to be standing outside conducting business on the front porch. Are you out there talking about me?"

Abby flushed with embarrassment. "I'll be right there, Mother." Then she turned back to Deb Howell and Joanna. "My mother has a few security issues. I have a caregiver who usually stops by several times a day to check on her when I'm at work, but when I'm here, Mother doesn't like having me out of her sight. If you don't mind coming inside . . ."

Abby allowed her voice to trail off before she finished her less than enthusiastic invitation. It was plain to see that she wasn't eager to welcome them into her home. As the daughter of a sometimes difficult mother, Joanna understood the woman's reluctance. In public, Abby Holder appeared to be totally in control. It had to be difficult for her to be treated with such open contempt at home.

The polite thing for Joanna and Detective Howell to do would have been to walk away and let Abby Holder deal with her mother's issues in private, but this was a homicide investigation. As someone who had worked with the victim day in and day out for years, Abby Holder might well have insights into the workings of Debra Highsmith's life that no one else could provide.

There was another series of raps on the closed door. "Abigail? Are you still there?"

"We don't mind at all, do we, Deb?" Joanna said with a bright smile. "Any information you can give us at this stage would be a huge help."

Reluctantly, Abby opened the door and allowed them to enter. Just inside the door a tiny woman sat hunched in a wheelchair. She gripped a colorful cane in one hand and was clearly within seconds of staging another assault on the door, whose marred surface already gave clear evidence of several previous blows. The woman appeared to be afflicted with a severe widow's hump, one that left her face permanently pointing into her lap. Thin gray hair did little to conceal the balding spot on the top of her head.

"It's about time you came inside," she complained, peering up at them sideways due to an inability to raise her head. "You told me you were going to make some tea. I'm still waiting."

Looking at her, Joanna was reminded of a time when, as a little girl, she had climbed into a cottonwood tree to spy on a nest of newly hatched crows. Joanna had gotten only the smallest peek at the naked, angry, and demanding little things before an infuriated mama crow had shown up on the scene to drive the interloper away. Abby Holder's mother wasn't naked, but she had angry and demanding down to a science.

Abby gestured Joanna and Deb into the living room. "Could I interest you in some tea?"

"Please," Joanna said, accepting for both of them. "That would be great."

While Abby retreated into what must have been the kitchen, Joanna and Deb seated themselves side by side on a chintz sofa. The living room was small and crowded with too much oversize furniture. There were two large easy chairs that matched the sofa. A huge glass-fronted buffet was shoved up against one wall with a flat-screen television perched on top of that. On the muted screen the cast members of some afternoon soap opera were going through their paces. Every available inch of wall space was covered with framed artwork—notably oversize desert landscapes done in vivid oils.

To Joanna's way of thinking, none of the colorful furnishings in the crowded room quite squared with plain-Jane Abby Holder who always dressed in black or gray, whose hair was always pulled back into an old-fashioned, simple French twist, and whose face never showed a single hint of makeup. The furniture seemed far more in keeping with Abby's mother, who was dressed in a vivid orange muumuu and whose thin lips and cheeks were garishly colored with bright red lipstick and rouge.

Despite the limited floor space in the room, Abby's mother propelled her hand-powered chair through the maze of furnishings with practiced ease.

"I'm Elizabeth Stevens, Abigail's mother," she announced. "I can't imagine what possessed her to go rushing off without bothering to properly introduce us. Who are you? What are you doing here? Not selling something, I hope. Maybe you're a pair of those Bible-thumping missionaries? They're forever showing up on the front porch and ringing our doorbell. I've told Abby a hundred times not to let them inside. You're not some of those, are you?"

"No," Deb said with a laugh. "Definitely not. I'm Detective Deb Howell, and this is Sheriff Brady."

"Oh, that's right. I forgot we have a lady sheriff these days," Elizabeth said. "Call me old-fashioned, but I can't imagine that a woman could do as good a job of running the sheriff's department as a man would, and you still haven't mentioned what you're doing here or what it is you're after."

Joanna knew that Abby Holder was a few years younger than her own mother. That meant that Elizabeth was somewhere in her eighties or even nineties. Somewhere along the way, she had decided to turn off her self-editing applications. She would say whatever came into her head and let the chips fall where they may. Not wanting to divulge the purpose of their visit, Joanna made a gentle stab at changing the subject.

"Have you lived here long?" she asked.

"Longer than I ever wanted," Elizabeth shot back. "I'm afraid Abby made this bed. Now we both have to lie in it."

Out of Elizabeth's line of vision, Abby had come into the room and was collecting a set of cups and saucers from the buffet.

"Mother!" she exclaimed. "Please! Give it a rest."

"Well, it's true," Elizabeth sniffed. "If you hadn't gone against your father's wishes and married that Freddy Holder, we wouldn't have to live in this dump."

It was easy to see that this was a long-established pattern, with Elizabeth Stevens bullying her daughter and with Abby taking it. This time, maybe for the first time ever, Abby seemed prepared to fight back, countering fire with fire.

"If Daddy hadn't made such spectacularly bad investments," she said, "you wouldn't have had to sell the big house on the Vista and come slumming with me."

Elizabeth seemed both astonished and dismayed by her daughter's response. All the natural color drained from her face, leaving only the bright red clownlike layer of rouge glowing on otherwise stark white cheeks.

"I won't have you speaking about your father in such a disrespectful manner," she declared.

Abby didn't back off. "I won't have you speaking disrespectfully about Fred, either," she returned. "He and I found this place together, and he paid for it with his life. Just remember, if it weren't for your being able to come here to live with me, you and all your furniture would have been out on the street. How about a little gratitude for a change?"

"Well," Elizabeth huffed. "I never!"

With that, she spun her chair into a sudden about-face and sped from the room.

"I'm sorry you had to witness that," Abby said. "Most of the time I just let what she says wash over me. Today I couldn't."

I don't blame you a bit, Joanna thought. She said aloud, "Fred was your husband?"

Abby nodded. "My father was the superintendent of the mines. Fred's father was an underground miner.

That's all Fred ever wanted to be, too—a miner, just like his dad, Daniel. Fred knew he wasn't cut out for college; his grades weren't good enough, but he knew that working underground he'd be able to support us. Naturally my parents despised him. They thought I could do far better in the matrimony department than marrying some guy who worked underground. They did everything they could think of to break us up. I know my father told the guys at the company employment office that Fred wasn't miner material, but I figured out a way around it."

"What was that?" Joanna asked.

"I told Fred we should pretend that we had caved. I came home from a date one night in April, crying my heart out. I told my parents that I had broken up with him, and it worked like a charm. They were thrilled. Two things happened after that. Suddenly—magically—Fred was no longer persona non grata in the employment department. The strike was over by then. Fred got a job working underground, and I set about signing up for the fall semester in Flagstaff.

"Back then, it was still called the Northern Arizona Teacher's College. It wasn't even a university. My mother was in her element, though, shopping like crazy to get me properly decked out to go off to school in the fall, but I fooled them. Two weeks after high school graduation, on the day I turned eighteen, Fred and I eloped. We got married in Lordsburg. Fred had already moved out of his parents' place and rented this one. When we moved in here, my parents had a conniption fit. My father officially disowned me. He never spoke to me again, not even when Fred died a few months later."

"He died?" Joanna asked.

Abby nodded.

"What happened?"

"He died in a mining accident less than two months after we got married. The stope he was in collapsed. The other miners managed to dig him out, but it was too late. He was already dead. Fred's parents were always as good as gold to me, right up until they both died. All of which made the way my parents acted that much worse. My parents didn't even bother coming to the funeral.

"With Fred gone, I was completely on my own. I had taken typing and shorthand in high school. Luckily I managed to get hired as the school secretary at Greenway Elementary School. My father wasn't speaking to me at the time, and he wasn't on the school board, either, but for all I know he might have helped engineer my being offered the job so I'd at least be self-supporting. A few months later, when Fred's life insurance paid off, I went to my landlord and offered to buy this place. Paid cash for it. I've been here ever since."

"How long has your mother been living with you?" Joanna asked.

"Six years now," Abby said. "When my father retired from Phelps Dodge, my mother signed the paperwork saying it was all right for him to take a lump-sum distribution instead of a pension. The trouble was, he got all caught up in day trading and lost the money."

"He lost all of it?"

Abby nodded. "He used creative money-managing techniques to keep my mother from finding out how bad things were, but once he died and was no longer able to juggle things around, his financial house of cards finally collapsed. That's when my mother discovered she was destitute. The house on the Vista, the one mother had lived in all her married life, was mortgaged to the hilt. Since there was no pension, all she had coming in were the Social Security checks that came to her as my father's widow. The bank was foreclosing on the house. They were going to throw her and all her worldly goods out into the street, so I took her in."

"Under the circumstances, you did more than most people would have," Joanna said.

Abby shrugged. "She's my mother. What else could I do? I had planned on retiring in the next year or two.

Now, with Mother living here and with my hours cut back to just four days a week, that's not going to happen anytime soon."

From the kitchen the shrill whistle of a boiling teakettle demanded attention. Stacking the cups, saucers, plates, and teapot onto a tray, Abby hurried into the kitchen to tend to it.

"If I had been in her shoes, I think I would have told my mother to piss off," Deb Howell muttered.

Joanna nodded. "No one would have blamed you, either."

"I always thought people who lived on the Vista had perfect lives," Deb added thoughtfully. "This sounds anything but perfect."

That had been Joanna's perception, too. She'd had no idea of the steep price that someone like Abby, one of the seemingly privileged few, might have paid living as a virtual prisoner, first as a victim of her parents' demanding expectations and later as the target of their unrelenting disapproval. It pained Joanna to think that all the time she and the other kids had secretly made fun of Abby Holder's perpetually grim outlook on the world, the poor woman had been coming to work, day after day and year after year, with a permanently broken heart, mourning the loss of both the love of her life and the love of her parents.

Generations of schoolkids had mistaken that sadness for anger.

By the time Abby returned from the kitchen, Joanna Brady regarded her with a whole new respect.

She came into the living room carrying a tray laden with tea makings, including a plate of carefully trimmed, triangular cucumber sandwiches. She set the tray down on the coffee table in front of Joanna and Deb.

"If you'll excuse me for a moment," she said, "I'll take something in to my mother."

She dosed a cup of tea with cream and sugar, took it and a plate holding three sandwiches with her, and went off in the same direction in which her mother had departed. She returned a few moments later. If she'd had to endure another tirade from her mother in the meantime, it didn't show on her face or in her actions. She sat down and served tea in a fashion that not even her highly critical mother could have faulted.

"I don't believe I ever said a proper thank-you to your father, Sheriff Brady," Abby said quietly as she passed Joanna a delicate bone china cup and saucer. The cup was filled to the brim with fragrant tea. It took real concentration on Joanna's part to keep from slopping some of it into the saucer at this unexpected turn in the conversation.

"Thanked him for what?" Joanna asked.

"For digging Fred out of the stope the day he died," Abby answered. "Your father was one of the crew of miners who pulled him out of the muck and tried to revive him. Of all those guys, your father was the only one who had balls enough to come to Fred's funeral. Everyone else was so afraid of what my father might do that they didn't dare show up.

"As a consequence, it was a very small funeral," Abby continued. "Your mother came, too, by the way, but it was your father whose job was on the line. Your parents were a little older than I was, but back then we were all relatively young. I was barely out of high school and already a widow. I didn't really understand the risk your father ran by going against my father's wishes, and I never made a point of telling your father how much it meant to me. I'm thanking you because I never thanked him."

It wasn't the first time in Joanna Brady's years in law enforcement that she had heard stories about her late father, D. H. Lathrop, being a stand-up kind of guy. She could count on one hand, however, the number of times her mother, Eleanor, had been mentioned in that regard. Now she wondered if being at odds with the superintendent of the local mining branch, the town's major employer, might have had something to do with her father's leaving the mines to go into law enforcement.

Everyone had always maintained that D.H. had stopped working underground because he had wanted to.

Was that really true? Joanna wondered now. *Or was he forced out?*

"When did your husband die?" Joanna asked.

"August 4, 1968," Abby answered without the slightest hesitation, as though the date were indelibly engraved on her heart the same way the date of Andy's death was engraved on Joanna's.

"We were newlyweds who didn't have any money," Abby continued. "All the miners in town were broke because of the strike, and nobody could afford to go on vacation, us included, but because it was so hot, we decided to go camping in the White Mountains during shutdown. The accident happened the day after Fred went back to work. The mine inspectors said that something must have shifted during the shutdown and that caused the stope to collapse."

In the old Phelps Dodge days, the word "shutdown," in Bisbee, had meant that the mines simply ceased operation for two weeks during the summer, and everyone who worked for the company went on vacation at the same time. Joanna's father was already working for the sheriff's department by the time she was born. So even though her family wasn't directly affected by the shutdown, Joanna remembered how long and lonely those two weeks seemed to be when it had felt as though she were the only child left on Planet Bisbee.

Now Joanna made a mental note of the date Abby Holder had mentioned. It was obviously a pivotal one in Abby's life, but Joanna wondered if perhaps it might be important in her own family's history as well.

"More tea?" Abby asked, reaching for Joanna's empty cup.

"Yes, please," Joanna said. "Now, perhaps we could go back to your telling us what you know about Debra Highsmith."

Chapter 7

Deb and Joanna sat in Abby's overstuffed living room for the better part of another hour, asking questions and taking notes. Abby allowed as how Debra Highsmith had seemed to be out of sorts for the past several weeks, although, as far as her secretary knew, there was nothing specific that had caused any kind of problem, at least nothing that had filtered down to the secretarial level. Abby knew of no fractious relations with any of the faculty members. Bisbee High School students, as a group, had performed well on their standardized tests, scoring several points better than they had a year earlier. Debra's relationships with the school board and the district office were fine . . .

Abigail Holder abruptly stopped speaking as a thoughtful but telltale frown flitted across her face.

"What?" Joanna prodded.

"Well, there was that one situation with the board."

"What situation was that?"

"Ms. Highsmith suspended a student, and the board made her back off."

"Would the student in question happen to be Marty Pembroke?" Joanna asked.

"Why, yes," Abby said, blinking in surprise. "That's the one. How did you know?"

"Word gets around," Joanna said, answering Abby's question in a fashion that was only one small step short of a terse "no comment."

"Although," she added, after a pause, "I don't think I remember seeing anything about it in the *Bisbee Bee*."

"That's right," Abby said. "Most of the discussions were conducted behind closed doors because the student involved is still a juvenile. The only thing that was made public was that the terms of a suspension had been adjusted so that schoolwork and exams could be made up after the fact. When Ms. Highsmith came to work the next morning, she was absolutely livid. In all the years we worked together, I never saw her as upset as she was that day until a couple of days later."

"She was more upset later? Why? What happened then?"

"Even though the paper didn't publish anything on the subject, that didn't stop the kid from going public. I haven't seen it, but I've been told Marty wrote a blog entry about it and posted the whole story on his Facebook page, complete with an utterly despicable video of Ms. Highsmith."

"You saw it?"

Abby nodded. "That really frosted Ms. Highsmith. The school board protected Marty's privacy, but he had no compunction about bandying about his own version of things to anyone who would listen. According to him, she was the real villain of the piece. I wasn't the only one who suggested she sue him for libel."

"Did she?"

"No, she said the damage was already done. She didn't want to draw any more attention to the incident than it had already engendered."

"What did she mean by that?"

"I'm not sure."

"You don't think the action she took with Marty Pembroke was out of line?" Joanna asked.

"By suspending him? No," Abby said flatly. "Not at all. She was simply trying to hold him accountable for his actions."

"Marty claims somebody else put the beer in his locker as a joke."

Abby Holder shook her head. "I don't believe that for a minute. Neither did Ms. Highsmith."

Joanna looked at Detective Howell. "Do you mind seeing what you can do to track down Marty Pembroke's Facebook page?"

"Not at all," Deb said with a nod, jotting down a note to herself. "I'll go to work on that once we get back to the office."

"Wait," Abby said. "Are you saying that you think Marty Pembroke might be involved in what happened to Ms. Highsmith?"

Abby Holder was at least twenty-five years older than Debra Highsmith. Joanna found it interesting that, although the two women had worked together as boss and secretary for years, they had never become friends and had never progressed to being on a first-name basis, either. Even in death, Abby continued to maintain a respectful distance. Was that due to Abby's naturally subservient nature or was it something that had been enforced from the top down?

"It's possible," Joanna said. "The fact that there was a disagreement of some kind between them in the weeks leading up to Ms. Highsmith's death means we need to take a look at those interactions and see if it leads us to anything useful. In the long run, that history may or may not be important, but at this point in an investigation it's our job to follow up on every lead, no matter how small or seemingly unimportant. So tell us, were there similar problems with any other students?"

"No," Abby answered. "Not that I remember."

"All right, then," Joanna said. "Tell me what you can about the Pembroke situation. When did it come to a head?"

"The locker infraction happened back toward the end of February," Abby answered. "Because we've had problems with illegal substances showing up at school, Ms. Highsmith instituted a program of conducting unannounced but mandatory locker inspections. She maintained that having a locker on the school premises was a privilege, not a right, and that if students wanted a locker they had to sign a paper agreeing to periodic inspections.

"It was during one of those routine inspections that she found the can of beer. It was Marty's first offense, but having alcohol on school property is grounds for an automatic ten-day suspension, and that's what she did—she suspended him. Marty is a smart kid who's used to getting good grades. During his suspension he missed several important tests that he couldn't make up. He also wasn't allowed to hand in papers. Those two things together meant his GPA was going to drop like a rock. Some grades that would have been solid fours would go to threes, and in one case to a two, and that's when the phone calls started."

"What phone calls?"

"First from Marty's mother and later from his dad. When the phone calls didn't work, Dr. Pembroke himself came to school complaining about the situation and demanding that Marty be allowed to make up the work. According to Dr. Pembroke, his son's new GPA would put Marty's entire future in jeopardy, starting with his not matriculating at the college of his choice."

Abby took a deep breath. "Believe me, it was not a pleasant conversation, but Ms. Highsmith was adamant. She told him that the suspension stood. Since she wouldn't back down, Dr. Pembroke appealed to the superintendent, who supported Ms. Highsmith's position all the way. Dr. Pembroke's next step was to go directly to the school board. All this backing and forthing took time. Dr. Pembroke's appeal didn't make it onto the school board agenda until the April meeting."

"When was that?" Joanna asked.

"A few weeks ago. The school board meets the first Wednesday of every month. I have it on good authority that the Pembrokes are pals with several of the board members. Why wouldn't they be? They're all neighbors on the Vista. As a consequence, they attempted one of those King Solomon routines where you cut the baby in half. They let the suspension stand but with the proviso that Marty would be allowed to turn in any required papers and to make up any missed tests."

"I don't suppose Ms. Highsmith was happy about that," Joanna suggested.

"No," Abby agreed. "She said that the board's action amounted to teaching kids that actions had no consequences. No, wait. What she really said was, 'no meaningful consequences.' "

"It's safe to say that between February and now, there were several contentious encounters between Ms. Highsmith and various members of the Pembroke family?"

"Yes," Abby agreed. "Several, raised voices and all."

"It might be helpful to know what went on during those discussions. Was any written record made of those meetings?"

"Not an official one," Abby said. "Not a tape recording or anything like that, but Ms. Highsmith kept a leather-bound calendar, one of those with two pages for each day. She has a whole shelf full of them. After a meeting or a phone call, she'd usually make a few notes in that to serve as a reminder of what had been discussed and what if anything needed to be done."

That resonated with Joanna. Her father had recorded the events of his life in a series of leather-bound volumes that Joanna had eventually inherited. In cleaning out the garage to make room for her new husband's belongings, Joanna's mother, Eleanor, had been prepared to dump them. Instead, George Winfield had bundled them up and handed them over to Joanna, who treasured them. They were a touchstone for her, a point of contact with a father who had died when she was only fifteen. In the years since, Joanna had sometimes been tempted to turn to her father's record of events in his life to help unscramble something in her own. Maybe Debra Highsmith's jotted notes would serve the same purpose in helping to solve her own murder.

"Are those calendars at school?" Joanna asked. "I don't remember anyone mentioning something like that yesterday during the search at Ms. Highsmith's house."

"Yes, she keeps them in her office." After a pause Abby changed the wording slightly to "kept."

"If you don't mind, I'd like to take a look at them," Joanna said.

Abby seemed to draw back. "I'm not sure I should show you. Those are private. Shouldn't you have a search warrant or something?"

Abby was right, of course—a search warrant was a very good idea—but she was right for the wrong reason. No doubt Abby's main concern was protecting Debra Highsmith's privacy. Joanna's was making sure that any evidence found would be usable when it came time to bring the perpetrator to court.

The previous day, when officers from the Bisbee Police Department had arrived at Debra Highsmith's home for that first welfare check, no warrant had been necessary. Later, however, when they returned for the missing person call, they had come armed with a search warrant. Joanna thought it possible that, at the time they obtained a search warrant for the house, they had also obtained one to search Debra Highsmith's office at school. Had such a search been executed, however, it seemed likely that Abby Holder would have known about it.

Laying hands on a properly drawn search warrant was essential, but Joanna didn't want to walk away from Abby Holder long enough to get one. Up till now, Abby had been nothing but cooperative. Left to her own devices, however, it was possible the school secretary might have second thoughts about that. Joanna had seen plenty of instances in which witness interviews, once interrupted, never got back on track.

Joanna glanced at Deb. "Would you mind taking care of the warrant?" she asked.

"Right now?" Deb asked, rising to her feet.

Joanna nodded. "I'll call Judge Moore and let him know you're coming."

When it came to search warrant requests, Judge Cameron Moore was Joanna's go-to guy, and she had all of his numbers—work, home, and cell—stored in her phone. When Joanna called his office, she was told he was gone for the day. She tried his home number next.

"Looks like old Arlee hit the DeLong case out of the park for you," Judge Moore said when he came on the line.

Managing to restrain herself, Joanna didn't say, "For a change."

"Yes," she said. "He certainly did, but that's not why I'm calling. Have you heard about the Debra Highsmith homicide?"

"Did," Judge Moore replied. "Just a little while ago. I went up to the Copper Queen for lunch, and the whole place was abuzz with all kinds of talk about the murder. It's too bad. A real loss to the community. From everything I've heard about the woman, she was doing an outstanding job. So what's up?"

"When the Bisbee PD requested the search warrant for her home yesterday, did they ask for one that included Ms. Highsmith's office at school?"

"No, but considering the circumstance, I assume you need one."

"Yes," Joanna said.

"When?"

"ASAP. I'm sending Detective Howell to bring you the paperwork right now. She has blanks in her trunk, and she'll fill them out before you see them."

"Have her get right on it, then, and have her stop by the house," Judge Moore said. "It turns out today is our anniversary. The little woman and I have dinner reservations at McMahon's, in Tucson. We're leaving shortly so we can run a few errands in Tucson before dinner."

"Okay," Joanna said, nodding toward Deb and pointing her out the door. "Deb Howell is on her way to your house right now."

The fact that the judge was at home was a stroke of luck. Driving out to the Justice Center would take at least twenty minutes. Judge Moore's house at the bottom of Arizona Street was only a few blocks away.

"More tea?" Abby asked.

"Please," Joanna said, but when Abby went to pour it, the pot was empty.

She rose and headed for the kitchen. The moment Abby walked through the swinging door into the kitchen, her mother came rolling down the hallway.

She parked her chair just inside the living room and turned her glare on Joanna.

"Just because my father was a doctor doesn't make me a doctor," Elizabeth Stevens said sourly, "and just because your father was a sheriff doesn't make you a sheriff."

Joanna Brady had never been any good when it came to turning the other cheek.

"You're right," she said. "The people of Cochise County are the ones who made me sheriff. They elected me to the office, not once but twice. Did you want to be a doctor, Mrs. Stevens?"

Elizabeth seemed surprised to have her mean-spirited comment pointed back in her direction.

"Well, no," she stammered. "Not really."

"If you had wanted to, you could have gone to school and studied and made that happen, couldn't you?"

"I suppose, although back in those days, not many women studied medicine."

"I've attended the Arizona Police Academy," Joanna said, ignoring Elizabeth's self-serving excuse. "My firearms rating is one of the best in my department. I maintain that by practicing on the shooting range each week. I've attended any number of law enforcement continuing education seminars to update my skills and to keep my department apprised of the latest advances in forensics and law enforcement technology. So you see, Mrs. Stevens, my being sheriff has almost nothing to do with my father, and everything to do with me."

Abby returned from the kitchen and stopped short when she saw her mother's frowning countenance. "What's going on?"

"Your mother was just telling me that she believes that the only reason I'm a sheriff now is because my father was a sheriff," Joanna answered. "I was explaining to her why that's not true."

Abby was aghast. "Mother!" she exclaimed.

"That woman was rude to me," Elizabeth said, pointing an accusing finger in Joanna's direction. "Make her leave. I want her out of the house, now."

Joanna didn't doubt that previously Abby Holder might have knuckled under to all of her mother's demands, no matter how outrageous, but somehow, today, the dynamics of their situation had changed slightly, shifting in Abby's favor.

"Sheriff Brady is a guest in my home, Mother," Abby said firmly, "and so are you—a guest. You should probably remember that from time to time. Now, if you'd like more tea, I'll be glad to get you some."

"That's no way to speak to your mother!" Elizabeth said petulantly.

"If you don't wish to be spoken to in that fashion, then don't be rude to my guests," Abby told her. "So, do you want more tea or not?"

"Not," Elizabeth replied. Again, she spun her wheelchair around and sped away down the hallway.

"I'm sorry," Abby said. "She's a little difficult at times."

A supreme understatement, Joanna thought.

"Yes," she said. "I can see that."

She was also realizing that, compared to Elizabeth Stevens, when it came to being troublesome, her own mother, Eleanor Lathrop Winfield, was a rank amateur.

This time, when Abby retreated into the kitchen to the whistling summons of the teakettle, Joanna followed her. It was a tiny place, old-fashioned but spotlessly clean. Instead of a dishwasher under the counter, a dish drainer sat on top of it, stacked with what was most likely a collection of washed and drying breakfast or lunch dishes. The cabinets had been built for someone far taller than Abby Holder, whose height matched Joanna's own five feet two. To help make up for the height deficit, a kitchen stool was stationed in the corner next to the stove. Trying to stay out of Abby's way in the confined space, Joanna perched on the stool while Abby poured boiling water over a strainer filled with tea leaves.

"You were saying earlier that you sometimes wondered if Ms. Highsmith was in the witness protection program. Were you serious about that or were you just kidding?"

"A little of both, I suppose," Abby Holder admitted. "She never talked about where she lived when she was growing up or how they celebrated Christmas or where they went on vacation. When people started talking about things like that, she just clammed up or else left the room. I never asked her about it, though. She was my boss. I wanted to keep my job, and it seemed to me that I was better off minding my own business."

Joanna's cell phone rang. When she answered, Deb was on the line.

"While the judge was going over the paperwork for the warrant, I went online to Marty Pembroke's Facebook page. We'll be sending you the YouTube link for the video clip. You might want to take a look at it as soon as you get it."

"Why?" Joanna asked.

"Because I'm worried that it might be taken down any minute."

Joanna's text message warning sounded. "Okay," she said. "It's here."

She opened the message. Once loaded, the film images were a little blurry, but she could still make them out. There was a video of a furious Debra High-smith leaving the board meeting. Underneath the film a ticker ran a message: DIE, BITCH!

Joanna called Deb Howell back. "Okay," she said. "Once we execute the search warrant, we both know where we need to go next."

Chapter 8

When the tea finished steeping, Abby led the way back into the living room and poured the next round. "At the time Ms. Highsmith had her various dealings with the Pembroke family, did you ever overhear anything that might be construed as a threat?" Joanna asked.

Abby clearly found the question offensive. "I'm a secretary, not an eavesdropper," she said.

"But if there were raised voices . . ." Joanna objected.

"Raised voices I heard," Abby conceded. "What those raised voices were saying? No, I didn't hear that."

"What about the gun?" Joanna asked.

"What gun?"

"Were you aware that Ms. Highsmith had obtained a concealed carry permit and that she had a loaded weapon in her purse?"

"Oh, no," Abby Holder said, shaking her head. "Definitely not Ms. Highsmith. She wouldn't have had one of those on a bet. You must be mistaken."

"What about her dog?" Joanna asked.

"What dog?" Abby responded. "Ms. Highsmith never mentioned having a dog. At least she never mentioned it to me."

"I have it on good authority that she did have a dog. His name is Giles."

"Amazing." Abby shook her head. "I don't remember hearing one word about him."

That seemed odd. Every time a dog had come into the Brady family's life, the new addition was a constant topic of conversation. For the seven years since Debra Highsmith had been hired as the high school principal, she had worked with Abby on a daily basis. Yet she had never confided in her secretary that she was carrying a loaded weapon in her purse or that she had acquired a dog. Maybe there had been some kind of difficulty between the two women that had yet to surface.

Before anything more could be said on that subject, however, Detective Howell turned up, search warrant in hand. It had taken her just under half an hour, which, in Joanna's view, had to be an all-time record. She handed the warrant over to Abby Holder, who read through the whole thing.

"Do you need me to come along to let you in?" she asked, handing the warrant back to Deb.

"That would be a huge help," Joanna said.

"I'll just go get my purse and my car keys."

"You're welcome to bring your purse," Joanna said, "but we'll be glad to give you a ride to and from."

"I'll still need my keys to get into the school," Abby said, "and I'll let Mother know that I'll be out for a while."

Abby disappeared into the interior of the house. Shortly thereafter, from down the hall, they heard Elizabeth's querulous response. "How long will you be?" she wanted to know. "Will you be back in time to make dinner? If I eat any later than five, I'll be up all night with indigestion."

Deb shook her head. "That woman has the patience of Job."

"She needs it, too," Joanna observed.

As Joanna and Deb walked out to their respective vehicles, Joanna's cell phone jangled. Tom Hadlock's number appeared in her caller ID window. "I have to take this call," Joanna told Deb. "Why don't you take Abby with you?"

"Got it," Deb said.

"Hi, Tom," Joanna said into the phone. "What's up? Are we making any progress?"

"Detective Carbajal got hold of the school district office. Didn't do squat for the next-of-kin problem. The beneficiary on Debra Highsmith's group insurance is some tree huggers' group."

"A conservation group, then?"

"Something called the Malpai Borderlands Group. Never heard of them."

Joanna had. They were a group of ranchers in the southeastern part of Arizona and the southwestern part of New Mexico who had banded together to fight the forces aligned against them—wind, rain, fire, and cross-border thugs who, along with federal oversight bureaucrats, all seemed determined to put them out of business. Finding themselves shunned by the well-heeled national conservation groups whose one-size-fits-all version of biological diversity ignored the ability of ranchers to earn their livelihoods, the people who formed the Malpai Borderlands Group had developed their own localized solutions to the various problems confronting them.

They had cleared out forests of invading mesquite trees, allowing the desert to return to its earlier grassland state. They had fought to protect the small band of jaguars that had turned up in their midst. They had waged a life-and-death struggle with marauding drug dealers who had gunned down unarmed ranchers working on their own property. It was in the aftermath of one of those crimes that the Malpai Borderlands Group had first come to the sheriff's department's attention.

"That's interesting," Joanna said. "I wonder what's the connection."

"Like I said. Sounds like tree huggers to me."

"Not if the tree in question happens to be mesquite," Joanna said. "Where's Jaime now?"

"On his way to the M.E.'s office," Tom said. "Dr. Machett is about to do the autopsy, and Detective Carbajal will be there to observe."

"So things are under control," Joanna said.

"Not exactly," Tom Hadlock replied. "The media natives are restless. Marliss Shackleford is camped out in the public office, raising hell as usual, and my phone is ringing off the hook. I've had at least a dozen requests for information from media outlets all over the state in just the last half hour."

Joanna could tell from the stress in Tom's voice that the pressure was starting to get to him. She couldn't help feeling a little guilty on that score. One of the reasons she had gone along on the Abby Holder interview was that she had wanted to avoid having to deal with Marliss. She didn't doubt that her presence at the interview had made possible the fact that they now had a search warrant in hand, but Tom's inexperience was showing and he was obviously in over his head.

"Sorry to leave you hanging out to dry like that," Joanna told him. "I know it's a lot to handle."

"What I need to know is this," he said, sounding exasperated. "Are we making any progress at all on notifying next of kin? Everybody's demanding that we come out and release the name of the victim. I've been doing what I can to stall on releasing information, citing the next-of-kin issue, but it's not working out very well. I can tell from what reporters are saying to me that they already have Debra Highsmith's name. It's apparently common knowledge all over town, and I'm not sure how much longer I can keep these people from putting it on the air."

It's common knowledge because my own darling daughter helped spread the word, Joanna thought as a momentary spark of anger shot through her. In a high-profile case like this, what went on in the media was as important as what was going on with the detectives. The photo Jenny had sent to her friend made handling the media far more problematic.

"Do the best you can, Tom," Joanna advised her chief deputy as she put the Yukon in gear and pulled in behind Deb Howell's Tahoe. "We've got a search warrant for Debra Highsmith's office, and we're on our way to the high school right now to execute it. I'm sorry the school district angle didn't give us what we needed. I'm hoping we'll find something in her office that will help us locate her next of kin. Otherwise, we're out of luck, out of time, and out of ideas. Much as I hate to do things this way, if we haven't found a family member by the time Machett is done with his autopsy, we'll have to go ahead and release the name. See if you can find out when he expects to be finished, and schedule a press conference immediately thereafter."

"He's not going to talk to me," Tom Hadlock said. "You know that, and I know that."

"Yes," Joanna said. "Unfortunately, you're right. Let me see what I can do."

It was a little before three on Friday afternoon. That meant that Dr. Machett's secretary, Madge Livingston, was still on duty. "Can you ask Dr. Machett when he thinks he'll be finished with the autopsy?" Joanna asked when Madge came on the line.

"No point," Madge said. "He'll say these things take time and that they can't be rushed."

"What's your best guess?"

"Two hours flat," Madge pronounced in her smoke-damaged rasp. "He'll be done by five on the nose."

"Why do you say that?"

"Because it's Friday," Madge answered. "Trust me on that. He's out of here by five on Friday afternoons, come what may."

By then the two-car sheriff's department caravan had arrived at the chain-link gate blocking the driveway entrance to the school grounds. Abby Holder stepped out of Deb Howell's Tahoe. With keys in hand, she stooped to unlock the padlock on the security chain that held the swinging gate shut. Once Deb and Joanna were through the entrance, Abby carefully put the chain back in place and refastened the padlock.

Abby Holder, Joanna noted, was nothing if not thorough.

As they made their way through the empty parking lot, Joanna called Tom Hadlock back. "Schedule the press conference for five thirty," she said.

"He'll be done that fast?"

"I have it on the best authority," Joanna answered.

"Will you be here for it?"

"Yes," Joanna said, again thinking longingly about how much she missed Frank Montoya's capable presence. "I'll be there."

Disregarding the no-parking zones, Joanna and Deb pulled into the drop-off lane just in front of the school's main office. Abby used her fistful of keys to let them into the building, then led them inside, switching on lights as she went.

Joanna fully expected an alarm to sound the moment they entered. None did, although something that appeared to be an alarm keypad was built into the wall right next to the door.

"What about the alarm?" Joanna asked. "Don't you need to shut it off?"

Abby laughed. "It's already turned off," she said. "Permanently. When it came time for the school district to cut costs, the alarm company contract went away."

Abby dropped her purse on the desk Joanna knew to be hers—had always been hers—and then walked as far as the entrance to the principal's office. There she stopped short.

"Oh, no!" she wailed, stepping back, groping for the doorjamb, and swaying visibly on her feet. "Oh, no, no, no!"

"What's wrong?" Joanna demanded.

There was a moment of confusion when all three women tried to occupy the doorway at once. Eventually Abby retreated, going back into her office and sinking onto a chair while Joanna and Deb Howell stood in the doorway and examined the shambles that had once been Debra Highsmith's office. Furniture was upturned and or smashed. The floor was littered with a layer of loose paper that had been liberated from overturned files and emptied drawers. There was shattered glass everywhere. What looked to have been a glass-fronted bookshelf lay in broken pieces on the floor. Maybe a hundred or so textbooks lay scattered in the debris, but there was nothing—not one volume— that looked like a leather-bound calendar.

Joanna was already punching Alvin Bernard's speed-dial number into her phone. "We're at the high school," she said tersely when he came on the line. "We came to Debra Highsmith's office to execute a search warrant, but evidently someone else got here first. The place is a mess."

"I'll send some uniforms right away, but how did this happen? We haven't had any reports of an alarm going off."

"There is no alarm," Joanna said. "The school board evidently discontinued the service."

"Breaking and entering?"

"No need. If the killer had Ms. Highsmith's keys, all he had to do was let himself in and out."

Ending the call, Joanna went into the outside office where Abby Holder sat, fanning her flushed face with a stenographer's notebook.

"There are no calendars in the office," Joanna said. "How many were there?"

Abby seemed to consider before she answered. "I'm not sure. She's been here for seven years—almost seven. She used one a year, but there were more than seven. Fifteen maybe?"

"The calendars are gone. Can you tell if anything else is missing?"

Abby Holder got unsteadily to her feet and came as far as the doorway. "I don't know," she said, shock still visible on her face. "It's such a mess, it's hard to tell."

"Did Ms. Highsmith keep anything of value in here—jewelry, for instance?"

"Definitely not," Abby answered. "She didn't wear jewelry."

Joanna had noticed at the crime scene that there had been no jewelry visible on Debra Highsmith's body. At the time she had simply assumed that robbery had been part of the motivation for the murder. Now it seemed that the absence of jewelry was more a result of the victim's personal sense of style than it was of some criminal enterprise.

"Interesting," Joanna said with a glance in Deb's direction. "Why tear up her office when we saw no evidence of this kind of destruction at the victim's house?"

"The killer must have known that whatever it was he wanted, Debra Highsmith kept it here at her office rather than at home."

"He?" Abby Holder asked. "You know for sure that the killer is a he?"

"We don't know anything for sure," Joanna said.

"Would you say that as far as faculty members are concerned, you would be the one who was closest to Ms. Highsmith?"

"I'm staff, not faculty," Abby replied. "As far as I know, she wasn't especially close to any of the faculty members. That might have lent itself to playing favorites, or, at least it might have been construed that way."

"So who were her friends?"

"I'm not sure. She didn't mix her school life with her personal life. It's no exaggeration to say she was a very private person."

Abby Holder might not be able to reconstruct her boss's social life, but Joanna knew that her cell phone records would make Debra Highsmith's social network an open book. "We'll need those cell phone records ASAP," Joanna said to Deb.

Abby frowned and looked around the room. "Wait," she said. "Where are the computers?"

"As in more than one?" Joanna asked.

"She had a desktop and a little notebook computer that she carried with her. She used the desktop for school correspondence. The other one was for personal use."

"It's possible there's some crossover," Joanna said. "Especially in e-mail accounts." She turned to Deb. "Her computers are also covered on the warrant, right?"

Deb nodded. "They are," she replied, "but we need to be able to find them first. Does the school district have any kind of automatic system-wide backup?"

"Yes," Abby said. "The computers back up every day."

"I'll follow up on that, too," Deb said.

"What's the meaning of this?" an irate male voice demanded from the room behind them. "Chief Bernard called me and said there had been a break-in. Why didn't you call me to begin with, Abby? How dare you bring police officers onto the school grounds without consulting me? It's outrageous that I should be the last to know."

The three women turned as one to face the new arrival, William R. Farraday III, the Bisbee School District's superintendent of schools. At five six or so, the man was barely four inches taller than Joanna. His diminutive appearance was at odds with both his bellowing voice and his belligerent attitude.

It was always possible, Joanna supposed, that when Farraday went golfing at the Rob Roy Links maybe he let down his hair enough that members of his foursome could call him Bill. Maybe his wife called him that in the privacy of their own home. On all other occasions, when he was out in public and most especially in a work setting, he was known as Mr. Farraday, with special emphasis on the MISTER part. Joanna had had some dealings with him through the years and thought he was a twit—a vindictive bully who ruled his small bureaucratic fiefdom with an iron fist. It occurred to Joanna that Farraday and Dr. Machett were birds of a feather.

Since Joanna was evidently more than he wanted to handle, Farraday kept his wrathful gaze focused on Abby Holder.

"What in the world were you thinking, Abby?" he demanded.

Terrified of the man and looking as though she wanted to sink through the floor, Abby shook her head and didn't answer.

"We were executing a search warrant regarding the Highsmith homicide," Joanna explained, quickly coming to Abby's defense. "We were engaged in interviewing Ms. Holder at the time our warrant came through. She was kind enough to offer to accompany us to the school and use her keys to give us access to the office area. When we saw the interior of Ms. Highsmith's office, we immediately called in a report to the

Bisbee Police Department. Their officers should be here any moment."

Joanna carefully avoided mentioning to *Mr.* Farraday that their obtaining the office search warrant was due in large part to information that had come to them from Abby Holder. Joanna already knew Abby's financial situation dictated that she was in no position to retire, much less to have her employment terminated. As a consequence, Joanna tried to draw Farraday's attention to herself and away from the hapless secretary.

"So far, the only items we can determine to be missing are Ms. Highsmith's computers—a desktop and a laptop," Joanna continued. "Those and several years' worth of personal calendars."

"The laptop was hers, but the desktop is definitely school property," Farraday said. "As is the broken furniture. We'll have to file an insurance claim first thing, and somebody's going to have to clean this place up before school starts on Monday morning."

The look Farraday turned on Abby Holder then made it clear that he regarded the cleanup process as someone else's responsibility—most likely hers. It didn't earn him any points in Joanna's book that the school superintendent seemed far more concerned about property damage than he was about the death of his longtime employee. Even worse, he apparently had zero empathy for how the murder of Abby's supervisor might affect someone who had spent years working closely with Debra Highsmith.

"I don't see any broken outside windows. How exactly did the culprit or culprits gain access to the office?" he demanded. "Did they just walk into the building or what? Why weren't they caught?"

"We're working on the theory that whoever did this is also responsible for Ms. Highsmith's murder. Since her keys weren't found at the crime scene, it seems likely that the killer has her keys and used them to gain access here. If the school's alarm system had been functioning, just having her keys wouldn't have been enough, not without the disarm code. I may be wrong, but don't I remember hearing something about the school district discontinuing its contract with the alarm company?"

Joanna's question laid the blame squarely where it belonged—on the superintendent's none-too-broad shoulders—without betraying Abby Holder as the one who had mentioned the situation with the discontinued alarm.

At least Farraday didn't try to deny it. "We had to," he said quickly. "There was a problem. They were taking undue advantage of our situation."

"Now the bad guys have taken advantage of it, too," Joanna observed. "As far as the cleanup is concerned? That's going to have to wait until after my people have a chance to do a thorough crime scene investigation."

"Why your people?" Farraday wanted to know. "You're county. The school is inside the city limits. Shouldn't the Bisbee Police Department be handling the investigation?"

Joanna suspected that Farraday thought he had more ink with Alvin Bernard's department than he did with hers. No doubt he was hoping for a little better control of the narrative. Joanna didn't give him any.

"In Debra Highsmith's homicide, we have crime scenes in both the city and the county. As a consequence the investigation is being handled as a joint operation. My people will be handling the forensics. Detective Howell here is the lead investigator."

When it came to playing poker, D. H. Lathrop had taught his daughter well. When she called Farraday's bluff, he folded.

"All right, all right," he said, shaking his head. "Carry on."

While Joanna had engaged Farraday in conversation, Deb had been on the phone to the department, summoning the CSIs.

"They're on their way," Deb said.

Joanna nodded and then turned back to Farraday. "While we wait for my CSI team, it might be helpful if Detective Howell and I asked you a few questions."

He sighed. "I don't suppose I have any choice in the matter."

He did have a choice, but neither Deb nor Joanna bothered mentioning that fact.

"How long have you known Ms. Highsmith?" Deb asked.

"She's worked here for the past seven years. I met her a few months before she came onboard."

"You're the one who hired her?" Deb asked.

"Yes," Farraday said, "I am. She had just finished earning her master's in education at the University of Arizona. She had been an assistant principal in Tucson before that, but Tucson is a really desirable location. It would have taken years for her to move up to a principal's job there. She came to us highly recommended."

"To say nothing of her being a recent graduate," Joanna observed. "That meant she was also more affordable than someone with years of experience."

"That, too," Farraday admitted. "She may have been inexperienced initially, but she did a good job. No complaints about her job performance."

"Other than the Pembrokes'?" Joanna asked.

"Well, yes," he agreed. "There was that."

"Do you know of anyone who wished her harm?"

William Farraday crossed his arms. "Other than the Pembrokes? No."

Yes, Joanna thought to herself. *That's definitely our next stop.*

Chapter 9

C hief Bernard arrived with Detective Keller in tow as well as two uniformed officers, followed shortly thereafter by Dave Hollicker and Casey Ledford. Always a gentleman, Chief Bernard offered to take Abby Holder home, and she gladly accepted. For a while Farraday insisted on watching every move the CSIs made.

"I'm sorry," Joanna told him finally. "This isn't going to work. You need to go outside and let them do their jobs."

"You can't just throw me out. This is my school," William Farraday objected.

"Yes, I can," Joanna said with a smile. "This may be your school, but it's my homicide investigation."

Grumbling under his breath and citing a need for privacy, Farraday retreated to his car to talk on the phone. When Chief Bernard reappeared, Joanna was involved in bringing the new arrivals up to speed with what they had learned from Abby Holder as well as what they had found in Debra Highsmith's office.

Joanna was annoyed that the whole time they were trying to brief him, Matt Keller continued to fiddle with his smartphone. He was almost as bad as the kids in the restaurant.

At last he stopped and held up the phone. "Here," he said, handing the device over to Chief Bernard. "Take a look at this."

Alvin Bernard had to dig a pair of reading glasses out of his pocket before he could see what was on the phone. When he did, his eyes bulged. "Is that Debra Highsmith?"

Matt Keller nodded.

"Where did this come from?" he demanded, passing the phone over to Joanna. On it was a still shot from the video, complete with the DIE, BITCH caption.

"Go to the next one," Matt said.

Joanna did so. She was shaken but not surprised to see the photo Jenny had taken. The caption underneath the second photo said: BITCH DIES.

"Where did you get this?" Joanna asked, passing the phone along to Deb, who clicked back and forth between the two photos. "From Marty Pembroke's Facebook page?"

"Didn't have to," Matt said. "It's gone viral, just like the video. Those two photos and their captions are paired all over the Internet. I entered Debra Highsmith's name and this is the first thing that came up."

"Where did the crime scene photo come from?" Alvin asked again. "How did they get it?"

"From my daughter, I'm afraid," Joanna admitted. "Jenny found the body. She took the photo with her cell phone and sent it to a friend while she was waiting for me to show up. Next thing you know it's on the Internet."

"How can this be out on the Net when we haven't made any kind of official announcement?" Chief Bernard wanted to know.

"I'm sorry," Joanna said. "Believe me, I've already read Jenny the riot act about it."

In the meantime, Deb handed the phone back to Matt, who, with a purposeful frown on his face, immediately began fiddling with it again.

"It could be that our next-of-kin notification is going to be a lot harder than we thought," he added. "Here, take a look at this."

This time he handed the phone directly to Joanna, who read aloud from the screen. " 'Debra Jean Highsmith, born August 15, 1967, Bridgeport, Connecticut. Died September 21, 1967, New York City, New York.' "

"Died?" Joanna asked. "Is this someone with the same name? Maybe she's a relative."

Matt shook his head. "I don't think so," he said. "This has to be something else, because this Debra Jean Highsmith and our Debra Jean Highsmith have a lot more in common than just their names. They also share the same birth date and Social Security number."

"What are we talking about, then?" Deb Howell asked. "Identity theft?"

"Yes, unless there really is some kind of bureaucratic mix-up going on in Social Security," Matt said.

"Which could turn out to be the case," Alvin Bernard suggested.

"Possibly," Matt agreed. "Once the feds get their wires crossed, it's hell getting them uncrossed. Whatever it is, accidental or deliberate, it's been going on for a very long time. This was the name our Debra Highsmith was using when she graduated from high school at Good Shepherd Academy in Albuquerque. It's also who she was when she attended the University of New Mexico and later when she enrolled at the University of Arizona for her master's degree."

Joanna was impressed with Matt Keller's cyber-sleuthing. It was right up there with the kinds of wizard things Frank Montoya used to pull off for her. "You found all this out in, what, a little over three hours?"

"What can I tell you?" Detective Keller asked with a grin. "I'm a connected kind of guy."

"Okay," Joanna said. "If our Debra Highsmith isn't really Debra Highsmith, who is she?"

"That's the sixty-four-thousand-dollar question, isn't it?" Chief Bernard said. "I'll call Dr. Machett and let the M.E.'s office know this latest turn of events. He'll be taking dental X-rays, so we can put those into the national missing persons database, but this is a problem. How are we supposed to do a next-of-kin notification if the victim isn't who she pretended to be?"

"Cell phone records," Deb Howell suggested. "Once we have those and know who she's been calling, we may be able to trace back through some of those folks."

Keller nodded in agreement. "So what's our first step, Detective Howell—tackle Marty Pembroke?"

Joanna was doubly impressed. He had been surfing the Net, but he had also been listening.

Deb nodded and then turned to Joanna. "Are you going on this one?"

Joanna shook her head. "I was already part of an earlier, somewhat contentious meeting with him at lunchtime. Marty is less likely to have his guard up if he's talking to people other than me. If I were you, I wouldn't bring up the 'Die, Bitch' bit. Let him think that you're in the process of interviewing everybody who knew our victim, students and teachers alike."

"That might work for Marty," Chief Bernard put in, "but only as long as he's officially a person of interest. If Dr. Pembroke gets wind of it, he'll raise all kinds of hell."

"What do you mean?" Joanna asked.

"Let's just say he's been giving other people here in town plenty of grief, and not just the school district, either. He's filed planning and zoning complaints. He's in a beef with his next-door neighbor over an intruding laurel hedge. So if we're asking Dr. Pembroke's son questions about Debra Highsmith's murder and Daddy hears about it, I'd guess he's not going to like it one little bit. I'd expect him to land on your doorstep with a complaint, most likely with an attorney in tow, in two shakes of a lamb's tail."

"So he's not what you'd call a reasonable kind of guy?" Joanna asked.

"Hardly."

Joanna thought about that for a time. "Okay," she said at last, "just to be thorough, maybe you should think about establishing Dr. Pembroke's whereabouts on the night Debra Highsmith died. He got his way with the school district and made the board renege on parts of the suspension Debra Highsmith had given his son, but that doesn't mean he was happy about it."

"Good point," Keller said. He turned to Deb. "We'd better get cracking then. My car or yours?"

"We'll take both," Deb said.

"Looks like you've got a live one there," Joanna said to Chief Bernard.

"Yeah, he's great when it comes to using the Internet, but he's not much use when it comes to interviewing suspects."

"Give him time," Joanna said. "He'll get better."

Bernard glanced at his watch. "Speaking of time, don't you have a press conference coming up in a little over half an hour?"

"I do," Joanna said. "The problem is, I know even less now than I did before."

"Wing it," Alvin Bernard said. "You should be able to do that with no problem. I used to play poker with your dad. He could bluff like crazy. It looks to me like you're a chip off the old block."

William Farraday returned, went back into Debra Highsmith's office, and came out a short time later, still fuming. "The way those two are working, it's going to take hours."

Joanna felt like telling him that's what it took to be a CSI—supreme attention to detail, for both what was at the crime scene and what was missing. She settled for changing the subject.

"When you hire new principals and teachers, do you run background checks?"

Farraday frowned before he answered. "Didn't used to," he said. "We do now."

"Did you run one on Debra Highsmith?"

"I'm sure at the time we hired her we checked her school transcripts and that sort of thing, but we didn't institute the background searches until two years ago after the school district in San Manuel ended up hiring a registered sex offender. That situation got everybody's attention."

"I'll bet it did," Joanna said. "What about teachers and administrators who were already here?"

"They were grandfathered in," Farraday said. "The union saw to it that background checks applied to new hires only. Why, have you found something unsavory in Ms. Highsmith's past?"

That's the problem, Joanna thought. *We know nothing about her past.*

"Just wondering," Joanna said aloud. "We're trying to put the bits and pieces together. One more thing. I believe I was told the beneficiary of her group insurance policy is the Malpai Borderlands Group. Do you have any idea what her connection might be to those folks?"

"None at all," Farraday said. "Most of the time employees name their spouses or children as their beneficiaries, but we certainly don't discriminate against people who don't have regular family members when it comes to beneficiary arrangements. The person being insured gets to name the beneficiary."

Having worked for Milo Davis at the Davis Insurance Agency for several years, Joanna was well aware of that.

"Thank you so much, Mr. Farraday. You've been most helpful."

Unaccustomed to being dismissed, he seemed a little surprised, but Joanna didn't hang around long enough to check out his reaction. Instead, she went back into the office, where she paused in the doorway long enough to catch Casey Ledford's eye. Casey stopped what she was doing and came over to the door.

"What's up?"

"I know it's already looking like a very long day, but when you leave here, I'm going to need you to stop by Ms. Highsmith's place in San Jose Estates. When the city cops went by there yesterday, they thought they had a missing person case. They had no idea that she was a homicide victim. I have a feeling their forensics work was less than adequate."

"Do you think?" Casey returned with a wry smile. "You want Dave and me to give the whole place a going over?"

"Please, and if it's overtime, it's overtime or comp time, your choice."

Joanna already knew that Casey, a single mom, would most likely choose comp time, while Dave, with a wife, a mortgage, and a baby on the way, would most likely take the money. Of the two, Joanna preferred comp time because it was easier on the budget.

Leaving them to it, Joanna checked her watch and headed back to the Justice Center. She wasn't looking forward to the press conference, especially since she was concerned there would be questions about Jenny's photo. Leaving Tom Hadlock to deal with those wouldn't be fair.

As Joanna drove through the parking lot toward her covered reserved parking place in the back, she spotted a bright red Miata tucked in neatly among the collection of media vans. It was parked with the top down, near the front door. Joanna knew it had to be her mother's. Eleanor Lathrop drove the only red Miata in town. Joanna had considerable experience in handling dangerous crooks, but dealing with her mother was often tougher.

"Crap," Joanna said aloud. Having her mother show up at the office was not unheard of, but with a complicated press conference due to start in the next half hour or so, Joanna needed some time to pull her thoughts together. In truth, her relationship with her mother was somewhat better now that Eleanor and George spent nearly half the year tooling around the country in their RV. Their May 1 estimated departure date was only a few weeks away, and for Joanna, it couldn't come soon enough.

She ducked inside through the back door that opened directly into her office. Once she put down her purse, she picked up her phone and dialed Kristin. "I take it my mother is here?"

"She told me she was going out to the lobby to talk to Marliss Shackleford."

"Great," Joanna said. "My two favorite people in the same place at the same time. Did my mother mention what this was about?"

"She said something about tomorrow night."

"What's tomorrow night?" Joanna asked. Then she remembered. The gala. Her mother was a pal of Maggie Oliphant, the mover and shaker behind the Bisbee Art League. Eleanor had asked if Joanna and Butch would be attending the gala. Joanna had offered to make a donation, but she had turned down the invitation. She worked too many hours during the week to want to spend weekend evenings away from her family if she didn't have to.

"First things first," Joanna said. "I have to get through Friday before I can think about Saturday. Have you heard anything from Jaime?"

"Yes, he's on his way down the canyon now."

"Good. Tell him to ring the bell on my back door and come in that way. I need to talk to him before I talk to the press."

"She's back, isn't she."

Joanna heard her mother's voice in the background. Putting Kristin on the spot wasn't fair, either. Eleanor Lathrop was Joanna's problem. "Go ahead and send her in," Joanna said with a sigh. "Let's get this over with."

Eleanor waltzed into her daughter's office as if she owned the place. Unable to help herself, she paused long enough to run a finger across Joanna's small conference table, looking for dust. Thanks to Kristin, there wasn't any.

Way to go, Kristin, Joanna thought. Aloud and as brightly as she could manage she said, "Hi, Mom. What brings you here?"

"Is there any reason I shouldn't stop by to see my darling daughter?"

There were plenty of reasons, not the least of which being that said daughter was busy working. There had been a homicide on her watch, and she needed to keep after it.

"No reason," Joanna said, hoping that her voice remained even and that her face was unreadable. "What's up?"

"Milo and Fanny Davis's daughter-in-law had an emergency cesarean up in Phoenix last night," Eleanor said. "They just left to go help their son look after the other two kids. Three kids under the age of five. If that isn't a family-planning nightmare, I don't know what is."

Joanna still held her former boss in high esteem. "Milo is great with kids," she said. "I'm sure they'll be able to handle it."

"That's neither here nor there," Eleanor sniffed. "The problem is, they were supposed to sit at our table tomorrow night. Since I'm on the committee, Maggie will be beside herself if there are empty places at my table. I'm hoping you and Butch will agree to come in their place. The food should be excellent. Prime rib at the Rob Roy is always top drawer. As an elected official, it's always good to be seen out and about and doing your civic duty."

Joanna was getting ready to decline when Eleanor added the knockout punch. "I called Butch first. He says he'll be glad to dust off his tux for the evening, but that it's up to you."

This wasn't the first time Eleanor had played divide and conquer by going to Butch behind Joanna's back, and it wouldn't be the last.

"We'd have to get a sitter," Joanna said, making the most obvious objection.

"Handled," Eleanor said. "I already talked to Jenny. She'll be glad to take care of her brother to earn some extra spending money. I'll order pizza for them, and I'll pay the bill for that, too."

"In other words, you really want us to come," Joanna said.

"Well, yes," Eleanor said. "You do hold a certain position in the community, and it would be a good idea to be seen in public when you're wearing something besides a uniform and a handgun."

Joanna got it. Eleanor was proud of her, but she probably would have been happier with Joanna in a more traditional "women's work" job. As for Butch, since his mother was more of a case than Joanna's was, he always capitulated when Eleanor showed up as a paragon of sweetness and light. If he hadn't meant what he'd said about going to the gala, he wouldn't have said it. He wasn't in the habit of leaving Joanna to be the bad guy.

"Okay," Joanna said. "If it's okay with Butch, it's okay with me."

"Thank you," Eleanor said. "Maggie Oliphant is having a conniption fit about this particular dinner. She needs it to be a huge success, and she's worried that it won't be. Having empty places at the tables when she's already given the final head count would make it that much worse."

Joanna didn't know Maggie Oliphant well, but she'd clearly been able to rope Eleanor into the process and make her feel personally responsible for a successful outcome. That meant Maggie had to be some kind of organizing genius.

"I can see why Maggie's worn out," Eleanor said. "Dealing with this particular group of artistic types has been especially challenging—a lot like herding cats. It's almost impossible to get them to move from place to place and show up on time. They had a guest speaker for this afternoon's workshop session, and they were all late getting back from lunch. Maggie was frantic."

Joanna knew that Junior Dowdle's meltdown had a lot to do with the Plein Air group's late lunch, but she didn't tell Eleanor that. For as long as Junior had worked at Daisy's, Eleanor had sniffed her disapproval on more than one occasion. Her opinions about the developmentally disabled were similar to her opinions about small children—they should be seen but not heard, and not seen too much, either. And there was no way Joanna was going to pass along what Daisy had said about Junior's possible Alzheimer's diagnosis.

Having accomplished her goal, Eleanor stood up to leave. "Marliss was just telling me about the situation with Mrs. Highsmith."

Joanna knew that the word "Ms." had never made its way into her mother's vocabulary, but Eleanor's comment reminded Joanna that no one knew Debra Highsmith's exact marital status, either. Single? Married? Divorced? Who knew?

"Yes," Joanna said. "It's terribly unfortunate, but we haven't released her name yet." She glanced at her watch. It was almost time.

Eleanor frowned. "Oddly enough, Marliss seemed to think I knew all about it. Surely she doesn't think you would blab sheriff's department business to me, does she? Why would she jump to that kind of conclusion?"

Joanna understood all too well. Marliss didn't suspect Joanna of being the leak. The reporter was convinced Jenny would have confided in her grandmother, except Eleanor and Jenny didn't have that kind of relationship.

"Maybe I should talk to Marliss about it," Joanna suggested.

"I didn't mean to get her in any kind of trouble."

"Of course not," Joanna said confidently, "but leaking information about a homicide victim before the family has been notified can cause difficulties later on."

Kristin tapped on the door. "Detective Carbajal is back from the autopsy," she said.

"Mom," Joanna said. "I'm going to have to chase you out of here. I need to meet with Jaime before the press conference."

"I'm going, I'm going," Eleanor said. She walked as far as the office door and then turned to look back at Joanna. "It's days like this when I'm really grateful George is retired. Whenever there was a homicide to worry about, it seemed like that was all he could think about."

Joanna knew that feeling from the inside out.

"You won't let this get in the way of your coming tomorrow night, now will you?" Eleanor asked.

"No," Joanna told her mother. "I gave you my word. I said Butch and I will be there, and we will."

Eleanor marched out of Joanna's office, and Jaime Carbajal sidled inside. "What's the news?" Joanna asked.

"What we already knew. Machett says she was shot four times with a thirty-eight," Jaime said. "She didn't die instantly. Probably bled out over fifteen minutes or so."

"Time of death?"

"Somewhere between one A.M. and three A.M. There was no undigested food in her stomach."

"So she probably hadn't eaten since noon?" Joanna asked.

Jaime nodded. "So that would be consistent with what the Bisbee cops told us. That the killer surprised her when she came home from work, where she was taken down before she had time to take off her ID badge or change clothes. From the injuries to her arms and legs, it appears she was restrained for some time prior to the murder. She evidently struggled against the restraints, but they were removed either before or after she was shot. She also has a single puncture wound in her right shoulder. It'll be a while to get the tox screen back, but Machett thinks she may have been hit with some kind of tranquilizer."

"Sexual assault?" Joanna asked.

Jaime shook his head. "No sign of that, but Dr. Machett says she's had at least one child, probably carried to term, and delivered by C-section."

Abby Holder hadn't mentioned Debra Highsmith's having a child, a spouse, or a former spouse. Neither had William Farraday. Joanna suspected that Mr. Farraday would draw the line when it came to hiring an unwed mother to serve as a school principal in a town where people expected their educators to double as role models.

Kristin knocked on the door. "Tom Hadlock is wondering if you're ready. The reporters are getting impatient out there."

Joanna nodded and then looked back at Jaime. "Anything else I should know?"

"There was some bruising on her upper arms, like somebody grabbed her from behind. There's also some bruising to her forehead, like maybe she fell to the floor. The head injury happened several hours before she died."

Joanna paused long enough to open her purse, take out her compact, and check her hair and makeup. Eleanor Lathrop Winfield probably didn't approve of her daughter's line of work, but her years of exhortations that Joanna "always look your best" hadn't fallen on deaf ears. Joanna had no idea what she was going to say in her press conference, but nobody would be able to say that she hadn't dressed for the part.

Chapter 10

Joanna had learned over the years that press conferences are a kind of stylized form of performance art, not unlike Kabuki. The idea is to be there, to act as though you're fully prepared to tell all, while at the same time divulging as little as possible. A certain amount of earnestness was always helpful. During the conference a few nuggets of information would be parceled out, but only enough to leave the attendees wanting more. That way, when the reporters went back to their respective computers to write their articles, they would do so with only the barest outline of what had happened.

Joanna went outside and back to the same shaded breezeway where she had stood side by side with Arlee Jones the previous day. Tom Hadlock still wasn't up to

Frank Montoya standards, and neither was she, but she made it through this one with no difficulty.

She started by making a series of remarks before opening up to questions. The body found earlier that morning on High Lonesome Road had been identified as Debra Jean Highsmith, Bisbee High School's principal, who had been reported missing on Thursday morning. She had died as the result of multiple gunshot wounds. The incident was being investigated as a suspected homicide.

Joanna had to resist the urge to smile slightly when she said that. Suicides hardly ever die of multiple gunshots, and multiple gunshot wounds generally ruled out death by natural causes. However, declaring death by multiple gunshot wounds as a definite homicide went beyond the stylized dance of accepted press conference protocol.

Toward the end of her remarks she delivered what she considered the red meat of her presentation. "As of this time, my officers have been unable to locate any of Ms. Highsmith's next of kin. If anyone hearing this announcement can offer any assistance in this regard, you are urged to contact the Cochise County Sheriff's Department."

When she finished and called for questions, most of them turned out to be questions she had already answered, but she answered them again anyway. That was another part of the press conference process.

During the Q and A, Joanna noticed that Marliss, prominently positioned in the first row, was busily taking notes, but she didn't raise her head or her hand. When one of the other reporters asked about the source of that unauthorized crime scene photo that was reportedly making its way around the Internet, Joanna replied with a firm "No comment." At that point Joanna more than half expected Marliss to jump in with a related question or to at least mention Jenny's possible involvement in the crime photo flap, but she did not. That seemed odd. It wasn't like Marliss to exercise that kind of restraint. Not at all.

It seemed to take forever. When the news conference finally ended, however, Joanna's phone rang before she could leave for home.

"I've got your dog," Jeannine Philips announced.

Jeannine was head of Joanna's Animal Control division. Animal Control had landed in Joanna's department several years earlier, on a supposedly temporary basis that was now regarded as permanent by all concerned.

"My dog," Joanna repeated. She was mystified. Lady was generally a quiet, stay-at-home kind of dog, and Lucky was deaf. Joanna found it difficult to believe that either of them had wandered away from High Lonesome Ranch.

"Which one?" Joanna asked. "Lady or Lucky?"

"Not *your* dog," Jeannine said. "Your murder victim's dog. His name is Giles. He's properly licensed and chipped and up to date on all his shots. A woman who lives just outside Huachuca City and works at the PX on Fort Huachuca came home this afternoon and found the dog cowering on her back porch. She's scared of dogs. Terrified of dogs. She dialed 911 and refused to get out of her vehicle until an ACO could be dispatched to the scene. Fortunately, one of my officers was already over in the Huachuca City area picking up a batch of kittens that had been abandoned beside the road. She ended up getting both the kittens and the dog."

"Is he okay?" Joanna asked.

"Giles? Not really. He has a snootful of porcupine quills and is badly dehydrated. I had my ACO transport him directly to Millie's. She put him on IV fluids, and she's removing the quills even as we speak. She says she thinks she needs to keep him overnight."

Millie was Dr. Millicent Ross, the same vet Jenny worked for. She and Jeannine were partners. As a consequence, Dr. Ross provided an astonishing amount of pro bono vet work for the animals who happened to come to the attention of Cochise County Animal Control.

"Did you say porcupine quills?"

"Yes, indeed." Jeannine chuckled. "Millie calls dogs like that carpet dogs or yard dogs. They get out in the wild and have no idea what's what. Giles probably got hungry and thought the porcupine was something good to eat. Small error on his part. Believe me, the porcupine got the better end of that deal."

Joanna had thought the Doberman was a goner, right along with Debra Highsmith. Who would kill the dog's owner and let the dog go? Giles had been found in Huachuca City—a good thirty miles from home. How had he gotten there? If he was from Fort Huachuca, maybe he had been trying to get back to his original owner, so had he walked there on his own or had someone given him a ride? Maybe Debra Highsmith herself had taken the dog there.

"If that poor woman thought she was getting herself a first line of defense by acquiring a guard dog, she didn't get much of a bargain," Joanna said.

"Now wait," Jeannine said. "Don't jump to any conclusions, and don't be so hard on the dog. It's not his fault. Millie says the dog has a seeping puncture wound on his right shoulder that didn't come from a porcupine quill. She says it's consistent with a wound from the kind of dart gun they use to tranquilize bears and cougars who happen to wander into suburban neighborhoods. She thinks someone took the dog out of the equation early in the game by tranquilizing him. Then the perp transported Giles and dumped him while he was still unconscious."

The moment Jeannine mentioned the tranquilizing gun, Joanna made a possible mental connection between what had happened to Giles and to Debra Highsmith as well.

"Can she do a tox screen and find out if there's any residue of the tranquilizer in the dog's blood?"

"Why would you need that?"

"Because the killer may have used the same tranquilizer to incapacitate both the dog and the dog's owner. If we know what the exact compound is, we may be able to trace it."

"I'll ask her, but it might turn out to be expensive. I don't want her to end up having to do it for free."

"My department will pay for the tox screen," Joanna said.

"What about next of kin?" Jeannine asked. "Any sign of them?"

"Not yet."

"I'm going to need to find someone to foster Giles until we can locate one of the victim's friends or family members who would be willing to take him," Jeannine said. "It's not fair to bring a dog that's been through this much trauma into the pound."

That was one of the difficult aspects of homicide. Unexpected deaths usually left grieving family members behind; some were human, some were not. It was no accident that the first people to come in contact with the bereaved animals—animal control officers dispatched to crime scenes—often ended up taking bereaved pets into their own homes on a permanent basis. After all, that was how Lucky had come into their lives—as the only surviving dog of a murdered animal hoarder.

"Good luck with that," Joanna said. "Let me know how it goes."

She grabbed her purse and had made it as far as her parking space when Deb Howell pulled into the parking lot with Matt Keller's unmarked city patrol car on her six. Joanna dropped her purse on the front seat of the Yukon and then waited for the detectives to park and come to her.

"How'd the Pembroke deal go?" she asked.

"About how you'd expect," Deb said. "We'd had about five minutes with Marty when Daddy Pembroke came flying into the driveway, jumped out of his car, and came inside to . . . let's just say encourage . . . his son to lawyer up."

"So you didn't get anywhere before that happened?"

"Not completely," Matt said. "Marty claimed he was with somebody last night. If his father hadn't come screaming to the rescue, I think Marty would have given us his alibi, which we could have verified or not."

"Check with the other kids," Joanna suggested. "Starting with the kids whose names I gave you earlier. With all this social networking going on, I think everybody probably knows what everybody else is doing at any given time, but don't worry about following up on that tonight. We've all had a long day, and tomorrow isn't going to be any better." She turned to Detective Keller. "Did Chief Bernard authorize overtime?"

"Yes, ma'am."

"Even so, let's go home," she suggested. "We'll get a good night's sleep, and hit it again in the morning. I want to have a task force meeting at eight sharp in the conference room. We'll have Dave and Casey give us an update on what they've found. By then we should have access to Dr. Machett's preliminary report."

"I'm hoping we'll have the phone records by then, too," Keller said.

"All right," Joanna said. "Let's see what the morning brings. We'll go from there."

"You want me to call everybody?" Deb offered.

"No. You go home. I'll have Dispatch give people a heads-up."

With that the two detectives headed home, and so did Joanna. Usually she looked forward to going home and settling in for a quiet evening with her family. This wasn't one of those times. All afternoon, in the background of whatever she was doing, she had continued to noodle away about how best to deal with Jenny and the crime scene photo. Caught in the cross fire between being a mother and being a cop, she dreaded the coming confrontation.

Due to the late-afternoon press conference and the subsequent meeting with the two detectives, Joanna had already missed eating with the family when she pulled into her garage at High Lonesome Ranch. Lady was the one who greeted her at the door, so she went looking for everyone else. Butch was closeted in the bathroom overseeing Dennis's bath. Jenny's bedroom door was shut. Not unusual, but given what had gone on that day, not a good sign, either. Joanna started to knock but then thought better of it. She and Butch would have to deal with the Jenny situation together, after Dennis was in bed.

Back in the kitchen, Joanna found her dinner plated and on the kitchen counter, ready to pop into the microwave. She was in the process of reheating it when Butch and Dennis showed up. Dennis threw himself at Joanna with a joyful exuberance that made her smile.

She grabbed him up in a bear hug, sniffing his damp hair, fresh with the unmistakable odor of Johnson's baby shampoo.

"So how's my boy today?" she asked.

Without answering, he slipped from his mother's grasp and darted over to Lady, who accepted his effusive greeting with a modest thump of her tail.

Joanna looked at Butch. "I guess that puts me in my place."

He grinned back at her. "It could be worse," he said. "At least you're ahead of the dog in Denny's estimation. Care for a glass of wine with dinner?"

"I'd like that, but shouldn't we deal with Jenny first?"

"That's already handled," Butch said. He pulled a bottle of wine from the rack and set two glasses down on the counter.

"Handled?" Joanna asked. "What do you mean?"

"Look," Butch said, peeling the foil off the cork. "With you and Jenny both calling me 'Dad,' I figured I'd better step up my game. I spent my whole childhood with a mother who was forever pulling the whole 'wait till your father comes home' routine. The last thing I want to do is be a clone of my parents."

Having spent some time with Butch's parents, especially his mother, Joanna had no argument on that score.

"So I took care of it myself," Butch said, expertly removing the cork. "You and I don't use texting. I called the cell phone people and asked how much we were paying for texting. Then I told Jenny she had a choice. If she wants to be able to text, she has to pay that part of the bill. She chose no texting, so that part of the service is gone as of this afternoon."

Joanna was impressed. "That's called making the punishment suit the crime."

Butch handed Joanna a glass of merlot, passed her the plate of food, and then sat down across the table from her with his own glass.

"What's she doing now?" Joanna asked. "Sulking in her room?"

"No," Butch said. "She's writing a eulogy for Ms. Highsmith."

"A eulogy, really?" Joanna asked. "Does she even know what a eulogy is?"

"Sure," Butch said. "She's a junior. I'm not sure why, but everybody has to read *Julius Caesar* when they're sophomores. That's the way it's always been, but just to bring her up to speed, we went over the whole 'I come to bury Caesar, not to praise him' bit. I told her that taking and sending the photo was wrong and that the way to make amends to Ms. Highsmith's family would be for Jenny to write a eulogy, something that the family could use at the woman's funeral if they chose to. I told her that even if she thought Ms. High-smith was the scum of the earth, it's her assignment to find something good to say about her."

Joanna was looking at him with something akin to slack-jawed wonder. One of Eleanor Lathrop Win-field's objections to Butch as marriage material was the fact that he had never been a father before. She had doubted he was up to the task of taking on a ready-made family, especially one that included a potentially headstrong teenager. Joanna couldn't imagine any bio-logical father, including Andy Brady, doing a better job in this instance, which Butch had handled with com-plete aplomb.

"How'd I do?" he asked.

"Not bad," Joanna said, raising her glass in his direction. "Not bad at all. You're definitely top-drawer daddy material, but about my mother . . ."

"Oh, that," Butch said offhandedly. "The gala thing."

"Yes," Joanna said. "The gala thing. Are you really going to wear your tux?"

"It's black tie optional," he said. "Since I already have a tux, I might just as well get some use out of it."

Butch had bought the tux for the Edgar Awards ban-quet when his first book, *Serve and Protect,* had been nominated for a First Novel Edgar from the Mystery Writers of America. Of course, he hadn't won, and the tux had languished accusingly in the far corner of his closet ever since.

"Besides," Butch added, "it's for a good cause. The school board and the superintendent of schools think of art as an expendable afterthought. Maggie Oliphant is in the process of proving them wrong."

"Good point," Joanna said. "If it's something that's going to put William Farraday in a bad light, I'll go with a happy heart."

Chapter 11

O ver glasses of wine, Joanna brought Butch up to speed on the investigation into Debra High-smith's murder, including the fact that the victim apparently wasn't who she had claimed to be. Along with the identity-theft aspects of the case, there was also the disturbing knowledge that Debra had, somewhere along the way, borne a child whose very existence was a mystery.

They stayed up talking until the ten o'clock news came on. Not surprisingly, the murder of Bisbee's high school principal was again the lead story on the broadcast. The segment included Joanna's press conference plea for help in locating family members.

"That's unusual, isn't it?" Butch asked as they headed off to bed right after the news.

"What's unusual?"

"To release the victim's name without first notifying the next of kin."

"Everything about this case is unusual," Joanna said, "but with Jenny's photo all over the Web, we really didn't have a choice. Since everybody in town already knew the victim was Debra Highsmith, it made no sense to continue referring to her as an 'unidentified woman.' Besides, it's possible someone will see the story and come forward."

"Possible but not likely," Butch said.

His pessimism wasn't unfounded.

"Stranger things have happened," Joanna agreed, "but I'm not holding my breath."

Surprisingly enough, the story bore fruit slightly more than an hour later. Joanna was in bed and sleeping soundly when her cell phone, hooked to a charger on her nightstand, started its ungodly rooster-crowing racket. Butch, who despised that particular ring tone, rolled over and covered his head with a pillow as Joanna answered. Tica Romero, the nighttime dispatcher, was on the line.

"What's up?" Joanna mumbled as she got out of bed and stumbled into the living room to take the call.

"I've got a woman on the line whose name is Sue Ellen Hirales from the Falling H Ranch over in New Mexico."

The name sounded familiar, but still half asleep, Joanna couldn't put it together. "What does she want?"

"She says she's a friend of Debra Highsmith and she may have important information for us. I offered to put her in touch with one of the detectives on the case, but she wants to speak to you—to you and no one else. She's also on her way here."

"To the department?" Joanna asked.

"Yes," Tica replied.

"Right now?" Joanna demanded. "In the middle of the night?"

"That's what she said," Tica replied.

Joanna sighed. Going into the office on a middle-of-the-night wild-goose chase was exactly what she didn't want to do, but she also didn't seem to have a choice.

"All right," she said. "I'll be there. Do me a favor. Start a fresh pot of coffee in the break room. I don't want to drink the stuff that's been sitting there cooking since the swing shift came on duty."

"Do you want me to call out Detectives Howell and Carbajal?"

"No," Joanna said. "Whatever this is, I'll handle it. I'm going to need them to be on their toes tomorrow. Better for one person to be dragging instead of the whole crew. Besides, you said she asked for me by name, right?"

"You're the one she wanted."

"Okay. I'll be there ASAP."

Joanna tiptoed back into the bedroom to get her clothes. "Somebody dead?" Butch asked.

A reasonable question for a middle-of-the-night call-out. "Someone with information about Debra Highsmith," Joanna answered. "She wants to give it to me and nobody else."

"Couldn't it wait until morning?"

"Evidently not."

Joanna managed to pull on her clothing without turning on the light. Once she was dressed, she paused long enough to give Butch a kiss on the top of his head.

"Be safe," he murmured.

"Will," she replied, then she hustled out to the laundry room, where she collected her weapons from the wall safe Butch had installed over the washer/dryer. As the ten-minute drive in the cool night air cleared the cobwebs out of her head, she remembered that the Falling H Ranch in the Animas Valley was part of the Malpai Borderlands Group. It was possible that the woman coming to see her might be able to explain why that organization in particular had been designated as Debra Highsmith's life insurance beneficiary.

By the time Joanna arrived at the Justice Center, she was already second-guessing her decision to interview the unexpected witness alone. Having more than one investigator present was a good idea, not only in terms of asking the questions but also for remembering the answers.

"I have a witness coming in," she told her watch commander, recently promoted Sergeant Ted Lang. "I want you to set up interview room one."

"Do you want me to have a deputy come sit in?" he asked. "I can call someone in from Patrol, or I could do it myself."

"No," Joanna said. "Don't bother. I don't foresee this witness causing any kind of difficulty, but at the same time, I want to be sure that I don't miss anything. If we tape it, I can go back over it later, and so can my detectives. When the witness—Sue Ellen Hirales— gets here," Joanna added, "have her taken directly to the interview room as though it's standard procedure."

"You got it, boss," Lang said.

Joanna had come into the building through the secure door into her private office. After stopping by the break room to collect a freshly brewed cup of coffee, she returned to her office and settled in to wait. She didn't know exactly how long it would take to get from Animas to Bisbee—probably the better part of two hours—but she also had no idea if Sue Ellen had called the department while already in transit. Joanna sipped her coffee, knowing as she did so that it would probably make sleep difficult later on, providing there was time to sleep.

Since she was at her desk, she decided to make good use of the time. She had been out of the office most of the day. That meant she was behind on her paperwork. She looked through the watch commanders' summaries of what had gone on. Other than an accident down by Greenbrush Draw involving a DUI and multiple non-life-threatening injuries, there wasn't much to report. She soon found her attention straying from the routine paperwork. Putting it aside, she stared at the eerie moonlit desert outside her window and struggled with the unanswered but essential questions of the Debra Highsmith case. Who was Debra Highsmith? How old was she? Where had she come from? It seemed to Joanna that the only way to get some traction in finding out who had killed the woman was to find out who she was and why she had been in hiding.

Joanna returned to Abby Holder's half-kidding suggestion that perhaps Debra Highsmith had been in a witness protection program of some kind. Since all of her school records had been done under the alias, Joanna was left to wonder what she could possibly have known as a girl—what damning evidence could a mere teenager have provided—that would have required placing her in a witness protection program? And what about her child? Dr. Machett claimed that she had given birth to a child, but where was it? Was Debra's murder somehow related to this unknown child? Had she given him or her up for adoption? Had the baby died in childbirth? What?

Lost in thought, Joanna was startled when Sergeant Lang tapped on her door. "Witness is ready and waiting in the interview room," he said. "I offered her coffee. She declined. Watch yourself. She looks tough—as though she wouldn't mind taking on a couple of black bears single-handed."

"I'll keep that in mind."

Joanna stopped in the hallway outside the interview room and peered in at Sue Ellen Hirales through the two-way mirrored glass. Ted Lang was right. It was hard to tell the woman's age. Her weathered skin made her look to be somewhere in her sixties. Her iron-gray hair was cut in a short, straight bob. She was dressed the way cowboys dress for cold weather—long-sleeved flannel shirt, worn jeans, and a pair of dusty boots that had seen plenty of stirrup use in their day. On the floor next to the boots sat an old-fashioned piece of luggage, one that Joanna's mother referred to as a train case and which Eleanor still preferred to use when transporting makeup and hair equipment on long hauls in the RV.

Clearly this was a working cowgirl who spent hours in the sun and wasn't likely to have a close relationship with anyone in the cosmetics industry, including a neighborhood Avon lady. There was no lipstick on her thin, parched lips, and Joanna doubted she squandered time, money, or energy on moisturizers or sunscreen, either. After a quick mental calculation, Joanna chopped twenty years off what she had initially assumed to be the woman's age. Sue Ellen Hirales was probably only in her forties.

She waited quietly at the small Formica table in the interview room. There was no fidgeting. Her hands rested in her lap. She exhibited no interest or curiosity in her surroundings. This was a woman who was accustomed to waiting out the seasons. For someone like that, a few minutes spent in an interview room were of no consequence.

Joanna opened the door and let herself into the room, holding out her hand as she did so. "Ms. Hirales? I'm Sheriff Brady. I understand you wanted to see me."

Sue Ellen Hirales stood up. Her handshake was beyond firm. Her skin was dry and rough. Her palms were callused from doing hard manual labor. Joanna suspected that she was someone who had not only ridden fence lines but had built them as well.

"Can I get you something?" Joanna offered.

Sue Ellen shook her head. "Pretending this is a social visit won't make it any easier. I'm here because my friend is dead, and I'm doing what she asked me to do. That's all."

"I'm sorry for your loss," Joanna murmured, taking a seat.

"Thank you," Sue Ellen said, nodding stiffly and wiping away a tear as she resumed her seat. She looked too tough to be susceptible to tears.

Is that the big secret? Joanna wondered. Were Debra Highsmith and Sue Ellen Hirales a gay couple? William Farraday probably wouldn't have approved of having a gay high school principal any more than he would have liked having one with an out-of-wedlock baby.

Joanna had been prepared to ask questions. That proved unnecessary. Sue Ellen had come there to tell her story and did so with no prompting.

"I spent the last five days out on the trail with some well-to-do assholes from back east who think they're great white hunters but who didn't have brains enough to take a shot when I gave 'em one. We got back home late tonight. Mom was watching the news and saw the story about Debra. I was out feeding and watering the stock when she came to the barn to tell me. When I finished with the horses, I got cleaned up and headed out."

The hunting part was what finally allowed Joanna to pull the pieces together. Cougars poaching livestock were an ongoing problem for ranchers in both the San Bernardino and Animas Valleys and in the Peloncillo Mountains, which stuck up like a rocky spine between the two. For years Augusto Hirales, one of the ranchers in the area, had offered guided cougar hunts to big-game hunters. If Sue Ellen was Augusto's daughter, it appeared she had now taken over that aspect of the business.

"Augusto is your father?" Joanna asked, just to be sure.

Sue Ellen nodded.

"If you don't mind my asking," Joanna said, "what is the nature of your relationship to Ms. Highsmith?"

"It's a long story," Sue Ellen said.

"That's all right," Joanna told her. "I'm in no hurry. We've got all night."

"If that's the case, maybe I'll take you up on that offer of coffee after all."

Joanna recognized the request as a delaying tactic. "Cream and sugar?"

"Just black. It's too much trouble to drag all that stuff along on a hunt. I've learned to do without."

Joanna went back to the break room, poured herself a second cup, and brought another one along for Sue Ellen.

"Are you recording this?" Sue Ellen asked when Joanna set the cup down in front of her.

"Taping it, yes," Joanna answered. "You asked for me, but I have a team of homicide detectives who are handling the case. If anything you tell me is applicable to the case, they need to have access to the information."

Sue Ellen nodded her understanding. "All right," she said, "but first tell me. How did Debra die? The news said something about her being shot."

"Several times," Joanna said. "In the leg and in the back. She was alive when she was taken from her home in town and then held for several hours. Sometime later she was transported to a deserted area out along High Lonesome Road where she was shot, maybe while she was attempting to escape. We can't be sure about that. There was evidence that restraints had been used, but no restraints were found on the body."

"Not somebody local, then," Sue Ellen said.

"What makes you say that?"

"High Lonesome Road. That's where you live, isn't it—on High Lonesome Ranch? A local would have to be dumb as a stump to shoot somebody just up the road from the sheriff's place."

It was an astute observation, and one that didn't exclude either Marty Pembroke or his father. They were new to town. Joanna doubted they had any idea about where she lived.

"You're right, of course," Joanna said. "I sometimes forget that this is a place where almost everybody knows everybody else. Except for Debra Highsmith, that is. What I've learned so far is that she was a very private person and hardly anybody knows much about her. I'm hoping you're the exception to that rule."

"She was my best friend," Sue Ellen said with a sudden burst of emotion. "The first real friend I ever had. I can't believe she's gone."

"Tell me about her," Joanna urged. "Where did you meet?"

"At Good Shepherd Academy in Albuquerque," Sue Ellen said. "It's a boarding school. Expensive. Two girls to a room, but none of the other girls wanted to room with me because I was a dyke. They acted like being queer was contagious or something. When Debra showed up as the new girl that fall, the nuns put her with me, and she didn't seem to mind. I'd lived on the ranch all my life. I'd been friends with ranch hands and the like, but I'd never been friends with another girl before, and not friends with benefits, either," she added, giving Joanna a hard look. "Just friends.

"She told me that she was alone—that her whole family, her parents and a younger brother, had died in a car wreck in Michigan a year earlier. They were on vacation without her when the driver of an eighteen-wheeler fell asleep, lost control, and smashed their car flat. Other than a grandmother somewhere back east, Debra had no one. The grandmother was the one who had sent her to Albuquerque to Good Shepherd. Later on that fall, she told me the grandmother had died, too. It turns out that was a lie, but I believed it at the time. I believed it until tonight."

Sue Ellen looked down at the train case at her feet. She paused for a moment. Rather than pushing her, Joanna let the silence linger. Finally, Sue Ellen resumed her story.

"Because she had no family left and nowhere to go for the holidays, when Christmas came around that year, I invited her to come home with me. My family loved her as much as I did. From the moment she walked through the door, they treated her like she was another daughter, which, as far as my parents were concerned, she was. They gave her a room of her own. That's where she stayed whenever she came to see us, and that's where I found this tonight." She nodded toward the train case. "It was on the top shelf of her closet, just where she said it would be."

Sue Ellen paused and sipped her coffee, which had already gone cold in the heavy china Mickey Mouse mug Joanna had pulled out of the break room dishwasher.

"From then on, that's how it was. She came home to the ranch for holidays and for summer vacations. I worried that with her grandmother gone, she'd have to drop out of school, but she said Granny Dora, short for Isadora, had taken care of her tuition in advance before she died, and that she had set aside money for Debra to go on to college as well. From looking at these, that's evidently the one true thing she told me, by the way," Sue Ellen added bitterly. "Isadora Creswell is her grandmother's real name."

"Is?" Joanna asked. "You're saying the grandmother is still alive?"

"She was as of two months ago," Sue Ellen said. "The last letter from her is dated March eleventh."

Joanna felt a surge of relief. Sue Ellen had provided exactly what was needed—the name of Debra's next of kin. "Where does she live?"

Sue Ellen shrugged. "I have no idea. Until tonight, I didn't know Debra had any kind of family connections. I thought we were it."

She paused then. Sensing there had to be more to the story, Joanna waited for Sue Ellen to continue.

"Have you ever seen someone you love walking toward the edge of a cliff and you couldn't do anything to stop it?"

Joanna nodded.

"That's what happened to me our senior year of high school. I could see Debra was headed for trouble and I couldn't do a damn thing about it. Good Shepherd was an all-girls school, but that didn't mean there weren't plenty of boys around. Debra was so pretty, and the guys tended to clump around her like flies to honey. There were good ones and bad ones in the mix. Naturally, she fell for a bad one. I tried to tell her he was just out to make a conquest. We had a big fight about it—the first fight we ever had. She told me I was a queer and didn't know anything about boys. I told her if she went to bed with him, she was a stupid slut. She did sleep with him, though. Maybe we weren't what you could call 'good' Catholic girls, but we weren't so bad as to use birth control."

"She got pregnant?"

Sue Ellen nodded. "It turned out the dyke's assessment about the creep was on the money. Once Debra slept with him, he dropped her like a hot potato. We were young and naive. It took a while for her to figure out she was pregnant. She didn't tell me at first, but she finally had to tell someone, and I was it. When she told me what he had done to her, I went looking for the asshole. I found him in a bar and beat the living crap out of him with a pair of brass knuckles my dad had given me. Nothing ever came of that. He couldn't very well press charges. After all, he was a big-deal tough guy and I was only a girl. If his buddies had found out I was the one who knocked him for a row of peanuts and took out two of his front teeth in the process, he never would have lived it down. Instead, he stuck to the story that after he and I talked outside the bar, I left and some other guys came along and beat him up.

"By May of that year, Debra was starting to show. Some of the girls may have figured out what was going on, but I don't think anyone let on to the nuns at Good Shepherd. After graduation, Debra came back to the Falling H with me because, again, according to her, she didn't have anyplace else to go. My mother took one look at her and figured out what was going on. Debra and I had spent hours talking about what she should do. Obviously, getting an abortion was out of the question. She never would have done that, no matter what, but she couldn't see how she'd be able to go on to school and take care of a baby at the same time. She talked about giving the baby up for adoption, but we didn't have the first idea about how to arrange something like that.

"That's when my parents stepped in. They're good people. They offered to take the baby and raise him as their own. His name is Mike, by the way," Sue Ellen added after a pause. "We call him Mikey. He's twenty-six now. He joined the marines fresh out of high school. That was the third fight Debra and I had. He wanted to go. Debra was against it, but she didn't really have any say in the matter, either.

"When he finished his enlistment, he came back home and got his BA degree in a little less than three years. Now he's in his first year of law school at the University of New Mexico. The only condition Debra made was that, under no circumstances, were we to tell him that she was his mother. As far as Mikey is concerned, I'm his big sister and Debra is his Aunty Deb. He loves her to distraction . . . Loved," she corrected. "That's why she's spent every holiday and every Christmas vacation on the ranch with us. I taught her how to rope and ride at the same time I was teaching Mikey."

"What about guns?" Joanna asked. "Did you teach her how to shoot, too?"

"Never," Sue Ellen said. "Debra hated guns. That was the second fight we had—when she found out I was teaching Mikey how to shoot. I told her he was being raised as a ranch kid, and being able to shoot was part of the deal. When you run into a rattlesnake out on the range, you can't use a spitball. She shut up about it after that. We never discussed it again."

"Would you be surprised if I told you Debra bought a handgun, had obtained a concealed carry permit, and had the weapon in her purse?"

"Are you kidding?" Sue Ellen demanded. "I don't believe it. Mikey won't, either." She paused again and shook her head. "Poor Mikey. This is gonna break his heart twice over. My folks always told him he was adopted. They said that they hoped someday he'd be able to meet his birth mother, but I think Mikey stopped believing in that about the same time he stopped believing in the tooth fairy and Santa Claus. I'll probably be the one who has to tell him the real story."

Overcome, she stopped, and sat there for a long time, unable to continue.

"You'll need to do that right away," Joanna said gently. "There's a particularly vile photo out on the Internet—one that should never have been posted. You don't want him to find out about it that way."

"What kind of photo?"

"A crime scene photo."

Sue Ellen swallowed and nodded. "I'll tell him," she said. "I'll call him once we're finished here."

"I could probably get someone from the Albuquerque police department to go by and talk to him in person," Joanna offered.

"No," Sue Ellen said, shaking her head. "I need to be the one. I need to tell him all of it, not just that she's dead."

"You said earlier that you came here because she asked you to," Joanna said. "What's that all about?"

"Debra told me a few weeks ago that if anything happened to her, I should go in her closet and find a case with some packets of letters in it. She said I should take the letters to the cops—actually, to you specifically. She said you'd know what to do with them. Here they are."

She picked the case up off the floor, put it on the table, and pushed it toward Joanna.

"So she believed she was in some kind of danger?"

Sue Ellen shrugged. "I guess so. I asked her at the time if there was something wrong. She said it was no big deal. I believed her about that like I believed her about everything else. So tonight I got down the case, opened it, and read what was inside. It broke my heart," she said, tapping the top of the case. "She lied to me the whole time—lied to me about everything. What I can't figure out is why."

Chapter 12

I t was after one when Joanna escorted Sue Ellen Hirales into the conference room so she could place a call to her adopted brother in private. Once she was gone, Joanna opened the train case. What she found there were packets of letters, held together by rubber bands and labeled by year, dating back as far as thirty years. Unfortunately, the letters had been stored sans envelopes. That meant there were no return addresses visible.

The letters themselves were handwritten, not typed. They were composed in a spidery cursive that became shakier as the years went by, as if the hand that wrote them was developing an increasingly serious tremor. That as well as the fact that the correspondence was entirely of the snail-mail variety suggested that this was an older person who hadn't quite gotten a handle on the digital age.

Over the years, several different generations of upscale stationery had been used to write the multipage missives, including several changes of colors and styles, but always, the top of the first page was embossed with the sender's name, Isadora Creswell. The typeface on that had changed some over the years, but it was usually some variation of a font that resembled calligraphy. Unfortunately, beyond the woman's name, the stationery revealed no additional information.

After turning the problem of tracking down Isadora Creswell over to Margaret Mendoza, her nighttime records clerk, Joanna began thumbing through the letters. The brittle rubber bands holding the packets together splintered at the slightest touch. As she scanned through them, Joanna noticed that some of them began with the words "My Darling Debra" or "My Sweet Girl" or "Dearest Debra," but the signature never varied. "Love and kisses, Granny D."

The contents of the letters were utterly commonplace, offering a window on Isadora's life in a small town. Her cat, Mr. Rufus, had taken ill and she'd had to put him down. The garden club was holding their next meeting at her house. Isadora had collected her second grand slam in a lifetime of playing bridge. Fall was coming. She loved fall but dreaded winter. There were comments about things Debra had told Isadora in letters she wrote—tales about school and teachers and classes, but nowhere were there any references to phone calls in either direction. Nowhere was there any mention that Debra had given birth to an out-of-wedlock child.

Joanna had always marveled at the inherent beauty and strength of spiderwebs, and it occurred to her that these letters were like that—an unbreakable filament of love that linked Isadora to her granddaughter across miles of distance and an expanse of years.

Joanna's door opened. Sue Ellen came back into the room. "Did you reach him?" Joanna asked.

Sue Ellen nodded. "I told him," she said.

"All of it?"

"All of it. Not surprisingly, he's broken up about it. He had only one question. Why didn't she tell him? I told him I didn't know, but that she must have had a good reason. I do know that she loved him with her whole heart. He's coming down, by the way. He said he'll leave first thing in the morning. He'll stop by the ranch to see the folks, then he wants to come by and see you."

Joanna nodded.

"I was planning to drive straight back home tonight, but Mikey made me promise that I'd get a hotel room and spend the night here. He's a smart kid. He's been out on hunts with me, and he knows how wearing they can be. He's right, of course. I was bone tired before I got into the car to drive here. So I've got a room at the Copper Queen. If you need me, that's where I'll be, although I'll probably head out early, too. I didn't call my parents after I talked to Mikey. I didn't want to wake them, so I want to get home before he turns up."

"Sounds like a good idea."

"Do you need anything else?" Sue Ellen asked.

"Not right now. Do we have your contact information in case we need to reach you?"

"I thought I gave my cell phone number when I called in earlier, but here it is again."

Joanna jotted it down. When her phone rang, she saw Sue Ellen out the door before she answered.

"Got it," Margaret Mendoza said. "Clara Isadora Creswell, 450 Spruce Street, Altoona, Pennsylvania."

Once Joanna had written down both the address and the phone number, she looked at her watch. It was half past one, Arizona time. With the East Coast on daylight saving time, it was three hours later than that in Altoona. Should she wait a few hours before making the phone call? Ultimately she decided that the best thing to do was to go ahead and contact the Altoona Police Department. When they agreed to send out a uniformed officer to make the notification, Joanna gave them her cell phone as the preferred contact number. She packed the letters—the ones she had read as well as the ones she hadn't—back into the train case and left it locked in the evidence room for safekeeping.

Then, mindful of her early-morning task force meeting, she headed home. The house was quiet when she let herself into the laundry room from the garage. She crept into the bedroom and slipped into bed. Now that Lady had deserted Joanna's bedside to sleep in Dennis's room, Joanna could come and go in the dark without having to worry about stumbling over a dog.

Butch acknowledged her presence by turning over in bed and flopping his arm across her waist. She was tired enough that she should have been sleepy, but the encounter with Sue Ellen Hirales left her awake and wondering what it was that had caused Debra High-smith to strike out on her own so far from what must have been her home. Joanna's first guess went to the possibility of some kind of child abuse. More often than not, that was the reason runaways took off.

The collection of letters from Isadora, literally decades' worth of letters, made this an unlikely run-away situation. Most kids who disappeared did so com-pletely. They cut all ties, either because their home situation was so bad that they wanted to or because something in their new life—often a homicide—made it impossible for them to return.

What about the young man who had fathered Debra Highsmith's son? Where did he fit in? Did he even know Debra had gotten pregnant? Did he care? Had he known about it, would he have insisted on being involved in the child's life? He might have objected to his son being adopted by anyone and refused to relinquish his parental rights, but not if he had no idea that he had parental rights. Maybe that was what this was all about. Maybe twenty-six years down the line, he had finally discovered the existence of his son. Was that the answer? Had Debra Highsmith been murdered in an act of naked revenge by her son's outraged biological father?

The last time Joanna looked at the clock, it was after three. Her ringing cell phone awakened her at seven. Butch was out of bed. The aroma of bacon frying leaked into Joanna's senses along with the appropriately early-morning rooster crow of her phone.

"Hello," Joanna said, trying to clear the sleep from her voice.

"Are you Sheriff Brady?"

"Yes," she answered.

"My name is Isadora Creswell, Debra's grandmother. Those bastards finally got her, didn't they!

The officers who came to the house told me to call you, but it was the middle of the night where you are, and I decided to wait until a less ungodly hour. Besides, I needed to make some decisions as well as some travel arrangements."

"I'm sorry for your loss," Joanna began.

"Of course you are," Isadora replied crisply, "but we don't need to waste time talking about that right now. It's Saturday morning. My vet's office doesn't open until nine. That's the earliest I'll be able to check Pixie in for boarding. Pixie is my cat, by the way."

Joanna had already read about Mr. Rufus, Isadora's previous cat, going to kitty heaven. It stood to reason that her post-Rufus pet would also be of the feline variety.

"After that it's more than a two-hour drive to get to the airport in Pittsburgh," Isadora continued. "Trying to catch the eleven forty-five flight was just cutting it too close what with all these new TSA security regulations. The first flight I can catch out is the one that goes through Dallas/Fort Worth. That one should get me into Tucson around seven thirty or so. I googled Bisbee. It's supposed to be about two hours from the airport. How far from there is your office?"

Joanna sat up straighter in bed as her assumption about Isadora being digitally illiterate went out the window.

"My office is in the Justice Center," Joanna said. "It's a few miles east of Bisbee on Highway 80."

"The airline schedule says I'll get in at seven thirty, but with the time zone changes, it'll be far later than that as far as my body is concerned. Since I'm not wild about driving on strange roads in the dark, I'll rent a car at the airport, get a hotel room in Tucson, and then drive to Bisbee first thing in the morning. I know it's Sunday, but will you be able to meet me at your office?"

"Of course," Joanna said. "If you call this number when you come through the tunnel, we'll arrive at the Justice Center about the same time. If you'd prefer, however, I could have one of my detectives come to Tucson to pick you up."

Joanna's offer may have sounded like a bit of common courtesy, but it was also sound law enforcement practice. Having Isadora in a vehicle for two hours with either Deb Howell or Jaime Carbajal would give them an opportunity for uninterrupted questions and answers. It turned out, Isadora wasn't having any of it.

"If you have detectives working on Sunday, I want them out looking for Debra's killers, not hauling me from place to place. I'm perfectly capable of driving myself wherever I need to go."

Killers plural, Joanna thought, plucking that one critical word out of Isadora's answer.

"Ms. Creswell," Joanna said, "it sounds as though you have some idea of who's behind this."

"Call me Isadora, but you're right, I do know!" the woman declared forcefully. "I most certainly do, but let's not discuss any of this on the telephone. They might be listening."

"They who?" Joanna pressed.

"Why, the CIA of course, who do you think?" Isadora demanded. "Although it could also be whoever's on the other side. They never made it clear exactly who that was. As I said earlier, I refuse to discuss this any further on the telephone."

She made that one stick by simply disconnecting the call.

Joanna was crawling out of bed, aware that she'd had far too little sleep, when Butch appeared in the bedroom doorway with a very welcome mug of coffee.

"I heard your phone," he said. "I figured with the amount of sleep you'd had, you could use some coffee."

She took it gratefully. "Thank you."

"Who was that on the phone?"

"Debra Highsmith's grandmother," Joanna answered. "I managed to track her down late last night. She's flying in from Pennsylvania today. She'll come to the office to meet with us first thing tomorrow morning." She paused and glanced at the clock.

"I have a task force meeting at eight," she told Butch. "Since I'm the one who called the meeting, I'd better be there."

"Breakfast to go then?" Butch asked. "I can do you a homemade McButch BELT."

When it came to breakfasts to go, Butch's special concoction—bacon, egg, and tomato sandwiched between two slices of lettuce and two slices of whole wheat buttered toast—was Joanna's all-time favorite.

"Sounds good." She brushed his cheek with a kiss on her way to the bathroom. "There are real advantages to marrying a short-order cook."

Joanna stood for a time in the hot shower, letting the water pound some of the weariness out of her body and thinking about her conversation with Isadora Creswell.

The CIA? she wondered. *Why would someone from the CIA target a harmless high school principal in Bisbee, Arizona?*

That made no sense—none at all. Did that mean Isadora was a paranoid nutcase and completely delusional? Possibly, although during the rest of the conversation, given the kind of bad news she'd just gotten, the woman had seemed to have her wits about her and a good grasp on reality. Joanna had no intention of bringing any outside agencies—most especially the CIA—into her investigation until she had to, and that wouldn't happen until she had a better idea of Isadora's state of mind.

Meanwhile, there was something else about the conversation with Debra Highsmith's grandmother that Joanna found disturbing. Debra had left home, presumably in Pennsylvania or somewhere else back east, a good twenty-seven years earlier. Joanna's brief scan through the train case of letters had shown no indication of a visit—of Isadora coming to visit Debra in Albuquerque or Tucson or Bisbee or of Debra going home for a holiday visit, either. So why, now that her beloved granddaughter was dead, was Isadora suddenly ready to hop the first available plane and come to Bisbee? Why now? Why come to oversee funeral arrangements instead of coming to visit a living, breathing, and apparently well-loved granddaughter? Why honor the dead more than the living?

That makes no sense, either, Joanna told herself as she stepped out of the shower and began to towel herself dry.

By the time Joanna was dressed and ready to leave, the rest of the family was gathered in the kitchen. Jenny was at the table, poring over her driver's training manual. Denny was on the floor, attempting to teach

Lucky to hold a Cheerio on his nose. It wasn't working. Butch was loading the dishwasher.

"Here you go," Butch said, handing her a lunch bag with the still-warm breakfast sandwich sitting at the bottom.

"What's on the agenda for you guys?" Joanna asked.

"Dad is taking me out for a driving lesson this morning."

"Yes," Butch agreed, beaming just a little. "If I had hair, I could count on it turning white by the end of the day. I'm sure my knuckles will be, too."

His natural hairline was sparse enough that he had worn his head shaved for as long as Joanna had known him, but she was eternally grateful that he was the one giving Jenny her manual-transmission driving lesson.

"Carol's going to come over and look after Dennis while Jenny and I go out for our ride. What about you?"

Joanna glanced at her watch. "Murder and mayhem starting in about ten minutes. I'd better go."

"Yes," Butch said, "but remember. I don't care how many people croak out in Cochise County today. When it's six thirty P.M. and time for us to make our appearance at the Plein Air gala, I expect you to be at the Rob Roy Links, properly dressed and in my Outback rather than arriving in uniform in your Yukon. Got it? This is a social occasion, and we're going to treat it as such."

Joanna looked at him and laughed. "You're just worried about what my mother will do if I turn up late."

"Or don't turn up at all," Butch said, "which you and I both know has happened before. I don't want tonight to be one of those times when I'm left holding the bag while Eleanor Lathrop Winfield goes on the warpath."

Joanna held up the lunch bag. "I won't stand you up," she said. "Why would I? Aren't you the same guy who just made me this sandwich?"

"That's me," Butch said with a grin. "Now get going, or you'll be late."

Chapter 13

That Saturday morning, Joanna left the regular morning shift-change briefing to Tom Hadlock while she huddled in her office with the investigators and CSIs working the Debra Highsmith homicide. Dave Hollicker and Casey Ledford had finished up their crime scene investigation of the victim's San Jose Estates home about the same time Joanna had gone back to bed. They were at the meeting on time, but they were also swilling coffee and looking every bit as bedraggled as their boss.

Usually in those kinds of briefings, Joanna functioned more as an observer and moderator than as an active participant. This time, however, she was the one with news to impart, including the identity of the homicide victim's grandmother as well as the unanticipated existence of Debra Highsmith's biological son.

The meeting started with the assembled officers settling in to watch the Sue Ellen Hirales interview. When that ended, Joanna went on to tell them about tracking down Isadora Creswell and asking to have officers from the Altoona Police Department do the actual next-of-kin notification.

Jaime raised his hand. "Does the M.E. know about the next of kin? Machett is real touchy about who knows what when."

"I'll call him when the meeting is over," Joanna said. "He fancies himself a Monday-to-Friday kind of guy. He won't be happy being called at what he probably thinks of as the crack of dawn on Saturday."

She then recounted a brief summary of her early-morning conversation with Isadora Creswell.

"She really said that?" Deb Howell asked when Joanna ended her presentation. "That she thought the CIA was responsible for Debra's death?"

"Yes," Joanna said. "She also said that she thought whoever killed Debra might have people eavesdropping on her phone calls. My assumption would be that's why she's coming to Bisbee to talk to us in person. She's afraid her phones are bugged."

"Sounds like paranoia on the hoof," Jaime Carbajal observed, and everyone else nodded in agreement.

"What about the situation with the son? Is it possible that the father finally got wind that he was a father and came here demanding some kind of parental rights?"

"It's a little late for that," Joanna said. "According to Sue Ellen Hirales, the kid is twenty-six years old now and a first-year law student at the University of New Mexico. That makes him an adult. If the biological father wanted to have a relationship with his son, he could do so without having to ask for permission, and certainly without knocking someone off."

"Still, it sounds like there was bad blood there," Deb said. "Why else would Sue Ellen have dragged the guy out of the bar and beaten the crap out of him? Logical or not, we need to check this out and see if we can identify the guy. Even date rapes get reported."

"Good luck with that," Joanna replied. "Date rapes still don't get the kind of reporting they deserve, and all this happened more than two decades ago. Times have changed, but I'm guessing that back then a senior at Good Shepherd Academy wouldn't have been caught dead telling the cops she had been having sex, especially consensual sex. Dealing with the cops would have been one thing. Dealing with the nuns would have been a nightmare."

As they talked, the train case—brought over from the evidence room for the meeting—had been making the rounds, with the investigators plucking out one or another of Isadora's notes and briefly scanning through them.

"Hey," Jaime said. "I've got an idea. If the grandmother thinks the CIA was after Debra, maybe this is all written in code. When she's writing about the garden club or the Friends of the Library, maybe she's talking about something else."

Deb looked at him and shook her head disparagingly. "You thought Isadora Creswell was paranoia on the hoof? What about you?"

"Leave the letters with me," Joanna said. "There's no sense in taking the time to read through them since we'll be able to talk to Isadora in person tomorrow. In the meantime, what's happening with Debra Highsmith's dog?"

"I checked with Dr. Ross just before you got here," Deb said. "She says Giles is going to be fine."

"What kind of name is that for a dog?" Dave Hollicker said.

"It's what he answers to, which is surprising considering how long Debra had him," Deb replied. "Dr. Ross says she'll be ready to release him later today, but she'd rather not send him to the pound while he's still recovering from all the porcupine damage. She's worried about him picking up an infection or maybe passing one along to the other dogs. Since the puncture wound is infected, he's on antibiotics. She's taken a blood draw for the tox screen, but after this much time has passed, it's not likely that anything will show up on that."

"What puncture wound?" Dave asked.

That's the reason we all need to be in the same room, Joanna thought. *So we all have the same pieces of the puzzle.*

"From a bear-tranquilizing dart," Joanna answered. "Dr. Ross thinks that's what knocked the dog out."

"Who would have access to something like that?" Dave wanted to know. "And why use it?"

"Depending on how it's deployed, it could be lots quieter," Jaime said. "Some of them are fired out of pistols or shotguns, but I've also seen blowguns that can bring down small game. If the guy had a dog in his face, taking him down with a dart could be a lot less obvious than using a gun in a residential neighborhood. What I think is most interesting here—and more than a little odd—is that whoever killed Debra Highsmith went to considerable effort to neutralize her dog without killing him."

"What color is the dog?" Dave asked.

"Mostly black," Deb answered at once. "It's a Doberman. Why?"

"What about the victim's hair color?"

"Brown," Jaime answered. "With some lighter streaks."

"Women call those streaks highlights," Deb said. "We pay good money for them."

"Okay," Dave said, ignoring the hair-color byplay. "I collected several hairs that were caught on the metal frame of the doggie door at Debra Highsmith's house. Under the microscope, it's easy to see that the black ones belong to the dog. Then there's a slightly longer light brown or even auburn one that's definitely human."

"So maybe that's how the perpetrator gained access to the house—through the doggie door?"

"Maybe," Dave agreed. "With any luck the guys in the crime lab will be able to develop a DNA profile. The truth is, it could also belong to the victim."

"Why would Debra Highsmith be crawling through her own doggie door?" Deb wanted to know.

Dave shrugged. "Maybe she forgot her keys and had to let herself in that way. Not that it's ever happened to me," he added with a sheepish grin.

"By all means, get that sample to the crime lab," Joanna said, stepping into the discussion. "In the meantime, what about the victim's phone records?"

"Got 'em right here," Deb said, tapping her finger on a stack of faxes sitting in front of her that she had been shuffling through during the meeting. "They came in overnight from Debra Highsmith's cell phone provider. Turns out she didn't have a landline at home, which probably explains why she didn't have an alarm system. Besides, it's tough to find security alarms that can differentiate between the family dog and an intruder.

"While we've been sitting here, I've been scanning the phone records. If what Sue Ellen Hirales told you about being close friends with Debra Highsmith is true, why aren't I seeing a single phone call from Debra's phone to New Mexico or from New Mexico back to her? I'm not seeing any calls to Altoona, Pennsylvania, either. So she saves all her grandmother's letters, for years and years, but she doesn't pick up the phone and call her? Not ever? At least not in the last year's worth of phone records."

"What about e-mail records?"

"I'm looking into those. The school district isn't eager to let us into their computer system, but so far I don't have any kind of personal e-mail account for Debra Highsmith, only the one at work."

"Did you ask Abby Holder about that?"

Deb nodded. "I asked her that specifically. She said that as far as she knew, Debra Highsmith didn't have an e-mail address other than the one at school. So we're going to need to get access to that."

"I'll tackle Farraday," Joanna said. "I'll try to get him to cooperate. If he won't, then we'll have no choice but to get the warrant."

Next Joanna turned to Casey Ledford. "Okay. Where do we stand on fingerprints?"

"Nowhere," Casey said. "I took elimination prints from the people who work at the school who would most likely have been in and out of Ms. Highsmith's office. Thanks to Dr. Machett, I have the victim's prints as well. So far I can't find any prints that shouldn't be there—not in her house, her office, or her vehicle. That tells me the guy was wearing gloves the whole time. If he went to the trouble of obtaining bear tranquilizer, this shows a whole lot of premeditation. The killer is organized. He planned this well in advance."

"I'd have to agree with that," Dave said. "We're seeing premeditation, but also plenty of rage. The guy was careful about going through the house, but demolished everything in sight once he got to the victim's office. What changed? Presumably he went to the house first. Then he killed the victim. I believe it was only after she was dead that he went to her office, because he wouldn't have had the office keys before that."

"Maybe he couldn't find what he was looking for and that made him mad as hell," Matt Keller suggested. All through the meeting, the Bisbee investigator had been sitting there, taking it all in, but not saying a word. "So far, the only things we know for sure that are missing are those calendars and the two computers."

"We also still don't know where the perp went after he left High Lonesome Road," Joanna said. "I understand from Terry that he and Spike lost the trail up by Grace's Corner. Terry's theory is that someone picked the guy up from there and took him to his vehicle, which would have to have been parked in an unobtrusive place."

"If you don't know the make or model of the vehicle you're looking for, any parking place is unobtrusive," Jaime said. "What do we do now?"

"I'd like everybody to spend the morning out in San Jose Estates. The neighborhood canvass that was done is just like the earlier crime scene investigation that was conducted at Debra Highsmith's house. When the City of Bisbee officers were questioning the neighbors, they were asking about a possible missing person. A homicide is a lot more serious. Talk to everybody. Maybe someone was missed, or maybe one of them will have remembered something important that he forgot to mention the first time around."

Joanna looked around the room as her investigators nodded in agreement. "What about the Pembrokes?" she asked. "Do they have alibis?"

"Unfortunately, Dr. Pembroke's is rock solid," Matt Keller said. "The M.E. puts the time of death between one and three A.M. From midnight to four, Dr. Pembroke was in the ER dealing with multiple injuries from that DUI down by Naco."

Joanna vaguely remembered seeing something about that incident during her middle-of-the-night scan of the previous day's paperwork. The accident victim's bad luck turned out to be good luck for Dr. Pembroke.

"What about his son?"

"Marty Pembroke is a snarky kind of kid, but I don't see him as a killer," Matt replied. "Posting something derogatory online is a lot more his style than hauling out a gun and shooting someone."

"If he has a verifiable alibi, why won't he talk to us?" Deb asked. "Why lawyer up instead of coming straight out and telling us where he was and what he was doing?"

"What about the other kids?" Joanna asked. "They all seem to be wired into this social networking business. If Marty won't talk to us, maybe someone else will, or maybe what we need to know is posted online."

"I tried questioning a couple of the kids and got nowhere," Matt said. "You're right. What we need may be online, but getting inside those groups isn't as easy as you'd think."

"Maybe we should talk to Marliss Shackleford," Joanna suggested.

Every person in the room, including Matt Keller, looked at her in utter amazement.

"She must have some kind of access," Joanna continued. "She knew about Jenny's photo being on the Internet before I knew about it because she was the one who told me. Let's ask her."

"Wait," Jaime said. "You're saying you want one of us to go out of our way to speak to that woman?"

Matt Keller came to Joanna's defense. "Sheriff Brady could be right," he said. "One of the guys in the department, a friend of mine, was getting a divorce. Somehow or other Marliss Shackleford knew about it before he and his wife had even signed any paperwork. He jumped all over Marliss and asked her where she was getting her information. She claimed it was from his daughter's Facebook posting."

Joanna regarded Marliss as her own personal cross to bear. "I'll handle talking to Marliss," she said.

"She's likely to hide behind the 'confidential sources' bit," Deb said. "I doubt she'll tell you anything."

What Deb didn't understand was that Joanna had a secret weapon in that regard—her mother. Eleanor and Marliss had always maintained a special kind of bond. Through the years and more than once Marliss had used that personal relationship to wage a PR war against Joanna. For the first time ever, Joanna was prepared to return the favor.

Joanna's phone rang. It was Lisa Howard, the weekend desk clerk from out in the public lobby. "Sorry to interrupt," the clerk said. "Someone named Sue Ellen Hirales just showed up here at the window. She claims she's a friend of Debra Highsmith and she wants to speak to you before she heads back to New Mexico."

"You were absolutely right to interrupt," Joanna said. "Send her in. You don't need to bring her back. Tell her to come to my office rather than to the interview room."

When Sue Ellen appeared in the room, she was wearing the same clothing she'd worn the last time Joanna had seen her. Although she may have taken a room at the hotel, Joanna doubted she'd slept much. The poor woman looked exhausted.

Joanna introduced her all around and then invited her to have a seat at the table.

"We haven't had a chance to access Ms. Highsmith's e-mail accounts, but we were wondering, did you correspond with her over the Internet?"

"The Internet?" Sue Ellen asked, shaking her head. "No. Never. We sent letters back and forth, but no e-mail."

"Do you have an e-mail address?"

"Of course," Sue Ellen said. "I have one. Debra just didn't use it, that's all."

"What about phone calls?"

"None of those, either."

"Doesn't that seem odd to you?"

"It's just the way she was," Sue Ellen said with a shrug. "For as long as I knew Debra, she was shy around phones. When e-mail came along, she preferred using the U.S. Postal Service to stay in touch. She told me once that just because the world had changed didn't mean she had to."

"I've told the people here what you mentioned to me last night—that your brother, your adopted brother, Michael, is Debra Highsmith's biological son. Is there a chance that his biological father might be behind what happened to her?"

"That worthless creep?" Sue Ellen said. "I don't think he even knows he has a son. I know for sure that Debra never would have told him."

"He may have found out some other way," Joanna said. "We need to be able to rule him out as a possible perpetrator."

Sue Ellen considered for some time before she finally answered the question. "His name is Ryan— Kenneth Ryan. I've kept an eye on him through the years because I always worried he might show up and cause trouble for Debra or for my folks."

"Do you know where he is right now?"

"He dropped out of college his sophomore year. He's been married and divorced three times so far. He runs a low-class sports bar in Las Cruces called the Goalpost. Could you do me a huge favor? I understand that you'll probably have to talk to him to find out if he was involved, but if he hasn't already figured out about Mikey, could you try to keep from telling him? Considering what's just happened to the poor kid, I don't want any more piling on, and I'd like to spare my parents some additional grief over this. If someday Mikey asks me about his father, I'll be the one to tell him, but not right now. Not until he's ready."

Joanna glanced around the room. "Can we do that, people?"

There were nods all around.

"No promises, then," Joanna said, "but we'll do our best. If we can discreetly rule Ryan out of the homicide, then contacting him directly might not be necessary. You need to know, however, that I have been in touch with Debra's grandmother."

Sue Ellen's eyes widened. "You found Isadora?"

"She's flying into Tucson tonight. She'll be here in the morning. Do you know if she's aware that Debra had a child?"

"I doubt it."

"Someone will have to let her know," Joanna said. "Do you want to do it, or should I?"

"I suppose I should do that, too," Sue Ellen said. "She's coming here?"

Joanna nodded. "To make funeral arrangements."

"We were planning to do that, too," Sue Ellen said.

"You'll have to sort that out among you," Joanna said.

"Now that I think about it," Sue Ellen said, "maybe it would be better if you told her about Michael. That way she'll have some advance notice."

"All right," Joanna said, looking at her watch. "This is the kind of news that's probably best given in person rather than over the phone, but right now she's already in transit."

"Okay." Sue Ellen rose to her feet. "Now, if you don't need anything more from me, I'll head home. I want to be there before Mikey arrives."

Sue Ellen hustled out the door. Joanna turned back to her investigators. "There you have it," she said. "Sue Ellen is Debra's best friend in the world. Her parents are the people who raised her son, yet she makes no phone calls to them and sends no e-mails even though e-mail is readily available. What do you think?"

"If Debra Highsmith didn't use e-mail for correspondence, that means she made a serious effort to maintain a low profile on the Net," Deb said. "No wonder she was so provoked when Marty Pembroke posted the 'Die, Bitch' video that ended up going viral."

"Wait," Joanna said. "When was that exactly?"

"Two weeks ago. The same night the school board ruled in Marty's favor. Why?"

"Do we have a date for when Debra Highsmith applied for her concealed weapons permit?"

"The permit is dated eight days after the school board meeting. There's no waiting period in Arizona for concealed carry permits, but that's still lightning-fast service. How did she make that happen?"

"I understand the Bisbee Police Department helped her obtain it," Matt Keller put in. "Debra Highsmith wasn't officially part of city government, but she was a prominent person in town."

Joanna nodded. "What about the dog? When did Giles turn up on the scene?" she asked. "Call Dr. Ross and find out when Debra Highsmith brought Giles in for his first visit."

Deb picked up her phone and called the vet's office. She asked a single question, waited for an answer, and then put the phone down. "The receptionist says Giles's first visit was on April sixth."

"In other words, right about the same time," Joanna mused. "Okay, guys, let's hit the bricks. It's looking more and more like the situation with the Pembrokes may have triggered Debra Highsmith's taking defensive measures. The question is, was she scared of them or was she scared of someone else?

"By this afternoon, I want to know everything there is to know about the Pembroke family—where they came from, how long they've been in town, if Marty had any run-ins with the law prior to their moving here. They don't have any concealed weapons permits, do they?"

"Nope," Jaime said. "I already checked."

For the next few minutes, the detectives discussed who would handle what. As they filed out of Joanna's office, she picked up her phone. The call to Guy Machett went straight to voice mail. She left a message letting him know that the next-of-kin notification had been accomplished and gave him the details she had about Isadora Creswell and Mike Hirales. Her next call was to William Farraday. That one also went to voice mail. Joanna had no intention of opening a discussion about having access to the school's e-mail accounts in a voice mail message. Finally she dialed her mother's number.

"Hey, Mom," she said brightly. "I was wondering if you'd mind if I stopped by for a cup of coffee."

Eleanor was immediately on the defensive. "Joanna Lee," she began. Her use of Joanna's full name usually indicated the beginning of a tirade. "Don't you dare think you can just drop by to deliver some cockamamie excuse for backing out of going to the gala tonight—"

"No," Joanna said quickly. "It's nothing like that. I told you yesterday that Butch and I are coming to the gala, and we are. Right now, though, I'm looking for a little information on a case."

There was a small hesitation before Eleanor spoke again. "The Highsmith homicide, maybe?" she asked.

"Yes," Joanna answered. "That's the one."

She tried to make sure that her reply sounded like a grudging admission on her part. She did that deliberately in the hope that her seeming reluctance would set the hook. There was nothing Eleanor Lathrop Winfield liked more than being in the know. In this case, it worked like a charm.

"If you're coming right now," Eleanor said, "I'll go straight to the kitchen and start a new pot. That way it'll be ready by the time you get here."

"Thanks, Mom," Joanna said. "Looking forward to it."

She called out to the lobby. "I'm leaving," she told Lisa Howard.

"Will you be back?"

As sheriff, she didn't qualify for overtime no matter how many hours she put in. Joanna knew that if she didn't grab a nap sometime during the day, she'd be a mess when it came time to show up for her command performance at the gala.

"That depends," she said. "I was here late last night. I'm going out to chase down a lead in the Highsmith case. If it doesn't pan out, I may call it a day."

Chapter 14

For as long as Joanna had been on the planet, her mother had lived in the house on Campbell Avenue, in a blue-collar part of Bisbee's Warren neighborhood. Initially Eleanor had lived there with Joanna's father, D. H. Lathrop. For a number of years after his death, she had lived there with her daughter, followed by an even longer period of living there alone. Now the long, narrow house, built on a long, narrow lot, belonged to Eleanor and George Winfield together.

After Joanna's father's death, Eleanor had allowed the place to turn into a time capsule. Nothing changed. The furniture remained the same. It was quality stuff and well cared for, but over the years it had gradually gone out of fashion. The humdrum fifties-era kitchen remained a fifties-era kitchen. For years Eleanor had made do, working around the one burner on the electric stove that no longer functioned. There was no dishwasher. Had there been one, the house's aging wiring and glitchy plumbing probably would have caused problems.

All that had changed once George and Eleanor tied the knot. Upon first moving in, he had installed a replacement burner in the kitchen stove, then he had dusted off D. H. Lathrop's long unused patio grill and put it to good use. George knew his way around tools, and he made remaking his wife's house the focus of his retirement. Working mostly by himself, he had updated the kitchen with new cabinets, plumbing, wiring, and state-of-the-art appliances. He had redone both bathrooms, and managed to talk Eleanor into furnishings that were far more modern and far more comfortable that the ones she'd had originally. His most recent efforts included a brand-new roof and a new coat of exterior paint on both the house and the fence.

That morning, walking up to the house and seeing how the flaking old paint had been scraped away and replaced, Joanna found herself marveling at George Winfield's energy and industry, to say nothing of his patience. She wasn't sure how he had managed to persuade Eleanor to make all the necessary decisions surrounding those changes, but he had. In the process, George Winfield had put his own particular stamp on the place. It was now his house every bit as much as it was Eleanor's.

When Joanna rang the bell, Eleanor came to the door with a telephone in her hand. She let Joanna into the house and used hand motions to indicate that there was coffee in the kitchen and that Joanna should go get some. Joanna poured herself a mug and then returned to the living room where her mother was still on the phone.

"You can't take it so personally, Maggie," Eleanor was saying. "You probably need to make the admission requirements stiffer. When you advertise it as a 'master' class, people need to understand that a certain level of expertise is expected. It's not fair to Mr. Coleman or to the other participants to have rank beginners involved in the classes and wasting everyone's time.

"The problem with rank beginners, of course, is that they have no idea how bad they are," Eleanor added. "As that old proverb says, 'They who know not, know not they know not.' Delusions of adequacy and all that. Having a panel of judges vet the work of all the applicants before they're admitted may seem cumbersome, but it would prevent this kind of thing from happening in the future."

There was a drawn-out pause on Eleanor's end as Maggie Oliphant spoke at some length. While she listened, Eleanor mimed that Joanna should bring her a cup of coffee, too. Following directions, Joanna returned to the kitchen, poured a second cup, and doctored it with her mother's dollop of cream and two spoonfuls of sugar.

"No," Eleanor was saying when she returned. "You don't need to worry about any of that. It's handled. I've been in touch with Myron Thomas out at Rob Roy Links several times so far today. There will be plenty of food. If more people than expected show up, he'll have a table in reserve that can be brought out and set up in a blink. Myron's a professional. He won't let us down. As for the floral centerpieces, they should be delivered sometime in the next hour or so."

Joanna waited through another long pause.

"That's probably a good idea," Eleanor said eventually. "Take one of those pills and then lie down and treat yourself to a nap, but only if you're sure the antidepressant won't knock you on your butt. I know this week has been tough on you, Maggie, but we need you on your feet tonight, keeping things together. If you fall apart, the gala falls apart. With all the big spenders coming down from Tucson and Phoenix, we can't afford that kind of bad publicity. We need you, Maggie. Bisbee needs you. Okay. See you tonight."

Eleanor put down the phone, covered her eyes with her hands, and shook her head. "Maggie Oliphant," she explained unnecessarily. "The poor girl is losing it. She's under tremendous pressure to make things work. Unfortunately, this Plein Air group has been a hassle. One of the so-called artists is so bad, he's only one step beyond second-grade finger painting. He acts like it's okay to skip classes completely or else he shows up late. If we're going to make this idea work long term, we're going to have to develop a more sophisticated admissions policy."

Joanna tried to feign interest, but the current difficulties of the Bisbee Art League weren't any of her concern. Debra Highsmith's homicide was.

Eventually Eleanor must have come to the same conclusion. "Sorry," she said. "I didn't mean to go on so. What was it you said you wanted?"

"It's about Marliss and Jenny," Joanna said. "I suppose you've heard about the photo Jenny took yesterday morning."

Eleanor nodded. "Then sent it out to all and sundry. I'm afraid I did hear about that. I should have thought you'd have taught her better than to pull a dumb stunt like that."

"I should have thought so, too," Joanna agreed.

Her mother's instant assumption that it was all Joanna's fault was par for the course. "It turns out she didn't have better sense, but she didn't send it to 'all and sundry.' She sent it to one person only—to her friend Cassie."

Joanna didn't let on that there was a good possibility that Cassie Parks was now Jenny's former friend. She didn't want to give Eleanor that kind of ammunition.

"Cassie is the one who sent it along to someone else, and before you can say chop-chop, Marliss Shackleford shows up at my crime scene already knowing Debra Highsmith is the victim even though we've made no announcement to that effect. As she was leaving, she made some veiled comment about Jenny that didn't make sense to me until later, when I found out about the photo. What I can't figure out is how Marliss knew about the photo. I understand that the kids are all involved in every social networking site you've ever heard of, and some you haven't, but where does Marliss Shackleford come in? What's her connection?"

Joanna stopped then. Maintaining a poker face was a useful skill her mother had never quite mastered. The small twitch near Eleanor's mouth said Joanna was onto something.

"Jenny's not in any trouble, is she?" Eleanor asked.

"She's in trouble with me," Joanna declared. "It could have been a lot worse. Fortunately, we were able to contact Ms. Highsmith's next of kin before any of them saw the offending photo on the Web, but I still want to know how Marliss knew about that photograph before I did."

Eleanor sighed. "If I tell you," she objected, "I'll be betraying a friend's confidence."

"How did she know?" Joanna pressed.

"She's a reporter," Eleanor hedged. "Reporters have to know things."

"How did she find out?"

Eleanor sighed again. "Her granddaughter," she said.

"Which granddaughter?" Joanna asked. "The one who's going to school in Flagstaff?"

Eleanor nodded.

"How would she know about any of this?" Joanna asked. "She doesn't even live here."

"She was here last summer," Eleanor explained, "and was hanging around with some of the kids from the high school. She . . . let me see, what's it called again? Oh, yes, that's right— she friended some of the kids in Marliss's neighborhood. When the granddaughter went off to Flag, she let Marliss take over her account, the one she used for her summer friends here in Bisbee."

"So she's been going to the various sites all this time, pretending to be her granddaughter?"

"I believe that's what she's been doing," Eleanor agreed. "Marliss says she gets all kinds of insider information that way, especially from the cheerleaders' page. She says paying attention to what the kids are saying to each other gives her a head start on what's really going on here in town. It's not against the law."

Joanna happened to know that in Arizona impersonating someone on the Internet with the intent to harm, even with the other person's permission, could be grounds for being charged with a class four felony. Whether something like that would hold up in court was another issue. Not wanting to push Eleanor into defending her friend, Joanna mentioned none of that.

"It strikes me as unethical," Joanna said. "I wouldn't have expected Marliss to stoop to that kind of behavior. I would have thought she'd have higher standards."

Eleanor looked alarmed. "You're not going to go see Marliss, are you?"

"Yes," Joanna said, carefully setting her cup down on the coffee table. "I believe I am."

"If you tell her I told you—"

"Don't worry, Mom. I won't rat you out. As far as Marliss is concerned, she'll think I figured it out all by myself."

Marliss Shackleford and Dick Voland lived on a steep street in Old Bisbee. Once Joanna left her mother's place, she headed straight there. Driving up Tombstone

Canyon, however, she spotted Marliss's Toyota RAV4 parked on Main Street, just down from the offices of the *Bisbee Bee*. It may have been Saturday, but Marliss was evidently hard at work.

Joanna got out and hiked up the narrow stretch of Main Street with its wall of brick-fronted buildings on either side. Storefronts that used to house clothing or furniture or jewelry or hardware stores had morphed into art galleries or antiques shops. The *Bisbee Bee* still had offices in its original location, but the hulking press that used to rumble away in the back had been removed. The paper's layout and printing functions were now handled in a newer facility in Sierra Vista, while circulation, advertising sales, and reporting were still done out of the old office in Bisbee.

The door was unlocked, but when Joanna let herself in, there was no one at the reception desk. Instead, she found Marliss alone in the back of the office and hunched over a computer on an old-fashioned wooden desk where the printing press had once stood. She looked up in surprise when she saw Joanna walking toward her.

"What are you doing here?"

"Not 'How are you?' or 'How can I help you?'" Joanna asked. "Is that any way to treat someone who's come to call?"

Had they been in a public venue, Joanna had no doubt that Marliss would have exuded charm. In private, however, she didn't bother.

"What do you want?"

Without waiting for an invitation, Joanna took a seat on the chair next to Marliss's desk. "You knew the identity of our victim before there was any public announcement," Joanna said. "I want to know how you gained access to Jenny's photo."

"So you admit it was Jenny's photo? You gave her open access to the crime scene?"

"Jenny found the crime scene," Joanna corrected. "Yes, taking the photo and sending it to someone didn't show very good judgment on her part, but she's a teenager, after all. Occasionally teenagers do stupid things. So do grown-ups."

"What's that supposed to mean?"

"Masquerading on the Internet as somebody else isn't smart, either," Joanna said. "I'd guess that some of the kids you've been fooling by pretending to be your granddaughter would be upset if they found out who their trusted correspondent really is."

"Who told you that?" Marliss demanded. "Your mother?"

"I may not be an official detective," Joanna said, "but I'm smart enough to put two and two together. When you came out to the crime scene yesterday morning, you knew more than you should have. Then when you were leaving, you asked about Jenny. That seemed out of character. So later in the day, when I found out about the photo, it wasn't difficult to make the connection."

"I haven't broken any laws," Marliss said. "It's not like I'm a child predator or something."

"A court of law might have a different take on that," Joanna said. "But since you're married to a former cop, you probably already know all about that, and you've decided it's worth running the risk."

Marliss said nothing.

Joanna had come here for the express purpose of lighting into Marliss and setting her straight. Now, however, it dawned on Joanna that having access to what the town's teenagers were up to through Marliss's involvement in their social networks might prove beneficial to both Joanna and her department in the long run. Rather than threatening Marliss Shackleford with arrest, Joanna decided to back off and attempt to enlist the woman's help.

"As far as the kids at school are concerned," Joanna said, "my investigators are running into a brick wall. The kids know stuff, but they won't talk to us. With your unique access to that particular community, you might be able to help us."

"I'm a journalist," Marliss objected. "I'm supposed to report what's going on. I'm not supposed to be involved in it."

Joanna shrugged off her concern. "Journalists have confidential sources," she said. "Cops have confidential informants. That's what I'm asking you to do—to use your granddaughter's identity to function as a CI and give me some access to a few of those kids' private lives. I'd consider it a huge personal favor. I'd owe you one, and you might even help keep one of those kids from being wrongly accused of murder."

Joanna knew that Marliss was into power trips in a big way. The idea of being one up on Eleanor's daughter would be tempting. Being able to consider herself the hero of the piece would be more than she could resist.

"What do you want me to do?" Marliss asked guardedly.

"I want you to go online and see if anyone has posted anything about Martin Pembroke's whereabouts the night Debra Highsmith was murdered."

"What if I don't?"

"I might be tempted to let it be known around town what you've been pulling all this time." She had more ammunition than that, but for the time being, she held on to it.

"Isn't that blackmail?"

"It's more like exerting pressure than it is black-mail," Joanna said. "Sort of like what you're doing is investigative journalism rather than identity theft, but you might want to be a little more careful. When you let the cat out of the bag about someone's upcoming divorce, you were leaking private information a trou-bled young woman was confiding to what she thought were a few close friends. She didn't expect that one of those supposed friends would broadcast news about her parents' upcoming divorce to the whole world. Come to think of it," Joanna concluded, "that shows almost as bad judgment as Jenny did in passing along the crime scene photo."

For several moments, Marliss stared at her computer screen without replying. Joanna knew from the look on her face that she had landed a telling blow.

"All right," Marliss said finally. "What do you want to know?"

"Because of his Web postings about Debra High-smith, Martin Pembroke is high on our list of suspects. He may have an alibi for that night, but when we asked about it, he lawyered up instead of just coming out and telling us. If he's got a verifiable alibi, he's off the list."

Marliss didn't have to go online to give Joanna her answer. "Dena Carothers," she said.

"One of the cheerleaders?" Joanna asked.

Marliss nodded. "According to what Dena posted, she and Marty were going at it hot and heavy down at the Rifle Range until the wee hours."

"In the middle of the night on a school night?"

Marliss nodded again.

"What do you mean, hot and heavy?" Joanna asked.

"What do you think I mean?" Marliss returned.

"Dena's only a junior," Joanna objected. "That means she's underage. They both are."

"Well, duh!" Marliss said. "Why do you think he didn't want to tell you?"

Now that Joanna had the information, it was something she really didn't want to know. Certainly, she had no room to talk, other than to pass along the old saw "Do as I say, not as I do." She herself had gotten pregnant at seventeen and had married at eighteen. When Eleanor learned about the pregnancy, she could easily have had Andy charged with statutory rape. Instead she had given Andy the choice of doing the right thing—or else. Once he did so, Eleanor had taken charge of putting together a hurry-up shotgun-style wedding.

Now Marty Pembroke was faced with a similarly complex choice. If he and Dena had been together doing whatever at the Rifle Range, then he might have an alibi that would remove him as a suspect in the Debra Highsmith homicide. If that information somehow got leaked to Dena's parents, he ran the risk of being charged with statutory rape and spending the rest of his life labeled as a sex offender. Joanna wondered if Dr. Pembroke knew about that. It could explain why he had opted for an attorney.

"What are you going to do now?" Marliss asked, breaking into Joanna's reverie.

"I'm not sure," Joanna said, "but thank you. I appreciate the help."

As she walked out of the *Bee's* office, she should have felt proud of herself, but she didn't. Yes, Joanna had talked her way around Marliss Shackleford. Yes, she was going away with the information she needed, but if Marliss was in the wrong for having the information, didn't that make Joanna even more wrong for using it?

Her former father-in-law, Jim Bob Brady, was forever talking about "the pot calling the kettle black."

If Marliss was the kettle, that made Joanna the pot. Unfortunately, for someone who liked to think of herself as being on the side of the angels, it felt uncomfortably close to being a hypocrite.

Chapter 15

Joanna was sitting in her Yukon, wondering what she was going to do next, when someone tapped on her passenger window. Her best friend, Reverend Marianne Maculyea, was standing on the sidewalk, grinning at her.

"Hey," she said when Joanna opened the window. "Your eyes were open, but you were a million miles away."

"I was," Joanna conceded. "It's been a tough couple of days."

"You are going to the gala tonight," Marianne said, "aren't you?"

"How'd you know that?"

"A little bird told me. One of our parishioners bought tickets and now can't attend, so she gave her tickets to Jeff and me. I called out to the house, hoping to hire Jenny to come babysit, only to be told that she's already taken."

"Sorry," Joanna said. "Did you find someone else?"

"Yes, Jeff called one of the ladies from church. Is Butch really going to wear a tux?"

Joanna nodded. "My mother would wring his neck if he didn't."

"I told Jeff that since he doesn't own a tux and since the invitation says 'black tie optional,' he should take them at their word and do optional. Is there assigned seating?"

"Not as far as I know," Joanna said.

"Good," Marianne said. "Maybe the four of us can sit together. I know Jeff will be happier being at a table with the two of you than at a table full of strangers."

"We're committed to being at my mother's table," Joanna countered.

Marianne grinned. As Joanna's friend and pastor, she knew where the bodies were buried in Joanna's challenging relationship with her mother.

"I'll check with her, then. Your mother doesn't bother me," Marianne added. "I can handle her a lot better than I can my own mother. Are you working, or do you have time for a cup of coffee?"

"Working," Joanna said. "I'd better pass. See you tonight." Because while Joanna had been talking to

Marianne, she had also reached a conclusion. She drove a short way up the canyon, made a legal U-turn, and then stopped her Yukon directly outside the door of the *Bee*. With her flashers on, she hopped out and poked her head in the front door. Marliss was still alone in the room and still seated at her desk.

"Any idea where I'd find Dena Carothers today?" Joanna asked.

Marliss didn't have to surf through any Web pages to answer the question. "The cheerleading squad is having a car wash to raise money for camp."

"Where?"

"At the new fire station."

The "new fire station" on Highway 92 wasn't really new, but it was a lot newer than any of the other firehouses in town.

"Dena will be there?"

"She's supposed to be."

It was as though the kids from the high school were pawns laid out on a chessboard, while Marliss, working behind the scenes, kept track of them all. For the first time Joanna began to wonder. Jenny's crime scene photo had been posted, but how much of what she and Butch thought of as their private lives was also being bandied about on the Internet? The thought flashed through Joanna's head, but she forced herself to not focus on it.

"What about Marty Pembroke?" Joanna asked. "Will he be there, too?"

"Trust me," Marliss said. "If Dena's there, Marty will turn up eventually."

Let's hope it's later rather than sooner, Joanna thought.

Back in the Yukon, she drove straight to the car wash. Two cars were already parked, waiting their turns. Joanna pulled in behind them, even though the idea of getting the Yukon washed was a hopeless proposition. High Lonesome Road was dirt. By the time she got back to the house, the newly washed car would be covered by a thin film of dust. Besides, if she wanted it washed, the guys at the motor pool would do it for free. Having the car washed by the cheerleaders was a way of being a good citizen while offering her the possibility of having a quiet word with Dena.

Armed with a bucket of soapy water, Dena had drawn hubcap duty. When the girls tackled the Yukon, Joanna positioned herself by the right-rear wheel and waited for Dena to come to her.

"I'm not supposed to talk to you," Dena said.

"On whose orders?" Joanna asked.

Dena didn't answer.

"Let me guess," Joanna said. "The answer to my question is Marty Pembroke."

"So?"

"So, you can talk to me, or I can go to your folks and tell them what you and Marty were doing out at the Rifle Range."

Dena's fair skin was already flushed from working in the sun, but now she blushed a bright crimson.

"We weren't doing anything wrong."

"Oh?" Joanna said. "You need to wise up, Dena. If you don't want your personal life to be public knowledge, you probably shouldn't post all the gory details on the Internet. Marty Pembroke strikes me as a smart-ass, but that isn't the same as being smart. You may be doing nothing 'wrong'"—Joanna said, using her fingertips to signal quotation marks—"but the real question is this: Is he smart enough to use a condom?"

Still blushing, Dena bit her lip. "He doesn't have to. We're fine. I'm on the pill. He got them for me. From his dad. They're like free samples or something."

So either Marty was lifting medications from his father without Dr. Pembroke's knowledge, or Marty was a cad and Dr. Pembroke was his enabler. Despicable? Absolutely! The very thought of it made Joanna furious, but her job right then was to investigate a homicide.

"Talk to me," Joanna warned, "or I go straight to your parents. Did they know you were out of the house?"

"No," Dena admitted. "I snuck out, after they were asleep."

Joanna Brady knew all about sneaking out of the house. As a teenager she had been an expert at doing that very thing.

"So tell me about that night," Joanna ordered. "All of it. I need the truth."

"My parents go to bed after the news—about ten thirty. I waited until eleven. When I was sure they were asleep, I climbed out through my bedroom window. Marty was waiting in his car at the end of the street. We went to the Rifle Range and we . . . well . . . you know," she finished with a shrug.

Joanna knew all about that, too. Dena Carothers and Marty Pembroke weren't the first, second, or even the third generation of Bisbee kids to use the abandoned Rifle Range south of Warren for those kinds of romantic, sexually driven assignations.

"How long were you there?"

"He dropped me off about two, and I climbed back in the window. It was a school night, but I'm lucky. I don't need much sleep."

"What's going on?" a male voice demanded from behind Joanna.

She turned to see that Marty had arrived on the scene. "Why are you talking to her, Dena?" he demanded. "I told you not to talk to anybody, but especially not to her."

"Why is that?" Joanna asked. "Why shouldn't she talk to me?"

Still blushing, Dena picked up her bucket and moved to the next vehicle in line, leaving Joanna and Marty alone.

"Because she's underage and you could go to jail for statutory rape?"

Marty's face twisted into a grimace. "I don't know what she told you . . ." he began.

"Why don't you tell me about Wednesday night?" Joanna suggested.

"I'm not supposed to talk to you without the lawyer."

"Then I suppose I have to go have a talk with Dena's parents."

That was really an idle threat on Joanna's part. These were two nonadults, but they were consenting nonadults. They were also taking precautions. Already struggling with being a hypocrite based on her own history, Joanna knew that turning them in for what they were doing wouldn't be in anyone's best interest. If the story came out, Dena's reputation would be shot, and Marty would end up spending a lifetime labeled as a sex offender. In this case, abiding by the letter of the law would have made things even worse for Sheriff Joanna Brady. Fortunately, Marty Pembroke didn't know that.

"We went to the Rifle Range," he admitted, shame-faced about it rather than bragging. "It wasn't anything serious. We were just messing around."

"Really," Joanna said. "I think the correct terminology would be 'screwing around' rather than 'messing around.' What time did you and Dena meet up?"

"Around eleven."

"What time did you drop her off?"

"Around two, I guess. I got home about two thirty."

"While your father was still at the ER?"

Marty nodded.

"Does your father know about this?" Joanna asked. "About your having sexual relations with Dena?"

Marty didn't answer that question, and Joanna was convinced she knew why.

"What if she gets pregnant?"

"She won't."

"You seem surprisingly confident about that. Why?"

"Because she's on the pill."

"Courtesy of your father?" Joanna asked.

Again, when Marty didn't answer, Joanna was able to sort the answer out for herself.

"I think I understand. Your father's afraid that if you knock up some hick girl from Bisbee, that might stand in the way of your future, sort of like your school suspension from Ms. Highsmith might have lessened your chances of getting the education of your choice. Even if you've been accepted by a school, that decision could be rescinded. Isn't that right?"

Marty Pembroke was a big kid, probably a full foot taller than Joanna's five two, but he seemed to shrink in size under her penetrating green-eyed gaze. He was one of the privileged few, and she doubted anyone had ever spoken to him in quite that tone before. He stared down at his feet for a time and then gave the tiniest nod.

"Your father told you that it would be easier to beat a murder rap than it would be to duck a statutory rape charge, right?"

Another nod.

"Okay, then, Marty, here's the deal." Joanna reached up and clapped him on one of his shoulders. "Dena Carothers has just backed up your alibi. She didn't like telling me that she was out at the Rifle Range or what she was doing out there, but she did. It turns out that you're telling me the same thing. Since you were out there in your car screwing your brains out, you couldn't very well have been ten or eleven miles away out on High Lonesome Road murdering Ms. Highsmith at the same time. That means you're off the hook on the murder charge, got it?"

Marty raised his eyes and looked at her. "Okay," he mumbled.

"It turns out that this is also Dena Carothers's lucky day."

"Why's that?"

"Because you're bad for her," Joanna declared, "and you're going to break up with her."

"You can't make me do that."

"Oh yes I can," Joanna told him. "Watch me. You don't have to do it today, but by the end of the weekend you're going to tell her that she's a great girl, but it's just not a good idea to get too serious when you're about to go away to college in the fall. From that moment on and for as long as you're in Bisbee, you're going to live a celibate lifestyle."

"What does that mean?"

"Celibate means no more screwing around—literally. If you mess with any of the other underage girls here in town, I'll know about it, and I promise you, I'll nail your ass to the ground."

"How do you know all this stuff?"

"Have you ever heard the saying 'What happens in Vegas stays in Vegas'?"

"I guess," he said with a shrug.

"Well, here's some news from the front, buddy boy. It ain't necessarily so. I know you kids think you're the only people surfing the Net, but if you believe that, you're way dumber than your father seems to think you are. I'm giving you one chance to walk away with your future intact. One chance, and that's it. Don't screw it up, literally or figuratively. Understand?"

Marty nodded.

With that, Joanna climbed into her Yukon and headed home. She was convinced that she could exclude Marty Pembroke as being a possible suspect in Debra Highsmith's murder, but one of the things she had said to him continued to resonate in her head—the part about kids not being the only ones surfing the Net.

Debra Highsmith had gone to a great deal of effort to keep away from electronic media. Almost immediately after Marty Pembroke had posted her face on the Internet, she had started taking defensive measures— obtaining the concealed-weapons permit; getting the dog. So something about being posted online had made her wary, but of whom? And why?

Joanna's phone rang. "Kenneth Ryan isn't our guy," Deb Howell said. "The night Debra Highsmith was murdered, he was under house arrest, serving out a DUI sentence complete with an electronic ankle brace- let. He's allowed to be at home or at work and nowhere else. They give him fifteen minutes of grace time to get from one to the other. Turns out that's been the case for the past two months. He's got one more month to go."

"So he's a thrice-divorced drunk," Joanna said.

It occurred to her about then that Debra Highsmith had been wise beyond her years in realizing that Kenny Ryan wasn't father material and in keeping the fact that she was pregnant away from the presumptive father.

She said, "I have a feeling that Mikey Hirales is way better off living with his adoptive parents on the Falling H than he would have been living with a drunk for a father in Las Cruces."

"I think so, too," Deb said, "but what do we do tomorrow when Mikey's biological grandmother shows up? What do we tell her?"

"As Jim Bob Brady is fond of saying, 'Let's cross that bridge when we come to it.' Right now, I'm going home to take a nap. I was up most of the night chasing after Sue Ellen Hirales and Isadora Creswell while the rest of you were sawing logs. Butch and I have a command performance at the Plein Air gala tonight, and I need my beauty sleep. I had a chance to check out Marty Pembroke's alibi. It looks like he's in the clear."

"Too bad," Deb said. "He was really our only lead."

"Did anything come from reinterviewing Debra Highsmith's neighbors?"

"Nada."

"Those are all finished now?"

"Yup."

"Who's on call tonight?"

"Jaime."

"All right, then," Joanna said. "Tell the guys to take the rest of the day off and go home. The budget can't handle running this whole investigation on an overtime basis. We'll take another look at things tomorrow morning when Isadora shows up."

"Sounds good," Deb Howell said, sounding relieved at getting some of her weekend back. "I'll let everyone know."

As Joanna headed for High Lonesome Ranch, she was thinking about her father. She remembered him telling her once that sometimes you had to do the wrong thing for the right reason. She was sure what she had just done with Marty Pembroke was an instance of that. And when it came to Marliss Shackleford? Ditto. Calling her on her Internet snooping was the right thing to do. Making use of that snooping was right or wrong, depending on your point of view.

Joanna was relatively sure that nothing short of a threatened jail sentence would make Marliss cede even so much as an inch of her Internet territory, and that was fine with Joanna. As long as Marty Pembroke was still in town, Joanna Brady intended to take full advantage of

Marliss's ill-gotten info to make sure Marty continued to walk the straight and narrow.

When Joanna parked in the garage and let herself into the house, Lady and Lucky came scrabbling into the laundry room to greet her.

"You're home early," Butch said.

"I'm beat," she told him. "I'm going to take a nap."

"Sounds like a good idea, but what's the smug look I'm seeing on your face?" Butch wanted to know. "What have you been up to?"

"I think I've just figured out that it's possible two wrongs do make a right."

"Tell me."

"Later," she said. "Right now, I need to close my eyes. If I'm not on my feet by five, come wake me. Mother wants me to appear for that dinner all gussied up. The way I'm feeling right now, that's going to take some time and effort."

Chapter 16

When Joanna and Butch arrived at the clubhouse at Rob Roy Links at six thirty on the dot, it was clear that the club's owner, Myron Thomas, had outdone himself. The nominally Scottish-themed lobby had been transformed into an upscale art gallery where open bar cocktails were being served.

Every inch of available wall space was lined with a series of vivid gold-framed paintings, both large and small, all of them with M. L. Coleman's signature in the corner. Many of the oversize pieces featured time-honored views of the Grand Canyon lovingly rendered in oils on canvas. Great care had been taken to adjust the focus of the track lights in the ceiling in a fashion that made each painting glow from within. Some of the pieces were scheduled to be auctioned later that evening, with a piece of the action going to Maggie Oliphant's beloved art league.

Checking out the crowd, Joanna discovered that, with few exceptions, most of the menfolk had shown up, as expected, in tuxes. One notable dress-code exception was the artist himself. M. L. Coleman stood in the midst of his array of paintings in a long-sleeved white dress shirt but still wearing a brown vest and a pair of well-worn jeans. Drink in hand, smiling broadly, and looking totally at ease, he greeted arriving guests and collectors in a fashion that was completely oblivious of the icily disapproving look Eleanor lobbed in his direction on her way past.

Eleanor zeroed in on Butch and Joanna like a heat-seeking missile.

Seeing her mother's approach, Joanna took a deep breath. She had shown up properly attired for the occasion in the green silk number—a floor-length sheath with a slit up the side—and matching three-inch stiletto heels Butch had bought for her on their honeymoon. While she was getting dressed there had been a moment when she thought the dress wouldn't fit and that she'd have to use her back-up-plan little black dress.

The last time she had worn the green gown had also been the last time Butch had worn his tux—when they had gone to New York for the MWA banquet for an award Butch hadn't won. Having had Dennis since then made her wonder, but the dress had slipped smoothly onto her body. Under that layer of shimmering silk, however, there was no room at all for her small-of-the-back holster. Over Butch's exaggerated eye rolling, Joanna had stuffed her Glock into her tiny beaded clutch. With the handgun inside, that left room for only a compact, a badge, and a single tube of lipstick. She tried fitting her cell phone in as well, but that didn't work. She had meant to ask Butch to carry it, but in the rush of leaving the house the phone had been forgotten on the nightstand.

Eleanor stopped directly in front of Joanna and Butch and gave them both an up-and-down appraisal. Finally, she smiled at her daughter, nodding in approval.

"Not bad," Eleanor said. "You look lovely."

Joanna was nothing short of amazed by Eleanor's unconditional compliment. It was unexpected enough to leave her momentarily dumbstruck. Fortunately, Butch came to her rescue.

"That's right," he said. "Not bad for a girl. She must be a chip off the old block," he added. "You're not bad yourself."

"Oh, go on," Eleanor said, flushing with pleasure. "You're such a tease." She stood still for a moment, examining the crowd. "I'm looking for Maggie Oliphant. You haven't seen her by any chance, have you?"

"We just got here," Joanna said. "You're the first person we've talked to."

Eleanor hustled off, intent on her search. "You've almost got her eating out of your hand," Joanna muttered under her breath.

"Yup," Butch said, grinning. "I told you I'd bring her around eventually. We're definitely getting there."

As Butch led Joanna around the lobby, she spent more time paying attention to her feet than to the paintings. No longer accustomed to wearing heels on a daily basis, she clung to Butch's arm to keep from losing her balance. When he stopped abruptly, Joanna came close to flying forward.

"Why, would you look at that!" he declared.

They had left the immense Grand Canyon pieces behind and were now in an area that featured groupings of smaller paintings, scenes of Paris.

"Look at what?" Joanna asked.

"That one—the flower stand. Don't you recognize it?"

The painting was twenty by thirty inches. It featured an outdoor flower stand, with vases of brilliant pink and yellow flowers standing on risers, glimpses of the Parisian skyline showing in the distance.

Joanna moved close enough to see the title: MARCHÉ D'ALIGRE—SUNDAY MORNING FLOWER VENDOR.

"Wait. Isn't that the market that was just down the street from our hotel?"

When Joanna and Butch were planning their wedding and honeymoon, Joanna had been surprised to learn that Paris was his first choice. She had also been amazed to discover that Butch spoke fluent French. When they went there on their honeymoon, they had stayed at the Hotel Plazza Bastille while Butch played tour guide all over the city.

"So you've been there?" a voice behind them asked. They turned and found Michael Coleman standing behind them.

"We honeymooned at the Plazza a few years ago, Mr. Coleman," Butch said. "We walked past this place almost every day."

"Call me Michael, or Mike," the artist said. "The hotel has been completely remodeled since then. It goes by a different name now."

As Butch and the painter struck up a conversation, Marianne Maculyea appeared at Joanna's side. Not completely comfortable in the cocktail party atmosphere, Joanna was glad to see her. Evidently Marianne was of the same mind.

"Your mother said we're good to go, so I slipped into the dining room and reserved four chairs at her table," she said. "I hope you don't mind."

"Are you kidding?" Joanna replied. "Anything that takes my mother's focus off me and onto someone else is all to the good."

Jeff was standing next to Marianne, wearing a suit, tugging at his bow tie, and looking as though he, too, was a little out of his depth. "I've been checking out the price tags on those paintings," he said. "They're all too rich for our blood."

"Ours, too," Joanna said, "but the prime rib should be great."

Across the room, Joanna caught sight of her mother meeting up with Maggie. They stood just inside the front door, huddling over some last-minute detail. That was the problem with any kind of event like this. It took plenty of concerted effort from any number of people to make it work. Joanna still thought it remarkable that Maggie had managed to rope Eleanor into the project.

When Marianne and Jeff moved off to chat with a pair of parishioners, George Winfield took Marianne's place at Joanna's elbow.

"Care for a drink?" he asked. "They're handing out free drinks in hopes of getting people to loosen up their wallets for the auction."

"Not too many drinks, I hope," Joanna said, "but a glass of champagne would be great."

She turned back to check with Butch, but he and the artist had wandered off to another part of the room and were standing in front of a different painting.

"Did you talk to Dena?" Marliss Shackleford asked, materializing from out of nowhere. She already had a glass of champagne in her hand.

Joanna nodded. "Thanks for your help."

"You're not going to tell me what was said?"

"No, I'm not," Joanna answered with a smile. "Maybe Dena will post a report of the conversation on her Facebook page."

When George returned with Joanna's champagne, Marliss found a reason to be elsewhere.

Watching her walk away, George shook his head. "I understand that Eleanor's friendship with Marliss predates my showing up on the scene, but for the life of me, I don't understand what Eleanor sees in that woman," he said.

Taking a sip of her champagne, Joanna nodded. "That makes two of us."

"I see Dr. Machett is here, too, dishing out doses of urbanity to people he can't help but regard as country bumpkins," George observed. "He's not my cup of tea, either."

Joanna laughed aloud at that. "Are you sure you're only my stepfather? I'm beginning to suspect you may have passed along some of your DNA to me."

"Maybe so," he said. "Eleanor's currently out of earshot, so can we talk shop for a minute? How's your latest case going? Debra Highsmith seems to be hot news all over the state."

"We hit a dead end this afternoon," Joanna admitted. "It turns out our two most likely suspects both have solid alibis. Now, at Mom's request, I'm officially off work and showing up here to do my daughterly duty. My detectives and I will be at it again tomorrow. What about you and Mom? When do you leave for Minnesota?"

"By May first at the latest. I had wanted to be on our way earlier, but Ellie got caught up in this whole art-conference deal. I'll be glad when it's over. Maggie Oliphant has been pushing panic buttons for weeks. She's been on the phone day and night, asking Ellie for advice. I suspect that your mother is the only thing that's been holding this can of worms together."

Joanna looked around the room filled with close to two hundred milling guests—local dignitaries, visiting artists and their spouses, as well as visiting art patrons—all of whom had paid good money to be there. For a very small town, this was an enormous undertaking. Joanna was Eleanor's daughter. Most of the time she found it easy to dismiss her mother as a pain in the neck, but now, for the first time, she caught a glimpse of the fact that Eleanor had chosen to be a wife and mother when there were other things she might have done instead.

Even now, Eleanor was on the far side of the room conferring with Myron Thomas about something or other, probably averting some last-minute disaster that might have derailed the festivities. Finished with that, she came looking for George.

"Maggie is having a bad case of nerves," Eleanor explained. "She's asked us to take charge of Mr. and Mrs. Coleman until she gets a grip. They'll be seated at our table. When the waitstaff opens the doors at seven fifteen, she wants us to lead the way into the banquet."

"Nerves?" George asked. "Or too much champagne?"

"A little of both, I think," Eleanor said.

Dutifully, Joanna went off and rounded up Butch, who was now chatting with Jeff Daniels, while Eleanor and George went to collect the artist and his wife, Sheri. They took the lead positions—Eleanor on Michael's arm and Sheri on George's—in the procession.

The banquet room was laid out beautifully. The floral centerpieces were spectacular. Next to a small dance floor sat a DJ playing music from the fifties and sixties.

"Great job, Mom," Joanna whispered in her mother's ear as Butch led Joanna to her seat at the table.

At seven thirty, while people were starting on their salad course, Joanna's mother stepped up on the podium. Playing mistress of ceremonies as if born to the role, Eleanor welcomed the attendees and introduced the honored guests and their spouses. Joanna saw the piece of paper she placed on the lectern in front of her as she stepped up to the microphone. No doubt it was a cheat sheet of names Maggie Oliphant had provided, probably at the last minute, but Eleanor carried off her pinch-hitting stint with an air of cool assurance.

Joanna noticed that William Farraday, the superintendent of schools and his wife, Jeannie, were part of the introductions. Joanna made a mental note to try to speak to him sometime during the evening to ask about gaining access to the school district's e-mail system.

Later, Joanna told herself. *Not right now.*

Resuming her seat, Eleanor continued to play hostess throughout the remainder of the meal, keeping conversation at her table on a lively but even keel. Deft questions aimed at the Colemans elicited interesting bits of information from the artist and his wife, both of whom told snippets about their lives before and after their move to Sedona. Sheri Coleman, a classy, blond former flight attendant with a wicked sense of humor, was seated between Butch and Jeff Daniels and kept both of them laughing with occasional wry comments.

Dinner was a leisurely affair. Myron and his staff had outdone themselves. The prime rib with all the trimmings, including Yorkshire pudding, was perfectly cooked and perfectly served. As dinner progressed, however, Joanna noticed that Eleanor was becoming increasingly tight lipped and anxious. Finally, as the waitstaff began delivering trays of crème brûlée, Joanna went over to her mother's chair.

"I'm going to go powder my nose," Joanna said. "Care to join me?"

A flush of gratitude suffused Eleanor's face. "What a good idea," she said. Excusing herself, she rose to her feet, and they set off across the dining room, threading their way between tables and dodging waiters carrying loaded dessert trays and pots of coffee.

"What's the matter?" Joanna asked. "You look upset."

"I don't know what's become of Maggie," Eleanor complained. "She said she was going outside for a smoke and asked me to look after the Colemans during dinner, but that was hours ago. I was happy to make the initial introductions and host the dinner, but I thought for sure she'd be back for the start of the auction."

"Maybe she was taken ill," Joanna suggested. "Would you like me to go take a look?"

"Please," Eleanor said. "She's probably in her car."

"What kind of vehicle?"

"A Lincoln Mark Eight," Eleanor said. "A maroon Lincoln Mark Eight."

"What do you want me to tell her when I find her?"

"That the auction's about to start."

"Is there a chance she had too much to drink?" Joanna asked.

Eleanor considered for a moment and then nodded. "It's possible."

Back at the table, Joanna collected Butch. "Mind if we get some fresh air?"

He gave her a quizzical look, but took the hint. "Sure thing," he said, excusing himself from a quiet conversation with Sheri Coleman.

Joanna felt a tiny twinge of jealousy. "It looked like the two of you were having an interesting chat," Joanna observed as they made their way toward the lobby.

"We were," Butch said without going into any further detail.

Once outside, they found that the desert's "fresh" air was more than fresh. It was downright chilly. When Butch felt the goose bumps forming on Joanna's bare arms, he shed his tux jacket and draped it over her shoulders.

"What are we doing?" he asked.

"We're looking for Maggie Oliphant," Joanna explained. "She's supposed to be running this show. Mom's worried that she's gone AWOL."

"Where do you think we'll find her?"

"According to Mom, she drives a maroon Lincoln Mark Eight. From what George was telling me earlier, there's a good chance she had a bit too much to drink and is passed out cold."

With Joanna clinging to Butch's steadying arm, they made slow work of covering the vehicle-crowded parking lot. Butch was the one who spotted the Mark VIII, parked some distance away from the other cars, at the far end of the gravel lot.

"There it is," he said, pointing. "If she came out here to have a quiet tipple, she parked far enough away from everyone else so people couldn't see what she was up to."

As they neared the vehicle, Joanna could see in the pale moonlight that someone was slumped behind the steering wheel. Tottering on high heels ill equipped for dealing with gravel, Joanna hurried over to the driver's side and rapped sharply on the window.

"Maggie," she demanded. "Are you all right?"

There was no response. Thinking the woman had probably passed out, Joanna tried the door handle. It wasn't locked. Once she wrenched the door open, a foul odor, mingled with years of stale cigarette smoke, erupted from the vehicle. A moment later, as the dim light from the open car door illuminated the car's interior, Joanna's eyes verified what her nose already knew—Maggie Oliphant wasn't just passed out in her Lincoln Mark VIII. She was dead. From the length of bloodied wire that was still twisted around her throat, Joanna knew that her death couldn't be anything other than murder.

Chapter 17

Butch, a few feet behind Joanna, was far enough away that the smell didn't hit him. "Is she okay?" he asked.

Joanna checked for a pulse, just to be sure. The woman's clothing didn't appear to be in any disarray, as one might have expected had this been an attempted rape, although there was a small triangular tear in the bodice of her dress where her skin showed through.

"She's not okay," Joanna answered, stepping away from the vehicle. "She's dead."

Instinctively, Joanna reached for her phone, but it wasn't there.

"I'll need your phone," she said.

Without a word, Butch pulled his cell phone from his pants pocket and handed it over.

"There's a flashlight in the glove compartment of the Outback, isn't there?"

Butch nodded.

"I'll need that, too. Then I want you to go inside and tell my mother that she's going to have to handle the auction, that Maggie isn't up to helping out. Whatever you do, don't tell Mom that Maggie is dead. If we do that, the auction is history, and Maggie and Mom will have done all that work for nothing."

"Got it," Butch said, "but if you don't come back inside, what am I supposed to tell your mother?"

"Tell her the truth—that I'm staying with Maggie for the time being."

"Do you need anything else?"

Joanna considered for a moment. "I'm going to contact the department. Jaime's on call tonight. I'll get my forensics people out here, but I'll also need the M.E., who, as it turns out, is here for the gala. Do you know him?"

"I've met Dr. Machett a time or two," Butch said. "I can find him, if you want."

"Good. Tell him I need to speak to him—that it's urgent."

Butch trotted away on the first of his several errands, leaving Joanna alone with the body. For a moment she stood where she was, peering into the car, acutely aware that she was tramping around a crime scene in her high heels. Any footprints would already have been obliterated by her stilettos, and because she hadn't been wearing gloves when she wrenched open the door, the crime scene had already been altered.

Moving away from the Lincoln but leaving the driver's door ajar and the light on, Joanna put Butch's phone to her ear. With her own phone all the numbers she needed would have been instantly accessible in her contacts list. With Butch's phone, she opted for calling 911. The emergency operator patched her through to her chief deputy.

"Hey, boss," Tom Hadlock said. "Not to worry. I've got everything under control."

"Unfortunately, you don't," Joanna replied. "I've got another homicide here in the parking lot at Rob Roy Links. I need Jaime Carbajal and Dave and Casey ASAP. I'll want a couple of uniforms as well. Have whichever deputy is closest to my place on High Lonesome stop by on his way here. I've got a complete set of crime-scene-appropriate clothing in an overnight bag in the back of my Yukon. I'll need someone to pick that up and bring it here. Doing a crime scene investigation in a silk evening gown and high heels isn't going to cut it."

"I'm on it," Tom said.

"Jenny is home babysitting. I'll have her put the bag out on the slab in front of the garage. Tell whoever you send to just pick it up from there. I don't want people stopping by and ringing the doorbell when Butch and I aren't there."

"Check," Tom Hadlock replied. "Bring the bag; don't ring the bell."

Butch trotted up just then and handed over the flashlight. As he started back toward the building, Joanna tried to hand him his jacket.

"Keep it," he said. "You need it a lot more than I do right now. I'll send Machett out once I find him."

As Butch hurried away again, Joanna called home. While she waited for Jenny to answer, she switched on the flashlight and sent the beam roaming around the dead woman's vehicle. A few feet from the open door something sparkled on the ground, reflecting back the light, but by then Jenny had answered.

"Dad," Jenny grumbled without waiting to hear who was on the phone, "Denny's in bed asleep. We're okay. You don't need to call and check on us."

"It's me," Joanna said. "I'm using Dad's phone right now. I need you to get my bag of crime scene clothing out of the back of the Yukon and leave it outside the garage door. Someone should be by in a few minutes to pick it up."

"Your crime scene clothes? How come? I thought you were going to some kind of fancy dinner."

"I don't have time to go into it," Joanna said. "Sorry. Just set the bag out, please."

Ending the call, Joanna stepped closer to what she had seen on the ground. Part of the reflection was due to what looked like a scattering of tiny pieces of shattered glass along with something metallic. Closer examination revealed that this was the back of some kind of brooch, complete with a broken hinge where the pin had once been.

Butch had found a green silk pocket square that matched Joanna's dress. Pulling the piece of silk from his jacket pocket, Joanna used that to retrieve the damaged brooch. It turned out to be a lapel watch, a tiny Lady Elgin attached to a diamond-studded fleur-de-lis. The front of the timepiece had been smashed to pieces, and the hands, broken and bent, were frozen in place at 7:35.

At the sound of approaching footsteps, Joanna looked up. "What's going on?" Guy Machett demanded. "Can't a guy have at least a moment's peace?"

Joanna motioned to the open car door. "Take a look," she said, "and then you tell me. I've got my people coming. You'd better call yours."

Machett bent down and peered inside the vehicle. "Crap," he said. "Two murders in two days? Are you kidding me? What the hell is going on around here?"

He straightened back up. "Any idea how long she's been here?"

"I saw her talking with my mother early on during the cocktail hour," Joanna said, "but look at this." Cradling the watch in the pocket square, she held it out and shined the light on the mother-of-pearl face so he could see the stilled hands.

Machett looked at the watch and frowned. "Gives us a reasonable idea about the time of death, then," he said. "Must have happened after everyone went inside. That's why no one noticed."

"Yes," Joanna agreed. "That's about the time my mother was making her opening remarks. I'm not sure we should accept this at face value. It looks like she was strangled from behind, inside the car. She was wearing the watch on her dress; why would it be broken and outside the vehicle? What if the killer reset it to deliberately mislead us as to the time of death?"

Machett glowered at her. "Are you trying to tell me how to do my job?" Then he plucked his phone out of his pocket. As he began summoning reinforcements, Joanna heard the first siren announcing the arrival of one of her patrol cars. She hurried to meet the vehicle as best she could, beckoning the car in the right direction and signaling for the deputy to cut the lights and siren. For right now, at least, she was hoping to keep news of the tragedy from spreading to the people who were supposed to be inside spending money.

Deputy Armando Ruiz, who usually patrolled the outskirts of Sierra Vista, was the first deputy to arrive. After pointing out where she had found the broken watch, Joanna left Deputy Ruiz to help Machett and to maintain what remained of the integrity of the crime scene while she herself headed back into the building, uttering evil imprecations to her high heels every step of the way.

She went looking for Myron Thomas. When she didn't catch sight of him in the dining room, she tracked him down in his steamy kitchen. Wiping his mouth with a napkin, he hurried toward her with an anxious expression on his face.

"Can I help you?" he asked. "Is something amiss out in the dining room?"

"The problem is in the parking lot," she said.

"What?"

Joanna shook her head and didn't answer. "I noticed a security camera over the front door," she said. "How many others do you have?"

"The system comes with ten cameras in all," he answered. "We have one on the front door, one on the back, and one in the lobby. The rest are focused on the course itself, on the first and tenth tees so we can see who has teed off. The others are scattered around the course so we can send out people to move golfers along if we've got slowpokes. Why?"

"If you don't mind, I'd like to get a look at tonight's video, both the front and the back door," Joanna said, "from say six thirty until nine or so."

"No problem," Myron said. "The computer and the video DVR are in my office, but what's going on?"

"There's been a homicide," she explained. "We just found Maggie Oliphant's body in the driver's seat of her car out in the parking lot."

"Maggie?" he repeated unbelievingly. "Are you sure?"

Joanna nodded.

"That's dreadful! This is her party. How could such a terrible thing happen? But of course you can look at the video." Myron stopped long enough to call back into the kitchen, "If anyone needs me, I'll be up in the office." Then he turned back to Joanna. "Right this way."

He led her out of the kitchen and then up a staircase that led to a loft-style office with windows that allowed anyone seated at the desk an unobstructed view of both the lobby area and the pro shop. On the opposite side of the room was a desk with a complicated console of computer components as well as an oversize screen. Thomas sat down at the computer table, motioned Joanna into a nearby visitor's chair, and started punching buttons on a remote. A moment later, the large-screen monitor before her came on with a low-throated *thunk*.

"What do you want to see first?" he asked.

"Front door," she said. "Between say seven and nine."

With Myron expertly using both the keyboard and the remote, it took very little time to fast-forward between the critical time periods on each of the cameras. For one thing, by seven fifteen most of the guests had arrived. There were two couples who were late and who came rushing in at what the time stamp noted to be 7:20. There were several people who came out and stood clustered around the front door where they availed themselves of the ashtray stationed there, but no one in that group looked especially furtive. Joanna and Myron watched clear through until Joanna and Butch emerged just before nine.

"What else?" Myron asked.

Joanna looked at her watch. It was after ten now. The auction was probably in full swing.

"Let's look earlier," she suggested. "I saw my mother talking to Maggie earlier, shortly after we got here, which was right at six thirty."

Again, Myron started operating the remote. At the earlier time frame, because there were so many arriving, it was impossible to fast-forward. At 6:40, Maggie appeared, leaving the building and having to sort her way through arriving guests to do so. She stopped near the ashtray and lit a cigarette.

"It looks like she's waiting for someone," Myron said. "See how she keeps looking at that thing on her dress?"

Joanna had noticed that, too. The lapel watch had been pinned to her dress in the same spot where Joanna had noticed that triangular tear in the material.

Eventually, Maggie ground out the butt of her cigarette in the ashtray. A moment later, she left the frame of the video and didn't reappear.

Myron and Joanna were still watching when there was a knock on the door. "Someone here is looking for Sheriff Brady. Is she with you?"

"Yes, she is," Myron answered. "We'll be right down."

"Can I have copies of these videos?" Joanna asked.

"Which ones?"

"Front door, lobby, and back door."

"No problem," Myron said. "I'll burn some DVDs and have them ready whenever you want them."

"You're probably in for a long night," Joanna said. "People are going to have to hang around for a while. You might brew up a few more pots of coffee."

"Will do," Myron said, and hurried off.

Casey Ledford was waiting for Joanna at the bottom of the stairs, holding Joanna's overnight bag.

"Jaime's already here. He and Delcia were having dinner at Ricardo's, in Hereford. She just dropped him off. He wanted me to let you know that we've already had a few people come straggling out of the building asking what's going on," she said. "We've been passing the situation off as a medical emergency, but once Doc Machett's meat wagon shows up, that's not going to wash. Jaime's hoping we can get statements from all the people who are here from the Plein Air conference. Some of them might know something, and if they're leaving town tomorrow, we need to know how to get in touch with them."

Joanna looked longingly at the bag. Her feet were killing her. There was nothing she wanted more than to be out of the silk gown and high heels and into something more comfortable, even if that something was nothing more than a bright orange crime scene jumpsuit.

"How's the auction going?"

Butch had appeared behind Casey. "When I left the room a few minutes ago, there were only a few more items. Paintings have been selling like gangbusters. It's a huge success."

Joanna knew right then that her decision to keep the situation in the parking lot quiet had been one hundred percent correct. What she really wanted to do was slip off the silk gown, morph into her sheriff persona, and go out to the parking lot to help her CSIs. This time, though, she couldn't do that. At that moment, the one thing Joanna Brady needed to do for the investigation was also what she needed to do for her mother.

"Tell Jaime I'm on my way inside to make an official announcement, then I'll go back out to the scene. Check with my mother. Either she'll have the official guest list or she'll know who has it."

"Counting waitstaff, there have to be well over two hundred people here," Casey objected. "We'll never be able to talk to them all."

"Let's hope someone saw something and will have brains enough to come forward. Now, do you happen to have an evidence bag with you?"

Casey nodded. Joanna retrieved the pocket square with the wrecked lapel watch from Butch's tux jacket and deposited it in the bag Casey had produced from one of the pockets in her own jumpsuit.

"I'll show you where I found it in a few minutes," Joanna said, then she peeled off Butch's tux jacket and handed it back to him. "Once I make the announcement, you'll look after Mom?"

Butch nodded. "I gave George a heads-up a little while ago. Everything has been going so well that she's on a real high. Hearing about Maggie is going to blow her out of the water."

As she and Butch slipped back into the banquet room, Eleanor was in the process of leading Michael Coleman onto the stage, where he and the auctioneer stood smiling and posing in a congratulatory handshake while cameras flashed as people in the audience rose to their feet. Most were simply standing and applauding, although a few of them seemed to be edging toward the door.

Seeing Joanna, Eleanor shot her daughter a small smile. When Joanna held up a hand as though it were a traffic signal, her mother frowned and looked puzzled. Joanna then held her hand as though she had a microphone in it and mouthed to her mother, "Ask them to wait."

With a shrug, Eleanor stepped to the microphone. "Thank you to everyone who made this auction such a success tonight, but I see my daughter stepping forward. Apparently she has something to say."

After meandering around in the parking lot in her heels, Joanna found the carpet in the ballroom a whole lot easier to manage. Butch handed her up the steps onto the podium.

"I'd like to introduce my daughter," Eleanor said. "Sheriff Joanna Brady."

Someone in the audience whistled. In her bright green gown, Joanna knew she didn't look the least bit like a sheriff.

"If you'd wait a moment before you leave, I have an important announcement to make," Joanna said, "but first, I'd like another round of applause for my mother, who has done a remarkable job tonight under very difficult circumstances."

The request was answered with a rousing round of applause. Eleanor nodded and smiled, but she still looked puzzled.

Joanna waited until the room quieted again. "Thank you for that," she said. "Now I have the misfortune of having to deliver some shocking news. Maggie Oliphant, the woman who has been the mastermind behind the Bisbee Art League and the one who made this whole weeklong Plein Air celebration possible, was found dead in her car in the parking lot a short time ago. Her death is being investigated as a possible homicide."

A collective gasp shot through the room. Joanna glanced at her mother. Eleanor seemed to sway slightly on her feet, and Joanna was relieved to see both Michael Coleman and Butch step forward. They each took one of her arms and steadied her.

"It's possible that some of you may have witnessed something out of the ordinary as you were arriving here tonight," Joanna continued. "It might not have seemed important at the time, but it could well mean the difference between our solving the case and our not solving it. So please, if you have anything to report, speak to one of the uniformed deputies you'll find outside in the parking lot; to my lead investigator, Detective Carbajal; or to me. As you depart, we would appreciate your leaving contact information so we'll be able to be in touch later should the need arise. As for the Plein Air participants, I'm afraid I'll need you to hang around for a while longer. Once my homicide investigators finish up outside, they'll want to speak to you individually."

"Do you know what happened to Maggie?" someone asked.

Joanna shook her head. "I'm sorry," she said. "This is an active investigation. I have no further comment."

By the time Joanna finished speaking, Butch and Michael Coleman had escorted an ashen-faced Eleanor down the steps and back to her chair. Joanna left the podium and slipped onto the chair next to her mother's.

"Mom," she said, "are you all right?"

"This can't be true!" Eleanor declared. "Are you sure there hasn't been some terrible mistake?"

"Sorry," Joanna said. "It's no mistake."

"I talked to Maggie just before the dinner started. She said she was going out for a smoke."

"She did that," Joanna said. "That's on the security video. She was murdered sometime after that."

George Winfield made it through the crush of people. When he put a comforting hand on Eleanor's shoulder, she rose to her feet and melted, sobbing, into his arms.

"There, there, Ellie," he said, holding her. "It's okay."

With her mother in George's capable hands, Joanna decided it was time to bail. "I've gotta go, Mom," she said, but she doubted Eleanor heard a word of it.

Grabbing her overnight bag and slipping out of her heels for better traction, Joanna made a beeline for the nearest restroom.

Inside one of the stalls, she shed her slinky dress like a snake slipping out of its skin. Usually she wore the jumpsuit over her uniform. This time there was no uniform—only the jumpsuit and a grubby pair of tennis shoes. Once Joanna had her jumpsuit on, she retrieved both her badge and her Glock from the beaded purse. The badge went over the jumpsuit's breast pocket. With no small-of-the-back holster, the Glock went into one of the deep side pockets. That wasn't the safest way to carry it, but it beat putting it inside her bra or the elastic of her underwear.

Emerging from the restroom with the green dress slung over one arm, she found Butch waiting for her. "How about if I take care of the dress," he suggested.

"And the purse, too, please," she said, handing it over.

"I'll hang around long enough to do whatever your mother needs to have done. After that, do you want me to wait around or do you want me to go home?" he asked.

Joanna leaned over and kissed him on her way past. "You're wonderful, but go home," she said. "I'll be there when I can."

Chapter 18

Grateful to be in tennies rather than heels, Joanna went back outside and was relieved to see that Jaime had taken charge of the scene, marking it off with crime scene tape, turning on generator-powered lights so the area around the car was completely illuminated. Joanna noticed that the Mark VIII's passenger-side door was open, and Dave Hollicker seemed to be examining the door handle.

Joanna walked up behind Dave just as Jaime appeared at her elbow. "What have we got?" she asked.

"The Mark Eight is a two-door," he said. "There's no sign of forced entry. It's an older model from the midnineties when they still used a keypad locking system. So either the vehicle wasn't locked or the perp knew the combination. I think the killer may have concealed himself in the backseat and then attacked her from behind. It could be nothing more than a crime of opportunity. We found at least a dozen of what appear to be picture-hanging wires in the floor well of the backseat, so it may be the killer simply used whatever was handy. Afterward he let himself out through the passenger door, leaving the front passenger seat leaning forward."

"Like he left in a hurry," Joanna suggested.

"Exactly. Luminol showed us some blood on the passenger-door handle. Dave is collecting it right now. We don't know if it belongs to the victim or the perpetrator. What was it you sent out in that evidence bag with Casey?"

"It's the remains of a watch," Joanna said, leading him over to the spot where a tiny debris field of watch crystal had been ground to pieces in the gravel. "The hands were stopped at seven thirty-five, but that's such a cliché that I don't quite believe it."

"But that explains where Machett is getting what he's calling the time of death," Jaime mused. "I thought it was early in the process for him to be able to be that definite. Casey said you were checking the security tapes."

"They give us zilch," Joanna replied. "No one coming to and going from the party at the time in question, if seven thirty-five turns out to be the right time. No one before that or after that, I noticed, either. The car itself is parked outside the range of any of the cameras."

"So it could be an outsider," Jaime suggested. "Someone who came to the party to see what he could rip off from the parked cars of a bunch of well-heeled guests."

"What about the victim?" Joanna asked. "We know the killer tore off her watch. Was she wearing any other jewelry?"

"Yes, she was. A diamond ring and what looks like an emerald."

"So it's not a robbery, then."

"Maybe an interrupted robbery."

"Cell phone?"

"As near as we can tell, that's the only thing that's missing."

"Leaves two rings behind and takes the cell phone?" Joanna asked. "That doesn't make sense."

The M.E.'s van arrived. As Machett and his helper prepared to transport the body, Myron Thomas came hurrying across the parking lot. He stopped abruptly when he reached the boundary of crime scene tape laid out in a wide circle around Maggie Oliphant's Mark VIII.

"Folks are getting restless in there," he said. "Is there a way to start letting some of them leave? My people need to get into the dining room so they can start cleaning up."

"Right," Joanna agreed. "We can't keep everybody waiting all night." She turned to Jaime. "As people leave, ask them if they've had any dealings with Maggie in the last two weeks or so. Anyone who says yes, we'll contact later for a more detailed interview. We'll talk to the Plein Air participants after everyone else leaves."

"Sounds good," Jaime said.

With Joanna posted at one entrance to the dining room and Jaime at the other, people began to file out of the room. It took the better part of an hour for most of the guests to be allowed to leave. Several of the women who had served on the Plein Air committee were noted as needing follow-up interviews, but none of them or any of the other guests admitted having seen anything unusual.

Once the other guests had been handled, Jaime took responsibility for interviewing the artists as well as the major players—Eleanor Lathrop, Michael Coleman, and Myron Thomas. He did that upstairs in Myron's office, while Joanna handled the spouses and significant others at the golf pro's desk in the pro shop.

Joanna's introductory query about recent dealings with Maggie Oliphant was enough to take most of the spouses and significant others out of the equation since Maggie's focus had been directed primarily at the artists. The only real exception to that came when the last person in line, Michael Coleman's wife, Sheri, took her seat in front of Joanna.

"This isn't my first rodeo," Sheri said with a smile. "Michael does several of these events in any given year. He takes them in stride, while the organizers end up being nervous wrecks. That seemed to be the case with Maggie Oliphant. She was wound very tight to begin with, and she seemed to become more so as the week went on."

"Was there anything in particular that set her off?"

"I heard her apologizing to Michael several times, saying she had discovered that one of the people in the master classes had gotten in under false pretenses. He didn't have the skill or background necessary to take advantage of the kind of instruction Michael was giving them."

Joanna remembered hearing Eleanor's side of what must have been a similar conversation.

"Did she mention anyone in particular?"

"Not really. Just that she was embarrassed about it and didn't want Michael wasting his efforts on someone who had no business being in the class to begin with. She was afraid that if the guy's stuff at the juried show tomorrow is really bad that it would somehow reflect badly on Michael."

"Would it?"

"No, but Michael suggested that if she was really worried she might consider giving the guy the option of bowing out of the show gracefully."

"To not have his work in the juried show?" Joanna asked.

"Exactly."

"How did that turn out?"

"Maggie didn't say—at least not to me. She might have mentioned it to Michael."

"If one of the participants was really unqualified, wouldn't Michael have been able to notice based on the work they did during the week?"

"That's the thing," Sheri said. "Most of the artists haven't shown what they've been working on to anyone else. Their stuff for the show is supposed to be dropped off at Horace Mann tomorrow morning at ten. It'll take an hour or so to get it all hung. Then the judges will come in to view what's on the walls and make their decisions. The end-of-conference show starts at two in the afternoon."

"Isn't that the point?" Joanna asked. "Didn't they come here to get help from Michael and from their fellow artists?"

"Most of the people here are still at the point where they worry that someone will steal their ideas or try to copy their work. They haven't figured out that if you point a group of artists at the same rock and tell them all to paint the same thing, what's going to come out of that exercise will be as many different paintings as you have people doing the painting."

"Hasn't anyone explained that to them?"

Sheri laughed. "That's not something you can tell someone. They have to learn it on their own."

"That was the only specific thing you heard her being upset about—that at least one of the participants didn't measure up?"

"The rest of it was all logistical details—where were people staying, where were they having meals, whether anybody needed anything. She was excellent at sorting out all those little items."

"Did you see any confrontations between her and anyone else?"

"Only the man here—what's his name, the owner?"

"Myron Thomas?"

"Yes, I heard her on the phone with him several times during the week, adjusting the number of guests as people who were late about RSVPing finally got around to doing so. He evidently wanted to shut down the guest list. She wanted to include as many people as possible."

That gave Joanna something to think about. Until that moment, she had neglected to see that Myron Thomas might need to be considered as a suspect.

"What about at dinner tonight?" Joanna asked.

Sheri frowned. "I never saw Maggie tonight, not once. I was surprised that your mother was asked to take such a commanding role. I don't think any of us had met her before she came up and introduced herself during the cocktail hour. That's not to say she didn't do a good job," Sheri added quickly. "It's just that there's usually a whole bunch of people making something like this come together, while Maggie had struck me as something of a lone ranger."

"My mother is more of a background person," Joanna said. "I admit, I was a little surprised, too."

By the time Joanna and Sheri emerged from the pro shop, Michael Coleman was still there waiting for his wife, while everyone else had gone home, including George and Eleanor.

"Myron and Detective Carbajal are in the kitchen, interviewing the waitstaff and kitchen help," Michael explained. "He said we can go, that he'll be in touch with us at the hotel tomorrow morning if anything else is needed. Your husband went home, too. He said he expected someone would give you a ride home if you need one."

"Yes," Joanna said with a weary smile. "That's one of the advantages of being sheriff. When I need a ride, I get a ride."

The Colemans walked away, leaving Joanna alone in a dining room that had been stripped bare. The dishes and tablecloths were gone. Left behind was a roomful of scarred banquet tables. On a tall cocktail table near the denuded podium sat an immense coffeemaker and a few clean cups and saucers.

Joanna helped herself and waited. With her minimal skills in Spanish, she knew she'd be less than no help in the kitchen. The kitchen at the Rob Roy was definitely a place where English took a backseat, and Jaime's fluent Spanish would do far more good than Joanna's textbook Spanish.

It was almost one in the morning before Jaime and Myron emerged from the kitchen.

"I thought you'd be gone by now," Jaime said.

"So did I. Now you're stuck taking me home."

"You mean Dave is stuck taking us both home," Jaime said. "I got dropped off, too. He came in his Tahoe."

Jaime turned to shake hands with Myron. "Thanks for all your help. It's been a tough way to end what must have started out as a nice evening. I'm glad you were there when I was asking the questions," Jaime added.

"If it hadn't been for you, the guys in the kitchen wouldn't have given me the time of day."

"I'm a little surprised to hear that they did," Joanna said.

"They're so worried about immigration coming along and checking their papers that their first response was no response. Myron runs a tight ship. He told them that having someone die in the parking lot was bad for business. If they wanted to save their jobs, they needed to help out."

"Did anyone see anything?"

"Maybe. One of the guys who was out on a smoking break around seven said he thought he saw a man get into the Lincoln. It was parked close enough that he could see the man walk up to the car but too far away to see who it was. He walked up, did something to the door, then got inside."

"As in maybe used the keypad?"

"Most likely," Jaime agreed. "We saw no evidence of any kind of forced entry. So he might have used the keypad or he might have had a key."

"That would mean someone Maggie knew."

They walked up to where Dave Hollicker was finishing loading the Tahoe.

"That's where the phone records will play a critical role," Jaime said. "Fortunately, Judge Moore was one of the guests here tonight. We were able to get him to sign off on a search warrant for Maggie Oliphant's telephone records. Dave says he'll fax it in to her telephone provider first thing tomorrow morning." Jaime paused long enough to glance at his watch. "Actually later this morning," he corrected, "after we all get some sleep."

It was after two o'clock in the morning when Dave dropped Joanna at High Lonesome Ranch. Tired and more than ready to hit the hay, she expected the house to be dark when she came home. Instead, she found Butch at the kitchen table with her father's journals spread out on the table in front of him.

"Still awake?" she asked.

"Couldn't sleep," he said. "I can write about dead bodies, but I don't usually look at dead bodies. How do you manage?"

Joanna shook her head. "I don't really think about it; I just do it."

She sat down across the table from him. "What are you doing with my father's journals?"

"I remembered what you told me about Abigail Holder tonight as we were driving to Rob Roy Links. When I couldn't sleep, I decided to look up the date you mentioned. Look at this. It's your father's journal entry from August 5, 1968."

He slid the book over to Joanna. Joanna's first venture into her father's journal had turned up the unwelcome news that he had been romantically involved with his secretary, Mona Tipton. Eventually D. H. Lathrop had made the decision to stay married because he hadn't wanted to lose his daughter. Learning those sordid details about a man Joanna had considered perfect had come as a shock. It had forced Joanna to readjust her long-held notions about who her parents had been. Since that jarring discovery, Joanna had mostly left the books alone. They sat, untouched except for occasional dusting, on the bookshelves in the home office that was currently Butch's work space rather than hers. Now, though, looking down and seeing her father's familiar scrawl on the page of his journal was almost like hearing his voice, speaking to her from across the years:

Freddy Holder died today, and it shouldn't have happened. We were just finishing lunch. He went down into an old stope, one we weren't using anymore. He went in by himself, and the whole damned thing came down on top of him. Just that one stope. Nothing happened in the main shaft, although it scared the hell out of all of us. It took more than an hour to dig him out. The way he looked, with his

*skull bashed in, it was probably already too late
when we started to dig.*

*I asked our foreman, Mad Dog Muncey, what
the hell happened, why'd he let Freddy go into one
of those old stopes? He said Fred probably needed
to take a dump and went into the stope to do it.
I said, "Didn't you tell him not to go?" He said,
"Freddy Holder's all growed up and he don't have
to ask nobody for permission to do nothing. Just
because he was too damned lazy to walk his ass to
the shit car don't make it my fault." Mad Dog is a
crass asshole. Always has been; always will be.
I hope he wasn't the one who gave poor Abby
the news. They've only been married a couple
of months.*

Joanna finished reading the entry. "That's about the
same story Abby recounted when Deb and I talked to
her."

"Right," Butch said. "Now look at this."

The entry was dated three days later:

*The mine inspectors came through today. First
time I've ever seen Wayne Stevens come into Campbell Shaft, or in any of the shafts, for that matter.
They blew the whistle to let us know that bigwigs*

were coming down the hoist. He was wearing boots and coveralls and a hard hat on his head. The way he was glad-handing the guys, you'd have thought he was a regular politician out there hunting for votes, but what he was really doing was running interference and making sure that the only person the mine inspectors talked to was Mad Dog.

After they left, though, the shift bosses came around to have what they called a quiet word. It turns out they supposedly found evidence that Freddy was high-grading and that was why he went into the stope—to hide that day's stash of turquoise and malachite. I don't believe it for a minute. If somebody told Mad Dog to plant evidence on his own mother, I doubt he'd give it a second thought. So since Freddy is supposedly a thief, on Mad Dog's say-so, word has come down from on high that Mr. Stevens will be looking for any possible accomplices, and that anyone who shows up at Freddy's funeral will be considered suspect. That SOB! Freddy was his son-in-law, his daughter's husband! I hope Wayne Stevens rots in hell.

"Your father had no strong opinions about that guy," Butch said sarcastically as Joanna finished reading and looked up from the page.

"Right," Joanna agreed. "None at all."

"Do you want to keep reading?"

"Why not?" Joanna said. "I had so much coffee tonight that I'm tired but not sleepy yet, either. What else have you got?"

"Read the next entry."

Obligingly, Joanna turned to the next page.

Ellie and I went to Freddy's funeral today. It was held at Higgins Funeral Chapel on Main Street. Almost nobody came. Abby was there, crying her eyes out, and so was Freddy's family—his dad, Daniel; his mother, Elaine; his older brother, Mickey; and his baby sister, Emily. That was it. As the service was about to start, his mother turned in her chair, looked around the room, and then turned back to her husband. "Why isn't anyone here?" she asked. "They must have gotten the time wrong in the paper," Daniel told her.

Daniel knew that wasn't true, and so did I. People didn't come because they were scared. After being on strike for seven months, most of the miners in town are hanging on by a thread. They can't risk losing their jobs because of something Fred Holder may or may not have done, and so they stayed away.

After the ceremony, while they were loading the flowers into the hearse, Freddy's older brother, Mickey, came over to where I was having a smoke. He asked me straight out what the deal was. Said he'd asked his father and Daniel wouldn't say. I told him about the rumored high-grading, and about the word Wayne Stevens had put out, warning people to stay away. "How come you're here?" Mickey wanted to know. "Because I think Wayne Stevens is a jackass," I told him.

Ellie spent some time with Abby. She was there all by herself. How her parents could be so heartless is more than I can understand. She's barely turned eighteen and already a widow. She looked so lost and alone. Made my heart ache just looking at her.

"What strike?" Butch asked.

"People always talk about that one as the big one," Joanna answered. "It happened in 1967 and 1968. It was a nationwide, industry-wide strike that lasted for seven months. Most of the families here in town were single-wage-earner families back then. I have no idea what kind of settlement was negotiated, but I can't imagine that anything in the contract made up for those seven months of lost wages."

"Which Mr. Stevens, as company management, didn't lose?"

"Correct."

"He also knew that people wouldn't dare cross him by going to the funeral," Butch surmised.

"True," Joanna said.

"I think your dad had it right," Butch said. "I hope Abby Holder's father is rotting in hell."

He said it as though he meant it, and Joanna couldn't help but laugh. She stood up then.

"I've got to go to bed and at least try to sleep," she said. "When morning comes, my department will be knee deep in two homicide investigations instead of just one."

She kissed Butch on her way by, stripping out of her jumpsuit as she went. When she climbed into bed and turned out the light on her nightstand, Butch was still in the kitchen, wading through D. H. Lathrop's journals.

Chapter 19

Joanna had no idea when Butch came to bed. He was still asleep and snoring in the morning when she intercepted Dennis on his way to bounce on the bed.

"Come on," she said, grabbing her son and leading him out of the room. "Let's go make some breakfast. What do you want?"

"Oatmeal" was his one-word answer.

"Oatmeal, please," she corrected.

Joanna didn't often cook these days, but when it came to breakfast, oatmeal was one of her few strong suits. She cut up some honeydew melon for Dennis to munch on while she busied herself starting a pot of coffee and rattling the pots and pans.

"You're cooking?" Jenny asked disbelievingly when she appeared in the doorway.

"Don't look so surprised," Joanna said. "We survived on my cooking for a long time before Butch and Carol came on the scene. We're having oatmeal. Do you want some?"

"I guess," Jenny said.

"Your show of enthusiasm is overwhelming. If you'll get out the milk and brown sugar and start some toast, it'll speed things along."

When Joanna finished dishing up the oatmeal and set the dishes down on the table, she found a folded sheet of paper sitting propped against her juice glass. She looked at Jenny questioningly. "What's this?"

"It's that thing I had to write about Ms. Highsmith for Dad. I thought maybe you could proofread it for me before he sees it."

Joanna sat down, covered her oatmeal with brown sugar and milk, and unfolded the paper.

Ms. Highsmith was my principal at Bisbee High School. I didn't know her well, but she was a good principal. Some principals only know the bad kids' names—the ones who get in trouble. She knew everybody's name. Some kids thought she was mean. I thought she was fair.

I don't think Ms. Highsmith had any kids of her own. That's why she spent so much time with us. If there was a football game, she went. She went to baseball games and track meets and basketball games. Once when I was barrel racing at Rex Allen Days in Willcox, she was there. I took second place. She came up to me afterward and told me I should run for rodeo queen, and this year that's what I did.

I'm sorry she's dead, and I'm sorry for taking the picture.

Joanna was taken aback. Yes, she'd had a somewhat prickly relationship with Debra Highsmith, most notably over the zero-tolerance firearms policy, which, it turned out, Debra Highsmith herself didn't observe. Still, how was it possible then that it had been Debra Highsmith's encouragement that made it possible for Jenny to win the title of rodeo queen? The rodeo in Willcox hadn't been a school athletic event. Even so, with one or more of her students involved in the competition, Debra Highsmith had made the effort to go there, put in an appearance, and be supportive.

"Well," Jenny asked, "what do you think? Is it okay? Will her family like it?"

"It's great, honey," Joanna said, "and yes, I'm sure her family will like it. The only thing I would change is that last sentence. We've located Debra Highsmith's next of kin now, so what I was worried about—that they'd learn about her death from the photograph—didn't happen. Just delete it."

"You really think it's okay?" Jenny asked.

Joanna got up from her place at the table, went around to Jenny's chair, and gave her a squeeze.

"I think it's terrific."

Jenny beamed with pride, and Joanna was struck by that. Jenny was as pleased by her mother's unconditional praise as Joanna had been by her mother's compliment the night before.

Memo to self, Joanna thought as she returned to her chair. *More praise and less criticism.*

"What's terrific?" Butch asked, stepping into the doorway.

"Jenny's eulogy for Ms. Highsmith, sleepyhead," Joanna answered. "If I were grading that paper, I'd have to give it an A plus."

Butch strolled over to the counter and poured himself a cup of coffee.

"I saved some oatmeal for you," she said. "It's in the microwave, but I don't think it's cold enough that you'll need to zap it. How late did you stay up?"

"Late," he said. "I've got some passages bookmarked for you. I think you'll find them interesting."

He brought his cup of coffee and bowl of oatmeal to the table, kissing the top of Dennis's head on the way by. Once seated, he picked up the piece of paper and read through the eulogy.

"Your mom's right," he said to Jenny when he finished reading. "This is top-drawer stuff." He turned to Joanna. "Will you be seeing any of the family members today?"

Joanna nodded. "Debra's grandmother is due to show up anytime now."

"Would you mind if your mother gave this to her?" Butch's question was aimed at Jenny.

"To Ms. Highsmith's grandmother?" Jenny asked. "Do you really think she'd want to see it?"

Butch nodded. "I have a feeling something like this from one of her granddaughter's students would mean the world to her."

"Okay," Jenny said. "If you think she won't mind."

"But do delete that last sentence and print a new copy," Joanna suggested.

Leaving Butch to finish overseeing breakfast and getting the kids ready for Sunday school and church, Joanna took off for the shower. With two homicides on the books, there was no question about her going to church that day. Forty-five minutes later, when she headed out the door, a fresh copy of Jenny's eulogy was safely stowed in her purse. Much to her surprise, however, Butch walked her out to the car.

"What your father wrote is interesting stuff," he said. "You'll never guess who went out and bought himself a brand-new Pontiac in October of 1968."

"Who?"

"Mad Dog Muncey. Your dad wrote about seeing it in the parking lot during shift change. According to him, nobody else in town was buying new cars that year. Not only did Mad Dog buy it; he paid cash."

"Did Dad seem to think the money for the car came from Wayne Stevens?" Joanna asked.

"He certainly did," Butch answered with a nod. "As a payoff for taking out Freddy. That was your father's theory, anyway, but he couldn't find any evidence to back that up. At least he didn't find enough evidence that would hold up in court."

"Wasn't Freddy's death ruled an accident?"

"Officially, yes," Butch answered. "The mine inspector gave the company a clean bill of health on the incident. They said Fred Holder had ventured into an unsafe area on his own and against his supervisor's direct orders. I'm going to keep reading, because I think there's more to the story than that, and I'm guessing your father did, too. By the way, in what I've read so far, after Fred Holder's death Muncey wrote your father up on phony safety violations three different times. Sounds like he was on a mission to push your father out."

"Again at Wayne Stevens's request?"

"That's what your dad thought," Butch answered.

"I guess what goes around comes around," Joanna said.

"What do you mean?"

"Wayne Stevens, who spent his years in Bisbee lording it over people he thought of as lowly peons—Dad included—ended up dying broke. He left his widow, Elizabeth, completely penniless and living off the kindness and charity of the daughter they had both once disowned for marrying Fred Holder. Abby has spent the past seven years working as Debra Highsmith's secretary."

They had been carrying on this conversation in the garage, with the garage door open and her car running. Now her phone rang.

"It's the grandmother," Joanna said, looking at the caller ID. "She's on her way to the office. I'd better get going, but let me know if you find out anything more."

"Will do," Butch said. He leaned in the window and kissed her good-bye. "Be safe," he said. "No matter what, be safe."

Joanna answered the phone.

"I know I was supposed to call from the tunnel, but I must have dozed off. I'm already at your office," Isadora Creswell said in a tone that brooked no nonsense. "I told you I'd be here bright and early. I am, but it wasn't easy. It's been twenty years since I've had occasion to rent a vehicle. When I got to the car rental counters at the airport, they were all set to rent me a car until they took a look at my driver's license, which is still valid, by the way. Then they said I was too old, which seems like age discrimination to me. I made it here, but I had to hire a limo and a driver to make that happen."

"I'm sorry you had so much trouble," Joanna said, shifting out of reverse and closing the garage door. She headed for High Lonesome Road leaving a billowing rooster tail of dust behind her. "I had expected to be at the office by now," Joanna explained, "but we had another homicide last night. I didn't get in until very late."

"That's all right," Isadora said. "I'm perfectly fine waiting here in the lobby. Someone was kind enough to bring me a cup of coffee, and I'm enjoying the photographs."

The display cases in the lobby contained a collection of all the previous sheriffs of Cochise County. Most of the photos showed serious-looking men dressed in Western attire and glaring fiercely at the camera as if it were some kind of villain. There was only one female in the bunch—Joanna Brady. Her photo showed a red-haired child, grinning happily and dragging a Radio Flyer wagon loaded to the gills with Girl Scout cookies.

"I was a Girl Scout leader years ago," Isadora said. "The girls in my troop sold those cookies like crazy. I think they cost twenty-five cents a box back then. I wonder what they cost now?"

Two-fifty a box last I checked, Joanna thought. She said, "With two homicides on my plate, I'll need to have a short staff meeting with my people before I'll be able to speak to you."

"Don't worry about me," Isadora said. "I'll be fine. I'm also enjoying the view. Quite different from Altoona, especially all the red and gray hills. What's this huge flat thing that's right across the road from here? Is that what they call a mesa?"

"Mesas are natural formations. What you see in front of you is a man-made tailings dump," Joanna explained. "It's all the boulders and dirt the miners hauled out of the open pit mine you drove past as you came through town. At the time, the material stacked there was considered worthless because there wasn't enough copper in it to make it worthwhile processing down at the smelter in Douglas. Now they have a whole new system. They run water through the waste, and leach the copper out of it that way."

Even as Joanna spoke, she understood what was happening. Having a discussion about the scenery was an effective way for both of them to avoid talking about the real reason for Isadora's visit. For her part, Joanna was happy to carry on with that little charade. It delayed the moment when, for good or ill, she would have to find a way to tell this already grieving woman that she had a great-grandson she had never met.

Joanna dreaded that part of the conversation. It promised to be an emotional minefield. If Isadora didn't already know about Mikey Hirales's existence, how would she take the news? She would either be thrilled or be devastated. This was a situation where there was likely to be very little middle ground.

"How much did you know about Debra's life out here?" Joanna asked.

"I know she loved it," Isadora said. "She loved the wide-open spaces and the blue skies, but most of all, I think she loved the kids."

"What did she talk to you about?"

"We didn't talk," Isadora corrected. "We wrote letters. I wrote to her. She wrote to me, but never directly. That was too dangerous."

Not wanting to spook the woman, Joanna backed off. "Okay," she said. "I'll meet with my people first, then I'll come collect you from the lobby."

Joanna parked in her reserved spot, let herself in the back door, and went straight to the conference room where her team was already assembled and waiting.

"Bring me up-to-date," she said, taking her place behind the lectern. "What are the results from yesterday, and what's on the agenda for today?"

"Yesterday we reinterviewed all the neighbors, as well as Richard Reed, one of the Plein Air guys who's been in the neighborhood painting all week long. Nobody saw anything out of the ordinary. For today I've got the autopsy at the top of my to-do list," Jaime Carbajal said. "Doc Machett is pissed that he's having to work on Sunday. Too bad. If we have to work on Sunday, he has to work on Sunday."

"I've faxed a copy of Judge Moore's warrant to Maggie's telephone provider," Deb Howell said. "Once I get the records and can start going over her calls, that should tell us a lot."

"I'd be interested to know if the phone records show that Debra Highsmith was somehow involved with Maggie Oliphant or the art league," Joanna said thoughtfully.

"Why do you ask?" Deb replied.

"This is a small community. We've had two homicides in as many days. On the surface it looks as though we're dealing with two separate cases, and until we know better that's how we'll continue to treat them, but let's keep our eyes and ears open. There's always a chance that there's some connection between the two that's eluding us."

"I'll check," Deb said, "but if she made calls to Maggie from her office phone, we won't have a record of that without obtaining another warrant. We got one from Judge Moore last night because he and his wife were at the function when Maggie was murdered."

"Do what you can," Joanna said. "If there's a link between those two women, we need to find it."

With that, Joanna turned to Casey Ledford. "What about fingerprints?"

"There are literally dozens of fingerprints in Maggie's car, but that's not surprising. She's been running a taxi service all week long for the people involved in the conference, carting them here and there. We'd need a whole bunch of elimination prints to even begin figuring out who all was in her vehicle, and it would probably be a huge waste of time and effort since the bloody smear on the door handle didn't have any prints in it."

"Which suggests the killer probably wore gloves?" Joanna asked.

"Exactly."

"Let's do this, then," Joanna said. "For right now, don't worry about getting elimination prints, but go ahead and enter the ones you find into the Automated Fingerprint Identification System. If we end up getting an AFIS hit on one of them, it might be a big step up, especially if our killer turns out to be some small-time repeat offender who was simply prowling the cars in the parking lot looking for easy pickings."

She turned to Dave Hollicker. "What are you up to?"

"Once Casey finishes collecting prints, I'll be processing the vehicle. After that, I'll run that bloody sample from the passenger door up to the crime lab in Tucson to get them started on DNA testing."

Nodding her approval, Joanna turned to Deb. "What about you?"

"When the phone records come in, I'm planning to take them home with me so I can work on them there. Maury's been here all weekend. He's been great about hanging out with Ben, but I've barely seen either one of them. Maury's a good man, and I feel like I'm taking advantage."

"By all means work at home," Joanna said, "but first, if you don't mind, I'd like you to come sit in on the interview with Debra Highsmith's grandmother. She's waiting out in the lobby."

Joanna looked around the room. "All right, people," she said. "It sounds like everybody's on track. If no one has anything else . . ." Seeing no indication of any further pending business, Joanna nodded in Deb's direction. "How about if you bring her to one of the interview rooms so we can video her statement."

"Wait," Jaime said. "Isn't this the same woman who claimed Debra Highsmith was killed by someone from the CIA?"

Joanna nodded.

"That's one interview I'll be sorry to miss," Jaime said with a grin. "It would be fun to see you and Deb here all decked out in tinfoil hats."

"Get out of here and go watch your autopsy," Deb told him with an annoyed glare. "Go bother Dr. Machett with your lame jokes instead of bothering us."

Deb Howell left the conference room, slamming the door behind her as she left. Jaime Carbajal was still chuckling under his breath as he exited the room. Left on her own, Joanna couldn't help but think that Jaime just might be right. The idea of a CIA hit man showing up in Bisbee didn't seem at all likely.

Chapter 20

Joanna was waiting in the hallway outside the interview room when Deb led Isadora Creswell through the door from the public lobby. Isadora was a tall, spare, and stiffly upright woman who walked with a slight limp and with the aid of a metal cane with a multicolored shaft. The slight tremor that had first manifested itself in her handwriting seemed to have turned into a slight but visible shaking that affected her whole body.

She wore a double-breasted charcoal-colored suit over a crisp white blouse. On her feet were a pair of what Eleanor referred to as "sensible shoes," sturdy heels of the lace-up variety. There was no doubt that these were all designer duds, well maintained but several decades out of date.

Looking at the woman as she came down the hall, Joanna estimated that she must be well into her eighties. Artfully applied makeup effectively shed years off a face that must once have been stunningly beautiful. Her thinning silver hair was pulled back into a French twist and fastened with a stylish jeweled comb. Suspecting that the blue jewels in question were real sapphires as opposed to the fake variety, Joanna upped the ante on what she had previously thought to be Isadora's net worth.

A faded beauty, Joanna thought, but someone with the air of assurance—the savoir faire—that comes from having lived a life that included some degree of both wealth and position.

Isadora stopped short when she reached Joanna. "You must be Sheriff Brady," she said, smiling and holding out a trembling, bony hand whose thin fingers were gnarled by arthritis. "They didn't allow lady sheriffs back in my day, or even lady detectives, but I'm glad to see they do now."

Smiling back, Joanna was careful to return Isadora's handshake without squeezing too hard. This woman and Abby Holder's mother, Elizabeth, were most likely members of the same generation, yet their respective attitudes toward women in law enforcement were diametrically opposed.

"Won't you come in," Joanna said, gesturing toward the door of the interview room. Pausing at the doorway, Isadora peered inside. When she caught sight of the camera, for the first time she seemed to have second thoughts.

"Do you have to record this interview?" she asked. "There's always a chance that it might fall into the wrong hands. Couldn't we do this in your office with a civilized conversation?"

Joanna thought about it for a minute and then made up her mind. "Of course," she said with a nod in Deb's direction. "No problem."

Turning around, she ushered Isadora and Deb Howell back to her office. Settled into one of the visitor's chairs in front of Joanna's desk, Isadora stared out the window at the ocotillo-studded landscape that eventually gave way to a towering wall of limestone cliffs that sprang up out of the desert floor a mile or so away.

"Are those plants all dead?" Isadora asked.

"Which plants?"

"The ones with those long, spiky gray branches."

"The ocotillo?" Joanna asked with a laugh. "No. They're not dead, although they certainly look dead. They lose their leaves when it gets too dry, but they leaf back out again when it rains."

"Not just in the fall and spring?"

Joanna said, "Regardless of the time of year, within twenty-four hours after a rainstorm, they're green again."

"Fascinating," Isadora said, turning back to Joanna. "Debra loved this place," she said, "but she never mentioned the . . . what is it again?"

"Ocotillo," Joanna repeated.

"She mostly talked about her work and school. That's what interested her most. Her kids."

Joanna reached into her bottom drawer and pulled Jenny's eulogy out of her purse. "My daughter, Jenny, is one of your granddaughter's 'kids,'" Joanna said. She walked the paper around her desk and handed the eulogy to Isadora. "She wrote this yesterday."

Isadora reached into her own purse and plucked out a pair of reading glasses. Joanna and Deb Howell waited patiently while Isadora read through it, moving her thin lips slightly as she read. When she finished, she carefully refolded the paper and placed it in her purse, then withdrew a lace-edged hankie and wiped away the trail of tears that had blossomed on her carefully rouged cheeks.

"So you're Jenny's mother," she said. "This year's rodeo queen, right?"

Joanna nodded.

"Debra often spoke about her, thought she was a promising young woman, but then she took a keen interest in all the kids, not just the ones singled out for some kind of honor."

Joanna nodded. "From what I can tell, your granddaughter was a wonderful principal. The whole community is feeling her loss, but it turns out we've discovered that there's a lot we don't know about the woman we all thought of as Debra Highsmith. Maybe you'd care to enlighten us. For instance, it might be helpful if you told us her real name."

Isadora looked up sharply. "So you know about that?"

"We know that your granddaughter was using someone else's name and Social Security number from the time she was a freshman in high school."

Isadora drew a deep breath before blurting out her answer. "My son was a spy," she said simply. "A contemptible traitor to his country. He worked in the defense department in Washington, D.C., as an intelligence analyst. This was back before the end of the Cold War, back when there were all kinds of Russian spies on the ground in this country, and Gunnar worked for them."

"Gunnar was Debra's father?" Joanna prompted.

Isadora nodded. "You can google him if you like. That will give you some idea of what we're dealing with. It'll give you an overview of his part of it anyway."

Joanna's computer was right there on her desk. "That's G-U-N-N-A-R?"

Isadora nodded. "Lloyd was my husband. His father's forebears came from England. His mother's hailed from Denmark. Gunnar was his maternal grandfather's name."

Punching the letters into the computer, Joanna waited for the search engine to find the article.

Gunnar Lloyd Creswell, born October 10, 1937. Died March 26, 1979.

Joanna looked away from her computer screen and shot a questioning look in Isadora's direction.

Isadora seemed to understand exactly what she was thinking. "I was twenty when my son was born," Isadora explained. "In some circles I'm considered to be very well preserved for my age."

Joanna upped Isadora's estimated age by another decade. "And still driving," Joanna said.

"Yes," Isadora agreed with a nod, "just not at night, and not, as it turns out, in rental cars."

Joanna returned to reading the article.

The only son of Lloyd and Isadora Creswell, Gunnar Creswell was raised in Altoona, Pennsylvania, where he was considered to be an outstanding student as well as an all-around athlete who won an appointment to West Point. Graduating as a second lieutenant, he served two tours of duty in Vietnam. Returning from overseas, he was posted to the Pentagon in Washington, D.C., where he served as an intelligence analyst for the Department of Defense during the Cold War. Suspected of spying for the USSR, he was taken into federal custody in March 1979. He died two days later of an apparent suicide. No charges against him were ever filed.

"As you can well imagine," Isadora observed as Joanna finished reading, "that's a highly sanitized version of what happened. Most of the real story is still classified."

Joanna turned her computer screen far enough around so Deb could read the article for herself. If the guys at Wikipedia believed Gunnar Creswell was a spy, maybe there was something to the CIA story.

"Tell us what you can of the unsanitized version," Joanna urged.

Isadora sighed. "My first daughter-in-law, Gunnar's first wife and Debra's mother, was named Alice. She died in an automobile accident a few months after Debra was born. My second daughter-in-law was a money-grubbing gold digger. Isabelle came from Indiana—a farm girl with delusions of grandeur who ended up being Miss Indiana.

"She assumed that since Lloyd and I had money that Gunnar had money, too. She may not have been born with a silver spoon in her mouth, but you couldn't tell that from the way she acted. Not long after they married, Isabelle made it abundantly clear that Gunnar wasn't living up to her high expectations. His job at the Pentagon didn't earn enough to allow him to keep her in the manner to which she wanted to become accustomed. She insisted that he buy her a house in what she regarded as the right neighborhood in D.C. regardless of whether they could afford it. She wanted expensive cars. She wanted expensive clothes. She wanted the best schools for Alyse and for Jimmy."

"Who are Alyse and Jimmy?" Deb asked.

"Alyse was Debra's given name," Isadora explained. "Her original given name. Jimmy was her baby brother."

"Was?" Deb asked. "Is he dead, too?"

"Not as far as I know. But back then, whenever Gunnar's salary didn't stretch quite far enough to suit her, Isabelle fully expected him to come to us for a handout. He must have gotten tired of having to ask us for help. Instead of doing that, he went looking for another source of funds. Unfortunately, he found one."

"And a spy was born," Joanna said.

"Yes," Isadora agreed. "The problem is, Gunnar wasn't very good at it. He got caught."

"How?"

"Alyse," Isadora said simply.

"She turned in her own father?"

"Not exactly. You have to understand that even before Jimmy was born, Isabelle treated Alyse like so much extra baggage. Whenever Isabelle lit into Alyse, my son always took his wife's part. I couldn't help but feel sorry for the girl. She was a sweet thing. Lloyd and I were more than happy to have her spend a few weeks with us each summer, and she never gave us a bit of trouble. As my husband got older, he was ill and house-bound much of the time. Whenever Alyse visited us, she was our little ray of sunshine.

"One day when Alyse was thirteen, the three of us were having breakfast when she announced, out of the blue, that she thought her daddy was a spy. Lloyd choked on his coffee. I thought he was going to have another coronary on the spot. He may have been a retired banker, but he was a true patriot. Before he could go off on a rant, I managed to step in and ask Alyse whatever would give her such a strange idea.

"She said she was coming home from the library with some friends. They were taking a shortcut through Book Hill Park when she saw him sitting there on a bench with a woman—a beautiful woman— Alyse had never seen before. She thought it was odd that he would be there then because he was supposed to be at work. She started to go over to him and then something made her stop. Instead, she stayed where she was and watched.

"Knowing men, my first assumption, of course, was that Gunnar was playing around and maybe having an affair, but Alyse soon disabused me of that notion.

" 'It was just like in the movies,' she said. 'When he got up to leave, he took her briefcase and left his with her.'

"When breakfast was over, Alyse went on her way, leaving Lloyd and me sitting there shattered. I tried to pass it off as a case of a thirteen-year-old with an overly active imagination, but Lloyd took it seriously, and he went into overdrive. He fought in World War Two, you see. He was there on D-day and at the Battle of the Bulge. The idea that his own son might be a traitor to his country was more than he could tolerate.

"Lloyd had a friend of a friend look into Gunnar's finances. It took some time to pull all the facts together, but sure enough, he was spending half again more than he was making. He wasn't even smart enough to hide it. The Russians must have been keeping an eye on things, too. They knew he was compromised even before the people on our side did. Whoever the woman was, they pulled her out and sent her back home.

"That left Gunnar to take the fall all by himself, and, believe me, he was by himself. Lloyd and I never spoke directly to Gunnar after he was arrested, but we made it abundantly clear to Isabelle that we wouldn't be lifting a finger to help, and that included footing any bills for defense attorneys. Isabelle ended up screaming at me on the phone, telling me what a terrible person I was and that she'd see to it that I never saw my grandchildren again because she was taking them with her and going back home to live with her parents in Indiana.

"Speakerphones were new then, but we had one," Isadora continued. "Lloyd heard every word. When Isabelle hung up, he had me call our attorney to come make a house call and rewrite our will. Lloyd was determined that that woman would never inherit one thin dime of our money.

"Then, within days of that phone call, Gunnar died. It was dreadful. Since there was already so much ill will involved, Lloyd absolutely refused to attend the funeral. Between the time Gunnar died and the time of his funeral, the friend of a friend got back to Lloyd and told him that the authorities suspected that the woman Gunnar had been involved with was a top Russian spy and that they might have to interview Alyse in hopes of identifying her."

"It sounds like your 'friend of a friend' was well connected," Joanna commented.

Isadora nodded. "He was, very, and don't expect me to give you his name because I won't. Our big worry, of course, was Alyse. She was little more than a child who, because of her father's reckless behavior, was in danger of being turned into a Cold War pawn. If the CIA thought Alyse could give them information, it was only reasonable for the opposition to do everything in their power to make sure that didn't happen. Maybe Gunnar committed suicide, maybe he didn't, but believe me, the people involved on both sides were utterly ruthless, and so was Isabelle.

"As I said, Lloyd refused to go to the funeral, so I went by myself. There was a reception at the house after the funeral. I went to that, too, even though I hadn't been officially invited and knew I wasn't welcome. I went because I wanted to see Alyse. She spent most of the day in her room, crying her eyes out. That's to be expected. She had just lost her father. But it turned out that Isabelle blamed Alyse for it. Told her it was all her fault that Gunnar was dead since Alyse was the one who raised questions about her father being a spy. Alyse was devastated.

"Right then, I could see the writing on the wall, and I think you can, too," Isadora added. "Think about every evil stepmother story you've ever heard. I knew that's how Alyse's future was going to play out. Once they got back to Isabelle's hometown folks in Indiana, Alyse would have been an outcast. I had already seen that Jimmy was the favorite. He would be the perfect child and Alyse would always be the 'other' one, tolerated rather than loved. And young as he was, Jimmy got it. He'd do mean little things to Alyse, and Isabelle let him get away with it, usually blaming her for whatever happened.

"And he did it again at the reception. I saw it happen. Jimmy spilled someone's glass of wine and blamed it on his sister. Isabelle went ballistic. That's when and why I made up my mind—completely on the spur of the moment. I asked Alyse if she wanted to go to Indiana with her stepmother. She said no. I told her that there was a chance dangerous people might be looking for her. Which, it turns out, was all too true. I also told her that if she wanted to come with me right then, that very minute, her grandfather and I would do our best to protect her."

"You took her from her father's funeral reception?"

"Yes, I did, and I'm not sorry, either. I had her pack a suitcase and smuggle it out to the car. When it was time to leave, I had her get in the backseat and lie down on the floor, and away we went."

"Just like that?"

"Just like that. My best friend from grade school was in charge of a parochial school in upstate New York, the St. Giles Preparatory School. I stowed Alyse with Sister Benedict for a few days while I went home to face the music. I thought Lloyd would be furious with me, but I was wrong. He was the exact opposite. By then he knew far more about Gunnar's situation than I did, and Lloyd thought I'd done the right thing. In fact, he was the one who came up with the idea of changing Alyse's identity. We had some help with that, of course."

"Let me guess," Joanna said. "From your friend of a friend."

"Exactly," Isadora said, beaming. "That was in April of that year. With his help and with Sister Benedict's, by September Alyse Creswell had become Debra Highsmith and was enrolled at age fourteen as a freshman in Good Shepherd in Albuquerque."

"Did anyone suspect you of being involved in Alyse's disappearance?"

"No. Not at all. From the beginning, she was regarded as a runaway. Isabelle was all over network TV begging for Alyse's safe return, but that was just for show. I did feel a little guilty when I knew there were police officers and volunteers out searching the parks and dragging the river, but that didn't last long. The runaways that stay in the news are the ones who have family members out there lobbying for their return. Isabelle had her hands full. By the time the funeral was over, the bank was already foreclosing on their house. Even with the extra money Gunnar was making, Isabelle had managed to spend it faster than it came in. By the beginning of May she and Jimmy were off to Indiana—Fort Wayne, I think."

"You didn't stay in touch with Isabelle?"

"I tried to, at first, for Jimmy's sake. The letters and cards and gifts I sent were all returned unopened."

"Where's Jimmy now?"

"I have no idea. I finally gave up, but I still had Debra. She's gone by that name for so long now, I barely remember she was once Alyse."

"Over the years the two of you communicated strictly by letter?"

"Always. Through Sister Benedict at first, and later through Sister Benedict's successor. We both sent our letters to the convent, and they passed them along. It was the only way I knew to keep Debra safe." Isadora paused a moment. "At least I thought it would keep her safe, but now we know I was wrong. Someone found out. Just because the Cold War is over doesn't mean a thing. The people running the show may change, but a spy is still a spy. I keep wondering if Gunnar's female friend from back then is a VIP of some kind in the new Russia. It could be that anyone who might be able to tie her back to what she did in the old days could still be considered a threat."

"You're saying you still believe Debra's death to be some kind of holdover from the Cold War."

"I do indeed."

There was a small pause in the conversation, and Joanna knew it was time to change the subject.

"In her letters to you, did Debra ever talk about the Hirales family?"

"Of course," Isadora said. "I was incredibly grateful to know that those kind people had taken her into their home and into their hearts. I couldn't risk letting her come home or have me come visit her, so it meant everything to me that the Hirales family let Debra come stay with them over the holidays and during summer vacations. There was always a chance the phones were bugged or that someone had put listening devices in my house. I couldn't even risk hearing the sound of her voice. I slept better at night knowing she had someone on this side of the country who treated her like family."

"How much do you know about them?"

"The Hirales family? Quite a bit, I suppose," Isadora said, then she paused and frowned. "Well, there's Sue Ellen, of course. She was Debra's first roommate and her best friend. Then there are Sue Ellen's parents, Nancy and Augusto, who adopted a son, much later in life. Michael, I believe his name is. He was in Iraq or Afghanistan or one of those places for a while, but he's back home now and going to law school. He sounds like a very bright young man."

Yes, Joanna thought, *and he's also your great-grandson.*

Joanna knew that Sue Ellen Hirales and her little "brother" would be here soon, coming to start planning Debra Highsmith's funeral. Was it her job to tell Isadora Creswell the truth or was it someone else's?

"I believe he is bright," Joanna said softly, "but there's something else you need to know about Michael Hirales, Ms. Creswell, something Debra may have neglected to tell you."

"What's that?"

"Your granddaughter got pregnant when she was a senior in high school," Joanna said. "She had the baby out of wedlock, and Nancy and Augusto Hirales adopted him. Michael Hirales is really Debra's child, your great-grandson."

For a moment after the words landed in the room, nothing at all happened—like the pause between a flash of lightning and the distant rumble of thunder.

Then, Isadora Creswell seemed to slip from her chair, falling onto her knees on the carpeted floor in front of Joanna's desk.

"Praise be!" she exclaimed. "Praise be!"

After that her tears began to flow in dead earnest.

Chapter 21

Deb chose that moment to make a graceful exit to check on Maggie Oliphant's phone records. Eventually Isadora regained her composure. "I always blamed myself that Debra never had a chance to have a family," she said regretfully. "I was just so concerned about getting her out of one messy situation that I didn't realize I was inadvertently putting her into another, one that was equally difficult."

"She did have a family," Joanna pointed out. "She had you, and she must have treasured that relationship since she evidently saved every letter you wrote her through the years. She also had a stepmother and a half brother. Whatever happened to them?"

Isadora dried her tears and shrugged her shoulders. "As I said, after years of getting my cards, letters, and packages back marked 'Return to Sender,' I decided I was done. The notation on the outside of the envelopes and packages was always written in Isabelle's handwriting. My former daughter-in-law was not a pleasant person. It seemed likely to me that she would have poisoned Jimmy against me as well. It was less painful for me to simply stop thinking about them than it was trying to stay in touch and being rejected over and over.

"I certainly hope you don't expect me to notify Isabelle now that Debra is gone," Isadora added. "As far as she's concerned, Alyse is someone she didn't care that much about to begin with. Besides, Alyse went away decades ago, and Debra Highsmith is someone Isabelle Cameron—she took back her maiden name after Gunnar's death—never knew."

"What about the other side of the family, Alice's side?" Joanna asked.

"I stayed in touch with Alice's parents for some time. Not much more than annual Christmas cards, but they're both gone now. I'm sure it seems selfish on my part, but it was easier to live the lie when I didn't have to keep lying to people's faces. Does that make sense?"

Joanna nodded.

"So am I given to understand that Sue Ellen Hirales has now told Michael the truth about Debra? Does he know about me, too?"

"I believe she told him most of it last night—at least as much as she knew—and that you exist. She learned that from reading your letters, but I doubt she has any idea about the rest of what you've told us this morning concerning Debra's background. I expect Sue Ellen and Michael will turn up later this afternoon. I'm sorry to say that most likely the first thing you'll be doing with your great-grandson is planning his birth mother's funeral."

"I don't blame Debra for not telling me about him, or him about me," Isadora said. "I hope he understands that, too."

"Why didn't she?" Joanna asked.

"I'm sure she was afraid that the people who were after her might use him to get to her."

Joanna had to refrain from rolling her eyes. Maybe it was time to go ask Jaime Carbajal for some of those tinfoil hats after all.

"Look," she said reasonably. "So far our investigation has turned up nothing at all to indicate this is a situation with any kind of national intelligence overtones. It's far more likely that Debra's death has something to do with a disgruntled student from the high school, but let me ask you this. Does the name Maggie Oliphant ring a bell?" she asked.

Isadora shook her head. "No. I don't think so. Why?"

"My department is investigating another murder," Joanna explained, "one that occurred two days after Debra's death. Maggie Oliphant is the second victim. I was wondering if there might be a connection—if Debra might have mentioned their having any dealings with each other."

"Not that I know of. How did this Maggie die?"

"She was strangled."

"Debra was shot. So it's probably two different people, right? That's how it is on TV at least. People who kill multiple times generally use the same MO. Still," Isadora added with a frown, "with a distinctive name like Maggie Oliphant? I'm quite certain that if Debra had ever mentioned her to me, I would have remembered it, and I don't."

Isadora stood up abruptly and then paused for a moment, straightening her skirt and jacket. "I suppose I look a fright," she said. "Some people can manage to look decent when they cry. I'm not one of them."

It was true. Her carefully applied makeup had literally come to grief. As a result, Isadora's advanced age was definitely showing.

"I managed to get a room at the Copper Queen for tonight," Isadora said. "That's what the people at the hotel in Tucson recommended. I called on my way through town, and they said I can have an early check-in in an hour or so. In the meantime, I'd like to see Debra's house and her school."

"You can't go inside either one. They're both still considered active crime scenes."

"Of course. I just want to drive by. If you'll give me the addresses, the limo driver will be able to locate them on his GPS. After that, I'll have him drop me off at the hotel. My room should be ready by then. I think I'll go there and have a rest and put my face back on. You said that Sue Ellen and Michael are coming over from New Mexico later today?"

Joanna nodded. "This afternoon."

"Tell them that's where I'll be, then, at the hotel," Isadora said. "Let them know that I'm looking forward to meeting them both."

"Would you like me to show you out?" Joanna asked.

"Not necessary," Isadora said. "I'm perfectly capable of finding my own way."

As Isadora made her determined way out of the office, Joanna was again struck by the differences between her and Elizabeth Stevens. In the face of a terrible tragedy, Isadora was staunchly self-contained while all Elizabeth could do under far less difficult circumstances was whine and berate her daughter for no good reason. It seemed to Joanna that Abby Holder would have been a far better daughter to Isadora and Lloyd Creswell than Gunnar had been a son.

Thinking about mothers and sons and daughters made Joanna think again of her own mother and of the telephone call from Maggie that had been under way when Joanna arrived at her mother's house the previous day. Joanna had heard her mother's part of the conversation. Now she needed to know the rest of it. A glance at her watch told her that it was late enough in the morning that her mother and George were probably already home from church. When she dialed their house, however, George was the one who answered.

"Ellie and I came home in separate vehicles," he said. "With Maggie gone, your mother is the one in charge, and she's determined to keep things at the Plein Air tea from falling apart. The last I saw of her, she was on her way to the school to supervise setting up the art display for this afternoon's closing reception and to make sure the judges are on the job. You can't have a juried show without judges."

Joanna considered calling her mother to say she was coming. Instead, she decided to simply show up. She was on her way there when her phone rang.

"Great news, boss," Dave Hollicker said with unrestrained glee. "You'll never guess what we found in Maggie Oliphant's car."

"I give up."

"Her cell phone. It was shoved down between the driver's seat and the center console, completely out of sight. There was no other obvious trace evidence. Now that she's done with the prints, Casey is going to continue searching the car. In the meantime, I'm dropping the phone off with Deb, and then I'm on my way to Tucson."

Larger departments might be able to have CSI personnel who did only one aspect of the job. In Joanna's, both Dave and Casey had to wear multiple hats.

"All right," Joanna said. "I'm going up to the Plein Air reception to check out a couple of loose ends. Tell Deb I'll be in touch later."

In exchange for providing art education for local school children, the Bisbee Art League operated out of space rented from the school district at a price well under market value. Their main offices were in the old Horace Mann School, a former junior high school situated in the upper reaches of Old Bisbee. Joanna parked in a lot that still had faded signs reserving the spaces for TEACHERS ONLY.

The open house was due to start at two P.M. Since it was barely noon, Joanna wasn't surprised that the doors were still locked, but a wave of her badge was enough for the silver-haired gatekeeper to allow her to enter.

Upon pushing open the door, Joanna's nostrils were assailed by the familiar smell. Years after the last middle school child had left the building, the apparently indelible odor of overheated lunch-box bananas and apples still lingered. The wooden floor of the hallway was polished to a high gloss, and the long passage with its antique overhead fluorescent fixtures had been converted to a make-do art gallery of sorts, with paintings mounted on easels strung from one end of the hall to the other.

Eleanor Lathrop Winfield stood in the middle of a beehive of activity. Still dressed in her Sunday go-to-meeting finery, she barked a steady stream of orders to minions who jumped to do her bidding.

Leaving her mother alone for the moment, Joanna made her way down the middle of the hallway, pausing here and there to view the paintings on either side of the long, narrow room. Clearly the fluorescent fixtures didn't show the paintings in the best possible light. Even so, a few of the pictures exhibited genuine talent.

Because Joanna knew Bisbee's cityscape intimately, as only a native-born resident would, she knew the sights and could see where things worked and where they didn't. One artist had attempted but not quite captured the untidy clutter of Brewery Gulch and OK Street buildings, huddled in stark contrast to the steep sides of the red shale hill with Bisbee's school letter, B, standing delineated in white limestone.

An attempt to paint the front facade of the Copper Queen Hotel didn't quite work because the perspective was out of whack, making the hotel appear larger than the buildings in front of it. Several paintings focused on the town's sole statue, the figure of a copper-covered, bare-chested miner known as the Iron Man. All of those were crookedly out of kilter. A painting of Lavender Pit did a better job of capturing the actual subject matter, but the immense and decaying hole with its collapsing walls and levels was hardly a thing of beauty, and Joanna found herself wondering why anyone would bother.

The painting of San Jose Peak rising in purple mountain's majesty out of the dusty plain of Sonora, Mexico, was nothing short of stunning. That one, painted from what was evidently the top of Vista Park, was easily the best of the bunch. A close second was a painting of the cliff-covered limestone hillock generations of Bisbee kids had called Geronimo. With a distinctive double hump at the top of the peak, Geronimo looked like a gray Valentine gone bad, looming over the reddish brown flattened expanse of the tailings dump.

Of all the paintings, that was the one Joanna liked the most, perhaps because climbing Geronimo had been a triumph of her youth when she and Marianne Maculyea had conquered it together during a daring junior high school mountain-climbing expedition.

The painting at the end of the hall, the last one Joanna viewed, was also an odd man out. All the others, although often imperfectly executed, were nonetheless clearly representational. This one was not. Here three wide stripes of paint covered the whole canvas. It was reddish brown on the bottom, gray in the middle, and blue on top. There was no definition; no shading, no telling details. A slightly darker smudge in the reddish part might have been a shadow or it could have been the vague outline of a house. It was impossible to tell.

As far as Joanna was concerned, there was nothing in the picture that made it work, nothing that made it speak to her. The title printed on the card said: LIME-STONE CLIFFS SOUTH OF BISBEE. The name scratched in yellow in the lower-right-hand corner was "Richard Reed."

Joanna was still studying the painting when her mother walked up behind her. "Don't say it," she said. "I already know. If this is art, then so is second-grade finger painting. I'm almost embarrassed to put it up, but I have to since he came and paid good money to be here."

"Is this the same guy Maggie Oliphant was complaining to you about on the phone yesterday when I stopped by the house?"

Eleanor nodded. "That's the one. I told Maggie that in the future we need to have prospective artists give us a portfolio of their work prior to their being accepted into one of the master classes. After all, if you want to maintain any kind of quality, the process of being admitted to something like this should be more like auditioning for a part in a drama production than just forking over fifteen hundred bucks for tuition and walking into the conference sight unseen. That's what we'll do next year."

"We?" Joanna asked.

Eleanor gave her a look. "Yes, *we*," she said. "Somebody has to keep this thing running. What happens to the kids if we don't? Poor Maggie. She was always totally focused on the bottom line and on bringing in as much money as possible, but if we expect to create any kind of credibility in the art world, we're going to have to insist on an official selection process instead of simply doing a cattle call."

"Which is how this guy got in?" Joanna observed, nodding toward the painting.

Eleanor nodded. "Exactly. Richard Reed evidently signed up at the very last minute, just days before the Plein Air conference began, but he wouldn't have made it to first base—at least not as far as his art is concerned."

"Wait," Joanna said, tuning in to her mother's sarcasm. "What do you mean by that?"

Eleanor shook her head. "There's no fool like an old fool. Maggie was a little over the hill—aren't we all—and having a younger man pay attention to her was most likely more than she could resist. Putting a little romance in someone's life never hurt anybody. Look what it did for me."

A younger man, who was enrolled in the conference. That's when Joanna realized that she had met Richard Reed. Two days earlier, he had been the man at the cash wrap in Daisy's Café, the one who had given her first the leer and then the unexpected compliment. And yes, he was definitely closer to Joanna's age than he was to Maggie Oliphant's or Eleanor Lathrop Winfield's.

"You're saying there was something going on between Maggie and this guy?"

"Of course," Eleanor sniffed. "You can't look at that painting and tell me there wasn't."

"Did you mention this to anyone last night during the interviews?"

"Why would I? Just because Maggie is dead doesn't mean I have to drag her reputation through the mud. Besides, I know good and well Richard Reed can't be the killer."

"I don't know that for sure; how do you?"

"Because of the time. Maggie was killed at seven thirty-five. That was when I was at the podium, intro-

JUDGMENT CALL · 359

ducing the artists. Richard Reed was right there in the audience with the rest of the participants."

"The timing of Maggie's death was a deliberate holdback, Mother. How did you find out about it?"

"Dr. Machett told George and George told me."

By then, though, the alarm bell ringing in Joanna's head overcame her momentary annoyance with her mother and with George Winfield. She remembered that Jaime Carbajal had said something about interviewing one of the Plein Air painters at the same time he was speaking to Debra Highsmith's neighbors.

Reed's painting didn't reveal any details, but based on title alone, it was likely that he was the one who had been out in San Jose Estates, painting away, just up the street from Debra Highsmith's home. Reed was also a late enrollee with negligible artistic skill. Was being a bad artist enough to merit putting him on a list of possible murder suspects? No, but the fact that he had been in the vicinity of the crime scene meant that he should at least be given a second look.

"Who handled enrollment for the conference?" Joanna asked.

"Maggie did all of that."

"With help or without it?"

"Without," Eleanor answered.

"She has an application for each enrollee?"

"I'm sure she does. They're probably here in the office if you want to take a look at them."

One of Eleanor's worker bees trotted up with some kind of time-critical question about where the judges should be and when. Joanna waited while Eleanor finished putting out that particular logistical fire.

"Where were we?" Eleanor asked at last.

"You were going to show me the enrollment forms."

"Oh, right. This way."

Eleanor led her daughter into the room that had once been the principal's office. Joanna stopped in the doorway and looked around the grubbily appointed room. The massive wooden desk and oddball collection of wooden filing cabinets looked old and hard used enough to have been original equipment when the school first opened somewhere in the early twentieth century. A broken-down stool on wheels provided make-do seating for whoever was working at the desk.

"I don't see a telephone," Joanna said, looking around.

"Maggie didn't want to have to spring for a landline," Eleanor said. "She conducted all business over her cell."

Joanna nodded.

Eleanor opened several drawers in one of the filing cabinets. Eventually, after riffling through a set of folders, she pulled one out.

"Here's the file for this year's Plein Air," Eleanor said, handing it over. "Knock yourself out. I need to go deal with organizing the judges."

Joanna sank down on the stool, opened the file, and laid the stack of applications out on the surface of the desk. Considering that the artist in residence, Michael Coleman, was from Sedona, it wasn't surprising that most of the applicants came from towns in Arizona— one each from Prescott, Lake Havasu, Kingman, and Nogales. There were three from Scottsdale, two each from Sun City West, Mesa, and Gilbert. One hailed from Santa Fe, New Mexico, and one from Palm Springs, California. The California application for Richard Reed was dated April 12.

Joanna plucked her cell phone out of her pocket and dialed Deb Howell's desk in the bull pen. Obviously, she had yet to make it home.

"Did Maggie Oliphant's phone records ever come in?" Joanna asked.

"Her phone and her phone records," Deb answered. "I was about to pack up and go home with them. Why?"

Joanna consulted Richard Reed's application. "Here's a number for you." She read it off. "It's the cell phone listed for one of the Plein Air painters. When's the first time you see this number on her phone records?"

"It'll take some time to find the first call, but that number isn't hard to find. It shows up in the phone record several times. Wait a second." Deb paused. "I just counted them," she resumed. "Make that seventeen calls in the past week. Calls from Maggie to that number and calls from that number to Maggie's phone. From the looks of it, that's more than Maggie talked to anyone else at the conference. That would indicate a certain level of personal involvement."

"Yes," Joanna agreed. "It certainly would."

"Where's Reed from?" Deb asked.

"Palm Springs. That's what he lists as his residence on the application."

"The area code on his cell phone says L.A., but maybe he bought the phone in L.A. and that's why it got assigned an L.A. number," Deb said. "What's really interesting is that now that I have the phone itself, I'm looking at a whole cluster of calls—six in all, two each to three different numbers—that were placed late yesterday afternoon from Maggie's phone to various numbers in the 760 area code. I happen to know that's the area code for Palm Springs because I just looked it up. The only way I know about these calls is because we found the phone. None of them would show up on the billing information I got from her cell phone provider."

"Why not?"

"Because none of them went through. That made me curious, so I tried dialing them myself. All three of them go directly to a recording that says the number you have reached is not in service at this time."

Nonexistent numbers? Joanna's alarm bell started ringing even more urgently. "Read them to me, please," she said.

Deb did, dictating the numbers aloud while Joanna compared them with the information listed on Richard Reed's Plein Air application. The first turned out to be Richard Reed's home number. The second was his work number. The third one was the number of his emergency contact.

"If the phone numbers on his application are all bogus, everything else about him is probably bogus as well," Joanna said. "Look back through and see if you can locate the first time Reed's cell phone shows up in Maggie's call history."

There was a long pause on Deb Howell's end of the line. In the background, Joanna heard papers shuffling. "Okay," Deb said. "Here it is. As far as I can tell, the first call from that number is dated April tenth."

"The application is dated two days later," Joanna said. "So Richard Reed called one day, had the application faxed to him, and enrolled two days later."

"How did he pay?" Deb asked. "Visa? MasterCard?"

"The application is marked cash."

"How much is the tuition?" Deb asked.

"Fifteen hundred bucks."

"So what did he do?" Deb asked. "Send fifteen one-hundred-dollar bills in a FedEx envelope? Show up in person?"

The unorthodox method of payment, combined with the bogus phone numbers and Richard Reed's apparent lack of artistic skill, shifted into a disturbing pattern. "I know you were expecting to go home," Joanna said, "but I think we need to have a talk with this guy."

"Where are you?" Deb asked.

"I'm up at Horace Mann. The reception is due to start at two. Why don't you come here? We'll track Mr. Reed down and ask him a couple of questions."

"Do you know where he's staying?"

"Not yet, but I will by the time you get here."

When Joanna ended her call to Detective Howell, she immediately dialed Margaret Mendoza, her records clerk. "Here's a date of birth for you," Joanna said, reading off the information from Richard Reed's Plein Air application. "The name is Richard Loren Reed. Date of birth is November 25, 1975."

"Do you have a place of birth?"

The Plein Air application didn't ask for that. "No," Joanna said. "Only what's supposed to be a current address, 3242 South Calle de Maria, Palm Springs, California."

In the background Joanna could hear the clerk keyboarding the address information into her computer.

"No such address," she said a moment later. "There's no 3200 block on South Calle de Maria in Palm Springs. Are you sure you gave me the correct address?"

"I read it right off his application," Joanna said. "But since the phone numbers weren't legit, it's not too surprising. I wonder how much else about him is also phony-baloney."

She waited a while as Margaret's fingers clattered on her keyboard.

"I've got one Richard Loren Reed in the database," the clerk reported. "His date of birth is July 5, 1923, not November 25, 1975. So they're definitely not the same guy."

Suddenly it became blazingly clear why Richard Reed had paid his enrollment fee in cash instead of with a check or credit card. These days banks didn't establish checking accounts without some form of verifiable identification.

"Thanks," Joanna said to her clerk.

Hanging up, she immediately went looking for her mother, who was dealing with some kind of issue over the layout of various refreshment tables.

"What now?" Eleanor asked impatiently. "Can't you see I'm really busy here?"

"I'm busy, too," Joanna answered. "I need to know where Richard Reed is staying. It's urgent."

"You still think he may have something to do with Maggie's death?"

"He may," Joanna answered. *And a whole lot more besides,* she thought.

"All right, then," Eleanor said. "I'll get you a copy of the class roster, but I don't see how he could have done it when he was right there in the banquet room along with everyone else."

But Joanna did. If Richard Reed was the killer, he didn't need to suspend the laws of physics. All he had to do was change the time on the watch before he destroyed it.

Chapter 22

Again Eleanor shuffled through one of the file drawers in what had been Maggie Oliphant's office. Eventually she came away with a class roster that listed each participant's name, city of origin, accompanying guest, and lodging arrangements for the week. Richard Reed was listed as a solo, and he was staying at a place called Miner's Camp Lodge.

"Where's this?" Joanna asked.

"Above OK Street," Eleanor said. "It's a B and B, minus the second B. They don't serve breakfast, and it's a bit grim. As the old song says, 'no phone, no pool, no pets.' It's lodging only."

"There isn't anything above OK Street," Joanna objected.

"There may not be any streets above OK Street," Eleanor corrected, "but there are houses, and that's what these are—refurbished miners' shacks that are accessible by stairs only. The rates at Miner's Camp are dirt cheap for that very reason. If you're lugging your own suitcase up B Hill to get to your room, the higher you go, the more affordable the rate."

"Thanks, Mom," Joanna said, taking the paper. "Now, can you make me a copy of this?"

"I've got things to do," Eleanor said. "You'll have to do that yourself. The copy machine is over by the window."

It took what seemed like a very long time for the ancient copy machine to come on and spit out a copy of the roster. Once it had, Joanna hurried to the door of the school as Deb Howell pulled up outside in her Tahoe.

"Where to?" Deb asked as Joanna climbed into the patrol car and fastened her seat belt.

"Miner's Camp Lodge on OK Street."

"That's where Richard Reed is staying?"

"Supposedly," Joanna said. "At least according to the roster Maggie had in the file."

Shaking her head, Deb put the Tahoe in gear. "That property—including the main house, a parking lot on OK Street, and three additional cabins—was listed for sale when I bought my new place at the far end of Brewery Gulch. I didn't realize someone was dumb enough to buy it."

"They not only bought it," Joanna said, "they're evidently running it."

Since the Brewery Gulch/OK Street part of Bisbee was Detective Howell's home turf, she had no difficulty navigating to the parking lot at Miner's Camp Lodge, where a series of threatening signs insisted that parking was for REGISTERED GUESTS ONLY. ALL OTHERS TOWED AWAY AT OWNER'S EXPENSE.

On a street where parking was at a premium, a lot that would have held six cars held only one, a wizened VW bug with enough rust damage on the underside to indicate it was a recent arrival from much snowier climes.

"It looks like they're not exactly doing land-office business," Joanna said as Deb pulled into a spot in the almost deserted lot. "Leave your flashers on just in case."

The building next door, another aging wooden structure, boasted a sign that said OFFICE along with an arrow that pointed up a steep set of stairs. Before they could start up them, however, a woman appeared on a landing ten steps above them. She was dressed from head to foot in Spandex and looked like she was ready to take off on a bicycle at a moment's notice.

"You can't park there," she said, pointing a finger at the offending Tahoe. "Didn't you read the sign? Everybody thinks they can park here for free."

Joanna pulled out her badge wallet. "This is police business," she said. "I'm Sheriff Joanna Brady and this is Homicide Detective Deb Howell. We need to speak to one of your guests."

"You must mean Richard Reed," the woman said. "He's the only guest staying here at the moment."

With that, she darted down the steep flight of steps with all the grace of a bighorn sheep. The muscles on her calves looked like she did those stairs, all of them, several times a day with no apparent difficulty.

"Is that his car?" Joanna pointed at the rusty VW.

"No. That's mine. Mr. Reed is driving a Honda, a blue CR-V with California plates. Since his car isn't here, he's probably out painting somewhere, or maybe not painting since today is the last day of the conference. He's due to check out tomorrow, but I can tell you for sure that he isn't in his room right now. I was just up there changing the bedding and replacing his towels."

"I'm sorry," Joanna said. "I didn't catch your name."

"Denise," she said, holding out a tanned, leather-tough hand. "Denise Fuller. My partner and I are relatively new here in town."

"You're sure Mr. Reed's vehicle had California plates?" Joanna asked.

"Absolutely." With that Denise Fuller reached into an invisible pocket and withdrew an iPhone. "I can even give you the number on the plate."

With just that much notice Deb had a notebook and pen in hand, ready to take dictation. Denise read off the plate number while Deb wrote it down.

"I always keep a list with me so I can be sure that the people parking here are registered guests," Denise explained. "There isn't much parking on this street, and I make it my business to make sure that what's on the registration form matches what's on the vehicle. With Mr. Reed, for example, I discovered that he had inadvertently transposed two letters. Maybe he's dyslexic or something. I've done that myself on occasion."

From across the canyon, Joanna heard the sound of a wailing siren on some emergency vehicle. She knew what county sirens sounded like and the sirens on the local ambulance service. This was most likely a City of Bisbee patrol car. That meant whatever was happening was the city's problem, not hers.

Joanna gave Deb a brief nod. Understanding Joanna's unspoken command to check out the vehicle registration, the detective took herself out of the conversation, heading for the Tahoe with her phone to her ear. Meanwhile Joanna turned back to Denise Fuller.

"So the number you just gave Detective Howell is the one on Mr. Reed's vehicle, not the one on his registration form?"

Denise Fuller smiled a toothy smile. "They're both the same now," she said. "I fixed the registration form."

A second siren joined the first, and maybe that of an ambulance as well, both of them echoing back and forth across the narrow confines of Tombstone Canyon.

Joanna shut out the noise and concentrated on Denise Fuller. "You're telling us that Mr. Reed has been here all week?" Joanna asked.

"Let's just say he paid for the whole week," Denise said with a knowing wink. "From the looks of the bedding, I'd say he hasn't been here much of the time. Some people rent rooms from us and then don't want to admit that they can't handle going up and down those seventy-eight stairs. I do it every day, carrying loads of laundry back and forth. I'm used to it. I'm guessing Mr. Reed wasn't willing to admit that and ended up finding somewhere else to stay that didn't entail climbing stairs. Part of the problem is the altitude. People come here thinking that Bisbee is in the desert. They don't realize that it's a mile-high desert."

Down by the Tahoe, Deb Howell was nodding emphatically. Then she looked up, caught Joanna's eye, and motioned for her to come. Immediately.

"What?" Joanna said as Debra held the phone away from her ear, motioning that she was on hold.

"Margaret Mendoza just got a name on that plate number. You're not going to believe it."

"What?"

"Richard Reed's CR-V is registered to one James Gunnar Cameron of Palo Alto, California," Deb said. "Wasn't Cameron Isadora's former daughter-in-law's maiden name, the one she took back when she returned to Indiana?"

Joanna felt the blood drain from her face. "You mean Richard Reed is really Debra Highsmith's long-lost half brother, Isadora's grandson?"

"That's how it looks. With a name like Gunnar, it couldn't very well be anyone but him, could it? But what's he doing here?" Deb asked. "Why here? Why now?"

"It's obvious, isn't it?" Joanna answered. "He came here to kill his sister."

"How did he find her?" Deb asked. She signaled to Joanna that Margaret Mendoza was back on the line.

"Okay," she said into the phone. "No criminal record other than traffic infractions. You can get me a list of those later. In the meantime, give me his address." Joanna waited while Deb scribbled a long series of notes.

Joanna thought back to everything they had learned about the man known as Richard Reed. He had come to the Plein Air conference at the last minute, apparently dropping everything to come for a weeklong stay. Paying cash for his tuition. Paying cash for his room. Coming to town under a pseudonym. Pretending to be an artist when he wasn't even a talented amateur. It was all beginning to add up, and Joanna didn't like where it was going.

By then Joanna had her own iPhone out and was googling James Gunnar Cameron. He turned out to be Professor James Cameron of Stanford University, with a doctorate in computer science engineering, one of the country's best-known experts in developing facial recognition software.

Over the years Joanna had taken several continuing education classes that dealt with cold cases—cases that involved using artistic techniques to artificially age both suspects and missing persons. The resulting sketches had shown how someone might look decades after they had disappeared from view. What Joanna had learned in those classes was that although facial features changed over time, the foundations did not; the basic bone structure did not. If James Gunnar Cameron, once James Creswell, was an expert in facial recognition . . .

Then it came to her. Only a few weeks earlier, Marty Pembroke's "Die, Bitch" video had shown up on YouTube. The video that had gone viral. Nobody had needed to be listed as Marty's friend on Facebook to watch it. The video had been out there on the Internet for all to see. Suddenly Debra Highsmith, a woman who had done her best to keep her presence out of all kinds of electronic media, was all over it. If Jimmy had been prowling the Internet systematically, using facial recognition software in hopes of locating his sister, Martin Pembroke's video meant he had finally hit pay dirt. Once he had done that, he moved heaven and earth to come to Bisbee. To murder his long-lost sister? Why? What kind of sense did that make?

While Joanna had been lost in thought, the two sirens had turned into a cacophony. It seemed as though every emergency vehicle inside the city had suddenly been summoned to some incident down on Main Street, where they had converged in a spot that was totally invisible behind a collection of intervening buildings.

Deb was still on the phone with Records. "Switch over to Tica if you can," Joanna suggested, almost having to shout over the racket of the continuing emergency response. "See if she knows what's going on here in Old Bisbee. Find out if they need officers from my department to render assistance."

It took longer than Joanna would have expected to get through to Dispatch.

"Hey, Tica," Deb began. Then she fell utterly silent. A moment later, she handed the phone over to Joanna. "You need to hear this," she said.

The dismayed look on Detective Howell's ashen face spoke volumes. Joanna took the phone at once. "What?" she said.

"There's been a carjacking at the Copper Queen," Tica said. "The hotel, not the hospital. An elderly woman was sitting in a limo while the driver carried her bags into the lobby. While the driver's back was turned, someone jumped into the limo and took off in it with the woman still inside. So far the woman hasn't been identified," Tica continued.

Maybe no one else knew who the victim was, but Joanna did. How many limos were dropping elderly passengers off at the Copper Queen Hotel on that particular day?

"We're hearing all kinds of sirens . . ."

"The carjacker raced away from the hotel. First he turned down Subway, then he ran the stop sign at Main Street. Halfway up the street he lost control for some reason. He drove the limo up onto the sidewalk and smashed into a group of pedestrians who were gathered outside one of the galleries. The scene is chaotic. One suspected fatality and several injuries, some of them serious. EMTs are on the scene. More are coming."

"What about the limo?"

"Hit-and-run. The guy stepped on the gas and kept right on going. One of the victims didn't fall off the hood of the limo until it rounded the curve up by Castle Rock. He's the fatality."

"You put out an APB?" Joanna asked.

"Already done. That's what I was doing when Deb was trying to call in."

"I want every available officer we have on alert to help with this, whether they're currently on duty or not," Joanna ordered. "How long ago did it happen?"

"The first call came in to 911 seven minutes ago."

Joanna thought about times and distances. If the guy was northbound through town, the first turnoff would have been at the top of Tombstone Canyon where Cameron could get on Highway 80 in either direction—northbound or southbound. Enough time had already elapsed that he would already have reached that intersection. If he had turned southbound, even on the highway he wouldn't have had enough time to get all the way back downtown.

"We need roadblocks, ASAP," Joanna said into the phone. "Where's Jaime?"

"Back at his desk, I think."

"Tell him to take one other officer and set up a roadblock at Lavender Pit. If the guy doubles back through town on the highway, we need to nail him before he gets to Lowell or the Traffic Circle. From there, the bad guy will have a lot more choices and be harder to find. Call Chief Deputy Hadlock at home and let him know we need him to come in and hold down the fort. Call me back after that."

By then Deb was already at the wheel, with the engine running. "Where to?" she asked as Joanna jumped into the passenger seat. Joanna's Yukon was still parked at Horace Mann. With traffic on Main Street stopped, it might have been possible to go up and over School Hill to get it, but she didn't want to take the time.

"Go out to the highway and head north."

With no further urging, Deb charged out of the Miner's Camp parking lot with her lights flashing and siren blaring. The intersection to the highway was only a block or so behind them, but at that point OK Street was a narrow one-way road, going in the wrong direction. A blind curve at the entrance to the street made going the wrong way out of the question. The last thing they needed to do was crash into someone coming up the hill.

"He's got too much of a head start," Deb objected. "We'll never catch him."

"Try," Joanna urged.

As Detective Howell maneuvered up the narrow, shoulder-free street and down the hair-raising curves of Youngblood Hill, Joanna held on to the grab bar for dear life. As they started down Brewery Gulch, Tica called back. "Detective Carbajal and Deputy Ruiz are on their way to the Pit," Tica said, "with an ETA of two minutes out."

Joanna looked at her watch. "Good enough," she said. "That should work."

"Chief Deputy Hadlock is on his way in. Is there anything else you need?"

"Who's coming from Sierra Vista on Highway 90?"

"That would be Deputy Stock. He's just leaving Sierra Vista now."

"Have him set up a roadblock east of the San Pedro River. He should be able to get that far before the carjacker does. Then call the Border Patrol. We'll use their inspection station at Davis Road as our northbound roadblock. Tell everyone concerned that the carjacker is a suspect in not one but two homicides, and that the woman in the car with him is the grandmother of one of the victims. He is definitely to be considered armed and dangerous."

Joanna had worked hard to maintain a good rapport with the local Border Patrol guys. Whatever the head honchos in D.C. might do or say, the guys on the ground knew Sheriff Brady on an up-close and personal basis. When she asked for something, they paid attention.

"Tell Chief Deputy Hadlock to have everyone else stand by. If Chief Bernard says he needs assistance, we'll give him whatever he needs."

"He already asked," Tica said. "He needs people to divert traffic away from the downtown area. We've got people on their way there now."

Approaching the tunnel, Deb slowed and pulled over to the shoulder. Joanna watched as two speeding ambulances, sirens screaming, burst onto the highway from the entrance ramp behind them and then headed north, taking injury victims to other hospitals. The most seriously affected were likely headed for the trauma center at University Medical Center in Tucson. They were not Joanna's concern. Her problem was James Gunnar Cameron. Where was he going, and how much time did they have?

Joanna was convinced that time was running out for Isadora Creswell. If her grandson had his way, Jimmy's reunion with his grandmother was destined to end the same way the reunion with his long-lost sister had ended. Debra Highsmith was already dead; soon Isadora would be, too. Unless a miracle happened, Isadora Creswell was doomed.

"I'm sure we've missed them," Detective Howell said. "What do you want me to do now?"

"Pull over here," Joanna said, pointing to a parking spot in a decommissioned rest area.

"He's driving a limo," Deb said. "That should be easy to spot. He's never going to get away with this.

You've got roadblocks everywhere. We're bound to catch him."

It took a moment for Deb's words to sink in. When they did, Joanna was left feeling sick to her stomach.

"Maybe that's it," she said. "Maybe James Cameron has zero intention of getting away. That puts every police officer who comes across this guy in mortal danger."

Which made an already bad situation that much worse. If Cameron had made up his mind that he was on his way out, the only question was, how many people would he take with him?

Chapter 23

Joanna and Deb Howell sat in the car for a few moments. Joanna appreciated the silence. It gave her time to think. Seconds later, inspiration hit. Maybe someone could get a line on the limo's GPS.

She called Tica back. "Is the limo driver still at the hotel?"

"As far as I know."

"Give me the number of the hotel."

Once Joanna had the number, she dialed it. After several rings someone answered.

"This is Sheriff Joanna Brady. Is the limo driver still there?"

"He's busy. He's talking to a Chief Bernard right now. I'm not sure I should interrupt."

"Let me talk to Chief Bernard, then. It's important."

A moment later Alvin Bernard came on the phone. "Joanna, what's up?" he asked. "Do you really think the carjacker is the killer?"

"Yes, I do. How did he pull off the carjacking?"

"He was evidently sitting on the patio having a leisurely breakfast or brunch or whatever. When the limo pulled up, he waited until the driver went inside, then he jumped over the barrier and took off."

"So he knew she was going there. How?"

"The clerk says someone called earlier to ask if Ms. Creswell had checked in yet. When she told him no, he declined to leave a message."

"Because he was the message," Joanna said.

"So who is this guy? What's he up to?"

"Isadora Creswell is Debra Highsmith's grandmother. James Cameron, the carjacker, is Debra's half brother and Isadora's grandson. He signed up as one of the Plein Air artists under the name Richard Reed, but that was all a cover to get close to Debra. He killed his sister, and I believe he intends to knock off Isadora, too. Maggie Oliphant was collateral damage. She had to go when she discovered late yesterday afternoon that Richard Reed didn't exist. James Cameron registered for the conference under an assumed name."

"In other words, if we don't find him right away, the old woman is a goner."

"Exactly."

"We're already working on that," Chief Bernard said. "The limo isn't equipped with a GPS, but the driver's phone is. That was left on the front seat. We've got someone from the Department of Public Safety working with the cell phone provider to see if they can triangulate the position on the cell phone. If he didn't throw it out, that is. In the meantime, where are you?"

"On the far side of the tunnel."

"Tica told me that you had roadblocks set up everywhere, but that so far there's no sign of him."

"That's the problem," Joanna said. "What if he isn't going anywhere? He took Debra out into the desert to kill her. If he's doing the same thing with Isadora, somewhere between here and the San Pedro River or this side of Tombstone, there's nothing but wide-open spaces."

"Yes, but it's broad daylight," Chief Bernard replied. "Most of the roads out there lead to ranches or houses. We're putting out a news bulletin to all the media for people to be on the lookout for this guy. He's bound to turn up."

"How bad is it there?" Joanna asked.

"On the scene? One guy dead. Two critically injured are being transported by helicopter, but we have to get them down to the hospital here before that can happen. They're being transported to Tucson. Four more with serious injuries. Two are on their way to Sierra Vista. The other two are going to the hospital here."

"How come he lost control?"

"Speed, of course," Chief Bernard said, "but one of the witnesses reported that it looked like the old woman in the backseat was whacking him on the head with something, maybe a cane."

Despite the terrible toll the accident had taken, Joanna felt better knowing that Isadora hadn't taken the situation lying down. She had been fighting back for everything she was worth. That counted for something, didn't it?

"All right then," Joanna said. "If you get any information from the phone triangulation, let me know. You have my number."

"What now?" Deb asked.

"We've missed him," Joanna said. "We might just as well head back to town."

It was as Deb Howell executed a U-turn that Joanna caught sight of the communications towers crowning the top of Juniper Flats, the highest readily accessible point in the Mule Mountains. There were utility access roads on top of the mountain that led to the towers, but no one lived there. Of all those wide-open spaces she had mentioned to Chief Bernard, Juniper Flats was by far the most deserted.

"Turn around again," she ordered Deb. "When you get to the Old Divide Road, turn up that."

Deb complied. "You think he's up there?"

This was just a hunch, after all, but Joanna felt a surprising sense of certainty. "I'd almost be willing to bet on it."

Old Divide Road predated the tunnel, and wound along the side of the mountain with permanent no-passing zones laid down as the center line. The road was reasonably well maintained, but it was narrow and treacherous and didn't allow for any kind of speed. It took almost ten minutes for them to reach the remains of a long-deserted restaurant. A sign covered with graffiti still showed a faded shadow of the original content: THE TOP. Before the building of the tunnel, the Top had been an old-fashioned roadhouse and one of Bisbee's few fine-dining establishments. Now it was nothing but a burned-out hulk.

Deb turned off the road and drove past the building and onto a gravel access road. A few yards beyond the building they came to a mangled chain-link gate hanging from a bent metal post where a broken chain and a useless padlock testified that the gate had once been securely fastened.

As soon as Joanna saw the mangled remains of the gate, she knew she was right. James Gunnar Cameron had indeed come through here. With Isadora and her flailing cane loose in the backseat, he hadn't been able to risk getting out of the vehicle long enough to open the gate. Instead, he had simply used the powerful bulk of the limo to plow through the puny obstacle.

By then Joanna was on the phone to her chief deputy. "I need the Emergency Response Team now!" she ordered. "Top of the Divide. I believe the carjacker is on one of the access roads that crisscross Juniper Flats. Those roads are designed for trucks or for serious four-wheel-type vehicles. He won't get far. When he figures that out, all hell is going to break loose."

"Deploying the ERT is going to take time," Hadlock said. "With everything that's going on, I've got people scattered six ways to Sunday. Traffic on the highway leading in and out of Bisbee has come to a complete stop. It's a mess out there."

"Time is the one thing we don't have," Joanna said grimly. "Detective Howell and I are on the scene. Get people here immediately. Make that sooner than immediately!"

Joanna turned to Deb. "Stay here," she said. "Let me take a look." She walked through the gate. The gravel surface left no tracks for her to read, but about fifty yards beyond the gate, a crumpled black bumper with chrome-trim strips lay off to the side of the narrow dirt track. It had been torn loose by the gate but hadn't fallen off until sometime later.

Joanna went back to the Tahoe and signaled for Deb to shut it down. Then she called Tom Hadlock again. "Okay, Detective Howell and I are going in. Right now we have the element of surprise on our side. We're leaving enough room for the ERT to get past Deb's Tahoe, but be sure they know that there are four people out here—two friendlies, a victim, and a bad guy. Stay on the line. I'm turning my phone on speaker so you'll be able to hear what's going on, but maintain silence on your end. Got it?"

"Got it," Hadlock replied.

She turned to Deb. "We may not have time to wait for the ERTs," she said. "Lock up, turn your phone on silent, bring your shotgun, and let's go!"

They moved forward with Joanna on one side of the narrow road and Deb on the other. They walked along in dead silence, weapons drawn, taking cover under the scrub oak and low-lying juniper that gave the area its name. A hundred yards or so beyond the broken bumper, they came across the tread of a wide passenger car that had delaminated into the dirt. Joanna knew they weren't far behind it, because the smell of hot rubber still lingered in the air, and a trail of oil or water dribbled along in the middle of the dirt. If Cameron was limping along on three tires and a flat on a vehicle that was losing either oil or water, it wouldn't be long before they caught up with him.

Then they did. Joanna spied the limo when a splash of afternoon sunlight glinted off the back window. She held up her hand, signaling for Deb to stop.

"We've made visual contact with the vehicle, but not with the driver or the victim," Joanna whispered into the phone. "Tell the ERT that we're about three-quarters of a mile beyond where we left Deb's Tahoe. The limo appears to have suffered damage. I doubt it's drivable. We're going to move closer. Keep silent until I tell you otherwise."

Only a few years earlier cell phone reception in the Bisbee area had been spotty at best. Now, due in no small part to the towers just coming into view ahead of them, even a whispered conversation carried loud and clear.

"Good luck, Sheriff Brady," Hadlock whispered back. "Our guys are on their way, but I'll be holding my breath."

Me, too, Joanna thought.

The April air was sunny but cool. Still, Joanna felt cold sweat forming between her shoulder blades and under her arms, soaking through the khaki uniform. It dripped down her forehead and dribbled past her eyes. If there were any predators in the area other than James Gunnar Cameron, Joanna was sure they could smell the fear Joanna's body shed with every careful step.

The desert here wasn't completely silent. Overhead, a red-tailed hawk wheeled in the sky, occasionally letting loose with one of its distinctive shrieks. A flock of crows squawked their noisy objection to the presence of the hawk, while a male quail issued a stern warning to his covey that there was danger about. Joanna was sorry that it was too early in the spring for insects to be on the wing and in the grasses and brush, issuing sounds that might help cover the crack of a tiny broken twig or the telltale crunch of a foot falling on a clump of dried grass.

Of course, there was a chance that they were too late and that Isadora was already dead. They hadn't yet heard the sound of a gunshot. Cameron might have used picture-hanging wire to strangle Maggie Oliphant, but Joanna suspected that had been a weapon of convenience. There in the parking lot he'd had to use the first weapon that had come readily to hand, and one that ensured a certain measure of silence. Out here in the middle of nowhere, with silence not as much of a necessity, she suspected that a handgun of some kind would be more likely. A shot from one of those would let them know for sure that they were too late.

After a few more steps, Joanna heard Isadora's distinctive voice and breathed a sigh of relief. "Let me go!" Isadora demanded. "You have no right to do this."

"I have every right," he shouted back. "You crazy old battle-ax. What were you thinking, hitting me over the head with your cane like that? It's a miracle you didn't kill us both."

"I'm sorry I didn't," Isadora returned. "I would have done the world a favor."

They were close enough now for Joanna to see them through a break in the brush. They were in a small clearing, the slender metal structure of a tower soaring above them. Isadora was sitting slightly to the side of the tower, leaning against the crooked trunk of a scrub oak. James stood several feet away from her. A spiderweb of shadows from the steel structure overhead covered his body, obscuring some of his features. The wrecked limo sat in the foreground with its air bags deployed and its overheated engine still steaming. Clearly the once fine automobile had reached the end of the line.

"What are you going to do now," Isadora taunted, "shoot me like you did Debra or strangle me like you did that other poor woman? You killed her, too, didn't you?"

"Shooting's too good for you," he said. "I'm going to leave you here to bleed out the same way I did Debra Highsmith."

"Why?" Isadora demanded. "What did I ever do to you? What did Debra?"

"Don't you mean Alyse?" he asked sarcastically. "Don't you mean my dear departed older sister Alyse who turned my father in so the CIA could kill him and claim he committed suicide? He never had a trial, you know. They made sure of that. As for what became of Alyse? She simply disappeared. Vanished. How convenient! Mother always said you were behind it somehow, but we could never prove it. We could never figure out how you got Alyse away from the house or where you stowed her afterward."

"Your father was the one who was in the wrong," Isadora said, "and Alyse didn't turn him in. She happened to see something she shouldn't have and mentioned it to us. We're the ones who blew the whistle. We're the ones who called the authorities—your grandfather and I."

"Without Alyse, you wouldn't have," James insisted. "Her blabbing to you ended up costing Mother and me everything. We lost the house and the cars. We had to go live with Mother's parents on the farm. We left Washington, D.C., and ended up living with people who barely had indoor plumbing, even then. You never lifted a finger to help us."

"That's not true," Isadora said. "I tried to help. I sent letters with checks inside. I sent birthday cards and Christmas presents. Your mother always returned them unopened."

"She didn't," James said.

Isadora shook her head and said nothing.

"Mother committed suicide, you know," James said after a long pause. "I was ten. Think about how that helped me growing up. The other kids said I had to be some kind of freak to make both my parents commit suicide. I was the smart weird kid, the one with no friends. I hated the other kids. I hated Indiana. I hated my grandparents. They were stupid people. I left there the minute I graduated from high school and never looked back."

Joanna was close enough now to see that there was something odd about the left side of James's face. At first Joanna thought it was only the play of shadows across his features. Now she realized that his face was cut and bleeding. The wreckage of his wire-framed glasses sat perched crookedly on his face, but one of the lenses was missing, and the eye on that side was bloodied and almost swollen shut.

Seeing the damage, Joanna realized two things at once. There was no way to tell if the air bags had deployed when Cameron plowed into the people on the sidewalk or when he drove through the gate. Whenever it happened, however, the air bags had hit his glasses hard enough to smash them to smithereens. Since he was nearsighted enough to need glasses, that meant he was now at a serious disadvantage. He might be able to see fine out of his right eye, the one on Joanna's side, but maybe not nearly as well on the side where Deb was approaching.

"How did you find her?" Isadora asked.

"It took years," he said. "I've devoted my whole adult life to finding her. I'm what they like to call a visionary in the science of facial recognition, and now you know why. I knew that once the systems could be made to scan online photos that I'd be able to find her eventually. It was only a matter of time. You see, after Mother died, I found a picture of the four of us in a box of my mother's stuff. I think she sent it out with the Christmas cards that one year. I'm not sure why she kept it, but that's why I did, and I have it still. I took Alyse's image from that, and that's what I used to find her. I've had multiple computers scanning the Internet for years, looking for a match. When that video showed up, I knew I had to act fast before you made her disappear again."

"What video?" Isadora asked.

James laughed. "You don't know about that, do you? She pissed off some kid at her school, and he posted a video of her on the Net. He called it 'Die, Bitch,' which I thought was altogether too appropriate. Don't you?"

Isadora leveled a cold stare at him and again said nothing.

Behind her Joanna heard the smallest hint of an approaching siren. That meant that her Emergency Response Team had been summoned and was coming, but at this point in the proceedings, they wouldn't make it. Not in time. Their help would be too little, too late. By the time they reached the clearing, whatever was going to happen would already have played out.

Joanna stopped moving, concealing herself behind the final layer of scrub oak before it gave way to the clearing. She couldn't see Deb, but Joanna knew the detective was still off to the right, invisible behind a thick clump of low-growing juniper. Joanna was standing there, contemplating her next move, when Isadora chose to escalate the situation.

"Your father may have been my son," she said calmly, "but he was also a traitor to his country and a coward besides. You're just like him."

The utter contempt of the insult had its intended effect. With breathtaking speed, James closed the distance between them. As his raised foot connected with

Isadora's hip, Joanna heard the sickening and unmistakable crack of splintering bone. Isadora groaned in pain, but she didn't let up.

"Yes," she added through gritted teeth. "You're exactly like your father."

Despite the seriousness of the situation, Joanna couldn't help but feel a surge of admiration. Isadora may have looked frail—as though a strong wind could have blown her over—but she was tough as nails.

Up to that moment, there had been no sign of a weapon in the confrontation, but just then one appeared, as though on cue. Evidently James Gunnar Cameron was a killer who felt no need to stick with any previously used MO. Instead of drawing a handgun or producing a length of picture wire, he pulled a switchblade out of the pocket of his jacket. It flicked open with a chilling click that sent a shiver of dread down Joanna's spine.

"You'll never get away with this," Isadora gasped.

"You don't understand," he said. "I don't care about getting away with it. I'm going to end it here and now. With you and your precious Alyse wiped from the face of the earth, it'll all be over. It won't matter what happens to me."

"You're wrong," Isadora said. Her voice was suddenly clear and surprisingly calm. "It won't be over,

James. It will never be over. Debra had a son. His name is Michael. Everything I have will go to him."

That unwelcome news seemed to push James over the edge. "You're lying," he screeched back at her. "Debra Highsmith never had any children. I know. I checked!"

He held the raised knife by the handle. Before he could drive it home, Joanna chose that moment to step into view.

"Drop the knife," she ordered. "Get on the ground."

Startled, his one good eye jerked in Joanna's direction, but he didn't drop the knife. Instead, he reached down, grabbed Isadora by the collar of her jacket one-handed, and dragged her upright. One of Isadora's legs, the one he had kicked, dangled at a crazy angle. She howled in agony.

"No," James countered, now holding the knife at Isadora's throat. "You drop it. You can't shoot me without shooting her. You wouldn't want to do that to a helpless old lady, now would you?"

He stared at Joanna through his one good eye, squinting into the sun. Behind him Joanna caught sight of a slight movement. That meant Debra was closing in on him, coming at him from behind. Joanna's whole purpose now was to keep his focus on her no matter what.

"He's a monster," Isadora screamed. "Go ahead. Shoot him!"

With Debra behind him, Joanna couldn't have risked a shot anyway. Instead, she made a production of carefully leaning over and depositing her Glock on the ground at her feet. It was a calculated risk. If he slit Isadora's throat or if he charged at Joanna with the knife, either one or both of them might well be dead before Debra could make her move. Joanna was wearing her vest, but she knew that Kevlar offers far more protection from bullets than it does from knives. What she needed was some way to keep him occupied and talking rather than launching a deadly attack.

"Kick the gun here," he said.

Joanna complied. Her well-placed kick sent the gun skidding across the intervening open ground. It came to a stop at his feet. By then she had come up with what she hoped would be a plausible ruse. Once the gun stopped moving, Joanna simply turned her back on the man. She looked back the way she had come, trying to make it appear as though she didn't have a care in the world.

"It's okay, Michael," she called to the empty landscape behind her. "You can come out now. I want you to meet your great-grandmother and your uncle."

She stood there in the breathless silence with her back turned to James, counting on a combination of shock and curiosity about Michael Hirales, a man who wasn't there, to stall James Cameron long enough for Debra to make her move. Joanna had no way of knowing if her performance was good enough. There was always a chance that the long, thin blade would slice first into Isadora's throat and then into Joanna's back.

"Michael," Joanna called again. "Come on!"

Just then she heard a heavy thwack as the butt of Deb's shotgun slammed into the back of James's head. He groaned. As he fell to the ground, Joanna turned. At first, all she saw was a tangled heap of limbs, with James's body clearly on top. For a time Joanna thought she had misjudged the situation—and that while her back was turned, James had turned the blade on his grandmother. Instead, after a long moment, the old woman wiggled to life and began to squirm out from under James's dead weight. She scrabbled away from her fallen grandson, dragging her useless leg behind her.

Joanna hurried up to the injured woman. "Stay still," she ordered. "Let us get you some help."

"Where's Michael?" Isadora wanted to know. "Is he really here?"

Behind Isadora, Joanna caught sight of Deb, a pair of cuffs in hand, bending over James Cameron. Somehow, in the face of all that, Isadora's question struck Joanna's funny bone. Her grandson had almost murdered her, but all Isadora cared about was catching a glimpse of the great-grandson she had never met.

Somehow Joanna managed to stifle a completely inappropriate giggle. Pulling out her phone, she spoke up. "We're clear," she managed. "Repeat, we're clear. One in custody, one casualty. We'll need a MedEvac helicopter on Juniper Flats. ASAP. We're in one of the clearings up here. They'll have to find us."

"But where's Michael?" Isadora insisted through what must have been mind-numbing pain. "What have you done with him?"

"I'm sorry," Joanna said, and she truly was sorry. "Michael isn't here. That was just a trick."

"A trick?" Isadora asked uncomprehendingly. "What do you mean, a trick?"

"I had to do something to keep James looking in this direction."

"Oh," Isadora said as a sob of disappointment rose in her throat. "I was so hoping he was here. I really want to meet him."

With that Isadora fainted dead away.

Chapter 24

S eeing Isadora's pasty white face, Joanna dialed Dispatch again.

"I've got a serious casualty here," Joanna said. "Are any of those visiting EMT crews still in the area?"

Medical teams from Sierra Vista, Tombstone, and Douglas had all responded to the accident scene in Upper Bisbee.

"I think one of the units from Sierra Vista may still be there, or they might just be leaving. I'll try to divert them in your direction."

Hurrying over to the dead limo, Joanna opened the door and pushed the trunk release. She was gratified to see an emergency kit that included a lightweight blanket that looked more like tinfoil than cloth. She was just covering Isadora with that when Jaime Carbajal jogged into the clearing. He was the first member of Joanna's ERT to arrive on the scene, and he looked worried.

"Dispatch said someone was hurt," he said. "Who is it? One of ours? What happened?"

"Isadora Creswell," Joanna said. "Broken hip. I've called for a helicopter, but I've also called for any EMTs in the area to show up. Could you go help direct them?"

Joanna turned back to Isadora, who seemed to have regained consciousness. "Stay with us," she urged. "Help is coming."

Isadora whispered something that Joanna didn't quite catch. She leaned closer. "Say again?"

"Hurts," Isadora said.

Joanna nodded. "I'm sure it does."

"Could be worse," Isadora added through gritted teeth. "Broke my bad hip, though, not the one they already fixed."

Somewhere behind her, Joanna heard the distinctive squawk of an arriving ambulance. Joanna had some first-aid training, but not enough for a situation this serious. She was glad to know that professionals were in the near neighborhood.

Joanna dialed Dispatch again. "Any ETA on that MedEvac?" she asked.

"They're at least thirty minutes out," Tica replied. "Maybe longer."

Just then, to Joanna's relief, Jaime jogged back into the clearing, followed by two uniformed EMTs, one of them carrying a full kit.

Isadora was gone again. Kneeling beside her one of the EMTs asked, "What's her name?"

"Isadora," Joanna answered. "She may have a broken hip. I covered her because I thought she was going into shock."

"Okay," he said. "We'll take over from here. Isadora," he called, "can you hear me?"

Joanna was more than happy to relinquish her spot next to Isadora. By then the rest of the Emergency Response Team had made it into the clearing as well. They were clustered around Deb, who was busy hauling James Cameron to his feet.

"There's a knife around here somewhere," Joanna told Jaime. "He had a switchblade and was threatening to carve Isadora up with it when Deb whacked him on the back of the head with her shotgun."

"So no shots were fired?" Jaime asked anxiously.

"That's right," Joanna said. "No shots, and we both know that's going to make our lives a whole lot easier."

There was a complicated protocol for the aftermath of officer-involved shootings, and that was something Joanna was happy to avoid right about then. Once the media got hold of the story, a thump on the head was always a lot easier to explain than a stray bullet or two. While Jaime took off his ERT gear and resumed his more customary role of detective, Joanna hurried over to where Deb Howell was in the process of reading James Gunnar Cameron his rights.

Just then two people Joanna hadn't expected to see burst through the scrub oak and into the clearing. Sue Ellen Hirales was followed by a young man Joanna had never seen before, one who had to be Isadora's great-grandson, Michael.

"Chief Bernard told us what was going on," the young man said. "Where is she?" Surrounded by the EMTs, Isadora was entirely invisible from where he stood. "Is she all right?"

Joanna stepped forward. "I'm Sheriff Brady," she explained. "Isadora was injured. She's over there," she added, nodding in the direction of the EMTs. "Most likely a broken hip. The ambulance crew from Sierra Vista is looking after her for now, but we've called for a MedEvac helicopter to take her to Tucson. They should be here soon."

"What happened to her?" Michael asked.

The question was most likely intended for Joanna, but James Cameron was the one who answered. "I kicked her," he sneered. "Like I'd kick a rabid dog if

I had to. She deserved it, and so did my sister. Believe me, Alyse Creswell deserved whatever she got."

Michael looked first at him and then back to Joanna. "This is my birth mother's half brother?" he asked. "This is the man who killed her?"

Before anyone could answer the question, Sue Ellen Hirales flung herself at James Gunnar Cameron, ready to deck the man with her bare fists. "You son of a—"

Only a lightning-quick response on Michael's part kept the blows from landing.

"It's all right, Sue Ellen," he said, grasping her arm and holding her back. "Leave him be. Come on. We've got better things to do. Let's go meet my great-grandmother."

While Sue Ellen allowed herself to be led away, Joanna turned back to her officers. The sudden ending of the confrontation left her almost light-headed as the adrenaline rush dissipated. She paused and had to take a few deep breaths before she was able to begin issuing orders.

"Mr. Cameron here has received several serious blows to the head this afternoon," she told Deb. "Stop by the ER at the hospital on your way to the Justice Center. They're going to be busy, but we need to have someone check him out for a possible concussion and maybe stitch up the cut on his eye before you book him. For right now, he's to be jailed on suspicion of two counts of homicide and one count of vehicular homicide. He told us a little while ago that he doesn't care if he lives or dies, so I want to be sure he's under a suicide watch."

"Got it," Deb said.

Just then, Jaime approached Joanna, holding the switchblade in a gloved hand. "This is the suspect's knife?" he asked.

Joanna nodded. "That's it." When James had been holding it, the knife had seemed much larger and much more lethal than it did as Jaime first slipped it into an evidence bag and then, lacking a collection box, dropped the bag into a pocket of his jacket. By then Deb and Deputy Lang were in the process of setting off toward the vehicles with James Cameron locked between them. Jaime hurried after them.

"Hey, Deb," Jaime called, "hold up a minute."

"Why?"

"I want to check something out."

Approaching the prisoner, Jaime pulled up one of the sleeves on his jacket. From the cuff of his sleeve down, James Cameron's skin was fine. From the cuff up, however, his lower arm was covered with a tangled map of scratches.

Nodding, Jaime dropped the sleeve back in place. "That's what I thought," he said. "Just before all hell broke loose in town, Dr. Machett and I were finishing up with Maggie Oliphant's autopsy. There was all kinds of DNA evidence under her nails. She evidently fought her assailant like crazy. He was wearing gloves, so his hands aren't damaged, but his forearms are."

"Okay," Joanna said, finally switching gears out of confrontational mode and into analysis. "Detective Howell, when you book him, be sure you collect a DNA sample. I want that sample at the crime lab in Tucson ASAP. Got it?"

"Yes, ma'am," Detective Howell answered. "It'll be there this afternoon if I have to drive it up myself."

"Crap!" someone exclaimed behind her.

Joanna turned and found Police Chief Alvin Bernard examining the damaged limo. "I suppose my department is going to be stuck with the towing bill."

"You've probably got the limo for vehicular homicide inside the city limits. All I've got in the county is property damage, but I'll flip you for it," she offered.

Chief Bernard was peering at damage on the passenger side of the windshield, where it looked as though a rock might have broken the glass. "I'd say this is where my victim's head hit the glass," he said, "so no, this one is mine. I'll handle it."

"How are things in town?"

"Still a mess," Bernard conceded. "We've asked the Arizona Department of Public Safety to assist with their accident-investigation team, but since it's a fatality incident, that process is going to take hours. Tombstone Canyon is still closed to all traffic. Residents of the area are being allowed through, but we're continuing to divert all other traffic away from Upper Bisbee. Your mother came down from Horace Mann to give me an earful about it because, in her opinion, I was single-handedly wrecking some event or another. I doubt that's news to you. I suppose you're already aware that your mother can be a bit of a handful on occasion."

Joanna nodded. Eleanor Lathrop Winfield had always been a handful.

While Joanna and Chief Bernard had been talking, the Sierra Vista ambulance eased past the wrecked limo. "What's going on?" Joanna asked when Jaime came by again as well.

"The helicopter is almost here. The EMT crew thinks there's more room for them to land in the next clearing over than there is here. They've splinted her hip and stabilized it as well as they can. Now they're going to use the ambulance to transport her to wherever the chopper is able to land to pick her up."

While Joanna watched, a gurney with Isadora strapped to it was loaded into the ambulance. Once she was inside, Michael climbed in with her. With the blades of the arriving helicopter pounding overhead, the ambulance eased itself toward the next clearing while Sue Ellen came back to where Joanna was standing.

"She's something, isn't she?" Sue Ellen said admiringly. "She told them she wasn't going unless Michael went with her, and she was absolutely adamant about it. I'm guessing it'll be the same way with the helicopter. If he doesn't go, she doesn't go. No wonder Debra was so stubborn. The EMTs told me that the MedEvac crew will take her to TMC. Depending on the break, they may be able to do hip replacement surgery immediately or they may have to delay it. Either way, TMC is the best place for her. I told Michael I'd follow in the car and be there as fast as I can."

Joanna's phone rang. Caller ID told her it was her chief deputy. For a split second, she was worried that James Gunnar Cameron might have made some kind of break for it, but that wasn't the problem.

"Hey, boss," Tom Hadlock said. "Deb just told me that the whole top of the Divide is crawling with media vans. I have no idea how they got there so fast, but they did. Who's going to talk to them? I can come up there and do it if you want, but . . ."

"No," Joanna said. "You stay put and make sure Mr. Cameron gets booked into the lockup. This set of media relations is on me and Chief Bernard. We'll handle it together."

That's what they did, standing side by side in the clearing at the top of the Divide with the scrub-oak-studded red rock cliffs of the Mule Mountains glowing in the background. They didn't say much, only enough to get by. A suspect in two homicides as well as the afternoon's carjacking incident had been taken into custody without incident. Because Cameron had not yet been officially charged with any crime, his name would not be released. An elderly female relative of the suspect's had been injured and was currently being airlifted to Tucson.

That was Joanna's part of the proceedings. Chief Bernard's was a bit more complex. He had to deal with the ongoing traffic issues in town as well as with the fact that victims of the vehicular assault had been transported to various hospitals in the area. No names of any of the victims, including the fatality, could be released pending notification of next of kin.

By the time the impromptu press conference ended, Dave Hollicker had arrived to do the crime scene investigation. "Hey," she told him, "you guys don't need me hanging around and getting in the way. It's been a tough weekend so far, and I'm going to go home. If somebody wants to interview me, that's where I'll be."

It sounded good, but there was one problem. Joanna's Yukon was still parked in the lot at Horace Mann School.

"Hey, Chief Bernard," she called after him before he had a chance to get away. "Would you mind giving me a ride back down the canyon? I left my car in the art league parking lot, and I need to go pick it up."

"I will on one condition," he said.

"What's that?"

"If your mother comes out to the parking lot, you have to deal with her instead of me."

"Fair enough," Joanna said. "Let's go."

Chapter 25

When Chief Bernard stopped his aging Crown Victoria in front of Horace Mann, Eleanor's bright red Miata was parked outside, and she was busy loading what appeared to be a collection of plastic gallon jugs into the tiny trunk.

"Good luck," Chief Bernard said. "I trust you'll forgive me if I drop you off and keep on going. I've already had one tangle with that woman today. I don't need another one."

Eleanor stopped loading her trunk long enough to send a disparaging glare after Chief Bernard's departing vehicle. She stood, shaking her head, with both hands planted on her hips. If looks could have killed, Alvin Bernard would have perished on the spot.

"You'd think he could have made some exception for people trying to get to the reception," Eleanor said, "but no. That's not how it works. They shut down access to everything but local residents, so here I am stuck with gallons of Arizona punch and no telling how many dozens of cookies."

"Can I help you load something?" Joanna asked.

Eleanor picked up one final jug of punch. "This one won't fit. If you'd take that home, maybe your kids will drink it. Otherwise I'll have to leave it here in the street."

Joanna obligingly took the jug of punch.

"What on earth am I going to do with all those cookies?"

The boxes of cookies that were stacked next to Eleanor's vehicle were never going to fit in the Miata.

"I could take them home and freeze them, if that would help," Joanna offered.

"What a good idea," Eleanor said. "I hate to think of them going to waste."

Joanna knew that between Debra Highsmith's and Maggie Oliphant's deaths Bisbee would be having at least two major funerals in the next several days. That meant that no matter how many cookies hadn't been consumed at the Plein Air reception, all of them would be put to good use eventually. Joanna knew that but she didn't say it aloud. She was smart enough to real-ize that she and her mother would both be better off if Eleanor arrived at that conclusion on her own.

Instead, with no further discussion, Joanna and her mother set about loading a small mountain of cookie boxes into the back of Joanna's Yukon.

"I'm sorry the reception turned out to be such a fiasco," Joanna said.

"Not completely," Eleanor said. "It could have been worse. Right in the middle of the whole disaster, some-one from an art gallery in Tucson sent me a tweet."

Joanna's jaw dropped. That was her first hint ever that her mother had a Twitter account. Again she man-aged to keep her mouth shut.

"I don't know how, but he had heard that the sus-pect might be one of our Plein Air participants, which, unfortunately, I was able to confirm. It turns out he has a guy, a collector, who specializes in the artwork of suspected and convicted killers. It takes all kinds, you know. He asked me if any of the suspect's works were available for sale. I told him we happened to have one—the one Richard Reed painted of, it turns out, Debra Highsmith's house. It was in the show and our contract said we could sell it and keep fifty percent of the proceeds. When the tweet came in, it was marked at two thousand dollars. I quadrupled that, and the collector sent through his credit card number. So at least we made some money on the deal and the reception wasn't a complete loss."

Sheriff Brady had her own set of issues about anyone, most especially her mother's art league, profiting as a result of someone's murder.

Eleanor seemed to read her mind. "Believe me," she said, "Maggie would have approved. At least we got something out of the guy. Butch helped, too, of course."

"Butch?" Joanna asked. "He was here?"

"No," Eleanor said, "but believe me, he helped."

They finally finished loading the cookies. Joanna was grateful that Eleanor was so preoccupied with her own concerns she didn't ask a single question about what had gone on up on Juniper Flats, and Joanna didn't volunteer. Instead, she took her load of leftover cookies and headed home. She knew that the next day and the day after that and the day after that would be chock-full of paperwork and reports and meetings about what had happened on Main Street as well as what had happened on Juniper Flats. For right then, however, what Joanna needed more than anything was to step away from the job and return to a semblance of normal life.

She needed to reclaim her Sunday. She needed to see her kids and her dogs. She needed to see her husband. She needed to talk to someone who wasn't a fellow cop or a suspect or a victim. She needed to feel like an ordinary human being.

When she got home, however, no dogs greeted her in the yard. When she let herself into the kitchen through the laundry room, the house was uncharacteristically quiet. Dirty dishes from lunch were still on the counter. If Butch had set aside some dinner for her, it wasn't showing, and nobody seemed to be home. She knew too much about too many bad things to not find the oddly silent house disquieting.

"Hello," she called. "Anybody here?"

"Office," Butch called.

She went into the office to find Butch leaning back in his chair with both feet propped on the desk, reading one of her father's distinctive leather-bound journals. The bookshelf where the collection of journals usually sat was entirely empty, while the books themselves, some of them showing a trail of yellow Post-it notes, were stacked all over the desk and sofa. If he had managed to help out with the situation at Horace Mann, Joanna didn't see how it was possible.

"Hey, Joey," he said, looking at her over the top of the volume in his hand. "Did anybody ever tell you that your father was a hell of a guy?"

She cleared a space on the sofa and settled on it. "Someone may have mentioned that occasionally," she said with a smile. "Where is everybody?"

"Carol saw that I was busy with this, so she invited everyone over for popcorn and movies."

"Dogs, too?"

"Dogs, too. They're probably fine with the popcorn, although I don't suppose they're watching the movies."

"Busy with what exactly?" Joanna asked.

"Reading your father's journals," Butch said. "They're a gold mine. There's enough material here for me to write a dozen books." He closed the book he was reading. "That's my day. George called me a little while ago. I'm almost afraid to ask you about yours. Did you have lunch?"

Joanna shook her head.

"We had leftovers, and the kids ate like they were starvelings. How does a grilled cheese grab you?"

"Grilled cheese sounds great."

Joanna followed him into the kitchen. While he cleaned up the mess left from lunch, Joanna went out to the garage, unloaded the extra cookies into the freezer, and then brought the gallon of punch inside.

"Leftovers, from the reception that didn't happen. But then, I guess you know all about that. Mom said you were a big help."

"I try," Butch said.

While he grilled her sandwich, Joanna gave him a rundown of the whole day. Somehow, in the telling, she neglected to mention putting down her gun and turning her back on an armed assailant. There were some things about her job Butch Dixon didn't need to know. Joanna suspected that there were things in her father's life that might have made it into D. H. Lathrop's journals but which were never the topic of dinnertime conversation, either.

"That's what Debra Highsmith's murder was all about?" Butch asked when Joanna finally ran out of story and energy. "Some kind of long-term family feud?"

"Because James's father committed suicide while in custody, there was never a trial. James's mother evidently turned a technical 'not guilty' into 'innocent of all charges.' She poisoned James against both his grandmother and his missing sister. That's why he came here. To avenge his father's death. Unfortunately, Maggie Oliphant figured out something was off about him. We may never learn what. Once he realized she had started checking out his cover story, that was enough for him to turn her into collateral damage."

They had been sitting across the table from each other while Joanna gobbled the very welcome cheese-and-jalapeño sandwich. Butch took a deep breath.

"I think your father was collateral damage in another family feud," he said.

"What are you talking about?" Joanna asked.

"Elizabeth and Wayne Stevens," Butch said. "That's how come he got pushed out of working underground for PD, but there's more to it than that."

"Wait," Joanna said. "Are you saying they had something to do with his death?"

"Not at all, but they're the reason he lost his job and ended up going to work for the sheriff's department. He took Abby Holder's side against her parents. He and your mother went to Freddy Holder's funeral, and he spent the rest of his life trying to figure out what had really happened. Come look."

Butch led Joanna back into the office. "You need to read these," he said, picking a pair of journals out of the stack. "Take a look at all the Post-it notes. It's like following a trail of bread crumbs. Every time you open to one of the pages marked by a Post-it note, you'll find a passage leading back to Fred and Abby Holder or to her parents, Wayne and Elizabeth. From the moment your father and the other guys dug up Freddy's lifeless body, your dad was convinced there was something fishy about what had happened. Once he and your mother went to Fred Holder's funeral—against Wayne Stevens's express wishes—your father's job was on the line."

"And he pushed Dad out?" Joanna asked.

"Exactly, or at least that's what your father claims in the journals. He believed they ran him off on so-called safety violations. He was really lucky to be hired on as a deputy. After he was working in law enforcement, he tried again. Once he started asking uncomfortable questions about Fred Holder, they shut him down there, too, but Wayne Stevens didn't have quite the same amount of influence in the sheriff's department that he had in town. It wasn't enough to get your father fired outright, but it was enough to have him ordered to back off. That's why your father ended up running for sheriff."

"Because of what happened to Fred Holder?"

"Yes," Butch said. "Your dad was determined to get to the bottom of it."

Joanna picked up one of the journals at random. From the dates on the cover, she knew it was one that covered the better part of two years after D. H. Lathrop had won election to the office of sheriff. Three different Post-it notes stuck out of the top of the book.

"So all these Post-it notes are references to the Holder situation?" she asked.

Butch nodded. "In the journals he notes whenever he crossed paths with any of the people from that series of events—Abby and both her parents as well as Mad Dog Muncey."

"Did he put them under actual surveillance?"

"Not really," Butch said. "At least, not officially. Even so, he made it his business to run into them more

than you'd think would happen even in a small town.
More than once he mentions thinking that eventually he
was going to get a break in the case, and finally he did."

"When?" Joanna asked.

"That's the problem," Butch said, looking hesitant.
"The break didn't come until a week before he died."

"How?"

"Mad Dog Muncey's wife, Nelda, came to see your
father at the sheriff's department. She told him that her
husband was in the hospital and most likely dying of
emphysema. Mad Dog said he wanted to speak to your
father, and so your father went to the hospital. Do you
want to read the entries for yourself?"

Joanna shook her head. Once, much earlier, Joanna
had ventured into that particular volume—the last
one—of her father's journals. In the process, she had
discovered the unwelcome news that for years before
D. H. Lathrop died, he had carried on a love affair with
someone other than his wife. The fact that one of the
last entries mentioned his giving up the other woman
in favor of not losing his daughter had done nothing
to ease the hurt and shock Joanna had felt when she
learned about her father's duplicity. Butch held it out to
her, but knowing it was the same book, Joanna couldn't
quite bring herself to touch it.

"Tell me," she said.

"I'll read it to you," Butch said. He reopened the book and started to read:

Nelda Muncey came by to see me today. She didn't make an appointment or come into the office. She caught up with me outside as I was parking my car. She told me Mad Dog was in the hospital and wanted to talk to me. I knew he'd been dusted and had emphysema, but until I got to the hospital, I had no idea how bad it was. He's on oxygen and IV pain-killers and weighs maybe a hundred and twenty pounds. He used to be double that. Made me realize I was lucky to get out of the mines when I did.

On the way to the hospital I kept thinking, "This is it." When we got there, Nelda started to come into his room with me, but Mad Dog waved her away. "Go on out and shut the door," he told her. "Just me and D.H. We're the only ones who need to be here."

He waited until she shut the door. "She told you I'm dying?"

I shook my head, but all you had to do was look at the man to know it was close to the end.

"I done it," he said.

Just like that—with no introduction, no discussion of what he was talking about. It was like we'd been having this conversation all along for more than twenty years.

"I knew that one stope was shaky—that the support beams had come loose during shutdown. I put a come-along on one of them beams, then I sent Freddy into the stope to get something I said I'd left in there. When he went inside, I gave the come-along a yank and the whole thing caved in. The rest of us were lucky that whole damn shaft didn't come down on top of us."

"Why are you telling me this now?" I asked.

"Confession's good for the soul," he said. "I don't want to meet my Maker with this on my conscience. I done it. I'm sorry."

"I know you got a new car out of the deal," I said. "So who put you up to it—Wayne Stevens?"

I could see that he was getting tired, that the conversation was wearing him down.

"Nelda don't know nothin' about any of this," he said. "If'n I tell you that, her life won't be worth a plugged nickel. You find out the answer, I'll say straight out yes or no, but whatever you find can't come from me. You hear?"

He reached over and rang the little buzzer that was pinned to his pillow. A nurse came in, so did Nelda, and that was the end of it.

I was pissed when I left the hospital. It was what I'd always known—that he was the one responsible, the triggerman. In the old days Mad Dog Muncey wasn't scared of anyone or anything, leastways not for himself, but now he was scared for Nelda. She'd just gotten a new job at the company store, and he was afraid she'd lose it. There are only a couple of people in town who wield that kind of power, and Wayne Stevens is one of them.

It was a judgment call. At that point there was nothing about Mad Dog's supposed confession that would have held up in a court of law. There weren't any witnesses to what he'd said. It would be my word alone. So I'll have to find something to corroborate what Mad Dog said, but right that minute, I wanted more than anything for Wayne Stevens to know that the jig was up—that after years of getting away with murder he wasn't going to be dodging that bullet any longer.

Instead of lying low, I decided to beard the lion in his den. I went straight there—to the general office—and marched right into Stevens's private office, past his secretary who was chasing after me saying I couldn't go in there, but I did anyway.

Stevens was on his phone when I went inside, and he took his own sweet time getting off. "Good morning, Sheriff Lathrop," he says to me, cool as can be. "This is an unexpected visit. I don't believe I see your name in my appointment book. What can I do for you?"

"I just came from Mad Dog Muncey's room at the hospital," I said. "He told me the whole story."

"What story would that be?"

"I know who's behind the hit on Freddy Holder."

"Now, now," Stevens said to me. "No one around here is going to put any stock in the ravings of a dying man."

"I put stock in it, Mr. Stevens, and I intend to prove it. If it's the last thing I do."

So help me God, I will!

Butch stopped reading, closed the book, and placed it on the desk.

"That's it?" Joanna asked.

"Not quite," Butch said. "He spent the whole next week working on it, but he wasn't getting anywhere. He was building up his nerve to go talk to Nelda. That was on the following Friday. It's the next-to-last entry. You already know about the last one."

Yes, Joanna did know about it. That was the one that had turned her whole world on its head, the one that had confirmed D. H. Lathrop's long-term relationship with his secretary, Mona Tipton. When Joanna had been scanning through her father's journals, she had been so stricken by his infidelity that she had completely overlooked this other part of the story—that at the time of his death, he had been hot on the trail of a killer. Had that material been passed along to investigators at the time of D. H. Lathrop's death, they might have made the necessary connections, but Eleanor, D. H. Lathrop's widow, had made certain that the damning material didn't see the light of day. Had it not been for George Winfield's interference in passing the journals along to Joanna, it never would have.

Yes, Joanna had overlooked that part of the story once, but she wasn't overlooking it now.

"Is it possible Wayne Stevens was behind what happened to my father?" she asked. "Behind his death, I mean?"

Butch shrugged. "I suppose," he said, "but I always thought he died after being hit by a drunk driver."

"That's what I thought, too," Joanna said numbly, "because that's what I was told, but the timing suggests otherwise."

The drunk-driving part had been a given. Joanna, her father, and two other girls from her Girl Scout troop had been coming back from a weekend campout in the Wonderland of Rocks. They had all seen the disabled car parked along the road. Joanna's father had driven a little farther down the road, then he had made a U-turn and gone back. By the time they stopped, the stranded woman was trying to wrestle the spare out of her trunk.

It was summer. The car windows had been rolled down. "Here, ma'am," Joanna remembered hearing him say. "Let me help you with that."

As far as Joanna knew, those were the last words D. H. Lathrop said. Minutes later, with the woman's car up on a jack and with the woman and her kids safely away from the vehicle, another car had appeared from out of nowhere and come screaming past them. No matter how she tried, Joanna could never forget the sound of the impact as the car smashed into her father's kneeling body or the vision of him flying through the air like a broken rag doll. Memories of her father's death still haunted Joanna's dreams from time to time. They were the kind of nightmares that brought her awake, gasping for breath, and left her shaking and dripping with sweat.

At the time it happened, Joanna had blamed herself. It wasn't her fault that her father had been out changing that tire, but the reason he was there at all—on the road, coming back from the Chiricahuas—was because of her. As a traumatized teenager, Joanna had managed to block out some of what went on back then—

some but not all. It had been a hit-and-run. The drunk driver had been caught miles away in Benson. She didn't remember that there had been any kind of trial or legal proceedings. More likely some kind of plea bargain had been put into effect.

"So who was he?" Butch asked.

"The driver?"

Butch nodded.

"I have no idea," Joanna said, "but you'd better believe I'm going to find out."

Chapter 26

There was no sense in Joanna's going back to the Justice Center to look for the information she needed. Literally thousands of dusty boxes of county records sat in storage in the old courthouse, waiting to be turned into digital files. Instead, with her computer back on the dining room table, she logged on to the Internet. She knew the date of her father's death. Newspapers statewide had covered the event in gory detail, and their records had been digitized. Within a matter of minutes she found what she was looking for—the name of her father's killer, David Fredericks.

He was a former soldier stationed at Fort Huachuca and had been dismissed from the army with an other-than-honorable discharge. At the time of the accident, Fredericks was still living in Sierra Vista. An hour and a half after the incident, he had been arrested in Benson, more than sixty miles away, on suspicion of driving while intoxicated. When he was arrested, trace evidence from his high-speed collision with D. H. Lathrop's body was still embedded in the grille of his T-bird.

Further details about the actual investigation were sketchy, but, as Joanna had surmised, the case had ended swiftly with a plea bargain in which Fredericks had pled guilty to one count of vehicular homicide, one count of hit-and-run, and one count of driving while intoxicated. He was sentenced to five years in prison. Case closed. That was where the official news record left off. Joanna was just finishing reading the last article when Carol Sunderson dropped off Jenny and Dennis.

While Butch hustled Dennis off to the bathroom for a quick bath, Jenny settled down at the dining room table. "You were on TV tonight," she said. "You and Mr. Bernard. You caught the guy?"

Joanna nodded.

"Someone on the news said he's Ms. Highsmith's brother. Is that true?"

"The man hasn't been officially charged yet, so his name hasn't been released," Joanna said. "That kind of information shouldn't be out there, but yes, he's her half brother."

"So why did he do it?" Jenny wanted to know.

It frustrated Joanna to realize that once again the media was getting ahead of the law enforcement process. She shrugged. "I'm not sure. It's evidently something that happened between them when they were kids. He's spent his adult life consumed with anger and jealousy, plotting a way to get his revenge."

"Will that ever happen with Denny and me?"

Jenny was clearly nuts about her baby half brother and had been since the day he was born. Joanna smiled at her daughter and shook her head. "I don't think so," she said. "Never in a million years."

Jenny leaned over and stared at the photo—clearly a mug shot—that was visible on Joanna's computer screen.

"Is that him?"

"No," Joanna said, "that's a guy named David Fredericks."

"What did David Fredericks do?" Jenny asked.

The question wasn't a surprise. The presence of a mug shot made it clear that he must have done something.

"He was the drunk driver who hit and killed my father, your grandfather, when I was about your age." Joanna realized then that Jenny knew more about George Winfield, her stepgrandfather, than she did about her birth grandfather. One reason for that probably had to do with Joanna's continuing reluctance to talk about it.

"Were you there when it happened?" Jenny asked.

"Yes, I was."

"Did you see it?"

Joanna hesitated before she answered but only for a moment. "Yes," she said.

"So why are you looking at his picture now?" Jenny asked.

"Because things that happened a long time ago have a way of coming back to bite you in the butt."

"Sort of like Ms. Highsmith's brother."

"Exactly," Joanna said.

"Is that what you're going to do with this guy?" Jenny asked. "Get revenge?"

"I don't know," Joanna said. "I hadn't thought of it quite that way. I guess I'm more curious than anything else."

Dennis came out of the bathroom then, still damp from his bath, wearing his jammies and ready for his night-night kiss. When first Dennis and then Jenny slipped off to bed, Joanna returned to her computer. Now that she had David Fredericks's name, she put that into her search engine. Moments later, she hit the jackpot. There was an article about David Fredericks in a magazine called *Trucking Today*. It was accompanied by two photos. One was the same unvarnished mug shot she had seen in the online articles written shortly after her father's death. In those, Fredericks appeared to be an angry young man somewhere in his late twenties or early thirties. The other one looked to be an official company portrait of an at-ease, smiling, and well-to-do middle-aged business executive.

Twenty years ago, David Fredericks was released from the Arizona State Prison in Florence where, before being paroled on good behavior, he had served twenty-eight months of a five-year sentence for vehicular homicide. Unlike many of his fellow parolees, David Fredericks emerged from prison determined to turn his life around.

"While I was locked up, what I missed more than anything was the open road. I was also a guy with a felony conviction. I needed a job, but people weren't exactly falling all over themselves to hire me, so I decided to hire myself."

He sent himself to school and got a commercial driver's license. After patching together enough financial help to buy a rig of his own, he went to work hauling oversize equipment from one side of the country to the other. Two weeks ago, the company he built from scratch with that first vehicle was swallowed up in a deal that business analysts say is worth $7.5 million in Dave Fredericks's pocket.

"I wouldn't have been able to turn my life around if there hadn't been people who had faith in me and who gave me a hand up when I was down and out. That's one of the reasons I'm involved in a program that helps released inmates find meaningful work after they get out of prison. If they're doing something they love, they're a lot less likely to end up back in the slammer."

Mr. Fredericks met Donna, his wife of seventeen years, when he was driving a truck and she was working as a waitress at a truck stop in Nebraska.

"Every time he came through town," Donna says now with a smile, "he'd say, 'When are you going to give all this up and marry me?' Finally he wore me down, and I had to say yes."

The couple and their three adopted children live in Sahuarita, south of Tucson.

Joanna was still staring at the computer screen when her cell phone rang. "Hi, boss," Jaime Carbajal said. "I thought you'd want us to bring you up-to-date. We found James Cameron's CR-V parked in one of the lots by the Rec Center. It's a treasure trove. We found a thirty-eight, which we're hoping will turn out to be the murder weapon in the Highsmith case. We also found duct tape and a dress shirt with bloodstains on the arm."

"Sounds good," Joanna said.

"That's not the half of it. We also found a blowgun. It looks like the darts have been altered so they could be loaded with some kind of liquid, most likely bear tranquilizer, an unused bottle of which we also found in the vehicle. Company records show that two weeks ago tranquilizer doses matching that batch number were shipped to James Gunnar Cameron of Palo Alto, California. We also found Debra Highsmith's missing cell phone and her computers, along with her calendars, which are, as far as we can tell, nothing but calendars."

Joanna was surprised. "All this incriminating stuff was in his car? He just left it there for us to find?"

"Yup," Jaime replied. "I think he meant what he told you up there on Juniper Flats. He had no intention of getting away. Once he took out his sister and his grandmother, his job was done. He didn't care what happened afterward. Still doesn't."

"Has he asked for an attorney?"

"Not so far, and Deb and I have had him in the interview room for the better part of an hour." Jaime paused then added, "Have you heard from Arlee Jones yet?"

"No," Joanna answered. "Why do you ask?"

"He called the department thinking you'd be here. When you weren't, he asked to speak to Deb or me. He wanted us to run up the flag to him immediately if Cameron asked for an attorney. In the meantime, Arlee will probably call you next. He's got some bright idea about doing a plea bargain."

Joanna was surprised. "A plea bargain? Already? So far we've got three people dead. We don't even know if all the victims who were injured on the sidewalk are going to survive. How can he possibly be talking plea bargain this early in the game?"

"Beats me," Jaime said, "but I thought you should have a heads-up."

"Thanks," Joanna said.

Sure enough, when her phone rang again five minutes later, the county attorney was on the line.

"I understand you and your people have had quite a day of it," Arlee said, sounding hearty and enthusiastic in the hail-fellow-well-met fashion that only career politicians can ever fully master.

"Make that several days," Joanna said dryly, "and it's not over yet."

"You're right," Arlee said. "That's why I'm calling— with an opportunity for all of us to have it be over."

"I assume that means you're looking at a plea bargain?"

"Exactly. If we go for first-degree homicide in the Highsmith and Oliphant cases, we're talking about a possible death penalty trial. Undoubtedly that will attract big criminal defense guns from all over hell and gone. Cochise County will end up footing the bill for a multimillion-dollar trial that we can't afford. Besides, what happens if some doe-eyed defense attorney comes up with the brainy idea that Mr. Cameron is actually nuts—which I'm quite sure he is, by the way. They might end up getting the guy off on an insanity plea. That's something I don't want to see happen, and I doubt you do, either."

"If James Cameron is nuts, maybe that's why we have insanity pleas," Joanna suggested.

"Come on, Sheriff Brady," Arlee Jones said dismissively. "Don't be naive. What I'm prepared to do is take the death penalty off the table in exchange for life without parole. The good thing about plea bargains is there's no appeal. It can't be tossed out on some kind of technicality."

"One count?" Joanna asked.

"No, three. All of them first degree. The guy who was hit on the sidewalk died while Cameron was in the process of committing a felony. That means it's automatically bumped up from vehicular homicide to murder one. I'm also expecting that Cameron will plead guilty to one count of kidnapping, one count of assault with intent, as well as five counts of vehicular assault. Settling all those charges in one fell swoop is going to be huge—for your department, for Alvin Bernard's department, and for mine as well. Think of all the man-hours we'll be saving in paperwork alone if we take him down with what we have right now."

On the one hand, Joanna knew Arlee was rushing things. He wanted to have his plea bargain in place before James Cameron came to his senses and decided what he really wanted was a lawyer who might manage to beat the rap completely.

On the other hand, Joanna understood that the prosecutor had her between a rock and a hard place. If she didn't agree with the plea bargain plan, Arlee Jones would spend the next several months making life miserable for her and her investigators. She knew that her grounds for arresting Cameron were solid, but beyond that, the ball was in the prosecutor's court. As long as James Cameron stayed in custody for the remainder of his life, that was probably the best possible outcome for society in general and for Isadora Creswell in particular.

"I guess you'll do what you have to do," she said finally.

She had yet to put down the phone when it rang again. This time her chief deputy was on the line. "I'm on my way to Tucson with Cameron's DNA sample," he said.

"Good," she said. "Did he cause any trouble?"

"Nope, none at all. Went as quiet as a lamb. Have you heard anything about the grandmother's condition?"

"Not yet."

"Once I drop off the sample, do you want me to go by TMC to check on her?"

"Might be a good idea," Joanna said.

"Oh," Tom added. "Maggie Oliphant's daughter called the department. When you weren't in, the switchboard put her call through to me. She'll be in town tomorrow to start making final arrangements. Her brother is flying in from London. He won't be here until Wednesday at the earliest."

"Sounds like Bisbee is going to be funeral central this week."

"Yes, the school district is bringing in a whole armload of grief counselors to have at the high school tomorrow morning. The world is sure different. When I was a kid and somebody died, we talked to our parents. We didn't talk to grief counselors."

"You're right," Joanna said with a sigh. "The world really has changed."

"Staff meeting at eight in the morning?"

"Eight sharp."

Butch came into the dining room just then carrying two glasses of wine. The two side-by-side photos were still plastered across Joanna's computer screen. He passed her one of the glasses and then sat down beside her to peer at the photos.

"Isadora's grandson?" Butch asked, pointing at the portrait of the middle-aged man and making the same mistake Jenny had made.

"That's David Fredericks," Joanna answered. "He's the guy who killed my father."

"Any obvious connections back to Freddy Holder's in-laws?"

"Not obvious, but possible," Joanna said. "He served twenty-eight months in Florence. When he got out, he managed to start a trucking company doing long-haul trips of oversize construction equipment—a company he sold two years ago for a sizable seven-figure sum— seven and a half million bucks. Guess who uses oversize construction equipment? Mining companies, that's who," she concluded, answering her own question.

"You're thinking Wayne Stevens might have sent some of that business in Mr. Fredericks's direction?" Butch asked. "Thus turning an ex-con into an unlikely success story."

"It's worth following up," Joanna said.

"Is Mad Dog's widow still in town?" Butch asked after a pause.

"As far as I know she is," Joanna replied. "I believe Nelda Muncey lives over in Briggs in their old company house, one she and Mad Dog bought once the mines shut down."

"Your dad's journal said that no one besides him was in the room when Mad Dog confessed to killing Fred Holder."

"What are you saying?" Joanna asked.

"That there's a good chance Nelda had no knowledge of what her husband had been up to."

"There's always a chance she did, too," Joanna replied.

"I'm wondering, though, is it fair to Nelda to bring all this stuff up after such a long time?" Butch asked.

"What's fair?" Joanna retorted. "My father's still dead, isn't he? If Wayne Stevens was somehow behind my father's death, then the man got away with murder."

"Wayne Stevens is dead, too," Butch pointed out. "No amount of legal maneuvering is going to put him in jail for that crime now. So is Mad Dog. David Fredericks has already served his time in prison. Because of double jeopardy, he can't be tried again for the same crime, so what's the point? Reopening the case will certainly hurt Nelda Muncey, someone your father seemed to think was nothing but an innocent bystander. It's also going to throw you and your mother right back into all that ugly emotional turmoil. I'm not saying one way or the other, but I'm wondering if that's what you want to do."

Joanna shook her head. "I don't know, either," she said. "I'm going to have to think about it."

"I believe your father referred to it as a judgment call. The call he made at the time was to go straight to Wayne Stevens's office and raise hell about it instead of letting it be. I'm not so sure that was a good idea then, and I'm not sure it's a good idea now," Butch added thoughtfully. "There's a reason people say you should let sleeping dogs lie."

With that Butch drained the last of his wine, then he stood up and kissed the top of Joanna's head. "Are you coming to bed?" he asked.

"In a little while."

She sat there for a long time, listening to the quiet of their rammed-earth house and staring at the side-by-side photos. Finally, she made up her mind. It took only a few minutes for her to locate David Fredericks's telephone number in Sahuarita. Once she had it, she didn't give herself time to change her mind. It was a little before ten—late but not that late. She dialed the number. Once the phone started to ring, Joanna found herself hoping no one would answer, but then someone did. A man's voice came on the line.

"Hello," he said. "David Fredericks here."

Joanna took a deep breath. "My name is Joanna Brady," she said. "I'm the sheriff of Cochise County and—"

"You're D. H. Lathrop's daughter," he said, finishing the sentence for her. "I've been expecting your call for a very long time."

Chapter 27

From the time Joanna was fifteen years old, she had sometimes imagined what it would be like to finally confront the man who had taken her father's life. Yet that Sunday night, when it finally happened, the conversation was nothing like she had anticipated, because the first words out of his mouth were these:

"I'm so sorry."

That straight-out apology left Joanna with a mouthful of angry things she wanted to express and a sudden inability to say any of them. She had expected denials and weasel words. David Fredericks offered none of those.

"I was a troubled young man back then," he said. "I had planned on being career military, but they threw me out for a good reason. Believe me, I earned every bit of that other-than-honorable discharge. I was at loose ends, hanging around with the wrong people and trying to figure out what to do next, when someone suggested I might want to earn some money—a whole lot of money from where I was standing—by killing a crooked cop. It seemed like a good enough idea to me. After all, that's one of the things they train you to do in the military—kill people."

"My father wasn't a crooked cop," Joanna objected.

"I figured that out eventually," Fredericks said. "At the time, I believed every cop was a crooked cop, so I took the job. The person paying the bill gave me an article from the local paper that week. Small-town stuff. The reporter probably got paid by the number of names that were mentioned. Anyway, it was all about a Girl Scout troop going on a camping trip to the Chiricahuas—who was taking them there and who was bringing them back. Your father was one of the ones bringing people home. The plan was for me to follow him on his way to the pickup and force him off the road somewhere between Bisbee and the campout. The problem was, I ended up having car trouble that Saturday morning. By the time I caught up with your father, he was already coming back to Bisbee with three girls in the car."

"I was one of them," Joanna said quietly.

"I know that now, too," Fredericks said. "Once I saw there were kids in the car, I figured I was screwed.

I was being paid to take out one guy. I wasn't being paid to kill kids, so I backed off. Then I drove past the place where your father had stopped to change someone's tire. That's when I saw my chance to get rid of him without hurting anyone else."

Joanna listened in silence to Fredericks's story while unchecked tears streamed down her face. He must have noticed.

"Are you still there?" he asked.

"Yes," she managed. "I'm here."

"So that's what I did, but when I hit him, there was something about the sound of it that was so much worse than I thought it would be," Fredericks continued. "The plan was for me to take him out and then head for Mexico. The money was supposed to be waiting for me with the owner of a bar in Guaymas. Instead, I got drunk. I wasn't drunk when I hit him, but I was by the time they picked me up an hour or so later. Not just drunk, but roaring drunk. When they took me in, I tried to tell them that it was a hit job, that someone—a woman—had hired me to do it. I told them about the bar where I was supposed to pick up my money. Turns out, the bar didn't exist. She didn't exist. They thought I was hallucinating, operating in a blackout. I told them all about it, but no one believed me."

It took a moment before Joanna got it. Ever since she had read the passages in her father's journal, she had assumed that Wayne Stevens had been behind all of it. Now she wasn't so sure.

"Wait a minute. Did you say the person who hired you was a woman—female?"

"Yes, I did," Fredericks replied. "She was quite a bit older than I was, but good-looking. Now that I think about it, women who have money to burn always seem to be good-looking, even when they aren't. Once she gave me that first five thousand dollars in cash as a down payment, I thought she was good for it and that I'd get the rest of it later.

"Of course, for me there was no later. I was in jail. When I tried to track her down, she didn't exist. She had given me a phony name—Liz Hanson—and a phony address along with the phony bar in Guaymas. Besides, no one believed me anyway. If anyone went looking for her, I doubt they tried very hard. I didn't, either. For one thing, I was in jail. I had killed a cop. The judge offered me bail, but I had no way of raising the money. So I sat there and thought about what I had done. I decided that I was going to take my medicine—plead guilty, go to jail, and pay my debt to society. Even before I went to Florence, I had made up my mind that when I got out, I was going to turn my life around, and I did.

"Once I was out of prison, my brother, my parents, and my grandparents all pitched in to help me buy my first truck. The only truck I could afford at the time was a used equipment hauler, so that's the business I went into—hauling oversize equipment. My family stayed in the background as silent partners. As I did well, they did well, too. I've made plenty of donations to charity over the years. I always try to make them in five-thousand-dollar increments as a reminder that I need to give that amount back, over and over."

"So you're saying that five-thousand-dollar down payment was all you ever got? You never got the rest of your money?"

"Never, but you see, that didn't matter. Being sent to prison was what I needed. It's what it took to straighten me out. If I hadn't gone to jail, I'd probably be dead by now. I certainly wouldn't be talking to you on the phone."

"So how did you manage to make a fortune in the equipment-hauling business?" Joanna asked.

"By doing the best job I could for the lowest possible price. I always tried to bid low and do a top-dollar job. It paid off."

"You did work for mining companies?"

"I probably worked for all of them at one time or another," Fredericks said.

"Does the name Wayne Stevens ring a bell?"

"Not that I can think of. Why?"

"He was the superintendent of the mines here in Bisbee. He never steered any business in your direction?"

"Not as far as I know."

"Tell me about the woman who hired you."

"She told me her name was Liz Hanson."

"Where did you meet her?"

"At a bar in Sierra Vista—the Sundowner. It's long gone now. A few years after I got out of prison, I tried tracking her down. I just wanted to know who she was, but I was never able to find her."

Liz, Joanna was thinking, as in Elizabeth Stevens, maybe? Suddenly Fredericks's story was starting to make a lot more sense.

"Did she ever say what she had against the supposedly crooked cop?"

"Some kind of family problem. Something to do with a teenage daughter, I think. She was a little vague about that. I figured the guy had probably knocked up the kid."

"If I could show you a photo of someone named Liz, would you recognize her?"

"I don't know if I'd recognize her now. After all, it's been more than twenty years, but I do have one thing."

"What's that?"

"The note she gave me with the down payment."

"A handwritten note? You still have it?"

"It says, 'There's ten more where this came from.' Once I got out of prison, I had it laminated so I could keep it in my wallet. It's still there. It's one way of making sure I never forget where I came from."

Joanna took a deep breath. "If I could locate this Liz person, would you be willing to testify as to her part in the conspiracy to kill my father?"

"Absolutely, Sheriff Brady," Dave Fredericks said. "The law says I've paid my debt to society, but I don't believe it's true. I owe that much to you, and I certainly owe it to your mother."

Chapter 28

Joanna went to bed right after that. Not surprisingly, she didn't go to sleep—at least not right away. She lay awake thinking about her mother and Mona Tipton. Her father had assumed Eleanor knew nothing about his indiscretion, but it turned out that assumption was wrong. Eleanor had known enough to ban Mona from attending D. H. Lathrop's funeral. Which brought Joanna right back to Nelda Muncey. How much had she known, and when had she known it?

Butch was right, of course. Bringing all this up and having the late Mad Dog labeled as a confessed killer was bound to bring plenty of heartache into Nelda Muncey's life, but maybe not as much as might be expected. What if she had known about it all along—like Eleanor had known about Mona?

Looking at it that way, Joanna was finally able to go to sleep.

She slept because she had finally decided what she was going to do, and she was at peace about it. Her father had been right, this was a judgment call. She was making it—for him, for Fred and Abby Holder, and maybe even for Nelda Muncey.

When Joanna emerged from the bedroom showered and dressed the next morning, breakfast was well under way. "Your oatmeal is in the microwave," Butch told her as she poured a mug of coffee. "What time is the morning briefing?"

"Eight," she said.

"You have time then. Carol will get Jenny and the boys down to the bus stop."

The luxury of Butch usually having breakfast on the table when she came out of the bedroom was one of the side benefits of being married to the man, and one that she didn't take for granted, either. She zapped her oatmeal long enough to reheat it, then brought it to the table.

"You must have been awake a lot last night," Butch observed. "When I got out of bed, you were still sound asleep."

"I tossed and turned some," Joanna admitted, "but I'm good now."

"You've made up your mind about what you're going to do?"

She nodded.

"You're not going to tell me?"

She shook her head. "No, because you might not approve."

"Okay then," Butch said. "I hope it works. Be safe out there."

Joanna arrived at the Justice Center with five minutes to spare. She and her people were gathering in the conference room when Arlee Jones bounded into the room hours earlier than his usual Justice Center arrival time. He looked rumpled and disheveled—as though he had slept in his clothes—but there was no mistaking the triumphant look on his face.

"Got it," he said gleefully, slapping a sheaf of papers down on the table. "Signed, sealed, and delivered, complete with a handwritten confession and a plea agreement. Mr. Cameron claims he did it because, according to him, it was all his sister's fault that their father killed himself. He came here looking to hold her accountable for destroying their family. He's convinced that since there was never a trial about Daddy being a spy, his father was innocent. By the same token, I'm sure he's convinced that by doing a plea bargain, he's no more guilty than his father was."

"He really is a nutcase then," Joanna observed.

"Probably," Arlee agreed, "but what matters is that he took the deal. He was more than ready to kill other people, but he isn't willing to face the death penalty himself."

"His grandmother called him a coward to his face," Deb said. "She was right."

"Works for me," Arlee said. "Now I'm heading home to get some sleep. I haven't done an all-nighter like this since I was in law school."

He hustled out then, leaving the conference room in stunned silence. Deb Howell summed it up in a single word. "Unbelievable," she said, shaking her head, and that pretty well covered it. There was a palpable feeling of letdown in the room. Everyone had come to the staff meeting prepared to go to war, only to find that Arlee Jones had stolen their thunder.

"So it's back to business as usual," Joanna said after a moment's pause. "I want you to pull your paperwork together. It's time to do CYA in a big way. Let's be sure that everything we did or didn't do is properly documented. The county attorney seems to think that once he has his plea bargain in place, there's no way it'll be appealed or reversed. Unfortunately, in my experience, Arlee Jones doesn't always have all his ducks in a row."

Joanna turned to Tom Hadlock. "In other words, we still want to have that DNA report from the crime lab as soon as we can get it. We still want to connect all the dots on Debra Highsmith's murder and on Maggie Oliphant's."

"Yes, ma'am," he said.

"Did you go by TMC last night?"

Tom nodded. "Michael Hirales was flying back to Albuquerque from Tucson. He needed to be in class this morning. Sue Ellen is staying in Tucson for the duration. Isadora's surgery is scheduled for sometime today. It's probably happening as we speak. She signed over a power of attorney to Michael. That way he and Sue Ellen will be able to start making final arrangements for Debra Highsmith."

"Speaking of which, what's happening on that?" Joanna asked.

Jaime raised his hand. "Machett already released Debra Highsmith's body to the Higgins Funeral Home. They're expecting that the funeral or memorial service or whatever will be held sometime later this week, possibly in the high school auditorium."

Tom Hadlock nodded. "We won't know about Maggie Oliphant's arrangements until after her daughter arrives in town later today."

The remainder of the meeting was devoted to routine issues. When it was over and people started filing out, Joanna asked Deb Howell to hold up.

"What do you need?" Deb asked.

"I want you to do something for me," Joanna said. "I want you to go up to the *Bisbee Bee* and see if they have any stock photos of Elizabeth Stevens, preferably something from twenty-five or thirty years or so ago. She and her husband were in the top stratum of Bisbee society, so there should be pictures of them at events—balls at the country club or charity events of one kind or another."

"Elizabeth Stevens?" Deb asked. "Why?"

"It's a piece of unfinished business," Joanna replied. "Once you find one of her, I want you to locate photos of four other women taken around the same time so they're more or less contemporary in terms of clothing and hairstyles. Have them blown up so they're all the same size."

"This sounds suspiciously like we're putting together a photo montage."

"We are," Joanna said, "but don't mention that to Marliss Shackleford."

"Once I have the photos, what happens then?" Deb asked.

"Call me," Joanna answered. "By then I'll know what the next step is."

"You've got it, boss," Deb said. "On my way."

"I'm going to be out for a while," Joanna told Kristin as she headed from the conference room to her office.

"Any idea about when you'll be back?"

"None," Joanna said. "I may be gone for the rest of the day."

"What about calls from the media?"

"Send them to Chief Deputy Hadlock. Ball's back in his court."

Before Joanna headed out, she was forced to resort to using an old-fashioned phone book to locate Nelda Muncey's address. With that in hand, Joanna let herself out through the back door, got in the Yukon, and headed for Briggs. The house was situated on Cottonwood Street. An aging Honda sedan parked in the driveway served notice that Nelda Muncey was home, and the blue handicapped sticker dangling from the rearview mirror went a long way toward explaining why the tiny front yard was a weed-choked wasteland.

When the houses in Briggs and Galena had been built as company housing in the fifties, it was during a period when modest two- and three-bedroom bungalows were the order of the day. Stepping up on the small front porch, Joanna realized that Nelda Muncey's home was still a modest bungalow. A sign over the doorbell said it was out of order, so Joanna rapped sharply on a front door marred by sun-damaged varnish. There was a long pause before she heard movement inside the house. Finally the door cracked open.

"Who is it?"

"Sheriff Brady, Mrs. Muncey," Joanna said. "May I come in?"

There was no reply, only the sound of movement again as the woman walked away from the door, which remained open.

Joanna gave it a small push and opened it wider. "May I come in?"

"Help yourself." It was a grudging invitation, but an invitation nonetheless.

The living room Joanna entered was small and shabby and dimly lit. The faded flower pattern on the wooden-armed sofa was barely discernible. There was a battered wooden coffee table, covered with outdated magazines. Nelda Muncey sat in one of those ejection-seat recliners with a walker and several TV trays positioned close at hand. One held a collection of prescription medications; one held a coffee cup and a thermos of coffee; while the third held a Kindle.

Nelda caught Joanna eyeing the one thing in the room that didn't match.

"I love to read," she explained, "but these days it's hard to get out to buy books or even go to the library. By the way, I read your husband's first book," Nelda added. "Liked the story, don't much like his name. It must have been hell growing up with a fruity name like Gayle."

Because Butch's fictional protagonist was female, both his agent and his editor had advised him to use a non-gender-specific pen name—Gayle Dixon rather than Frederick W. or even FW. Joanna was already feeling ill at ease due to the nature of her business with Nelda, and the woman's unsolicited comments about Butch and his work didn't improve things. Besides, Joanna thought, how could a woman who had spent her married life with a guy named Mad Dog have nerve enough to complain about someone else's name?

"I'll pass that along," Joanna said. "May I sit down?"

Nelda gestured toward the couch. "As I said before, help yourself."

Joanna sat. Nelda was a relatively thin woman who, Joanna assumed from the extra folds of skin on her chin and neck, had once been far larger than she was now. She was dressed in a pair of knit pants topped by a brightly flowered print blouse. On her feet were a pair of bright green high-topped Keds. Maybe wearing running shoes was her way of thumbing her nose at the fact that she was now reduced to using a walker. Her thin white hair was pulled back in a pair of long, neat braids that wrapped around her head. Nelda might have had trouble walking, but braiding evidently wasn't a problem. She peered at Joanna inquisitively through a pair of thick glasses.

"What's this all about?" Nelda asked.

"It's about my father," Joanna said.

Nelda nodded but said nothing.

"I believe he came to the hospital to see your husband a few days before he died."

"Before they both died," Nelda pointed out. "Your father died on Saturday. Edward died a week later, also on a Saturday."

Edward? Joanna wondered. That was the first time she had ever heard or known Mad Dog Muncey's first name.

"Did you have any idea what they talked about?"

"Of course I knew," Nelda said. "I'm not stupid, you know. They talked about Fred Holder's death and my husband's part in it."

"As in the fact that he was responsible?"

"Yes, he was." It was a definitive statement.

"I was under the impression that you were out of the room when my father talked to your husband."

"Believe me, that wasn't the only time Edward talked about it," Nelda said. "The new minister we had at the church back then convinced him that confession was good for the soul. He talked about things right and left, but only to me and to your father. He wanted to die with a clear conscience, you see. Clearing his conscience may have been good for Edward. It wasn't much of a favor to me."

"What do you mean?"

"Come on, Sheriff Brady. You know how this works. A husband goes out catting around, he dies, and his widow is left holding the bag with whatever emotional damage his clearing his conscience may have left behind in her life."

"I thought we were talking about Fred Holder's death."

"We are," Nelda said. "Why do you think Edward did it? Oldest reason in the book. Because he was having an affair with Elizabeth Stevens, and whatever she wanted, she got."

"Did Mr. Stevens know about it?"

"Maybe," Nelda said. "Wayne Stevens had a serious problem—a wife who was several years younger than he was and a growing problem with not being able to get it up. At least that's what Elizabeth told Edward. Back then there was no such thing as Viagra. Wayne Stevens gave Elizabeth her head and let her do whatever she wanted because he didn't want to lose her and he didn't want word to get out that he wasn't man enough to keep his woman."

"You're saying Elizabeth Stevens is the one who hired your husband to kill Fred Holder?"

"That's what he told me. That she paid him cash money for doing the job. He went right out and splurged—bought himself that Pontiac and never had a moment's peace with it, either. That thing was a lemon from day one. Served him right."

"When my father died, only a few days later, why didn't you come forward?" Joanna asked.

"Why do you think?" Nelda asked in return. "He and Edward were both gone. It was over. I had no way of proving what Edward had told me. Besides, I had a lot of things on my plate at the time. If someone had come around asking me about it, I might have told them, but since no one ever did, I saw no reason for me to bring it up."

"Because you didn't want to deal with the whole tawdry affair," Joanna suggested.

Nelda nodded. "There was more to it than just that. When I realized Edward was dying, I knew money would be tight, so I went looking for a job. A few weeks earlier I had managed to land a job as a part-time check-out clerk at the company store. How long do you think that job would have lasted if I had blown the whistle on Edward and Elizabeth? Wayne Stevens would have had me fired in a heartbeat if I had gone to the new sheriff with that unsubstantiated story. Besides, what good would that have done? I didn't have any more proof than your father did about what had happened, and I had a whole lot less credibility. It would have been my word against Elizabeth Stevens's. You know how that would have gone over."

In Bisbee, Arizona, back then, little guy versus company bigwig? Unfortunately, Joanna knew exactly how those things worked. So had her father.

"Besides," Nelda added after a pause, "blowing the whistle would have meant letting our kids know about all of it, too. They were grown by then, but I didn't see any point in my telling them that their father was a two-timing jerk and a murderer besides."

"Let me get this straight," Joanna said. "As far as you know, Elizabeth Stevens was having an affair with your husband and she was the one behind all this rather than her husband?"

"Husbands or, in my case, wives are always the last to know," Nelda observed, "but I doubt Wayne Stevens had any idea about what had gone on between Edward and Elizabeth. If he had, I never would have gotten that checkout job. What I don't understand is why you're here asking all these questions. It has to be at least twenty years ago. Why bring it up now?"

"Because there's no statute of limitations on homicide, or on conspiracy to commit homicide, either," Joanna explained. "You and my father both believed Elizabeth was behind Fred Holder's death. I have reason to believe that she may have been responsible for my father's death as well."

"Wait a minute," Nelda said with a puzzled frown. "I thought D. H. Lathrop was killed by a drunk driver."

"So did I," Joanna said, "and so did everyone else, but it turns out that drunk driver may have been bought and paid for."

For a time the room was silent while the impact of Joanna's words settled around them. Then a slow smile crossed the old woman's face.

"I know the pastor would say that I'm not a good person, but when I heard Wayne Stevens had up and died, leaving Elizabeth penniless, I thought she was finally getting what she deserved. That seemed like the best I could hope for, but are you saying that now she might even go to jail?"

"Yes," Joanna said. "She might. The problem is, you may have to be called on to corroborate what your husband told my father. You might have to testify."

"With pleasure," Nelda Muncey said. "Between then and now, my kids have learned that their father didn't exactly walk on water. It's not going to kill them to find out the rest of it. After all, it didn't kill you to find out about your father and Mona Tipton, did it?"

Nelda's question rocked Joanna, and she couldn't help but blush. It seemed that everyone in town, including her own mother, had known about what was going on between her father and Mona Tipton. Joanna felt as if she was the only person involved who had been left in the dark.

"No, it didn't," Joanna agreed at last, "although I have to admit it was a real shock to the system."

"I'm sure it was," Nelda said kindly.

"You don't think this will be too hard on you—your possibly having to testify?"

"Oh, no," Mad Dog Muncey's widow replied. "Not at all. Your mother weathered that whole ruckus with your father like a champ. I expect the same thing will be true for me. I'll be fine. I'm not so sure about Elizabeth Stevens," she added with a broad smile. "We'll have to see about that, won't we."

When Joanna went outside, she sat in the Yukon for several long minutes before turning the key in the ignition. She was still sitting there with the gearshift in park and thinking about her mother when her phone rang.

"Okay, boss," Deb said. "I've got the pictures you wanted. They're not very good. Newspaper photos have changed a lot since the old days. What do you want me to do now?"

"Drive over to Sahuarita," Joanna said. "You're going to go see a guy named David Fredericks. Get Records to give you his name and address. I want you to show him the photos, and then call me with the results."

"Who is he?" Deb asked.

"He's the man who killed my father."

"That was years ago," Deb objected. "I thought it was an accident."

"So did I," Joanna said, "but it turns out the guy driving the car was a hired hand."

"Are you saying you think Elizabeth Stevens was behind your father's death? Is that even possible?"

"We'll know once Mr. Fredericks sees the photo. He's already spent years in prison for the crime, while the person who started this whole thing has been in the clear and free as a bird."

"It's a long way back and forth to Sahuarita. What are you going to be doing in the meantime?" Deb asked. "You're not going to go see her on your own, are you?"

"No," Joanna said. "I'm not going anywhere near Elizabeth Stevens without having backup in place. What I'm going to do instead will be a lot tougher than talking to her."

"What would be tougher than that?" Deb asked.

"I have to go talk to my mother," Joanna said. "She needs to know that what we both always thought was an accident was really cold-blooded murder."

Chapter 29

Joanna was tempted to call for backup to go see her mother, too. Butch would have been her first choice for that, but she didn't want to have to face up to his inarguable I-told-you-so. After all, this was exactly what Butch had suggested might happen—that in pursuing the possibility that D. H. Lathrop had been murdered, Joanna would bring all that painful history back into focus and reopen all the old wounds. Mad Dog's affair with Elizabeth Stevens would be out in the open, but from what Nelda had just said, so would D. H. Lathrop's relationship with Mona Tipton. Bisbee's gossipmongers would have a field day. With gossip, as with homicide, there is no statute of limitations.

It had now been several years since Joanna had first learned about her father's infidelity. Up to that point, whenever she had thought about her parents' relationship, she had always assumed that her father had been the wronged party. After finally realizing that her father, too, had feet of clay, she had come to appreciate how the two women involved—her mother and Mona—had survived the aftermath of the death of the man they had both loved.

As the widow of a slain police officer, Eleanor had maintained the field advantage of being able to put on a public show of bearing her grief bravely, while leaving her daughter puzzling over why she never saw her mother shed so much as a single tear over her husband's death. Now Joanna understood that her mother's behavior had been as much about fury and betrayal as it had been about grief, but public sympathy had always been on Eleanor's side.

If Nelda Muncey had known about D. H. Lathrop's affair, other people in town must have known, too, but when he died, there had been no public groundswell of sympathy for Mona Tipton. She had done her grieving in private. Some women would have left town. Mona didn't. She had continued to live in her house on Quality Hill, dealing with her grief in almost reclusive solitude. If the two women had run into each other at some time in the intervening years—in the bank or the post office or at a restaurant in town—there had been no words between them, no impropriety that would have brought anyone's attention to the situation. To the best of their ability, both of the women in D. H. Lathrop's life had tried to put him and his tragic death behind them.

Now they would both have to learn that his death hadn't been accidental at all. Joanna knew enough about human emotions to understand that the kind of closure people talk about in the aftermath of a sudden death is a figment of the public's imagination. Wounded souls scab over eventually. Broken hearts mend after a fashion, but there are always scars left behind. Joanna knew that when cold cases were suddenly solved—when, after years of nothing, a long-sought killer finally faced justice— "closure" was the word that was always on everyone's lips. Finding out at this late date that D. H. Lathrop had been murdered would bring two women the exact opposite of closure.

It would all be Joanna's doing.

She called her mother from the Traffic Circle. "Hey, Mom," she said, as cheerily as she could manage. "I was wondering if I could stop by for a cup of coffee?"

Eleanor wasn't exactly overjoyed to hear from her. "You'd think after the kind of difficult weekend we've had around here that a person could rest on her laurels for a single day at least, but that's not happening. Some of the women from the art league think we should donate the leftover refreshments from yesterday's tea to the funeral reception for Maggie. You don't know anything about what arrangements are being made, do you?"

"I'll see what I can find out on that," Joanna said, although she already knew no arrangements for Maggie's funeral had as yet been set. "Still, is it okay if I drop by for coffee?"

"Is something wrong?" Eleanor asked. "This is twice now in the last couple of days when you've stopped by for no apparent reason. I'm worried something's amiss."

"We'll talk about it when I get there," Joanna insisted.

"Oh, no," Eleanor said, automatically drawing a worst-case-scenario conclusion. "Don't tell me. Butch is leaving you!"

"Mother," Joanna insisted, "it's nothing like that. Things are fine with Butch and me."

"All right, then," Eleanor said, "but it sounds serious. Should George be here?"

Joanna thought about that. "It might be better if he wasn't."

It was only a few minutes later when she stopped outside her mother's place on Campbell. George was outside finishing painting the fence. He waved as Joanna went past, but she was relieved that he made no effort to join them.

Eleanor met Joanna at the front door. "What on earth is going on, Joanna Lee Brady?" she demanded frantically. "I've been dying a thousand deaths since you called. Is there something wrong with Jennifer? Is Dennis sick?"

"It's about my father," Joanna said quietly. "There's something you need to know."

"Your father!" Eleanor replied, lurching slightly and sitting down heavily on the arm of the sofa. "What about your father?"

Joanna took a deep breath. "We're reopening the investigation into his death," she said softly. "There's a good chance he was murdered."

In the past six years, Joanna had been involved in numerous next-of-kin notifications. Even though the momentous events in question were twenty years in the past, the news still came as a shock. Joanna delivered the information as best she could, determined not to be derailed by her mother's reaction. Nonetheless, she was amazed to see her mother dissolve into a spasm of unapologetic grief. Eleanor buried her face in her hands and wept in great gulping sobs. Gradually the sobs subsided.

"So you're saying this was all about Freddy Holder's death, then?" Eleanor asked at last. "I knew your father was back working on that again, but he'd been doing that for years. I never thought anything would come of it. I told him time and again that he had to stop obsessing about that case—that he needed to let it go."

"It looks as though once Dad went to see Wayne Stevens, all bets were off. Elizabeth Stevens must have been terrified that this time he'd finally be able to do something about it. When the drunk driver who hit Dad tried to tell people that someone had hired him to do it, no one believed him. No one ever bothered to look into the possibility that he was telling the truth."

"Are you going to arrest her?" Eleanor asked.

"I'm in the process of having my detectives pull together some other pieces of evidence, but you need to know that there's a good chance that Dad's journal from that time will have to be placed in evidence, too. Nelda's testimony can corroborate what Mad Dog told Dad about Freddy Holder's death, but the journal would need to be there. They're two different sources telling the same story. That's why I wanted you to know about this now. If you want me to drop it . . ."

"Heavens no!" Eleanor said. "If that woman has gotten away with murder all this time, you have to do this. You must. No question. Reliving all of it won't be a picnic for anyone, but it's about time somebody put her away."

Although they talked for another half hour, Joanna and Eleanor never did get around to having coffee. It was only as Joanna was leaving that her mother dropped the real bombshell.

"Are you going to go tell Mona Tipton?" she asked.

Joanna was thunderstruck. Going to see Mona had been the next thing on her list, but she'd had no intention of mentioning that to her mother.

"Yes," Joanna said uncertainly. "I thought I should."

"Good," Eleanor replied. "Having all of this come back up will be far worse for her than it is for me. After all, I have George and the kids and you. I don't believe that poor woman has anyone."

Joanna had been about to step off the front porch. Instead, she turned around, went back, and gave her mother a heartfelt hug.

"That's very kind of you, Mom," she said.

"Maybe age is finally catching up with me," Eleanor said with a shrug. "Maybe I'm finally getting older and wiser."

Chapter 30

D eb Howell called while Joanna was on her way up the canyon to see Mona. "Okay," she said. "I'm on my way—halfway back to Benson. David Fredericks picked Elizabeth Stevens's face out of the montage without a moment's hesitation."

"You recorded his making the ID?"

"Yes, ma'am. I videoed it with my iPhone. Sent it to Dave Hollicker. Fredericks also gave me the laminated note he told you about. We can have a handwriting expert work on verifying that."

Joanna glanced at her watch. "How can you already be halfway back to Benson?" she asked. "You didn't leave that long ago."

"When I called Fredericks, he asked to meet me at the Triple T. Yes, he's glad to help—he told me that again—but I think he wanted some time to break the news to his family. We did our business, and I headed home. What's the next step?"

Joanna looked at her watch. It was a little past noon. She had no idea whether the high school would be on a full-day schedule or a partial-day schedule, but she was hoping to stop by the house and deal with Elizabeth Stevens before her daughter came home from work.

"I'm running an errand right now," Joanna said, without any additional information. "When I finish that, I'll go back to the office and work on my paperwork jungle. Call me as you come through the tunnel. We'll meet at Abby Holder's place."

She pulled up in front of Mona's house on Quality Hill. The last time Joanna had come here and spoken to Mona, she had done so out of purely selfish reasons. This time it was different. This time she had something other than either curiosity or retribution in mind. This time she was here on an errand of mercy.

When Mona opened the door, however, it was as though no time had passed between Joanna's first visit and this one. Her father's onetime mistress was dressed in the kind of clothing she might have worn to work back in the day—a well-maintained suit that was years out of fashion, a carefully ironed white blouse, panty hose, and a pair of sensible heels.

"I'm sorry to show up unannounced," Joanna apologized. "If you're expecting someone . . ."

"It's fine," Mona Tipton said, opening the door wider. "I'm not expecting anyone. Please do come in and have a seat."

Like Nelda Muncey's living room, this one, too, was furnished with period pieces, ones that predated the fifties, but were in far better condition.

"What brings you here?" Mona asked when they were both settled.

"It's about my father," Joanna began.

Again she delivered the same painful information she had given her mother. When Mona heard the news, she didn't burst into tears. She simply nodded. "I always thought there was something to that guy's story," she said at last. "To the drunk driver's story, I mean, but everyone else's mind was made up about what had happened. They saw what they wanted to see and didn't bother looking any further."

"I wanted you to know about this in advance," Joanna said.

"Because you'll most likely have to use your father's journals as evidence against Elizabeth Stevens?"

"Exactly," Joanna said.

"Don't worry about me," Mona said. "I've lived with a scarlet A embroidered on my clothing for the last twenty years. Having it come out in public isn't going to bother me. Who knows, it might even help. Maybe people will finally figure out that there's a reason I've lived alone all this time. I really loved your father, Sheriff Brady. I wake up every morning of my life sorry that he's gone."

Somehow it was easier for Joanna to sit and talk to Mona Tipton than it had been to talk to her own mother. Eventually Mona went into the kitchen, returning with a tray laden with coffee, coffee cups, and saucers.

"I seem to remember you drink your coffee black, right?" she asked.

"Yes, thank you," Joanna said. "Black is fine."

She had just finished drinking her second cup when her phone rang. It was Deb. "I just came through the tunnel," she said.

"I'll be right there," Joanna said. "Don't go near the house until I get there."

She stood up.

"You're on your way to see Elizabeth Stevens now?" Mona Tipton asked.

Joanna nodded. "Yes," she said. "That's the next step."

"Do be careful," Mona advised. "Your father always said that a cornered rattlesnake was far more dangerous than one on the loose."

Joanna paused in midstep with a sudden catch in her throat. "He did always say that, didn't he?"

Chapter 31

Ten minutes later, Deb Howell's Tahoe and Joanna's Yukon were parked on the grassy parking strip in front of Abby Holder's house. The house still looked the same as it had the first time Joanna had seen it. Now she was struck by the fact that all this time, while Abby had been caring for her mother, she had also, without her knowledge, been harboring the person ultimately responsible for her husband's death.

"How do you want to handle this?" Deb asked.

"Elizabeth Stevens is in a wheelchair. Go around to the back and see if there's a ramp from the back porch."

Deb was back in under half a minute. "Twelve steps at least," she said. "So if she's in there, this is the way she has to come out."

"Okay," Joanna said. "Let's do it."

Joanna walked up the steps while Deb followed the seemingly meandering path of the wheelchair ramp up the steep incline. By the time she reached the porch, Joanna was already ringing the bell.

What seemed like a long time passed before there was any sign of movement inside the house. "My daughter isn't here right now," Elizabeth said from behind the closed door. "You'll need to come back when she's home."

"It's Sheriff Brady," Joanna said. "We need to speak to you."

"Why?"

"We have a few questions," she said. "About Debra Highsmith."

That was an out-and-out lie, but it was enough to get Elizabeth to open the door and let them inside.

"That woman never appreciated Abby," Elizabeth said. "I'm sorry she's dead, of course, but she could have treated Abby decently."

"What about you?" Joanna asked.

Elizabeth frowned. "What do you mean?"

"How do you treat your daughter?"

"Me? I thought we were talking about Abby's boss."

"Let's talk about you for a moment," Joanna said. "First, however, we need to read you your rights. Turn on the recorder please, Detective Howell, and then, if you'd be so good as to Mirandize Mrs. Stevens here, I'd really appreciate it."

"Read me my rights!" Elizabeth exclaimed. "You're both crazy. I'm in a wheelchair, in case you haven't noticed. I read all about Debra Highsmith's murder. She was shot to death somewhere out along High Lonesome Road. There's no way I could do that in a wheelchair. No way at all."

Undeterred, Deb did as she was told.

"I don't know what this is all about," Elizabeth said when the recitation of rights was completed. "You can't possibly believe that I had anything to do with Debra Highsmith's murder."

"I don't," Joanna said. "I'm here to arrest you for conspiracy in the murder of Freddy Holder and of my father as well."

"This is utterly ridiculous," Elizabeth sneered. "How anyone could believe something so far-fetched—"

"I have a witness," Joanna said. "In actual fact, I have two."

"That's not possible . . ."

"Does the name David Fredericks mean anything to you?"

"Nothing," Elizabeth said aloud, although the expression on her face told a different story.

"I'm surprised," Joanna said. "Because he's the guy you hired to kill my father when it looked like he had enough evidence to charge you with conspiring with Mad Dog Muncey to kill your son-in-law."

"Mother!" Abby Holder exclaimed. "Is this true?"

Unheard by the three women in the living room, Abby Holder had noiselessly entered the house through the back door and was standing in the kitchen doorway. Her face was dangerously pale, but her dark eyes blazed with anger.

"Abby!" Elizabeth exclaimed, looking first at her watch and then at her daughter. "What are you doing home so early?"

"Because of what happened to Ms. Highsmith, we only kept the kids for half a day today," Abby answered. "What's going on?"

Joanna was the one who answered. "A guy by the name of Edward Muncey, Mad Dog Muncey, told my father in a dying confession that he was responsible for your husband's murder and that your mother had paid him to do it. Shortly after that, my father also died when he was hit by a speeding drunk driver in what was always considered to be a tragic accident. Except I've learned just recently that it wasn't an accident at all. That supposedly drunk driver was hired to do the job by someone named Liz Hanson."

"Liz Hanson," Abby repeated. "That's your maiden name."

"Don't listen to her," Elizabeth advised. "None of this is true. She's making it up as she goes along. Sheriff Brady here is as much of a fruitcake as her father ever was. D. H. Lathrop told your father all about Mad Dog Muncey's wild story. Nobody believed it then, and nobody will believe it now."

But Abby Holder's body suddenly seemed to stiffen. She stood straighter. "I believe it," she said.

"You can't possibly," Elizabeth objected. "After all, I'm your mother."

"That's exactly why I do believe it," Abby declared with heat entering her voice. "You are my mother. You've lived here all this time, accepting my charity, all the while knowing that you had taken away the one person in the whole world who ever really loved me."

"Abby, this is ridiculous. Don't be silly."

"I'm not being silly. I'm dead serious."

"So am I, Mrs. Stevens," Joanna said. "You're under arrest. Cuff her, Deb."

Elizabeth's jaw dropped in amazement. "This is utterly astonishing. You're all making a terrible mistake. I demand to see my lawyer. Abby, give Burton a call, would you?"

"No," Abby said. "Burton Kimball is a friend of ours, and he's also a capable defense attorney, but I'm not calling him, Mother, and I won't pay for his services, either. You'll need to use whatever attorney they give you for free—one who's appointed for you, because you won't be able to afford one on your own."

"You can't do this to me, Abby. You can't abandon me like this!"

"Watch me," Abby Holder said. "I can and I will. You disgust me, Mother. Get her out of here," she said to Deb. "I can't stand the sight of her."

Joanna helped Deb wheel Elizabeth down the ramp. At the bottom they patted her down for possible weapons before loading her into Deb's Tahoe for transport. Once they drove away, Joanna went back up to the house where she found Abby Holder sitting on the couch staring vacantly across the room.

"Are you going to be all right?" Joanna asked.

"Yes," Abby said quietly. "I think I will. Knowing the truth is better than not knowing."

Joanna nodded, thinking of her mother and Mona Tipton.

"Yes," she said. "I think so, too, but here's my card just in case. If you need anything—anything at all— please call me. I lost my husband, too, you know," she added. "I know how this feels."

Abby looked at Joanna with tears brimming in her eyes. "Even after all this time?" she asked.

"Even after all this time," Joanna repeated. "It never goes away."

Chapter 32

Much later that night, while Joanna lay cuddled next to Butch's body in their queen-size bed, she told him the whole story.

"So it sounds like you made the right call after all," Butch said. "The right call for everyone concerned."

"My mother really surprised me," Joanna said. "I never expected that she'd unbend enough to give me permission to notify Mona Tipton."

"Miracles do happen," Butch said.

"Not only that," Joanna continued, "Mom's decided that she should send the remaining art league cookies to Maggie Oliphant's funeral reception. She arrived at that conclusion all on her own. If I had suggested it, it would have gone over like a pregnant pole vaulter, so maybe we're both finally learning not to boss each other around."

"As I said before," Butch muttered, "miracles do happen, but speaking of funerals, that reminds me. Sue Ellen Hirales called late this afternoon. She told me to tell you that Isadora came through her hip surgery with flying colors, but she was really calling to talk to Jenny."

"To Jenny?" Joanna asked. "Why?"

"It seems Isadora showed Jenny's eulogy to her great-grandson. Sue Ellen said Michael would like Jenny to read it at the funeral on Friday. The service is going to be held in the high school auditorium with Father Morris from St. Dominick's officiating."

"What did Jenny say?" Joanna asked.

"She said yes, of course. She's asked me to coach her on it so she can recite it rather than read it. I told her that's a lot more effective. She called your mother and asked if Eleanor would take her to Tucson tomorrow afternoon and help her find the right kind of dress. She says she doesn't have anything that would work for a funeral."

Joanna was dumbfounded. "Are you kidding? Tomboy Jenny wants to wear a dress?"

"That's what she said."

"What was it you were just saying about miracles?" Joanna asked.

"They happen," Butch mumbled sleepily. "Now shut up and go to sleep."

Epilogue

It was a busy week at the Cochise County Sheriff's Department. There were mountains of paperwork to attend to. After seeing the evidence, Arlee Jones agreed that there was enough to charge Elizabeth Stevens with conspiracy to commit not one but two homicides. Her court-appointed attorney asked for bail, which was granted. Like David Fredericks before her, she wasn't able to raise it. Instead, she stayed in jail, railing at everyone who came near her, complaining about the food, the bed, the air quality, and anything else she could think of. The more she complained, the better Joanna liked it.

Subsequent interviews with David Fredericks and with Nelda Muncey made it seem that Liz had been acting alone and without her husband's knowledge when the hits were arranged on both Freddy Holder and on D. H. Lathrop. It turned out that Wayne Stevens hadn't gotten away with murder because he hadn't committed murder.

Detective Keller, still on loan from the Bisbee Police Department, spent hours going through Debra Highsmith's two computers.

When he finished, he came into Joanna's office. "Find anything?" she asked.

Keller shook his head. "After the 'Die, Bitch' posting turned up on the Web, her browsing history shows that she looked up several articles on facial-recognition software programs, but none of those articles mentions James Cameron by name."

"What about her getting the dog and the gun?" Joanna asked. "Do you think she understood there was a specific threat?"

"I think her grandparents had convinced her that there would always be a threat," Keller answered. "After decades of being paranoid about it, the dog and the gun were more of the same."

"It turns out that Debra Highsmith wasn't wrong to be paranoid, and neither were her grandparents," Joanna said. "Too bad it wasn't enough to save her."

At one o'clock on Friday afternoon, the high school auditorium was filled to capacity with the overflow crowd listening to the service in the cafeteria, where it was broadcast over the school's public address system. The stage was awash in flower arrangements. In the middle of the stage stood a simple lectern with a microphone. Next to that stood a black-draped table that held a funeral urn and a three-foot-tall copy of Debra Highsmith's yearbook photo.

Because Jenny was one of the speakers listed in the program, Joanna and Butch sat next to her at the end of the second row. While a pianist played introductory music, the Hirales family filed down the aisle, with Augusto pushing Isadora in a wheelchair and Sue Ellen and Nancy walking behind him. At the very end was Michael, wearing a suit and looking somber, while at his side walked a magnificent Doberman.

"That's Giles," Jenny whispered as the dog padded past. "Isn't he gorgeous?"

Joanna thought Giles was far more fearsome than he was gorgeous, but his coat was brushed to a high sheen, and he was also exceptionally well behaved. When Michael Hirales sat, Giles sat, and at a hand sign from his new master, the dog settled into a contented down-stay, lying at Michael's feet, completely unconcerned that he was next to a busy aisle.

Joanna meant to pay attention to the service, but she was too distracted, too worried about how Jenny would do—would she remember what she and Butch had practiced for hours on end, or would she forget and flub her lines?

When Father Morris finally called on Jenny to come to the microphone, she walked up onto the stage in her sophisticated new black dress exhibiting a degree of composure that took Joanna's breath away. It wasn't until Jenny turned to speak that Joanna realized she didn't even have a copy of the eulogy with her. Instead, she spoke the words by heart and from the heart, and when she finished, Joanna joined everyone else in giving her a standing ovation. Jenny, however, seemed totally unfazed by the thunderous applause. Instead, she walked back down the stairs and then stopped in the aisle long enough to give Giles a reassuring pat on the head.

Butch was still applauding along with everyone else, but he leaned over long enough to nudge Joanna. "That's our girl," he mouthed with a wide grin. "That's our girl!"

After the funeral a reception was held in the high school cafeteria with William Farraday holding forth as though he was mourner in chief. It was all Joanna could do to keep from rolling her eyes.

Joanna went looking for her mother. "Beautiful dress," Joanna said. "Thank you."

"You're welcome," Eleanor replied, "but it takes a beautiful girl to make a dress beautiful. You must be very proud."

About that time, Jenny came bustling up. "Cassie's parents had to leave early. I told her we could take her home; is that all right?"

So things had changed for the better between Cassie and Jenny. Joanna was still perturbed by Cassie's passing along the photo, but it seemed right to let that go.

"Of course," Joanna said. "We'll be glad to give her a ride."

An hour later, as they were driving Cassie back to her parents' place near Double Adobe, Joanna was still marveling over Jenny's performance when something Cassie was saying in the backseat penetrated her wool-gathering.

"So Marty broke up with Dena," Cassie was saying. "Just like that. Wouldn't even tell her why. Maybe it's like one of his father's rules or something."

Unseen by the girls in the backseat, Butch Dixon reached over, took his wife's hand in his, and squeezed it.

"It's possible it has to do with Dr. Pembroke's rules," he said, sending a knowing smile in Joanna's direction, "but I doubt it."

"It's terrible," Cassie said. "It's the worst thing that could possibly happen."

"Don't be so sure," Butch counseled. "A couple of years from now, Dena Carothers may look back and decide that it was the best thing that ever happened to her."

"Are you teasing us?" Jenny asked.

"No," he said. "I'm not teasing in the least. I mean every word, and I'm betting your mother agrees with me."

"Yes," Joanna said, leaning back and closing her eyes. "In this case I believe you're absolutely right."

At Cassie's house, Jenny asked if she could stay for a while, and they let her. When Joanna and Butch got back to High Lonesome Ranch, a large wooden crate stood in front of the garage door, blocking the entrance.

"What's this?" Joanna wanted to know.

"It's this year's birthday/Christmas/anniversary present all rolled into one," Butch said. "I guess you need to open it. Hold on. I'll go get a crowbar."

While he went to his toolbox, Joanna examined the crate. It was marked M. L. COLEMAN, SUNSET PASS STUDIOS.

"It's a painting?" Joanna asked as Butch returned and started dismantling the crate.

Butch nodded. "It used up a big chunk of my next advance," he said with a grin.

"It's that expensive and they just dropped it off like this?"

"I arranged for Carol to be here to sign for it."

Eventually the wooden packing and the hard plastic foam peeled away. Inside was a gold-framed oil painting, four feet by five and a half, of the flower vendor across the street from their honeymoon hotel in Paris. It was breathtaking. The flowers glowed in the sunshine, while the pavement in front was still shiny from what must have been a passing shower.

"It's stunning!" Joanna exclaimed. "Absolutely stunning."

"You like it?"

"I love it. I thought it was smaller, though."

"You're right. The one they had at the auction was much smaller," Butch explained. "I thought about buying it during the auction, but then the auction didn't exactly go as planned. On Sunday, I called your mom and had her ask Mr. Coleman if he had a larger one. He did—this one—but it was back home in Sedona. He agreed to sell it to me and still give the art league their cut of the purchase price."

"So that's what Mother meant when she said you helped her."

Butch nodded. "I wanted it to be a surprise, and I was afraid she had given it away."

"It's a surprise, all right," Joanna said. "I had no idea, but where on earth are we going to put it?"

"I thought about that," Butch said. "I guess it'll have to go in the living room. It's way too classy to go with my model trains."

"Let's take it in and hang it, then," Joanna said.

Butch looked at his watch. "I thought you said you were going back to work for a while after the funeral."

"I changed my mind," Joanna told him. "The kids are gone. The dogs are gone. I've got better things to do this afternoon than go back to work."

"Amen, sister," Butch Dixon said, picking up the painting and following her into the house. "So do I!"

HARPER LUXE

THE NEW LUXURY IN READING

We hope you enjoyed reading
our new, comfortable print size and found it
an experience you would like to repeat.

Well – you're in luck!

HarperLuxe offers the finest in fiction and
nonfiction books in this same larger print size and
paperback format. Light and easy to read, HarperLuxe
paperbacks are for book lovers who want to see
what they are reading without the strain.

For a full listing of titles and
new releases to come, please visit our website:

www.HarperLuxe.com

HARPER LUXE